A NEWPORT

MESS

CHRIST~~MAS~~

A NEWPORT CHRISTMAS
~~MESS~~

A CHRISTMAS ESCAPE NOVEL

JESS HEILEMAN

VAGABOND PUBLISHING

Cover design: Melody Jeffries Designs

Library of Congress Control Number: 2022920775

ISBN Paperback: 978-1-7329851-7-9

ISBN Ebook: 978-1-7329851-6-2

Published By: Vagabond Publishing, LLC.

For Mom and Dad.
I owe so much of who I am to you.

And to all those who are seeking
love again. May you find it.

Bingo
Christmas Escape

Read all seven books in the series to get a Christmas romance blackout!

Broken elevator	Sleigh ride through the mountains	Allergic reaction	Snowstorm Power outage	A walk down main street
Candlelit house tour	Define the boundaries chat (multiple answers)	Ice Skating on a frozen pond	Mint hot Chocolate	"Highway to Hell" ringtone
Boat ride	"Fresh" chocolate milk	FREE SPACE	Reindeer Attack	Miniature Christmas Tree
Hot chocolate at a Christmas market	Trip to Ikea	Burning hot chocolate	Home Alone movie night (multiple answers)	Listening to Bing Crosby
An angry dachshund	Blanket fort	Snowy Beach	Mandalorian pajamas	Snowmobile ride through the mountains

ONE

QUINN

EVERYTHING APPEARED PERFECT THROUGH THE viewfinder of my camera, and I couldn't help but note the irony of what wasn't being captured. Maybe that was how I should start looking at my life—through a metaphorical viewfinder. Focus on the stuff worth capturing and pretend that the rest of my existence wasn't in absolute shambles. Too bad I wasn't sure there was anything worth capturing at the moment.

I sighed and pulled out the chair from the kitchen table to get a new angle. The marine layer hadn't burned off yet, causing the diffused light seeping through the windows to deepen the steel-blue icing of the cookies and brighten the white piping of the snowflake design. The dark, grained wood was one of my favorite backdrops lately—rustic, yet chic. I clicked a few more pictures and grabbed a quick panning video.

The narrator's voice blared from my Bluetooth speaker. "It seemed they had found their assailant. Or had they?" The eerie theme music trilled through the empty kitchen, and my arm hairs stood on end.

"It wasn't him," I said aloud, scrolling through the images I'd captured. "It's the boyfriend. He's the only one with a clear motive."

The subsequent advertisement for security cameras went silent mid-pitch, and a quiet laugh from behind sent me reeling in my chair. "Jeez, Ashlee!" My hand settled over my racing heart. "You scared me!"

Pure amusement lit Ashlee's dark features, her suitcase stationed behind her. "Girl, of all people to have an obsession with true-crime podcasts ..." Her words faded into laughter, her ponytail swinging with her shaking head.

"If I know how murderers think, I'm less likely to be killed by one." I tucked a mass of my blonde waves behind my ear, but it freed itself immediately, refusing to be tamed. "Besides, it wasn't the podcast that scared me. I just wasn't expecting you home until eleven."

Her chin lowered, and she peered at me through the tips of her black bangs. "Quinn, it's almost noon."

My gaze flew to the clock. How did time do that? Hours passing like minutes?

Ashlee scanned the piles of dirty dishes, the flour and powdered sugar dusting the countertops, and the trays of baked goods that cluttered her kitchen. It was absolute chaos. "You may have outdone yourself. This mess might even top the one you made during your Jane Austen dessert week posts. What with the"—she wiggled her fingers in front of her—"stiff Jell-O stuff you made in those hilarious shaped molds."

I laughed at the memory. "Flummery is a lot more difficult to make than I'd thought. And a lot messier, too."

Ashlee smiled and gestured around us. "Honestly, you should do a behind-the-scenes shot for your social media followers. I think they deserve to see what your creative genius looks like in action."

The camera strap tightened under the weight of the digital SLR, and I hopped down from the chair with an impish smile. "I'll clean it all up. Right after I finish."

She gave an airy laugh and shook her head again—her classic response to most things I said.

"Hey. You should be proud of me. I have the rest of November's posts scheduled, and this"—I gestured around us —"is half of December's. All of it accomplished while you were away."

Her brows lifted. "*You,* Quinn Cook, are ahead of schedule?"

My triumphant smile lessened when her eyes narrowed.

She crossed her arms, leaning a shoulder against the wall and crossing her foot at the ankle. Shoot. Interrogation stance. "And what prompted this sudden spell of motivation?" Her gaze bore into me. "Did you agree to make the gingerbread houses for that wedding in Newport Beach?"

Was I that obvious? I bit at my lip. "I was weak without you here."

"Quinn!"

With Ashlee's disbelieving stare on me, I shifted. "Nikki sent a message asking me to reconsider. She was so sweet and complimentary ..."

"And completely inconsiderate of the previous refusal that we spent hours discussing."

I tried an innocent smile. "She offered me more money."

Ashlee's eyes flicked to the ceiling. "Of course she did. She's apparently made of it."

Ashlee had never understood my admiration for Nikki. Not that she knew her, but she had a hard time believing a social media influencer with millions of followers could also manage to be an authentic and kind person. Though I knew differently, this clearly wasn't the moment to change Ashlee's mind about Nikki. I needed to try a new angle.

"It was you who first encouraged me to take this job. And I

think you were right. It will help take my mind off of ... everything."

"Need I remind you that *you* were the one who said you couldn't handle the extra stress this year?"

"I know, but I just kept thinking about the opportunity I was giving up. Nikki's audience is beyond massive, and doing the centerpieces for her wedding could be just the thing to revive my account and land me some sponsorships." When her expression didn't change, my shoulders dropped. "Honestly, it's a last-ditch effort. I can't keep putting so much time and money into this whole influencer thing if it's not going to pan out." Wow. I was starting to sound like the logical, reasonable person my parents were always encouraging me to be.

Ashlee considered me for a moment, then let out a resigned breath. "I just want to make sure you feel up to taking on something like this. But whatever you decide, you know I'll support you."

Her words pierced me. As my best friend, I knew she meant them, and yet a part of me wished for Cody to be here, offering his support like he'd vowed to do at our wedding. But he wasn't here. I pushed the thought away and gave Ashlee a cautious smile. "Even if it means your kitchen will be a disaster for the better part of December? Because I can always make the centerpieces at my parents'—"

"No. We don't need their well-intentioned guidance putting unhelpful thoughts into your head. You'll make them here."

I jumped forward, wrapping my arms around her. "Thank you."

Ashlee allowed my hug for a moment before giving me a stiff pat on the back and straightening her blazer. "Okay. Okay. I get it. You love me."

"More than you know." I stepped back. "Now, tell me, how was your trip? Did you get the clients?" Ashlee had gone to school for nursing, but for the last two years, she'd been helping her uncle run an at-home care company. She not only managed their entire nursing staff throughout California and oversaw the hiring and training of all the nurses, but she also helped convince established medical practices to contract with their company. Basically, she was amazing—and gone a lot.

Ashlee gave a timid nod. "We did."

"That's incredible." I took note of her absent smile. "So why don't you look thrilled about it?"

"They want us to start training their staff the second week of December so they can offer their patients the service beginning January first." She hesitated. "Which means I'll need to be in San Francisco through the New Year."

"Oh." Despite the heaviness that settled into my chest, I gave a dismissive wave of my hand. "That's okay."

Her head tipped to the side, and she gave a small frown. "I fully intend to fly home on Christmas Eve so the two of us can at least spend Christmas together like we planned."

Spending Christmas with Ashlee was the excuse I'd used to opt out of attending my family's annual Christmas gathering. I typically loved extended-family events, but that had changed this past year. Now, it seemed I spent the majority of time at get-togethers dodging comments about my *unfortunate situation* and fake-smiling through unsolicited advice. I didn't have the strength. Not at Christmas.

I shook my head. "You are not flying home for one day. You have family in San Francisco. Spend Christmas with them."

"But it will be your first Christmas ..." Her words trailed off, and her frown intensified.

"Alone. Yes. But I'll be fine. The divorce is official. Christmases alone will be my new normal." I meant my tone to be cheery, but it came off more depressing than anything.

Ashlee pulled her phone from her back pocket. "That's it. I'm booking my flight."

"Don't you dare." I lunged for the phone in her hands, but she lifted it above her head and out of my reach. I was a scrappy little thing, so I debated jumping for it but reconsidered when I remembered the thousand-dollar camera dangling around my neck.

"If you're here, then I'm coming home," Ashlee said resolutely.

Before I could argue, a distant ringing drew our attention. My phone. I turned toward the muffled sound, pushing aside stacks of used mixing bowls and baking trays in my search. I glanced behind a dish of white, red, and green confetti popcorn and around the oversized platter that held the cookie advent calendar that had turned out more darling than I could have hoped. The elusive ring stopped.

Ashlee's gaze lifted from her own phone.

I shrugged. "I'm sure they'll call back if it's important."

The ring started again.

"Where are you?" I asked in a sing-song voice, concentrating on the faint hum of the vibration instead of the tinkling ringtone. I neared the sink and peered around a stack of dirty pots to a discarded kitchen towel I'd used for raising cinnamon roll dough. I yanked at the corner, and, like a magic trick, my phone reappeared. "It's a 212 number." I glanced back at Ashlee with a furrowed brow.

She gestured toward the phone. "So answer it."

"Hello?"

"Yes, hello. Is this Quinn Cook?" The woman on the line had an East Coast accent that made me smile. I loved accents, despite that a clipped formality accompanied hers.

"It is."

"This is Irene Garrity, the wedding planner for Nikki Aker."

"Oh, yeah. Nikki said you'd be in touch."

"Yes. Well, I sent you an email two days ago, but seeing as I didn't hear from you, I thought I'd try calling."

"I don't remember seeing it ..." I put the phone on speaker and opened my email app, scrolling through the countless unopened emails that plagued my inbox. Sure enough, there it was. *Sender: Irene Garrity. Subject: Aker/Carrigan Wedding.*

Please respond at your earliest convenience. "Found it. Sorry, I'm not super great at checking my emails."

Silence.

I cleared my throat. "But I can check them more often if I need to."

"I would appreciate it, Ms. Cook. That way, we have our communications documented, and nothing gets missed."

Ashlee smirked from across the kitchen, and I scowled at her. Responsiveness was certainly not my strong suit, like it was hers. Neither was organization. Actually, my list of *non-strengths* was pretty extensive. "Great idea."

"If you will respond to my email as soon as possible with all the supplies you'll require, I think all I need from you now are your intended dates to travel so I can book your flights."

"Oh, I won't need to fly. Newport is only an hour and a half from where I live."

The silence on the line returned with an awkward vengeance.

I sent Ashlee an uneasy glance. "I promise I'll be careful getting the gingerbread houses there. My friend already agreed to let me borrow her SUV—"

"Aren't you from San Diego, Ms. Cook?"

"I am."

"The wedding is in Newport ... Rhode Island. I don't think you'll want to drive."

"Rhode Island?" I stared at the phone. "As in *one of the thirteen colonies*, Rhode Island?"

"That's the one," she said dryly, not even a little impressed with my sixth-grade knowledge of the state.

My mind skimmed over the brief communications I'd had with Nikki. "But I thought the wedding was going to be in Newport Beach. Isn't Nikki from Orange County?"

"She lives there now, but she grew up in Rhode Island."

I gave an absent nod, mouth open in dismay, only slightly aware that Ms. Garrity couldn't hear my response.

"The location of the wedding was on the electronic contract you signed." She paused. "If you cared to read it, that is."

Curse words. But honestly, who reads those things? "I didn't notice that. Which is totally my fault, but I can't do the centerpieces if the wedding is in Rhode Island. They'll take me weeks to create … and I would need to be there the whole time. And I'd need a kitchen … and all the supplies."

"I'll see to the arrangements." Ms. Garrity cleared her throat. "Though perhaps Ms. Aker will understand if you need to back out because of *extenuating circumstances*." Had I imagined it, or was there a touch of hope in her voice?

I glanced at Ashlee for an answer, but she only shrugged. "Can you hold a moment, Ms. Garrity?" I asked.

The woman exhaled sharply. "Of course."

I lowered the phone, hastily pressing mute, before sending Ashlee a pleading look. "What would you do?"

She shook her head, obviously unwilling to influence me.

I tilted my head back in disbelief. "You know how bad I am at making decisions."

Her lips were firmly pressed together.

"Please?"

She huffed. "Fine. Since you already committed to it, if it were me, I'd do it."

I stared at her, unblinking. "You'd just fly across the country to somewhere you've never been, all by yourself, at Christmas?"

She flung up a hand and gave a sardonic laugh. "Then, don't do it. At least that way, we can spend Christmas together."

I tapped my curled fingers mindlessly on my bottom lip, weighing my options. I refused to let Ashlee sacrifice Christmas with her family, flying home on her own dime, only to dry my tears and keep my thoughts from perseverating on Cody—on why he'd left me and how different this Christmas was supposed to be.

No. As it stood, I was going to be alone, so I might as well be somewhere that would prevent me from having to attend my family's annual Christmas party, ease Ashlee's unnecessary guilt, and render a healthy dose of CPR to my struggling social media account. Besides, it would be good to be away from all the memories that threatened to make this the most miserable Christmas in the history of my life—and that included the one when I got food poisoning from those darn eclairs and ended up in the hospital on IVs. My stomach protested at the memory.

I met Ashlee's watchful stare. "I'm going to go."

"If you're positive."

"I am." I pressed the mute button. "Ms. Garrity?"

There was no answer.

"Ms. Garrity?" I said again before noticing it was still on mute. Hitting the button, I tried a third time. "Ms. Garrity?"

"I'm here."

"I'll be able to do it after all."

"I heard the conversation. You didn't actually mute the phone —at least not until a moment ago."

"Oh." My face grew hot with embarrassment. So much for a good first impression, though, honestly, I'd pretty much sabotaged any chance of that from the get go. I drew in a deep, calming breath. "I'll need three weeks to complete all the gingerbread houses."

"I can get your flight out for December first?"

My palms grew clammy on the phone gripped in my hand. "Okay."

"And your return flight?"

I hesitated. "Sometime *after* Christmas would be ideal, if that isn't too long."

"I'll double-check with Nikki, but I'm assuming that would be fine. How about, for now, we say the morning of the twenty-seventh?"

The lump forming in my throat attempted to thwart me. "That will work."

"Wonderful. If you could reply to the other questions in my email, I will send the itinerary as soon as I discuss this with Nikki and book the tickets. Good day, Ms. Cook." A click sounded, and the words *Call Ended* flashed briefly on the screen before it dimmed to black.

"Are you sure about this?" Ashlee asked, pulling my blank stare from the phone. "Because you don't look very sure."

I pasted a smile onto my lips. "Oh, I am. It's going to be the perfect distraction."

It was official. I'd spend Christmas in Newport, Rhode Island.

Alone.

What had I done?

TWO

LANDON

THE LOS ANGELES SUN SHONE LIKE IT FORGOT IT WAS nearly December. I could get used to the idea of no snow, but the eighty-degree weather was a little harder to accept. Not that I was mourning the freezing temps in Rhode Island, but it felt strange blasting the car's AC when Christmas was just around the corner.

My stomach grumbled as I drove past the Thai place that opened last week. Reports were that it was worth the twenty-minute line, but I was eager to get back to the office. I had a few things to finalize before my two o'clock meeting, so eating would have to wait. Again.

The parking lot was relatively empty, but considering it was noon on a Friday, I assumed my fellow employees were actually satiating their hunger or had taken off early for the weekend. I nabbed a spot close to the front, grabbed my laptop bag from the passenger seat, and shut the car door.

"Hey, Landon!" Shawna beeped the car fob to her white Audi

Coupe and flashed her attractive smile. "Are you coming back from lunch?"

I groaned inwardly at her approach. Her knack for arriving at the same time as me was growing suspicious. This was the third time this week. "No. I went to the Planning Commission hearings."

She lifted her sunglasses when she reached me and rested them atop her head. "That sounds thrilling."

"Extremely." I gestured toward the building, hoping to end this delightful parking lot chat as soon as possible. "You headed in?"

"I am." Shawna's high heels clicked on the pavement at a slow, deliberate pace.

I didn't have time for this.

"So, do you have plans for the weekend?" Shawna asked, sending me a sideways glance.

"I have my sister's wedding in a couple of weeks, so I'm hoping to get ahead on a few work things."

She stepped in front of me, forcing me to stop mid-step or risk bowling her over. Her fingers brushed along my arm. "Why don't you let me show you a good time? All work and no play makes Jack a dull boy."

Did all beautiful women think a touch and a slight pout would get them whatever they wanted? My thoughts involuntarily turned to Eliza. How I used to be putty in her hands whenever she'd look at me like Shawna was looking at me now. Unfortunately for Shawna, I'd learned my lesson. "In that case, you'll have to excuse me for being dull. I have work to do."

Hoping to avoid an awkward elevator ride, I entered the lobby and took the stairs to the fourth floor.

When I strolled into the office, Anne gave me a bright smile from the front desk. Her hair looked different. Shorter, maybe? Or darker?

"How'd the hearing go, Mr. Aker?"

"We got approved."

"I'm not the least bit surprised. Oh, here." She handed me a sticky note. "Roger Carrigan called and said he needed to talk to you as soon as you got back."

I glanced down at the neon-green square with a number jotted on it. Why would Roger want to talk to me? I usually heard from the Carrigans' real estate manager or Frank, the head general counsel attorney, but rarely ever from one of the Carrigans. "Thanks."

I started toward my office but paused. "You did something with your hair," I said, hoping I was right.

She ran her fingers through her short bob, the corners of her eyes wrinkling with her smile. "I did. Those gray hairs were stealing all my thunder. I might be a grandma, but I don't want to look like I am."

"It looks great," I said with a wink.

Her cheeks rounded, a red color filling them, and she batted a hand toward me. "Oh, Mr. Aker. You're too kind."

When I stepped into my office, I dropped my laptop onto the desk and glanced around the small space. Those who strived for a corner office had obviously not seen this one. The view was a definite plus, considering it overlooked a well-manicured grass area with palm trees, but it was really the only benefit. The large desk took up most of the space, and because of the floor-to-ceiling windows along two of the walls, the bookshelf was crammed against the only free wall and prevented the door from fully opening. Thankfully, I wouldn't be here much longer. Only a week or two past the New Year most likely, and with Nikki's wedding and Christmas coming up, I would have a small break from the confining space.

I closed the door and dialed the number Anne had handed me.

"This is Roger."

"Mr. Carrigan, it's Landon Aker—general counsel."

"Oh, yes. Thanks for getting back to me. How'd the hearing go this morning? Are we on track?"

"They approved the building permit."

"Wonderful. That's great news." He cleared his throat. "I know you're right in the middle of all the legal stuff with this new build, but we're going to have Peter Jennings take it from here."

I stilled. "Peter? Isn't he in New York right now?"

"He was, but now he's headed there to take over for you."

I paused, my mind grasping at how to respond and whether I should have been worried about this unforeseen intervention. "Can I ask the reason I'm being taken off the project?"

"Don't worry. It's not anything you did. We need you in Boston for the Carrigan Enterprise annual board meeting. As our newest attorney on the general counsel, we feel it would be valuable for you to attend."

The tension in my shoulders lessened. "Of course."

"Perfect. If you could get Peter up to speed on where everything stands this next week, we'll get you a return flight to Newport for this Friday, the eighth. Does that work?"

"When's the board meeting?"

"The 13th."

My arrival seemed a bit premature. "Should I prepare something to present? Or—"

"Nope. Just be there."

Something felt off. "I'd be happy to take on another project in the meantime."

"Actually, with Kade and Nikki's wedding on the twenty-second, we've asked Peter to see to any real estate transactions and development issues that arise until after Christmas."

My jaw hung open. "But, Mr. Carr—"

"We insist, Landon." His tone was kind but unwavering.

That was over two weeks off of work with nothing but one meeting thrown in the middle. I stared blankly at my office door, trying to think of a response when my blood was now boiling. This wasn't some well-deserved vacation. This was orchestrated meddling. And I knew exactly who was to blame: Kade. "Thank you, Mr. Carrigan," I said through gritted teeth. "I'm sure my sister will appreciate your generosity."

"Well then, we'll see you in Boston ... and for the wedding."

My hand gripped the phone. "I look forward to it."

The moment the line went silent, I dialed Kade.

"Hey, Landon. To what do I owe this pleasure?"

I set the phone on speaker and placed it on my desk to avoid taking out my irritation on it. "Did you know your uncle called me today?"

"Really?" There wasn't an ounce of surprise in his amused tone. "Which one?"

"Roger. But that's not the point," I growled. "The point is, he insisted I abandon my current project to return to Newport—until after Christmas—for a single board meeting."

Kade chuckled. "It sounds to me like you just got yourself a few weeks off, and you're choosing to be upset about it."

"What I'm upset about is that my idiot brother-in-law—"

"Soon-to-be brother-in-law," Kade corrected.

My knuckles turned white where they pressed against the desk. "Sorry. My idiot, *soon-to-be* brother-in-law pulled his entitled, family-connection card to force me home."

"I don't see the problem."

"You wouldn't." My laugh was full of anything but humor. "You're an idiot, Kade."

"Three uses of idiot already? You *are* mad."

I paced the tight space right behind my desk, shaking my head in disbelief. "Yes, I'm mad."

Kade cleared his throat. "Okay, I get it. You're not thrilled with my interfering, but I didn't do it for you. I did it for Nikki. She misses you. You've only come to see us once in the four weeks you've been in SoCal. So yes, in hindsight, this probably wasn't the best idea I've ever come up with, but had I asked you, would you have gone home earlier?"

"No! I have a job. You know, one of those things common people do to earn money by showing up at work."

"Because the prospect of a vacation is obviously a high-stress situation for you, I'm going to forgive you for implying that I don't work, when, as we speak, I'm on my way to a client meeting."

"Is this meeting happening on a golf course?"

Kade chuckled again. "Eighteen holes of golf presents a lot of opportunity for talking business."

I released a heavy breath, unwilling to let him distract me from my irritation. "I can't believe you had me pulled from the project. Now, everyone in your family's company is going to think I'm being given special privileges because I'm related to you. That I only got hired because of our connection." I paused. "And I probably did, but I don't need others to be constantly reminded of the fact."

Kade didn't answer immediately. "I'm sorry, man. I should have gone about this a different way. I won't do it again ... most likely, anyway."

"Kade."

He huffed. "Fine. I'll refrain from using my *entitled card* to get you a much-needed vacation in the future. But since the damage is already done, will you stop griping and try to enjoy it?"

I refused to respond to that.

"Come on, Landon. How else am I supposed to measure up to *Nikki's favorite person* without going to such great lengths for her happiness?"

Despite myself, I smiled. "You'll always live in my shadow, Kade. Just get used to it."

He chuckled. "So we're good?" There was a smile behind his voice.

"No. But for Nikki's sake, I'll try not to kill you when I see you this weekend."

"That's an acceptable arrangement, and I thank you for it."

It looked like I was going home to Newport earlier than I'd expected.

THREE

QUINN

Baked gingerbread pieces filled every surface of the massive kitchen, the oversized dining table, and the three small tables in the living room. Some were on cookie sheets, but the bigger pieces were laid on wax paper with smaller pieces stacked on top of them. When I'd arrived in Newport a week ago, I'd thought the rental Irene Garrity had arranged for me was a bit excessive for one person's accommodations. But now I was grateful for all the space—at least when it came to baking.

The main part of the house where I was staying—the second and third floor—had a clean, modern look, like those attractive brothers on HGTV had remodeled it. The kitchen was massive and was separated from the large open space, which included a dining area and the family room, by a spacious island that could probably sit almost as many people as the over-sized table if there were more barstools. With the considerable size of everything, I felt a lot like Goldilocks who'd been put up in Papa Bear's swanky bachelor pad. Even the laundry room and second-floor bathroom were the stuff out of a magazine spread.

Upstairs, there were two decent-sized bedrooms, a bathroom, and a master suite. I'd almost opted to take the first room at the top of the stairs because the master was a bit intimidating, but there hadn't been a lock on the door, and there was a closet full of men's clothes, which was pretty unsettling. Besides, if I needed to use the bathroom in the night, I didn't want to have to walk down a long, dark hallway to get there.

Needless to say, as nice as the place was, I didn't feel at ease in it by myself. It might have helped to know if someone was renting out the first-floor apartment, since we shared an enclosed stairway that connected both front doors, but, then again, I guess that would depend on who the tenant was. So far, I hadn't heard or seen anyone come or go, and I'd been paying attention.

As it was, every noise made me pause, and when it came time to go to bed, I kept several of the lights on as I slept. I mean, I also did those things at Ashlee's when she was gone, but my nerves seemed more volatile here. So volatile, in fact, that I hadn't listened to a true-crime podcast since my arrival. It was all holiday music and feel-good Christmas movies for me.

I sat on the large sectional in my yoga pants, oversized sweatshirt, and bright-green-and-red-striped fuzzy socks, puzzling together the gingerbread cabin pieces that filled the coffee table's surface. The hand-drawn blueprint stationed on the floor next to the table helped me get my bearings, and I shifted the large, dense, gingerbread shape in my hand to resemble the correct placement. Once I confirmed the pieces for the cabin fit together correctly, I could move on to assembling all the structures. Which meant, if I started tomorrow, I was two days ahead of schedule. Or was today Friday? Either way, the benefits of isolation and the motivation of a looming deadline had been good to me.

I gave a heavy blink to refocus my strained eyes before realizing the ache wasn't from my intense focus, but the dimming light. The oranges and blues of the sunset outside were rapidly fading from the darkening sky. Quickly, I switched on another light and moved to the sliding door that led out to the second-floor deck overlooking the street. The handle was locked, and a thick wooden dowel rested on the lower track.

Refusing to dwell on how clearly someone from the street outside could see in, I threw the heavy curtains shut and moved to the nearby window, where I did the same—checked the lock and lowered the blinds—before moving to the others. Will Smith's character in *I Am Legend* would have found me a formidable ally with how efficiently I could secure a room at dusk. But I didn't want to think about that movie right now.

"Jingle bells. Jingle bells." My voice was artificially loud, which didn't help with my wavering pitch. "Jingle all the way."

I thought to check the rest of the house, but since I'd gone nowhere today—or all week, for that matter—and the image of apocalyptic zombies holding jingle bells was now central in my mind, I decided it would be best to wait until I Facetimed Ashlee tonight to do my thorough before-bed house check. Besides, though I couldn't see it from where I stood, I was absolutely positive the front door to my unit remained bolted. I'd checked it more than enough times to quiet my obsessive tendencies.

Flinging myself onto the overstuffed leather sectional, I flipped on the TV and resumed streaming *White Christmas* to fill the unnerving quiet and my wandering imagination. When my favorite part came on—where Judy convinces Phil to fake their engagement—I set down the gingerbread pieces, tucked my feet beneath me, and leaned back into the soft leather. This scene was not only comedic genius, it was romance at its finest.

After a few minutes, a distant sound drew my attention, and I paused the movie. In the quiet, I could hear the blood whooshing through my body, but nothing else. Stupid big houses and all their sounds. I lifted the remote to press play when the bang of a door closing stopped me. My pulse quickened. "Calm down," I whispered to myself. "It must be the tenants downstairs."

Heavy footsteps ascending the stairs sent me to my feet. Why would the neighbors be coming upstairs? Had they just arrived and mistaken the unit? That must be it. Or perhaps it was a misdirected food delivery person.

Keys jingled outside the door. Then, to my complete horror, the sound of metal on metal, like a key in the lock, nearly stopped my heart. The lock clicked.

I was as good as dead.

Adrenaline now pumping through me, I scanned the room. I needed somewhere to hide. Now. But the open floorplan gave me few options. Without another thought, I dove behind the far side of the sectional, near the wall, only to realize this was probably the worst place to be. I was literally cornered with no way out. Had I learned nothing from all those true-crime podcasts and documentaries? I should have attempted a drop from the second-floor balcony. That, or hiding in the kitchen would have given me a better chance at escape. Not only was there the large island that could have acted as a natural barrier, but it was closer to the only real exit. I was too scrawny a thing to put up much of a fight, but I was quick.

The door creaked opened, and heavy steps followed.

"What the ...?" a man's whispered voice traveled through the large space.

I scrunched down further and quieted my shallow breathing.

If only I'd had the sense to grab my phone. Or knew where it was. Had I left it on the coffee table? Or maybe the—

Clomp. Clomp. Clomp. His footsteps paused, and I resisted every pulling fiber inside of me to peek around the couch's edge to size up my captor. How many of those true-crime victims had made that novice mistake? I would not give my hiding place away. I would not become a statistic.

"Hello?" the deep voice boomed, and something heavy dropped that made me flinch. A bag of tools to dispose of the body—my body? "Is someone here?"

I swallowed, unwilling to fall prey to the tactic of an inviting tone. It was always the nice, unsuspecting person who was the perpetrator. Well ... not always ... or really even often, though that didn't mean it wasn't the case here. I'd recently heard of a man that rented out his home, only to fall upon his victims at night. The police had caught him, hadn't they?

I was growing dizzy from shallow breaths and fear.

The man started walking again. His steps were slow and calculated. Dangerous. Was he coming toward me? I couldn't tell with how the sound reverberated off the walls. This was not how I wanted to die. I mean, I didn't really have a preferred way of dying, besides living to old age and passing in my sleep, but if it had to be from something else, this certainly wouldn't be my choice. I squeezed my eyes shut, gripping the remote in my shaking hand. The remote. Perhaps I could throw it at him. Or maybe somewhere else as a distraction so I could make a run for it. It was an abysmal plan, but I didn't have a better option.

The sound of the wooden stairs creaking ignited a flicker of hope, preventing me from chucking the remote across the room. Was the man going upstairs? Another stair creaked, then another, and another. He must have been searching for me. Knowing I had limited time, I glanced around the side of the couch to be sure I was alone, then I quietly maneuvered my way out from behind it. The stairs leading up were across the room from the ones leading to the first-floor entrance—to outside—and I kept my eyes on them as I tiptoed toward salvation. Thank heavens I was wearing socks and was basically elf-sized.

Another creak halted me mid-step. Had the sound come from above or the staircase where I was headed? The doorway downstairs faced the kitchen, so I couldn't be certain from where I stood. A shiver of fear shot through me. What if I had been mistaken? What if the man was waiting on these stairs for me, knowing I would try to escape? I'd have to make a drop from the balcony. Backing away with silent steps, I tightened my fists at my sides, hoping to stave off the trembling that had consumed my whole body.

A voice barked from somewhere behind me, and like a deer

in flight, I took off, away from it, toward the kitchen. Glimpsing the iron skillet I'd used to make my dinner, I grabbed it and spun to face my pursuer. Except, there was no pursuer. Confused, my gaze landed on Bing Crosby's character moving across the screen and then shifted to the remote in my hand. Instantly, I realized my grave error and dropped it on the counter. As hurried footsteps made their way from one of the stairways, I tried to keep my tunneling vision from blackening. Ashlee had always teased that my spirit animal was a fainting goat, and with the way my legs tightened beneath me, I wondered if she was onto something. But now was not the time to keel over. I needed to fight.

Skillet extended, I glanced back and forth between the door that led to the first floor and the wooden banister that led up, waiting for the man to appear from one of them. When a large form barreled down the third-floor stairs, I shifted my body toward him. "Don't come any closer!"

His wide eyes landed on me, and to my utter amazement, I found an exceptionally handsome face staring at me. He wore a heavy winter coat, and a gray beanie covered all but a few ends of his dark hair. A well-manicured beard somehow made his prominent jawline stronger. More deadly.

"Who are you?" he asked, putting his hands up like I held a gun and not kitchenware. "And why are you in my house?"

"Your house?" My resolve wavered some, and I lowered the skillet a touch. But what if he was lying? What if that was some kind of ploy to get me to let my guard down? There was no unwritten rule that an attractive man couldn't also be a psychopathic murderer. In fact, the trait would probably serve him well. I lifted the iron skillet higher. "Prove it."

"Are you some sort of squatter?" His gaze dropped to the island between us, overflowing with gingerbread pieces. "That bakes in other people's kitchens?"

My head drew back at the strange comment. "No. But I'm not telling you who I am until you prove to me you own the place

... and that you aren't some serial killer who lures young, unsuspecting women into your rental properties."

"This is not a rental property. I only rent out the first floor."

I quirked a brow. "Then where have you been the last week?"

"In LA—for work."

It had to have been more than a coincidence that he claimed to have been in Southern California. He was definitely a stalker of sorts, attempting to get me to comply with commonalities. "Then why are you here?" I asked, keeping my skillet aimed at him.

"How is it I'm the one doing the explaining when you're the one in *my* house?"

"You haven't proven it's your house yet ... or that you aren't a killer."

"A killer?" he spluttered, shaking his head in impressively well-acted disbelief. "I have the key."

I shrugged. "So do I."

He tossed his head back. "This is ridiculous. How did you get a key ... unless ..." His gaze moved slowly across the haphazard stacks of gingerbread, then returned to mine. The crease in his brow deepened, though his arms remained up. "Are you the woman my sister hired to make the centerpieces for her wedding?"

My throat went dry. "What's your sister's name?"

His teeth clenched. "Nikki Aker."

The heat that had been pulsing through my body congregated in my cheeks. "You're Nikki's brother?"

He shook his head, and his nostrils flared.

"You're not?" I asked, suddenly confused.

"I am."

I took a step toward him, the skillet still extended. "Then why did you shake your head *no*?"

"Can I put my arms down now?"

"Call her," I said, unable to ignore the nagging voice inside me that needed further evidence of his innocence. "I need to know you're really who you say you are."

He stared at me before apparently realizing I was serious. His eyes flicked upward. "Permission to grab my phone?"

I gave a slow nod, ready to scramble to safety if he pulled out a knife or a gun instead. Could cast iron deflect bullets?

With overly intentional movements, he reached inside his coat pocket and retrieved a phone. I didn't miss the mischievous twinkle in his eyes, and I gripped the handle of the skillet more tightly, prepared for trouble.

"Siri, call Nikki," he said.

"Calling Nikki," the mechanical female voice responded.

A faint ringing sounded. He put the phone on speaker, wedged it onto a vacant spot on the counter between us, and then crossed his arms and glared at it.

The ringing stopped. "Hey, Landon." The feminine voice was definitely Nikki's, and my stomach knotted. Why had I insisted he call her?

"Hey, sis." The man's voice was dry and humorless. "Did you, by chance, let someone stay at my place?"

Her side of the line went quiet. "Why do you ask?"

"Well, I came home to find my house filled to the brim with gingerbread and a young"—he glanced at me—"what did you call yourself again? Oh, yeah ... *a young, unsuspecting woman* threatening my life with a frying pan."

"Quinn? Oh, the poor thing." There was sincere sympathy in Nikki's voice. "You must have scared her half to death."

Humiliation flooded over me, and I lowered the heavy skillet, finally convinced this man spoke the truth.

"I didn't realize you'd be home already," Nikki said.

"Kade hasn't confessed his interference?" he grumbled.

"He did. I just didn't realize when you were flying in."

A man, who I assumed was Nikki's fiancé, spoke in the background, though it was hard to distinguish what he said. The muffled sound of Nikki's answer made it clear she wasn't talking to Landon. "He's there." She paused, and the man's muffled voice came again. "Yeah." She cleared her throat. "Sorry about that.

Kade needed an update. And I'm so happy you're there! I can't wait to see you Monday."

Landon's jaw clenched. "I thought you were flying in tomorrow morning."

"That had been the plan, but there was a mishap with the wedding dress. They'll have it fixed bright and early Monday morning, and we'll be on our way as soon as we have it."

Landon didn't answer but pulled off his beanie and ran a hand through his dark hair that currently stuck out in odd directions.

"I feel so bad that you just barged in on Quinn like that. I meant to give you both a head's up that she was there before you arrived."

"And it just slipped your mind?" Landon's irritation was palpable.

"I guess so. I've got a lot going on right now. Is she there with you?" Nikki asked. "Can you put her on?"

His gaze locked on mine, and he gestured toward the phone with a stiff hand.

I stepped closer to the kitchen island between us, the skillet dangling in my still-trembling hand. "Hey, Nikki. It's Quinn."

"Oh, Quinn. I am so sorry about what happened. I hope Landon didn't scare you too badly."

"It's not a big deal," I said, ever the pacifist—unless I was threatening strange men in their own house with an iron skillet. "And I'm happy to stay somewhere else now that he's here."

"No. Don't be silly. His house is big enough for you both, and it sounds like you're already using the space. It'd be a pain to move all of your stuff now."

It certainly would be, but Landon's scowl made the effort a preferable option. Besides, I couldn't sleep in the same house as a man I didn't know—despite how the thought of his being close by was oddly comforting now that I was pretty sure he wouldn't murder me in my sleep. I swallowed my trepidation. "Really, it wouldn't be an inconvenience—"

"I'll sleep in the first-floor apartment," Landon interrupted, leaning toward the phone. "Unless you've also rented it out without telling me."

"Nope." Nikki's voice was light and cheery. "But remember, the groomsmen are going to be staying there the week of the wedding, so we might need to reassess the arrangements when I get there."

Landon grunted his answer.

"When was the last time I told you how much I love you?" Nikki said to her brother. "Because you are my favorite person in this whole world."

Kade's muffled voice returned, his tone teasing, though his precise words were still undistinguishable.

Nikki laughed again. "Fine. A close second to Kade. But I couldn't do this without your help."

The crease on Landon's brow disappeared, and his expression softened. "I'm glad you're aware."

"Speaking of," Nikki continued, "it's my understanding that Quinn has never been to Rhode Island. Make sure she doesn't spend all her time working. She needs to see Newport at Christmastime. It's like a dream, Quinn. You'll love it."

In a blink, Landon's scowl was back in full force.

My head started shaking before I could even form an excuse. I had no intention of forcing Landon to take me sightseeing around Newport, especially when he'd made it blatantly obvious he didn't want to. It was bad enough I had commandeered his entire house and forced him to the apartment downstairs. "I actually have lots to do if I'm going to get these gingerbread houses done in time, but thanks for the thought."

"When you need a break, please take it. Landon is happy to show you around our hometown. Aren't you, Landon?"

He didn't meet my gaze this time. "Of course." Though he'd agreed, his tone really said: '*I'd prefer the crazy woman put me out of my misery with the skillet.*'

"Well then, I'll come see you both as soon as Kade and I arrive.

In the meantime, Quinn, let Landon know if you need anything. He's the best of the best."

"And not a murderer?" I asked, mostly joking.

Nikki laughed. "Definitely not a murderer."

He crossed his arms over his broad chest. "We'll see if that changes when you and Kade get here."

"Oh, Landon. Play nice in front of our guest. We wouldn't want her thinking you're a disgruntled host."

"Too late for that," I teased, only to realize it came out sounding more sincere than playful. This time, I avoided looking at Landon.

In the quiet that followed my comment, I could make out Kade's voice telling Nikki they'd arrived wherever they were headed.

"Okay," Nikki said. "I need to go, you two. But try to have a little fun, and we'll talk soon. Love you, Landon. Bye, Quinn!" She made a kiss sound into the phone, and then the line went silent.

Hesitantly, I lifted my gaze to Landon's less-than-pleased expression. "I'm sorry I thought you were a murderer." I paused. "And I'm sorry for taking over your house. Had I known—"

"It's not your fault." He said it as a fact, not a reassurance.

"But I feel bad. I'm really fine to sleep in your rental downstairs."

His gaze scanned the cluttered counter again, then drifted to the table. "Won't you need to spend most days in my kitchen anyway?"

Of course he'd want to be downstairs where I couldn't infringe on his privacy. "It doesn't need to be this one, just a kitchen. Like I said, it wouldn't be too hard to bring the stuff down—"

"Really, it's fine." He shoved his beanie back on his head. "I'll be downstairs if you need anything."

Unsure how hard I should press the matter, I returned the skillet to the overflowing sink and followed him to the door.

A large duffel bag was on the floor—the object that had caused the thud when he'd first walked in, apparently—and he picked it up and flung it over his shoulder effortlessly, like some sort of dashing sailor about to bid farewell. He paused at the threshold. "I'll make sure the front door is locked. I'd hate for some unsuspecting robber to meet his untimely demise by frying pan." His tone was flat, unamused even, but there was a peculiar spark in his eyes, and an unexpected trill of pleasure shot through me.

"That's a good idea," I said dumbly, still reeling from my odd reaction to him.

His heavy snow boots echoed in the narrow stairwell.

"Night," I called when he reached the apartment door at the bottom.

He glanced up at me, and I thought I glimpsed a small flicker of a smile. "Night, Quinn."

I shut the door with more force than was necessary. What had just happened—the strange encounter; the attractive, disgruntled man; and that fleeting feeling brought on by a simple look?

And what would Cody have thought of the situation?

It didn't matter.

Cody had given up any rights to my heart when he shattered it a year ago.

I gave a resolute nod, as though that would convince my heart that Cody didn't still hold all its broken pieces in his grasp, and bolted the door behind me.

FOUR

LANDON

I slammed my laptop shut, aggravated I didn't have a single work email to respond to. I mean, I knew it was Saturday, but that never stopped people from contacting me. I wouldn't put it past Kade to have seen to it that a *do-not-contact* memo was sent to the whole blasted company while I was away from the office. Especially now that I knew he was a co-conspirator with my sister—or, more accurately, her lackey. I should have guessed his meddling meant he was up to something more sinister than getting me home early before the wedding. But, to both of their eventual disappointment, I had zero intention of allowing them to succeed. Nikki could scheme all she wanted when it involved other peoples' lives, but not mine. I'd been there, done that. I wouldn't be making that mistake again.

My fingers drummed mindlessly on the small kitchen table when a scraping sound from upstairs forced my gaze to the ceiling. What on earth was Quinn doing up there? Rearranging all the furniture in my house? Or maybe it was my lack of distraction that made me more aware of her constant movements upstairs. The ESPN highlights on in the background wasn't cutting it.

I pulled out my phone.

Landon: Hey, Peter. Just checking to make sure the contractors got the details about the property's easement yesterday.
Peter Jennings: They did.
Landon: Thanks.
Landon: If anything comes up, be sure to reach out.
Peter Jennings: I think we'll be good until you get back. Enjoy your time off.

I stared at the comment, that familiar tightness squeezing my chest. I wondered what Peter thought of my *vacation*. What the other employees thought about it. I enjoyed my job. Really. But it was moments like these I regretted taking a position at Carrigan Enterprises. The nepotism was undeniable (and rightfully so—it was a family business), and while I wasn't a Carrigan—my lack of hundreds of millions would attest to that—this wasn't the first time I'd been given special treatment because of my connection to Kade. And with how both he and Nikki liked to intervene in my life, it probably wouldn't be the last.

A loud bang from above had me glancing up again. Maybe I should go see if Quinn needed help with whatever she was doing to cause that racket. The last thing I wanted right now was damage to my hardwood floors. With how little I'd been home since the flooring had been put in, it was basically in pristine condition. Yep. That was why I was going up. To save my floors. Not to see the oddly endearing woman that was currently residing in my house.

I stood, and then I promptly sat back down. Was I that weak? My going upstairs right now would mean I was eating right out of Nikki's hands. It couldn't matter what bait Nikki dangled in front of me—even if the bait was extremely effective with big blue eyes, a contagious smile, and a face that refused to dislodge from my mind—I'd rather starve. Metaphorically.

I folded my arms, resolved. Besides, whatever matchmaking intuition Nikki claimed to have, Quinn was not my type. I mean, yes, she was gorgeous with that wavy, long, blonde hair and sun-kissed skin that was a rare sight in Rhode Island mid-December, but I was nearly certain she was one of Nikki's social media friends, and there was no chance I'd allow myself to fall for another influencer. I'd washed my hands of all of it after Eliza.

My phone chimed, and I read the incoming text.

Nikki: Hey! Did you get Christmas decorations up yet?

I groaned, knowing exactly where this was headed.

Landon: Nope.
Nikki: I'd like the place to feel somewhat festive for when the guys get there.
Nikki: And I'm sure Quinn wouldn't mind a few decorations either.

And there it was. Exactly like I'd thought.

Landon: I didn't put them up last year, and Christmas still came.
Landon: Besides, I can't remember that being part of the rental agreement.
Landon: Oh wait, that's right. There wasn't one. You put a stranger in my house without asking me.
Nikki: Grinch much?

My mind whirled with Grinch references, trying to create the perfect comeback, but Nikki's incoming text thwarted my attempts.

Nikki: Fingers crossed your heart will grow a couple sizes this year. *wink-face emoji*

I rolled my eyes. There was nothing wrong with the size of my heart. It was just closed off—and for good reason. A reason Nikki understood well. A reason that should have prevented her from interfering in my life again, and yet, here we were. Well, I hated to disappoint her, but there was no way I was going to let my adequately sized heart betray me and go upstairs. Not a chance.

FIVE

QUINN

The running faucet made it difficult to hear what Ashlee was saying. I turned off the water and threw the large mixing bowl in the dishwasher, pinning the phone between my ear and shoulder while I dried my hands. "Sorry, what was that?"

"The nerve of that woman! Putting you in her brother's house without telling either of you and then assuming you would continue staying there together. How unprofessional and totally—"

"It was a misunderstanding. I don't think she realized exactly when he'd be back in Newport."

"Either way, I can't believe you're not livid. Well, I can believe it. But if it were me, I would be on the next flight home, and I'd make Nikki pay for it. That, and I'd insist on some sort of compensation for the massive inconvenience."

I grabbed the broom from where it leaned against a chair. I'd swept under the dining room table earlier, even going so far as to move out all of the chairs, but I'd left the kitchen floor until I'd wiped off the sections of the counter not brimming with gingerbread—which wasn't much. "Honestly, it isn't a big deal. Nikki said she'd reassess the accommodations when she gets here, and for now, Landon seems ..." His handsome face flashed through my mind. "... nice enough."

"Who are you, and what have you done with my best friend? The one that refuses to open the door on the off-chance a sales-person is actually a human trafficker? You don't know this man. I can't believe you are okay with him being downstairs while in possession of a key to where you're staying. Unless ..." She paused. "He's totally hot, isn't he?"

My cheeks burned. "If you like the brooding type."

Ashlee's laugh was so loud I had to pull my ear from the speaker. "That's why you're cleaning—in case he drops by again. That should have been my first clue."

"I always clean up my messes ... eventually. Besides, it doesn't matter that he's decently attractive. My being here totally bugged him. I doubt I'll see him much after what happened last night, and even if I do, he legit thinks I'm crazy."

"You are."

I scoffed, trying to sweep something into my growing pile of dried-out cookie dough, only to realize it was stuck to the floor. "Wow. Thanks for the confidence boost, Ash." I leaned over and scraped the brown mass with my thumbnail until it dislodged.

"Oh, don't act offended. Your social media handle is *TheKookieCook.*"

She had a valid point, but I refused to acknowledge it. "Kooky is not crazy. Not exactly."

Ashlee went silent for a moment, and then she cleared her throat. "According to Webster, 'kooky is having the characteristics of a kook.' And a kook is" —she paused, obviously looking up the next definition on her phone— "'a crazy or eccentric person.' Own it, Quinn. No one rocks crazy like you do."

"Fine. I'm a little eccentric, but that's exactly my point—there's no way he'd be interested in me. He's stiff and serious ...

and, well ... I'm so not his type." The memory of his brief smile centered in my mind, and that same peculiar surge of energy shot through me. I ignored it and leaned the broom against the counter to go in search of the dustpan. "Not that I'd want to be, anyway. It's too soon."

"The divorce has been final for four months, Quinn. You've been separated almost a year. How is it fair that it's *too soon* for you when Cody is posting loads of pictures with his new girlfriend?"

My heart sank at her revelation. "Are you stalking Cody again?" I asked, trying for a light, disinterested tone but failing miserably.

"This new girl is worse than the last," Ashlee countered. "I'm pretty sure plastic surgeons need limits on how many procedures they allow a patient to undergo. She's probably half inorganic material."

AKA: the image of perfection.

I put the phone on speaker and stared at my Instagram app, my fingers itching to check Cody's feed despite the emotional bruising I'd experience. If this new girlfriend was as beautiful as the last one, I'd spiral into a whirlpool of self-doubt and uncontrollable weeping. I didn't have time for that right now. My thumb hovered over the app. *Or maybe I did.*

"Don't look, Quinn. It won't help." Ashlee's voice pulled me back to my senses. "I'm sorry I mentioned it. I only wanted to point out that it's not fair. You need to give yourself permission to date. Or, at the very least, to not feel guilty when you find a man attractive." When I didn't answer, Ashlee let out a long sigh. "I get that it's hard to move on—"

"Not for Cody." My chest buzzed. Perhaps Ashlee was right. Moping about and wishing things were different wasn't getting me anywhere. While my ex was out having the time of his life, all I had was my newly developed true-crime obsession and my stagnant social media following. All in all, I was not living my best life.

Or anything partially resembling it. Or anything even resembling a resemblance of it.

"What did you say Nikki's brother's name was again?" Ashlee asked. "Landon Aker?"

I groaned. Though, inwardly, I was grateful for the subject change. "Don't look him up."

The line went quiet momentarily. "Bummer. It doesn't look like he has an Instagram account. Let me try LinkedIn." Another pause. "Is he general counsel at Carrigan Enterprises?"

"I don't know. I just met him." Though Carrigan was Kade's last name. Maybe Landon worked for his family's company.

"This guy looks like a freaking GQ model in his profile picture."

That was probably him, then. "Does he have dark hair and copper eyes?"

"Yes. Here." She went silent again, then my phone dinged with a text from Ashlee.

I opened it to find a picture of Landon sporting a navy-blue blazer and giving an attractive closed-lip smile. "Yep. That's him."

"Holy hottie! Is he that handsome in real life, or did they use some kind of Photoshop magic on him?"

Despite myself, I smiled. Landon was incredibly handsome, and like Ashlee said, I didn't need to feel bad for thinking so. "Probably more handsome in real life."

"Honestly, Quinn, if you don't take advantage of this situation, I will never let you—"

A knock at the door drowned out the rest of Ashlee's threat. My whole body went on alert—not like a fight-or-flight response, but an I'm-oddly-too-excited-to-control-my-thinking-brain kind of response. "I have to go," I whispered. "Someone's here."

"It's him, isn't it?"

I started toward the door, trying to ignore the annoying fluttering in my stomach. "I don't know."

"It totally is. Go get your flirt on!" She ended her comment with a loud "whoop" that echoed off the walls.

"You're the worst," I hissed, quickly taking the phone off speaker and wishing I could hang up on her to make my point. "I'll call you back tonight. Answer this time. I had to do my night-time house check without you."

"I'm so sorry. I was out with potential clients."

The knock sounded again, followed by Landon's muffled voice. "Quinn, it's Landon. You in there?"

"Coming!" I called to preempt him from using his key.

"You'd better tell me every detail," Ashlee said.

"I will, but I've got to go." I ended the call and wedged the phone onto the counter between trays of gingerbread. My hand settled on the knob, and I drew in a calming breath, then another. If Cody could move on so easily, maybe I should give it a go.

Filled with resolve, I opened the door. Landon's large frame filled the small landing, a medium-sized cardboard box in his arms. My neck craned back to meet his gaze. With the distance I'd kept between us last night—me threatening him from the kitchen —I hadn't realized how tall he was. He had to be a good foot and a few inches taller than my five-foot-one-inch self—well, five-foot-one on a good day, which, ironically, was never on the days they measured me at the doctor's office. But my driver's license proudly displayed 5'1", and the few times I'd been pulled over, I'd never had a police officer challenge the extra inch when they inspected my license. So it was basically official.

"Morning." I leaned into the door, resting my head on my hand that held it open and channeling my inner Rachel Green from *Friends*.

Landon's dark, styled hair, dark brows, and short-trimmed beard framed his copper brown eyes a little too well—eyes that didn't even take notice of my flirty stance. "Nikki insisted I set up some Christmas decorations to liven the place up. But if this is a bad time, I can come back later."

I blinked, rewinding my mind to register what he had said. Nikki. Decorations. Now or later? "Now's as good a time as any." Thank goodness I'd had the foresight to spiffy up the place a little.

It wasn't clean by any stretch of the imagination, but it was presentable now—mostly.

"I'll get a tree on Monday, but I figured I'd bring up a few of the decorations I had in storage." He lifted the box, as if to indicate that was what was inside. "If you need to check the contents for your safety ..."

"That would be great. If you could just set it here." I pointed to the ground, hoping to pull that reluctant smile from him that I'd briefly glimpsed last night. "Strands of Christmas lights and glass ornaments can be deadly in the wrong hands."

Instead of the smile I'd hoped for, his brows lifted.

"I'm kidding," I said, though the uncertain tone I used even left me questioning what my original intentions had been. What was I doing? I was way too out of practice to attempt flirting ... or teasing ... or whatever this awkwardness was. Taking a big step back, I threw the door open wide to give Landon plenty of room to enter.

"I'll be in and out." He stepped through, careful to keep his distance from the *mad* woman occupying his house, and moved to the center of the living room. He glanced at each surface, and after realizing they were still all entirely occupied by gingerbread pieces and cookie sheets full of more gingerbread pieces, he set the box down in front of the fireplace.

"I'll just keep on working, then." I threw a thumb over my shoulder toward the kitchen and shut the front door with a muted groan at my continued idiocy.

The two of us worked in strained silence—me continuing to tidy up and Landon putting up decorations. I tried to keep my attention from drifting to him, but it was hard to break a lifelong habit of people-watching, particularly when he was so fascinating to watch. I mean, not just because he was easy on the eyes, but every time he pulled something from the box, he'd turn it over in his hands with a bewildered look, glance around the room, and then shove the object onto the overfilled fireplace mantel.

"They're stocking holders," I said, unable to stop myself as he studied two identical metal reindeer with a wary look. "You typically set them on the edge of the mantel and hang stockings on them." Though I wasn't sure if there was currently room for them amongst all the other posh Christmas knickknacks.

Without a word, he carefully scooted a few of the objects closer together and placed the reindeer on the mantel, directly in the middle. When he pulled two white, knitted Christmas stockings from the box, he stared at them with a guarded expression before placing them on the holders' hooks. "Thanks," he finally muttered.

Yep. He definitely had the brooding thing down.

With a garland in hand, he moved to the stair banister that led to the third floor and hastily weaved it through the iron bars. The final result was far too much garland at the bottom and a few loops that didn't lay correctly.

I rinsed off the washcloth I'd been scrubbing the counters with. "I'm happy to put up the decorations if you leave them here."

He eyed the lopsided garland. "That bad, huh?"

My mouth opened, but I couldn't muster any assurances. I'd never been very good at lying.

"Decorating isn't my strength," he said.

I looked around the magazine-worthy space. "Someone else did this for you?"

His jaw set. "My ex-wife."

I glanced at his empty ring finger as though I'd find evidence of a previous marriage there. "I'm sorry. I'm also divorc—"

His sardonic laugh cut me off. "Of course you'd be divorced."

The sucker punch to my gut stunned me, and I wrapped a hand around myself, trying to get my bearings.

Landon trudged to where the box sat and scooped it up. "I'll be back with the tree on Monday."

I clenched my hands at my sides, glad the dining room table was between us so he couldn't see the effect of his comment on me. "I don't need a tree." The high road was usually my path of choice, so I kept my tone casual. "In fact, I'm not planning on really celebrating Christmas this year."

I intended to stop there, but I hated unspoken tension and would rather just have it all out than risk encountering it with each conversation Landon and I had—not that I'd expect many to follow this one. "You don't need to care, but I came to Newport so my best friend wouldn't feel guilty about spending Christmas with her family instead of me. And so I'd have a valid excuse to miss a Christmas get-together where I'd be showered with pity and unhelpful comments about my recent divorce from my well-meaning family. But had I known I'd be staying in your house—that I'd be putting you out—I wouldn't have come. One thing I've learned about myself this past year is that I hate being an inconvenience. If I had the money, I'd find somewhere else to stay. I don't. I'm sorry that I'm here. Really. But until your sister or her assistant can find me new accommodations, I don't know what else to do."

He stared at me for a long moment before he shook his head —slowly at first until it grew more noticeable. "You don't need to leave. And you shouldn't be the one apologizing." He tipped his head back and then lowered it again to meet my gaze. "I'm sorry for my comment about not being surprised you're divorced. I didn't mean it how it sounded."

"Regardless, if you're upset I'm in your house, I'm fine to sleep downstairs. Really."

"This isn't about you being in my house." His hands drummed against the cardboard box absently. "It's the *reason* you're here."

I glanced down at the dining room table, full to the brim with gingerbread. "You're upset about my baking?"

"No." His eyes narrowed. "You really have no idea what I'm talking about, do you?"

Maybe he was the crazy one. "Apparently not."

He shifted the box to his side and ran a hand through his gloriously thick, dark hair—not that I was taking notice of how attractive he currently looked in his nicely fitted jeans and gray t-shirt that sat snugly against his broad chest. "How well do you know Nikki?" he asked, forcing my gaze back to his.

I shrugged. "We've only met twice in person. She was my mentor at a conference in San Diego a few years ago, then we met up at another conference this past summer. Other than that, we message occasionally and follow each other on social media. Why?"

His distant gaze focused before meeting mine. "So you aren't aware she is a self-proclaimed matchmaker?"

I tilted my head to the side, not sure why he'd bring up such a random thing, but suddenly, my eyes grew wide with understanding. "You think your sister is trying to set us up?"

"Why else would she put you in my house without telling me?"

"Because I needed somewhere to stay with a large kitchen, and she hadn't realized you would be here?"

"She would normally okay it through me. And between her fiancé, Kade, having me forced off my project so I'd be home earlier, her less-than-subtle hints that I should take you around Newport, and the fact we both just so happen to be recent divorcees ..." He shook his head. "She's undeniably trying to set us up."

Amusement bubbled up inside of me at the thought of Nikki Aker wanting to set me up with her gorgeous, grumpy brother. There was no way. Like, none. I clasped a hand over my mouth, but it didn't do its job at keeping my laughter from escaping.

"You think this is funny?" Despite Landon's serious tone, the corners of his mouth twitched. "It's only going to get worse when she gets here. She gets these crazy ideas in her head and does whatever it takes to see them actualized. I think she calls it manifesting or some nonsense, but really, it's just pure tenacity with a heap of sweetly applied manipulation."

"I'm sorry," I said after a moment, quieting my laughter but unable to lessen my smile. "It's obvious you're upset about this."

"And you're not? She flew you across the country for her own dubious purposes."

I wiped my eyes, sobering some at his comment. "Well, when you say it like that, I probably should be upset. I mean, if you're right—which I'm far from convinced you are—that's a huge hit to my pride. Not only because I thought Nikki hired me for my talent, but it's obvious you're less than thrilled by the idea of being set up with me."

He dipped his chin. "It's not you. You seem like a nice—"

I put up my hands, stopping him before he could finish with some half-hearted reassurance that would likely have the opposite effect on me than he intended. Maybe once Landon knew I wasn't a threat to his bachelorhood, he could stop being a surly beast at every encounter. "It's fine. Honestly, I wouldn't want to date me either. I'm currently a mess."

His gaze flicked to the kitchen behind me.

"That, too, but I meant emotionally." I'd already admitted more than I probably should have, but I could feel the explanation rising inside of me, trying to break free. And suddenly, it came rolling out. "It's been a long year. The first anniversary of my husband—ex-husband, that is—walking out on me is fast approaching. The day after Christmas, to be exact. I'd tell you his reasons to give further evidence of what a poor choice I am, but he never really told me what they were." I laughed in a way that probably made the point for me and squarely placed Landon in the *keep away* zone. Exactly where he should have been. Which was why I wouldn't regret my word vomit—until later.

"He just up and left." I gave an overdone shrug. "Until he remembered it was technically his house I was living in and kindly texted me to be out before the New Year. I've been living with my best friend ever since, relying on my super-meager income and picking up odd jobs to help contribute financially in what ways I can. I have a useless degree, and the one thing I love doing and had previously found success at—being a social media influencer— I'm now failing at. I'm also pretty sure I'm nearing an intervention-worthy level of addiction to true-crime podcasts and docu-mentaries. So there you have it."

He ran a hand over his beard. "Well, that was ... enlightening. But I—"

"Oh," I interrupted, remembering one last thing I needed to make clear. "I also have zero intention of dating right now. Cody and I were together for five years before we got married, so I don't even remember how to do the whole dating-other-people thing. I actually tried to flirt with you when you came to the door, just to test my skills, and we both know how that turned out. So, all of that to say, I'm right there with you on the not-being-set-up thing."

Landon's brow wrinkled. "You tried flirting with me?"

I pointed at the cardboard box. "The box situation—you putting it down so I could check it—and there was my cute lean against the door that you didn't bat an eye at."

That rare smile touched his lips. "Okay, maybe you're a little rusty."

Despite his stated disinterest, and my own, that darn smile of his enlivened the same onslaught of feelings I'd experienced when I first saw it. Construction on the wall around my heart would begin immediately. I'd meant every word I'd just said, and I was more than obviously not in a place to put myself out there yet. "That's exactly why I won't be flirting again—maybe ever."

To my utter amazement, he chuckled. "I'm not sure you should swear it off forever, but I'm glad we could come to an understanding."

I nodded. "*If* Nikki attempts to force us together, we will resist her every effort."

SIX

QUINN

THE SUGAR-GLASS WINDOWS WERE FINISHED, AND I'D nearly completed assembly on the first of the four gingerbread structures—a house that looked as unremarkable as the one I'd grown up in. I figured it'd make the most sense to start on the least-complicated building first. The cabin would probably be next, because I was still trying to figure out the best way to attach the four pillars to the front exterior of the other house—a large, three-story one. And then there was Rosecliff Mansion, which would certainly prove to be my greatest challenge with the countless design elements I'd need to incorporate to make it recognizable. None of my previous gingerbread creations had been as grand as Rosecliff, so as excited as I was to have a go at it, I was also terrified I might screw it up.

The sound of heavy steps in the shared stairwell sent me scrambling toward the door. I peered through the peephole, but before I could make out if it was Landon, the view went dark.

Why would Landon cover it? Or was it someone else? My palms grew clammy against the door.

There was a scratching sound followed by a loud thud. I jumped, and a second thud followed. "Who's there?" I asked, straining to hear over the drumming in my ears.

"It's Landon."

My whole body relaxed. When I opened the door, the smell of fresh pine overwhelmed my senses in the same moment branches filled the newly available space. Landon peeked around the massive tree. "Delivery."

I stared at the beast of a pine he supported. "Didn't we talk about this? I don't need a Christmas tree."

"Unfortunately, Nikki would disagree. And I don't have the patience to endure her barrage of texts until I comply." Without waiting for a reply, he maneuvered the trunk through. Pine needles scattered, and I pressed myself against the wall to keep from being maimed. When the whole tree was inside, Landon started toward the living room with it. "Considering you seem slightly less demanding than Bridezilla, I took a calculated risk."

"Slightly less demanding?" I shut the door. "And here I thought we decided to be nice to each other."

"We decided to thwart Nikki's matchmaking. I'm pretty sure being nice to each other is counterproductive to achieving that goal."

I followed him with careful steps to prevent the fallen pine needles from sticking to my socks. "Well, that's a huge relief. After our last chat, I was wondering how I'd cope with being deprived of your churlish behavior toward me. It seems I worried in vain."

He settled the tree at the end of the sectional, keeping his attention from drifting to me. "It seems so, but I admire your antiquated word choice."

A witty, Jane-Austen-worthy reply would have been perfect, but I had nothing. Instead, I pointed at the trunk. "It needs a stand if you intend for it to stay up."

He drew in a slow breath, his chest broadening with the intake of air. "I'm well aware. Thank you."

"Well then, I'll let you get back to it."

He finally locked eyes with me. "I left the stand in my truck."

"Oh. That's unfortunate." I took a step backward, entirely ready for him to beg. "Too bad we aren't being nice to each other, or I'd offer to hold the tree while you get it."

His brows went up, and his gaze trailed down my body—not in a way that made me blush, but in a way that made me stretch my neck a little taller. I knew exactly what he was thinking.

"I'm stronger than I look."

His slight smirk was full of condescension. "I'll just lay the tree on the floor."

I stepped forward again, chin lifted. "I can hold it." Before he could refuse my offer, I pressed myself into the branches and reached my arms into the thick boughs to find the trunk. With how the pine needles pricked at my bare skin, it was a good thing that my sleeves were mostly impenetrable and that I had safely secured my mass of curls in a messy bun. After one more hearty thrust into the unyielding limbs, I gripped the trunk with both hands. Widening my stance, I anchored through my legs. "Got it. You can let go."

"Are you sure?"

Two-thirds of the tree was situated above my hands, but the excessive doubt in Landon's tone ignited my determination. "Absolutely."

He removed one hand, surveying my hold. "Because I'd meant for you to grab the stand, not hold the tree."

Darn. That would have been an easier solution, but now I had a point to prove. "I've got it. Go."

Slowly, he released his other hand, though he didn't lower either of them. Instead, he kept them outstretched with his fingers splayed, like he expected the tree to come crashing down without his support.

When it didn't, I shot him a self-satisfied smile, though the strange angle I held my head at to avoid getting a mouthful of pine needles probably canceled out the effectiveness. "Small but mighty."

He assessed the tree again, then finally lowered his arms. "I'll be right back."

"Don't hurry on my account," I called to the sound of his retreating footsteps. Yet, despite my assurances, stabilizing the tree was more difficult for me than I'd admit. I was growing all too aware that the slightest movement could off-center the weight, and once that happened, there was no possible way I'd be able to keep it upright. So I just couldn't let that happen. I was a statue—an unmoving, arm-aching, determined statue. I refused to lose face in front of a man who thought me incapable—at least this particular man.

If only the spot on my cheek where the pine needles pressed didn't itch so terribly. Carefully, I lifted my chin and turned my head farther away from the assaulting branch. It slipped to my neck, which gave temporary relief, but after a minute, the itch started there and then intensified. My ears became unnervingly tuned to the void of sound in the stairwell. What was taking Landon so long?

The unbearable sensation was now radiating from my neck, back into my cheek, and down my arms into my hands. A moan escaped me, and I felt an irrational desire to let the tree fall and satiate the itch or scratch my skin off in the attempt. But I wouldn't do it. I could wait a few more minutes.

When footsteps finally sounded on the stairs, my breath came a little easier.

"You still good?" Landon asked from behind.

Besides how my skin screamed at me and how I was one slight movement away from the tree toppling? "Oh, yeah. Great, even."

"That was convincing." He kneeled down and placed the stand on the floor. "If I lift the tree, do you think you can help guide the trunk into place? Or have I maxed out your charity for today?" He stood and took hold of the tree with one hand, much higher than I held it, but his muscular arm was regrettably at eye-level. He flexed when the weight of the tree shifted to him, and it took me a huge heap of self-control to look away from the defined triceps peeking out of the bottom of his snugly fit sleeve.

I relinquished my hold and squatted down, rubbing my neck and cheek inconspicuously. Sweet relief. "Considering our current understanding to not be nice to each other, and the fact that you brought a tree when I told you not to, I feel it's impor-tant to say I'm only helping because I'm indebted to you for letting me stay here." It wasn't exactly true, but there was no reason for him to think otherwise. Besides, with my itch intensi-fying again, I wasn't feeling very generous.

"Fair enough."

I wiggled beneath the branches, doing my best to keep my messy bun from getting stuck. "Okay," I called. "I'm ready." The tree lifted, and I took hold of the trunk, easing it toward the middle of the stand. "It's centered. Lower it."

Landon slowly dropped it into place, and I shimmied further under the tree. My fingers felt oddly uncooperative, likely from all the work I'd been doing on the gingerbread, but I managed to tighten the bolts. "That should be good," I called when the clamps were secured around the trunk. With another quick scratch of my neck and cheek, I scooted backward, standing to face him with a self-satisfied smile.

"Thanks for ..." His brow wrinkled, and his focus went to my cheek. "What happened to your face?"

I placed my hand on the spot where he'd fixed his gaze—the spot that still itched despite having been scratched twice now—and the heat of it radiated into my hand. "What do you mean?"

His gaze dropped to my neck. "Are you allergic to pine trees?"

"Not that I know of. But my family always had a fake tree, so I guess I'm not sure. Why?"

He stepped closer, and I felt self-conscious under his careful consideration. "You're developing hives. Look at your hands."

My gaze dropped, and my stomach churned. Raised welts dotted the skin from where the wrist of my sweatshirt ended to the tips of my fingers, a pinkish-red color filling in the surface between them. Did my face look this bad? Instinctively, I covered my cheek and searched for a mirror.

"The closest mirror is in the bathroom," Landon said, apparently aware of what I was looking for.

I hurried to the half-bath and flipped on the light, mortified to find the same red splotches overtaking the entire left side of my face and neck. Leaning in closer, I stared at the hives congregated on the itchiest spots. Not only did it look awful, but my skin was abuzz and angry, begging to be placated. My fingernails made glorious contact.

"Don't." To my horror, Landon stood just outside the bathroom, watching me. "Scratching will only make it worse. And don't rub your eyes."

With one innocent warning, he somehow summoned the itch to reach my eyes. It took every effort to stop from shrieking in utter desperation at the sensation that was slowly consuming me. "And what do you suggest I do?"

"Are you having any difficulty breathing or feel you might vomit?"

I drew in a deep breath to test my lungs and shook my head.

"Good. Do you have Benadryl?"

I tapped my foot in a quick rhythm as some sort of release from the irritation. "Fresh out," I said with more of a bite than was necessary. Stupid itching.

"Go shower and change your clothes. I'll run and grab some medicine."

That was all I needed—to be further indebted to Landon. I glanced back in the mirror, allowing my eyes to rove over my unsettling reflection that now resembled an exaggerated version of my teenage self mid-breakout. My shoulders fell. "Thank you."

"I'll be back in fifteen. If you have a difficult time breathing or if you vomit, call an ambulance."

A wave of panic shot through me. "An ambulance?"

"They have epinephrine in case you go into anaphylactic shock. But I don't think you will if hives are your only reaction so far." He stepped back, leaving me plenty of room to exit. "Now, go shower."

I stepped out of the bathroom, stopping in front of him. "You're not going to go all Psycho and murder me while I'm showering, are you?"

He quirked his head and lifted his chin like he was thinking about it. "Nikki and Kade will be here tonight, so it would probably be best to keep my murderous rage bottled until then."

My grimaced smile made my cheek skin stretch, intensifying the itch, and I turned from him to make my way upstairs. Hopefully, a shower would ease this unbearable discomfort. When I reached the top, I glanced back to find Landon standing in the same place, watching me.

His gaze dropped, and he ran a hand over his jaw.

"Could you lock the door on your way out?" I asked.

"You bet." He stepped backward, out of sight.

"Thanks," I called, relieved to be free of Landon's perceptive gaze. My fingers settled on my cheek, eager to finally ease the unrelenting itch.

"Make sure you don't scratch," he called back, like I was the most predictable person he'd ever met.

I dropped my hive-speckled hand and groaned loudly enough for him to hear my immature reaction.

THE SHOWER HAD TAKEN the edge off the itch, but the hives hadn't faded. If anything, they'd grown more pronounced. And now, my eyelids had joined in on the fun. Looking at my puffy-eyed reflection in the steam-filled bathroom mirror, I fully regretted my moment of weakness—the moment after I'd removed my sweatshirt while I waited for the water to warm. My natural instincts had taken over, demanding I rub my aggravating eyes. I should have heeded Landon's counsel and restrained—at least until I'd rinsed off.

I was literally two swollen ears away from looking like Hitch after he'd eaten shellfish. I needed medicine—like, now. With a fresh set of clothes on and a towel still wrapped around my wet hair, I made my way downstairs to see if Landon had returned from the store.

The Christmas tree was gone, but there was no sign of him.

My phone's ring cut through the silence, and I searched the kitchen table where the sound originated, wondering if Landon had somehow managed to get my number. A glint of light off the bottom of a propped-up metal cookie sheet caught my attention, and I lifted it to glimpse the phone screen. Mom.

I snatched up the phone, carefully repositioned the tray, and pressed accept before I realized it was a video call. Mom's lovely face filled the screen, and then her eyes widened. "Quinn! What happened to you? Are you hurt?"

My gaze dropped to the thumbnail image of me in the corner, and I could see why she assumed I'd been jumped. "Did you know I had an allergy to pine trees?" I asked, forcing out an appeasing smile.

Her hand moved to her chest in obvious relief, though her worried expression remained in place. "No."

I shrugged. "Turns out I do."

"Oh, sweetie. You look awful."

I positioned my head to place my hived cheek and neck on full display. "I don't know. It's kind of a good look on me."

Mom didn't smile at my attempt. "You need to go to an urgent care. I know things are tight financially for you, but Dad and I could help pay—"

"Landon will be back any minute with Benadryl. He said it will help."

Mom's head flinched back, and I instantly regretted having mentioned him so casually. Though Mom and I didn't have much in common, our meager size meant we both shared a healthy dose of paranoia. "Who's Landon?"

"Nikki's brother. He owns the house."

"The house you're staying at?"

I nodded.

The emerging wrinkles on Mom's brow deepened. "Is he staying there with you?"

I tried not to be offended that she thought me naïve enough to stay alone in a house with a man I didn't know. "No. He's staying in the apartment downstairs. He was just here putting up a Christmas tree when"—I gestured to my face—"this happened."

Her expression finally relaxed. "Well, if the Benadryl doesn't help, promise you'll go in."

"I will." I paused, waiting to see if she would also drop a subtle reminder to keep my pepper spray on hand—the one the TSA had unfortunately confiscated—but she didn't. "So did you need something?" I asked.

"When do you get home again?"

"The twenty-seventh."

"Wait. What day is the wedding? On Christmas?"

"No," I said, bracing myself. "The twenty-second."

"The twenty-second? So why aren't you coming home before Christmas?"

"I thought it might be easier for me to be away this year."

Mom didn't answer for a minute. "I understand this Christmas is going to be hard for you, but that's why you should be with your family."

"As much as I love being with everyone, I honestly can't do it this year. I don't have it in me."

"What if we don't go to Santa Barbara?"

I stilled. "What do you mean?"

"Margaret had a great idea, and I think we should try it—just our small family together, here in San Diego, for Christmas."

"I thought Margaret and Michael were going to go on their belated honeymoon."

"They're postponing it until after the holidays. Margaret sent me an article the other day about establishing traditions as newly-weds. I'll have to forward it to you, but research shows that shared family traditions ground a couple and make for stronger, healthier marriages—something about weaving two separate lives into one. So Margaret was thinking, because Michael gets too overwhelmed with the whole extended family, we should start a new tradition and just have our immediate family get together for Christmas."

Thankfully, my swollen eyelids concealed my eye roll. Now that my older sister had started her PhD program in psychology, she was apparently an authority on all things that contributed to a strong marriage. If she hadn't already been accepted into the program before my divorce, I'd think my failed marriage was the sole motivation for her choice of study with how often she shared her *expert opinion.* "Isn't the point of a tradition to have done it for a long time—like us going to Santa Barbara?"

"It apparently doesn't matter if the tradition is long-standing or newly established, as long as those participating are committed to it. Besides, it's probably time we stop our large family gathering. Without Grandma here, I think the whole thing is over-whelming for Grandpa. I'm guessing he'd prefer to visit individual families for Christmas instead."

It was true that, the past two years, Grandpa had seemed out of sorts with all of us there. My aunts had all stepped up to fill the huge void that Grandma left, but it wasn't the same. And yet, the thought of it ending broke off a small piece of my heart. True, I hadn't planned on going this year, but that didn't mean I never wanted to again. "And what did Xena have to say about Margaret's *new* tradition? She loves going to Santa Barbara."

Mom smiled unapologetically. "Your sister will take one for the team."

A hollow laugh slipped out. There was no way I'd *take one for the team* this round. The past year had been torturous enough, helping to plan and then taking part in Margaret's wedding when I was still reeling from my own failed marriage. I didn't need to spend the anniversary of Cody walking out on me with a poignant, PDA'ing reminder of everything I'd lost. "As much as I'd like to be there, I don't think I can change my flight now."

"If you can't, Dad and I can pay for a return ticket."

A quiet knock sounded on the door, drawing my attention. Hallelujah. "Coming," I called. "Hey, Mom. I've got to go. Landon's back with the medicine."

"Okay." She paused. "But think about what I said. It would mean a lot to Margaret—to all of us—if you were here for Christmas."

Guilt wriggled around my resolve. "I can't make any promises."

"Thank you, sweetie." Before I could attempt a redo, she pointed at the camera. "And make sure you keep your pepper spray close by. I don't like the idea of some man you don't know having a key to the house."

"I'll be safe. Love you, Mom."

"Love you, sweetie."

I set my phone down, hurried to the door, and glanced out the peephole to confirm it was Landon. My hived hand resting on the bolt made me pause. Was I really going to let Landon see me like this—straight out of the shower with a towel on my head, swollen eyes, and hives covering half of my exposed skin? How low had I sunk?

"Quinn. It's me." Landon must have heard me at the door or seen the peephole darken when I'd looked through. "I've got medicine."

The secret code word—medicine—had been spoken, and I pushed my embarrassment aside. Besides, why should I care what Landon thought of me? He'd made it very clear that he not only didn't want to be set up with me, but that he didn't even want to be on friendly terms. With that reminder, I threw open the door without a care. "Hey."

He stepped through, bringing an assault of cold air and that delightful woodsy smell with him, but paused when his gaze dropped from my towel-wrapped head to my face. His widened eyes roved over every mortifying inch of my swollen, hived skin. "Are you doing okay?" The concern in his voice startled me, making me second-guess if I was. "Have you developed any more symptoms?"

"No, but I may have rubbed my eyes ... a few times."

His posture relaxed, and he closed the door behind him before gesturing to the living room. "Let's get you some medicine."

He removed his heavy coat as we walked, tossed it on the far end of the sectional, and took a seat facing me. I left one full cushion between us, knowing how he preferred his distance, and tucked my legs beneath me.

"Here," he said, dumping the contents of the bag onto the empty seat.

My stunned gaze went from the pharmaceutical jackpot to him. "I thought you said you were grabbing Benadryl. What's all this other stuff?" I grabbed a tube of cream to examine.

"That's hydrocortisone cream for the itching." He pointed to a pink bottle next. "And calamine lotion if you prefer that instead. Liquid Benadryl, of course. This one's an antihistamine to take for the next few weeks while you're here. And this"—he gestured to a pleated cloth sack with a plastic top—"is a reusable ice bag. A cold compress helps with the itch."

I blinked, taking in his haul one more time. "How much did all of this cost?" I asked, trying not to let my worry impact my tone. Maybe I would have to send the bill to my parents after all.

"Don't worry about it. I'll put it on Nikki's tab. Here." He grabbed the Benadryl box, opened it, and handed the plastic container to me. "The dosage is by weight."

I studied the dosing chart. I was right at the upper weight

limit of the lower dose, so it would probably be safe to take the higher one considering how intense my reaction had been. I poured two teaspoons into the included cup, downed it, and then went back for a second shot of the same amount.

Landon's attention remained on me. "It should kick in soon —maybe fifteen minutes or so. And you can take more in four hours if you need it."

I placed the measuring cup and Benadryl on the coffee table, wishing it would take effect sooner. The itch was slowly intensifying again. "Will it make my eyes stop itching?" Unable to stop myself, I rubbed the heel of my palms into the sockets. "Because I think I might scratch them out if not."

"It should, but I know something that might help in the meantime." Landon stood up and went into the half-bath. The sink turned on for a minute, then off again. When he came back out, he held a folded, wet washcloth. "Put this over your eyes."

I was careful to avoid touching his fingers when I grabbed the cold cloth. With one brief glance, and quieting my thoughts about how vulnerable putting something over my eyes would make me, I tilted my head back against the couch. Instant relief came from the frigid cloth. A sigh of contentment slipped from my lips.

"Better?"

I simply nodded, pressing the washcloth more firmly against my face. "You seem like quite the allergy expert. Do you deal with any?"

"My sister does."

"Nikki?"

"No. My older sister, Julie. Between her food allergies and her seasonal allergies, I've learned the drill." He paused. "Speaking of, we should probably get some cream on your hives and get you the cold compress."

His use of *we* had me sitting up straight, and the washcloth slipped down my face and into my lap. I plopped it next to the medicine on the glass surface of the coffee table. "I'll do it."

"Which do you want?" he asked, resuming his spot on the couch a cushion away from me. "White or pink?"

I glanced between the hydrocortisone cream and the calamine lotion Landon held. "Maybe I'll try them both and see what helps more, so I'll know for next time."

He extended them both closer to me, waiting for me to choose.

"I'll start with this one." I grabbed the hydrocortisone. Removing the cap and the aluminum safety covering, I plopped a decent amount into my palm and began spreading it onto my hands. The white paste was thick and slightly oily, but eventually, it rubbed in. I pulled up one sleeve of my sweater with my clean index finger and began dabbing it on the few hives there.

"Weren't you wearing long sleeves?" Landon asked, his eyes focused on my forearm.

"The needles poked through my sweatshirt in some places," I said, lowering the sleeve again and lifting my other one. I dabbed a bit of cream on a large hive near my elbow. "It's not too bad, though. Not like my face and hands."

Landon let out a heavy breath. "I'm sorry. Had I known you'd have a reaction—"

"Had I known, I wouldn't have offered to hold the tree. It's not a big deal, really." I twisted the lid back on the cream and grabbed the calamine lotion. "I'll do my face in the bathroom so I can see where I'm putting it."

He also stood, but to my relief, he started toward the kitchen.

The pink liquid refused to absorb into my skin, but the itch dimmed almost instantly at contact. "Is this stuff supposed to rub in?" I called.

"Not really," Landon called. "It coats the skin."

Perfect. If I had to have a few giant clusters of hives on my face and neck, why not draw attention to it with a pink, chalky mask? Thank heavens no one would see me like this—well, no one I needed to impress. When I finished the application, I shook my head at my pitiful reflection. "It just keeps getting better," I said, stepping back out into the open space.

Landon glanced up from where he was sweeping the floor, that smile of his, the one that made my insides flutter, making an appearance. "Pink's a good color on you."

"Isn't it?" I dropped onto the couch, my body unusually sluggish. A yawn escaped me, and I hurried to cover it. "I can help you clean up. I just need to sit for a minute first."

"I'm not letting you anywhere near these pine needles." He pointed to the corner of the coffee table. "There's your cold compress."

"Thanks," I said, picking it up along with the wet washcloth. The washcloth wasn't as cold as it had been, but it still brought relief when I laid it across my eyes. For several minutes, I leaned against the couch, listening to Landon move around the room and shifting the ice compress to whatever patch of skin most demanded it.

I yawned again. "Wow. I'm exhausted."

"The Benadryl is probably taking effect. It causes drowsiness in some people."

My head was nearly as heavy as my swollen eyelids, and my thoughts were growing muddled. I clearly was in the *some-people* category. "Had I known that, I probably wouldn't have taken extra."

The sound of his movements stopped. "How much did you take?"

The answer danced around my head, but each time I tried to latch onto it, it evaded me.

Hurried footsteps moved toward where I sat. "Quinn, how much did you take?"

I removed the washcloth for a moment to find Landon standing next to the couch with the dosing cup in hand and studying the Benadryl bottle with intensity. "I don't remember exactly," I mumbled. "Maybe four or five."

"Four or five what?"

"Tspppps." The idea of the sound made sense in my head but sounded wrong when I spoke it. What was the actual word? Tispons? No. Something like that, though. I was just too tired to recall it. "I need a nap." My words seemed to slur together in my mind. "Please don't kill me while I sleep."

SEVEN

LANDON

NIKKI'S CONCERNED GAZE REMAINED ON QUINN. "HOW long has she been out?"

"Almost six hours," I said quietly. Six horribly long hours. The hives had been one thing, but at least, with them, I knew how to help. When Quinn mentioned, in her medicine-induced state, she took extra Benadryl before proceeding to pass out, that was when I lost my cool. In my panic, I'd had Poison Control dialed before I'd had the sense to call my dad, who'd spent his career as an ER doctor. "Dad said an extra dose or two wouldn't be dangerous to an adult, but because she's so petite, he advised I watch her closely to make sure her breathing doesn't change and her heart rate remains steady."

Nikki glanced at me out of the corner of her eyes, and I was certain I saw her lips twitch like she was holding back a smile. "So you've stayed with her the whole time?"

"What else was I supposed to do?" I grumbled, refusing to give her the satisfaction of thinking her matchmaking intuition had been right. Nikki would never discover how attentive I'd been. And neither would Quinn. Quinn already thought I was some sort of closet murderer, so I didn't need her to find out I'd spent the better part of six hours in the room while she slept. Listening to her breathe. Occasionally feeling her wrist to check her pulse. And smiling to myself every time her light snoring interrupted my reading.

"I think she's waking up," Kade said, refocusing my attention on Quinn.

She tucked the blanket I'd draped over her up to her chin and rolled away from us with a groan of complaint.

"Quinn?" Nikki approached the couch. "Are you awake?"

A small noise escaped Quinn, but I couldn't see much from where I stood near the fireplace.

Nikki squatted next to the couch and touched Quinn's arm. "Quinn, how are you feeling?"

Slowly, Quinn's head turned toward Nikki. Her eyes blinked heavily a few times, focused, and then rounded. "Nikki. Hey!" She scrambled to sit, pushing the blanket off her legs, only to have the towel still wrapped around her head tip sideways. With clumsy movements, she quickly unwound the towel and freed the ends secured in its folds. "When did you get here?" she asked, running her hands through her hair and glancing around. Her gaze settled on me. "Have I been asleep long?"

"Six hours," Nikki said, saving me from answering. "Are you feeling okay?"

Quinn gave a slow, stunned nod, then returned her attention to my sister. "Much better. Thanks."

Nikki slid onto the couch next to Quinn. "I'm so sorry about all of this."

"It's fine." Quinn batted at the air dismissively. "It's so good to see you again. It's been way too long." She gestured to Kade, who stood a few feet behind Nikki, her voice unnaturally high and fast. "And I haven't met your fiancé. How was the flight? Did you get your dress?" Quinn's cheeks turned a darker shade of pink than the remnants of calamine lotion that still covered her face and neck.

Nikki smiled sweetly, obviously as charmed by Quinn's rapid firing of questions as I secretly was. There was something about this woman that constantly made me fight a smile.

"Our flight was great," Nikki said. "I got the dress. And this is my fiancé, Kade." Kade waved, and Nikki settled a hand over Quinn's. "And it's good to see you, too. Thanks for coming all this way. I hope you don't mind, but I peeked at your work." She gestured toward the gingerbread structure on the table I'd admired earlier. Quinn had done a remarkable job with it, considering that, even undecorated, I knew it was a replica of the house where Nikki and I had grown up here in Newport. The house my dad still lived in. "I can't imagine a better collection of centerpieces for our wedding."

Quinn ran a hand through her hair again and shifted in her seat. "Well, I'm glad to be here."

Nikki's gaze locked on me. "My brother hasn't been too terrible a host, has he?"

Quinn glanced at me, lifting her chin slightly as though resolving herself to our plan—well, not really a plan, but an understanding that we would thwart Nikki's scheme at any cost. "Other than when I thought he was breaking in and the whole Christmas-tree ordeal today, I haven't seen him much."

I tightened my already folded arms, trying not to shift under Nikki's glare. "You haven't shown Quinn Newport yet?"

I shifted. Shoot. "She said she had a lot of work to do."

"Unbelievable." Nikki shook her head and looked back to Quinn, her expression shifting from disappointment to apology. "I'll take you, then."

"Oh, you don't need to do that. I'm sure you have so much to do before your wedding."

Kade dropped onto the sectional next to Nikki and wrapped an arm around her waist. "She didn't hire the most uptight wedding planner on the East Coast for nothing."

Nikki dipped her chin, sending Kade a correctional look. "Irene Garrity is a dear. Besides, the wedding guests don't start arriving for another week. There's plenty of time to plan a night out." She pointed at me. "But you're not invited."

I wouldn't allow my sister to make me feel bad. Kade was the one that had forced me here, and she was the one who put some woman in my house without asking permission—and with ulterior motives, no less. But then why, if she meant to set me up with Quinn, had she banned me from going with them? Slightly confused, I shrugged like I didn't care.

Kade and Nikki shared a meaningful glance. I knew it. I knew she'd wanted things to go differently between me and Quinn. Nikki couldn't help but meddle in other people's lives, and I'd learned the hard way where that meddling would get me.

"I hope you don't intend to be Scrooge this whole time," she said, returning her attention to me. "There's someone I want you to meet, and I will be livid if you scare her away."

My stomach lurched, and I glanced at Quinn, whose parted mouth and surprised expression were probably not too different from my own.

"She's Kade's cousin," Nikki continued. "And she's perfect for you. Isn't she, Kade?"

Kade nodded like Nikki held his puppet strings. "I'm biased, but she's pretty amazing."

Nikki's hand tightened on Kade's knee.

"And also perfect for you," he added with an amused grin.

These two were up to something. "No offense, but being set up by you didn't exactly turn out well for me last time."

"Give me some credit." Nikki's head tipped to the side. "I know your type better now. Rachel is not only the whole package, but she's genuine to a fault. She's not like Eliza." Nikki kept her gaze focused on me. "Rachel will be here a few days before the wedding, and if the two of you hit it off like I suspect you will, I was thinking you could go together. She doesn't have a date either."

Quinn's thumb bounced on her clasped hands, and she looked like she wanted to excuse herself. Was she upset by the turn of events or relieved by it? Or maybe she was just uncomfortable talking about the details of someone's personal life, though that didn't seem to fit her zero-to-sixty personality.

I crossed my arms, ready to bring this to an end. "As great as that sounds, I think I'll pass."

Nikki's lips parted. "Come on. Just give her a shot. What harm can it do? At worst, you have someone to hang out with at the wedding."

"What if I already had someone in mind to take to the wedding?" I asked, just to be difficult. I didn't have anyone in mind.

Quinn's eyes narrowed in my periphery, but I kept my gaze locked on Nikki. "Honestly?" she said. "I'd be shocked—more than shocked, actually. I can't even remember the last time you took someone out on a date."

I drummed my fingers against my arms. "I guess you'll have to wait and see."

Nikki lifted her chin. "Fine. If you won't let me play matchmaker, I'll use my talents elsewhere." She shifted to face Quinn. "Do you have a date for the wedding yet?"

Quinn stared at her like she'd spoken in a foreign language. "I wasn't planning to go." Her cheeks grew pink. "I mean ... I didn't know I was invited."

"Of course you are. I had Irene email you to make sure you knew."

She bit at her lip, looking sheepish. Had she not seen the email? "Oh. Yes. Well ... as kind as your invitation is, I didn't bring a dress or shoes ... or anything like that."

"That's an easy fix."

Quinn blinked, her gaze going distant. Was she trying to think of an excuse? "I just don't know if—"

Nikki rested her hand on top of Quinn's a second time, giving her a well-executed pout. Part of me wanted to step in and save

Quinn from my sister's persuasive abilities, but the more reasonable part knew what Nikki would assume if I did.

"Please say you'll come," she said. "I have so many people I'd love to introduce you to. A lot of them are influencers like us."

I shook my head in amazement. She always knew the perfect carrot to dangle, and for a woman like Quinn, who had claimed she had a struggling social media account, Nikki had basically offered a lifeline. If I didn't know how genuinely good of a person my sister was, I'd be scared for anyone under her influence.

Quinn gave a timid nod of her head. "If you're sure."

"I'm positive!" Nikki clapped her hands together in front of her chest. "And I can't wait to introduce you to my friend Tyler."

My whole body tensed. "Tyler Baker?"

Nikki shot me a carefree smile. "Don't you think he and Quinn would have so much fun together?"

The tool would certainly try to have fun with her. "No." I uncrossed my arms and took a step toward Nikki. "Quinn's not Tyler's type."

Quinn's gaze flew to me, her insulted expression similar to the time she'd misinterpreted my 'I'm not surprised you're divorced' comment. Let her think what she wanted for now. I was trying to help her.

"You're wrong." Nikki looked at Quinn. "Tyler is fun, successful, and extremely attractive."

Kade leaned forward, catching Quinn's eye. "I don't know if I'd call him extremely attractive. I feel like that description should be reserved for ... I don't know ... one's fiancé. Decently attractive would probably suffice."

The corners of Nikki's mouth curved upward, and she discreetly fanned herself with the hand closest to Quinn. "He's super hot," she mouthed.

Kade shook his head and chuckled. "There you go, objectifying men again."

Nikki flashed a wide smile over her shoulder. "Don't tell me that Quinn and Tyler wouldn't make a beautiful—"

"I was going to ask Quinn to be my date," I blurted.

Quinn's head spun toward me, her eyes unblinking. She might have looked less shocked had I confessed to being a serial killer.

I shifted again but held her questioning stare. I couldn't tell her my reasons for this complete about-face. Not yet. She simply needed to trust me. But how was I supposed to convey that to her, especially after giving her so few reasons to do so?

She took in my expression for so long I wondered how I should react when she declined. "I ..." She gave a hard swallow. "I think that sounds fun." She glanced toward Nikki. "I mean, if that's alright with you?"

Nikki looked from Quinn to me and back again before pasting on a smile. "You don't need my permission if that's what you want." She genuinely seemed disappointed with how this had gone, so I couldn't regret my impromptu decision. But when I glanced back at Quinn's uncertain expression, I realized I was likely the only one with no regrets.

I CLOSED the door behind Nikki and Kade. They'd, thankfully, had dinner reservations and hadn't been able to stay much longer, which was perfect because I needed to explain my new plan to Quinn.

"Why did you ask me to be your date for the wedding?" Quinn asked, preempting me. I turned around to find her standing near the couch, her hands on her hips.

"Tyler is a player," I said, suddenly feeling defensive.

Quinn's expression softened like she suddenly understood why I'd said she wasn't his type. "And what about Rachel? Your asking me had nothing to do with avoiding her?"

I shrugged. "It's symbiotic."

She scrunched her nose. "Huh?"

"A mutually beneficial relationship—or, in our case, a mutually beneficial arrangement. I don't want Nikki to set me up, and you don't want to go to the wedding with Tyler, so we go together."

She crossed her arms, looking anything but intimidating with the pink remnants of calamine lotion that still covered parts of her skin. "How do you know I don't want to go with Tyler? Despite your opinion, Nikki obviously thinks highly of him."

"My sister doesn't know him like I do. Trust me. He's a tool. Besides, you were the one who said you had no intention of dating at the moment."

She gave a reluctant nod. "So where does that leave us?"

My head drew back. Did she think I actually wanted to take her to the wedding? I thought I'd made my intentions clear. Why did women always like to complicate everything? "What do you mean?"

"The whole *not-being-nice-to-each-other* thing? Are we still doing that?"

I breathed a sigh of relief. "You voided that with your whole damsel-in-distress, Sleeping Beauty routine."

She pursed her lips. "You mean my allergic-reaction-to-the-tree-I-told-you-I-didn't-want *routine*?"

Why did this woman make me want to smile at the most inconvenient times? "Again. I'm really sorry about that. But I'm glad to see the hives went away."

Her slightly puffy eyes grew wide, and her hand went to her face. Had she forgotten about the hives? With the way she raced into the bathroom, apparently, she had.

An audible gasp reached me, and she leaned out of the bathroom, piercing me with a glare. "Why didn't you tell me I looked like this?"

I allowed my gaze to rove over her. "Like what?"

She gestured to her entire head dramatically. "Like a rodeo clown that's seen better days!"

I couldn't restrain my smile a moment longer. "I think it's a good look on you."

"Really?" She disappeared from the doorway, and the sink turned on. "I'm glad to know your preference," she called over the running water. "Now I can replicate the look on our upcoming *date*." She reemerged, drying her face with the hand towel and tossing it back toward the sink.

"Perfect."

She scoffed, pulling her now-dry and slightly disheveled-looking hair into a ponytail. With one hand still holding her hair in place, she neared the dining room table and looked between the trays of gingerbread, her gaze searching for something.

"Are you looking for this?" I asked, grabbing a hair tie off the coffee table and tossing it to her.

To my surprise, she caught it and effortlessly wound it around her hair until a massive pile of waves sat atop her head in a sort of bun. "Thanks." Her tone was still a little clipped. But in my defense, I'd assumed she'd remember the calamine lotion on her face.

She stilled. "Is that from me?"

I followed her gaze to a few light-pink marks marring the brown leather. "I'm sure it will come off."

She hurried over to the part of the couch where she'd lain and frantically rubbed at a spot with her bare hand. It didn't budge. "Great. Now I'll have to spend the next five years as a receptionist at my dad's office, trying to pay off some crazy-expensive couch that I don't even own." She huffed and kept trying to wipe it. "What's in this stuff, anyway? Paint?"

I grabbed the slightly damp washcloth I'd given Quinn for her eyes earlier and stepped up next to her. "Here. This should do the trick." I leaned down and rubbed at one of the spots. With a little pressure and a few swipes, it vanished.

"Thank heavens." She grabbed the cloth. "I can finish cleaning it. It's my mess."

Her fingers grazed mine, and a strange electric pulse traveled up my arm. Had she somehow shocked me? With how motionless she was standing, both our hands still clinging to the cloth, she must have felt it, too. "I'm happy to clean it. I got you into this mess."

Her gaze slowly lifted to mine. After a moment of standing there, she dropped her hand and took a giant step back, like I was some kind of threat. "Thanks." She paced near the kitchen with a distant gaze, like a trapped animal in a cage. I must have crossed some sort of unspoken boundary. Or maybe she didn't like it being just the two of us here.

I quickly cleaned the rest of the marks, eager to be on my way. "Done."

She looked at me like she'd forgotten she wasn't alone.

I pointed toward the couch. "The marks came off."

"Oh." She nodded. "That's a relief. I guess I can cross 'indentured servant' off my to-do list." She was acting strangely. I couldn't pinpoint it, but something was wrong.

"Are you okay?"

"Me? Yeah." Her head bounced up and down. "Just hungry, I think."

That was my cue. Whatever was bothering her, it was obvious she didn't want me here. "I need to eat dinner, too, so—"

"You're welcome to join me."

I stared at her. Why would she ask me to stay if she wanted me to go? Was this one of those wrong-answer-either-way kind of things? If I left, she'd be upset, and if I stayed, she'd be annoyed? Apparently, she wasn't the only one who hadn't dated in a while. I was forgetting how women behaved. Or maybe it was just Quinn I couldn't read correctly.

She fidgeted with the sleeves of her sweater. "I mean, because you're here, and it seems like the right thing to do— invite you for dinner. Not because of ... anything else. Obviously. But we're friends now, so ... if you want to stay, you can, and if you don't ... well then, don't." At the end of her blurted explanation, her whole face scrunched up like she was momentarily in pain, but she quickly recovered, her cheeks now blazing red.

I had zero idea what she wanted, but for some inexplicable reason, I kind of wanted to stay. And now that I'd discovered Nikki hadn't intended to set me up with her, I didn't need to be as guarded. "I don't know how I could pass on an invitation like that," I said, testing the waters.

Her shoulders relaxed, and she gave a small smile. "Maybe you should wait to decide until I tell you what we're having—canned-chicken sandwiches with frozen green beans and carrots." She glanced toward the kitchen. "Ah! And I have tortilla chips still. I think."

Despite what I'd originally thought, I was kind of getting the vibe she wanted me to stay. "Wow. If you didn't sell it before, that certainly did the trick."

"It's not as bad as it sounds. I promise. I had the same thing for dinner last night."

"If it's good enough to eat two days in a row, I guess I need to try it."

She started toward the kitchen. "I mean, don't set your expectations too high. I've eaten through most of my fresh food in the last week and a half, so it's what I have."

I followed her, stopping on the threshold of the kitchen and leaning against the wall. "What do you mean you've eaten through most of your fresh food?"

She opened a cabinet and grabbed the canned chicken. "I knew I wouldn't have a car while I was here, so the grocery list I gave to Irene contained a lot of non-perishable items and freezer food."

"You know there are such things as ride-shares, right? And taxis?"

"I prefer eating canned food to getting into a strange car where I don't know the driver or what their intentions could be." She found the can opener and moved to the stovetop where there was nothing cluttering the workspace. It was odd seeing her look so at home in my kitchen while I stood on the outskirts like an outsider.

"I've found that their intentions are usually to take you where you want to go in exchange for payment."

The can hissed when the can opener punctured it. "*Usually* is the key word there."

I laughed, which pulled a reluctant smile from her.

"Go ahead and laugh." She cranked the handle of the can opener until the lid came free and then turned to face me. "But next time you are a five-foot female without a means of defending yourself, you might feel a little different."

My gaze trailed down her body with far too much enjoyment before I realized what I was doing and lifted my gaze to hers again. "That's fair," I said in appeasement. "But what about having groceries delivered? That wouldn't jeopardize your safety."

"I wasn't sure that was an option. And honestly, I don't think I have enough credit on my card to cover the cost until I could get reimbursed. It seemed easier to have Irene order non-perishables." She eyed me. "You really don't have to stay and eat a canned-chicken sandwich. I'm kind of sensing you don't want to."

"Have you left the house at all?" I asked, too intrigued by her admission to respond to her comment.

She busied herself by grabbing a bowl and emptying the contents of the can into it. "No. I really have had a lot to do."

"Have you at least walked down to the bay?"

She shook her head, pulling the mayo and mustard from the fridge. "Like I already said, I came here to make the gingerbread houses and get away for Christmas. I never planned to go sightseeing."

"Considering the bay is one street over, I'm not sure it would qualify as sightseeing."

She spooned some mayo into the chicken and threw in a little salt and pepper and a touch of mustard. I thought she might have been ignoring my comment, but her gaze met mine. "Honestly, I know it sounds strange, but I don't enjoy going out by myself. I met Cody—my ex—my very first week at college, and I've done everything with him or my best friend, Ashlee, since then. Before that, I was always with my parents, my sisters, or friends when I'd go out. When I'm home, I'll do errands by myself, but only if no one wants to go with me and only if I'm familiar with the place I'm going. Here, I'm across the country and alone." She paused, as if allowing her admission to sink in for me. "So no. I haven't even walked down to the bay yet."

Guilt settled over me like a suffocating blanket. If I hadn't treated Quinn like a piece in Nikki's game—a game, it turned out, I was wrong about—I might have realized her predicament sooner. Instead, I'd spent the weekend brooding like an inconsiderate jerk when none of this was Quinn's fault. It appeared I had a few blunders to redeem.

I rubbed a hand over the back of my neck and released a heavy breath when I realized Quinn was still watching me. "Can I help you with anything?" I pushed myself off the wall and walked into the kitchen. "I'm a revered expert on heating frozen vegetables."

She smiled and gestured to the freezer. "By all means. Have at 'em."

We worked in comfortable silence until the green beans were heated, the frozen sourdough bread was toasted, and our plates were loaded up. Quinn shoved the mostly empty tortilla chip bag under her arm, and I followed her to the couch, sitting one full cushion away from her like I'd realized she preferred.

She unrolled the bag of chips and positioned the opening toward me. "Excited?"

I only grabbed a few chips to ensure there would still be some left for her and pushed the opening back in her direction. "My mouth has been watering since you first mentioned canned chicken."

She laughed. "You'll regret that snark when you take a bite."

The crunch of the toasted bread was extremely satisfying, and I closed my eyes to make a point of it. The melted cheese was a nice addition, and the taste was … I opened my eyes. "It's surprisingly good," I said, my mouth still full.

Pride touched her striking smile, and she took a bite of her own sandwich. Her legs were wrapped under her on the sofa, and she looked the very image of contented comfort. "Told you."

I swallowed my next bite, curious to know more about Quinn and her reasons for wanting to be *an influencer*. She didn't seem like so many of Nikki's friends that I'd met over the years—always on their phones and desperate to get the next shot or to capture the perfect reel at whatever cost—but maybe she was. Maybe she was more like Eliza than I was inclined to think. "So tell me about your social media account." I glanced at the undecorated gingerbread houses on the table behind her. "I assume it involves baking."

"Mostly."

"Have you always enjoyed it—baking?"

"Since I can remember. My grandma taught me how to bake. When I'd visit, we'd spend all day in the kitchen, making cakes, brownies, candy … you name it." She grinned, her expression wistful, as though the memories were flashing through her mind. "And every year, as soon as school got out for Christmas break, my grandpa would drive down from Santa Barbara to pick me up. My grandma and I would spend the next few days baking all sorts of yummy things for our annual family gathering. I even went up the week before Christmas those first few years of college."

"So, being here, you're missing both of those traditions—the baking and the gathering?"

"The gathering, yes, but not the baking with Grandma." She paused and looked down at her plate. "My grandma died a few years back."

"I'm sorry."

She shrugged. "It's life. In all its ugly glory. It was actually two years ago, just before Christmas, that I started posting pictures and video clips of what I baked. It was just for me at first—a way to remember my grandma and document what I made—but one post went viral, and overnight, I hit ten thousand followers. I was honestly shocked anyone would care to see some random girl baking stuff, and yet, my audience kept growing and growing—until it stopped, that is. Now, it's sort of stagnant, if not quite firmly on the downward trend."

I sat there, not certain what to say. How did Quinn do it—be vulnerable so easily? We hardly knew each other, but she spoke without hesitation, without a thought to my judgment. And oddly, I wanted to reciprocate the honesty.

"I'm so sorry," she blurted. "I'm talking too much. Tell me about you. Your family or your work. Whatever you want."

And just like that, my aversion to revealing anything too personal—of opening up too much—took hold. "There's not a lot to tell. I worked at a few different legal firms until just after my divorce, and then I moved over to Carrigan Enterprises as a member of their general counsel. I oversee real estate transactions and development for them."

She crunched a carrot. "Carrigan. That's Kade's family's company?"

"It is. His grandfather started an investment firm over fifty years ago that did incredibly well and has expanded to all sorts of ventures—real estate, tech, pharmaceutical, backing start-up companies. The original Mr. Carrigan has retired, but his three sons and a daughter run it now. And several of his grandchildren, like Kade, also work for them, to some extent." I set my empty plate on the edge of the coffee table next to the assortment of medicine and leaned back into the couch. "And that's it."

"Tell me one thing you'd love to do if you had more time."

"Travel."

Her face brightened. "Really? Where to?"

"I've been to a handful of places in Europe and Central America, but I'd love to go to Peru. Or Thailand, maybe. How about you? Would you like to travel?"

"It's never really been on my radar, honestly. My family went on a lot of vacations, but they were always driving distance. And

Cody traveled while we were dating, but I never went with him. I assumed we'd maybe travel together eventually, but obviously that's not happening now. So, to answer your question, I'm not sure where I'd even want to go since I haven't really thought about it. Maybe England."

"England is pretty great. Make sure to hit up Scotland if you ever go. It's definitely worth a trip."

She gave a somewhat empty smile, like she wasn't sure that would ever happen. "What about your family? You have Nikki and ... Julie, was it?"

I nodded.

"Any other siblings?"

"I have a few step-siblings, but I've only met them a handful of times."

She waited patiently for me to explain, but when I didn't, she just nodded. "I also have two sisters: Margaret and Xena."

"Xena? Like The Warrior Princess?"

Quinn laughed. "My mom named all three of us after nineties TV characters. Well, Margaret is pre-nineties since her name comes from Major Margaret Houlihan on *M*A*S*H*, but *Xena the Warrior Princess*, and"—she pointed to herself—"*Doctor*—"

"*Doctor Quinn, Medicine Woman?*"

"The one and only."

I chuckled. "Are your sisters older or younger than you?"

"I'm your classic, overlooked middle child. Xena, my little sister, just went to college on a full-ride scholarship for soccer. She's got it all—brains, beauty, athleticism. Margaret, the oldest, is everything I'm not—organized, intelligent, driven. She graduated top of her class from USD and is now getting her PhD in psychology." Quinn's gaze flickered to her plate. "She got married this year."

She said it like she was happy for her sister, but her expression had sobered, and with it, I did too. Her gaze returned to me. "And then, there's me: The Queen of Chaos and Underachievement."

Once again, I didn't know what to say. From what little I knew of Quinn, she was slightly chaotic. And yet, somehow, with her, it was an endearing trait. Not that I could tell her that. But I found I wanted to say something that would make her smile again. "My sister has almost five million followers on social media and is about to marry one of the heirs to a multi-billion-dollar company. My other sister is a mother of four, actively involved in her community, and is a gifted artist when she finds time to paint, which is a lot more often than you'd think. So it looks like we have another thing in common."

It worked. Quinn gifted me a beautiful smile for my admission. "We should start a club or something. Or a support group. The Recently Divorced, Overlooked, Mediocre, Middle Children. We'll have to work on the name, obviously. It's a bit long. Or we could make it into an acronym." She whispered the name to herself, spouting off a letter with each finger she put up. "R-D-O-M-M-C. Ridommac," she said the letters like one word. "Nope. Not pronounceable. We'll have to shorten it." She laughed, and the sound was like magic with how it shifted the atmosphere of the room in an instant—or perhaps it had just shifted something in me.

The realization hit me like a rock-centered snowball. What was I doing? I couldn't let a woman have this effect on me. Not again. And especially one I hardly knew, who professed her very convincing *why-I-should-stay-clear-of-her* list at every turn. I'd obviously spent too much time here today, and my thoughts were muddled. I needed to go downstairs and clear my head. Remind myself of my priorities. Remind myself that Quinn also was in no place to reciprocate whatever this was I was feeling. Interest, maybe? Shoot. That could not happen.

Eager to be on my way, I stood. "I'd better be going. It's getting late." I glanced at my watch for proof and barely restrained my surprise.

"What time is it?" She looked around like she was trying to find a clock.

"Almost seven-thirty," I said, like there was no discrepancy between the early hour and my provided excuse.

"Oh." Her countenance fell, making me want to kick myself for not having come up with a better exit strategy. The last thing I wanted to do was leave more damage in my wake. But what was I supposed to say now? *Sorry for my abrupt behavior, but I'm strangely drawn to you, and I'm not comfortable with it?*

Quinn grabbed my plate from the table and set it atop hers. Then she stood and moved to the kitchen. "I'm sorry I kept you up so late with my endless chatter. I'll lock the door when you leave." Her tone was light, friendly almost, but it wasn't her genuine one.

I paused by the kitchen on my way out. "Thanks again for dinner," I said stupidly.

Quinn didn't look at me. "No problem. Night."

And just like that, I'd sabotaged our short-lived friendship.

EIGHT

QUINN

I turned up the Christmas music—ironically, "O Christmas Tree"—hoping to drown out my unhelpful overthinking. I hadn't seen Landon since his abrupt departure Monday evening, and now, two days later, I was still thinking about it. Perhaps I'd opened up too quickly or talked too much, but until he'd stood up and declared it was getting late, he'd seemed to be enjoying himself. Hadn't he? Or had I just thought he was and missed all the signals? That was more likely. Until Cody had left, I hadn't realized how unhappy he was in our marriage, how desperate he was to escape.

"Ouch!" My hand flew back when my skin made contact with the hot sugar mixture from the large gingerbread piece I held in place. "Concentrate," I hissed to myself. Several raw, red spots now dotted my fingers from where I'd accidentally touched the scalding liquid. This was exactly why I needed to stop thinking about Landon. It wasn't safe—for my fingers or for my well-being.

My phone chimed, and for once, it was sitting next to me.

Nikki: Hey! Are you free tonight? Kade and I would love to take you around Newport!

I closed my eyes, releasing a silent groan. I wanted to hang out with Nikki, but the idea of being chauffeured around in the freezing cold by a smitten couple made it far less appealing.

Quinn: Sounds lovely! What time were you thinking?
Nikki: Pick you up at four!
Nikki: If that works for you, of course.
Nikki: And come hungry.
Quinn: Perfect. See you then!

That meant I had three hours to finish the last gingerbread structure. The other three were done and waiting to be decorated, but Rosecliff was rightfully proving difficult. Perhaps I'd been a little too ambitious with the details, but I knew that if I could make it work, it would be worth it. I only hoped I was right.

A heavy knock broke through the blaring music, and I froze. That wasn't Landon's knock, and Nikki would have mentioned if she were here. I quickly muted the music and tuned my ears to any noises. Retreating footsteps sounded in the shared stairwell, but it wasn't until the distant sound of a car started that I found the courage to tiptoe to the door. There was no sign of anyone through the peephole. I pressed my ear to the door and listened again. Nothing.

With quiet movements, I unlocked the top lock and opened the door just wide enough for me to see out and, apparently, to let a rush of cold air in. No one was there. The instantaneous onslaught of thoughts about who had knocked and why sent a chill up my spine. Then, something caught my eye. Pressed up against the door were several bags of groceries.

But I hadn't ordered anything.

I thought to leave them there, in case the delivery person realized their mistake, when I caught sight of the bag of tortilla chips peeking out from one of the sacks—the same brand I'd served Landon. Had Landon had the groceries delivered? Quickly, I pulled the bags into the house and locked the door. My gaze roved over the haul, and sure enough, I noticed a sticker on a bag—L. Aker. Was this some kind of peace offering? Or was it simply Landon feeling bad for the odd girl who would rather eat canned chicken than leave the house?

Either way, I was grateful—especially with the smell of fresh pineapple and oranges wafting around me.

AN UNCONTROLLABLE SHIVER overtook me when I stepped out of Nikki's car. The heated leather seats had been divine, but the contrast now gave the air more of a bite. Or maybe it was the breeze off the bay that caused it. Either way, I pulled my coat more tightly around me and wished I had opted for more layers.

"I hope Kade can find a spot." Nikki glanced around the parking lot, where cars circled like vultures in eager search for a space, their tires leaving marks in the thin layer of snow.

"Looking for me?" Kade's voice came from the sidewalk behind us.

We turned toward the sound, and my stomach instantly wound into a ball of nerves when I noticed Landon standing beside him. Hadn't Nikki very intentionally not invited her brother?

"Landon." Nikki's gaze flicked to me. "I didn't realize you were coming."

He looked less than thrilled to be here, and his eyes remained fixed on Nikki. "Neither did I. Kade refused to drop me off at home after the board meeting."

Kade stepped forward with a mischievous smirk. "This forced-vacation thing has been rough on him. A night out is just what he needs."

"I suppose he can stay if he behaves himself." Nikki let out a puff of visible air. "How was the meeting?"

"Uneventful," Landon answered.

Kade chuckled. "He's just grumpy because I got the last prime rib at lunch. But in Landon's defense, bell peppers stuffed with kale and quinoa would make anyone irritable."

Landon leveled him with a scowl. "Almost as irritable as when I'm pulled from a project to attend a meeting where my presence isn't required—at all."

Kade's eyes danced with humor. "Not true. Roger asked you to report on the project in L.A."

Landon crossed his arms, unamused. "It took less than a minute to explain we got the permit approved and are on track for the build. And everyone there likely already knew that."

I freed my hair from behind my ears, hoping it would act as a blanket to the sides of my face. Another shiver jolted through me, and despite my best efforts, my jaw chattered this time, and my shoulders shook.

Landon's gaze finally turned in my direction. "We should start walking."

"Good idea." Nikki took hold of my arm and led me forward, leaving the men to follow. "You're going to love this place. It's like stepping back in time to a quaint little village. Every year, we'd come here to shop for our siblings' Christmas presents. It was one of my favorite traditions."

I leaned into her warmth. "What are some of your others?" I

asked, desperate to keep my thoughts on something besides the cold and my disconcerting awareness of Landon behind me.

"In the beginning of December, there's a tree lighting we'd go to here at Bowen's Wharf. There's the Christmas boat parade, which we also missed this year. And cutting down our own Christmas tree." She smiled at me. "But my favorite one was building gingerbread houses with my mom and my grandma before my mom died."

I stared at her, trying to find words. "I didn't realize you'd lost your mom. I'm so sorry."

"Last year was our first Christmas with her gone." Nikki bit at her lip. "And there's a part of me that dreads this one. It's just not the same without her, especially because my dad is now remarried. Sandra's a really wonderful woman, and I'm glad my dad is happy, but she's not Mom." Nikki sighed. "Christmas was my mom's favorite holiday, and she'd go above and beyond to make it magical for us kids—even when we were adults."

"Is that why you're having a Christmas-themed wedding?"

Tears formed in Nikki's eyes, and I worried I'd been insensitive or pried too much when she nodded. "I don't want to get caught up in the day's bustle and forget to think about her. That happens more lately—a whole day passing before I realize I was too busy to spare her a thought. And a part of me knows that's normal, but I don't want that on my wedding day. I want to remember her. I want to make her a part of it." Nikki batted at a tear that escaped. "Sorry, I still can't fully control the waterworks."

"You never need to apologize. Feeling is what makes us beautifully human."

She pulled me in closer. "I always knew we'd be friends in real life."

Despite the cold, the thought warmed me. But then again, Nikki was friends with everyone.

We passed a sign that read Bowen's Wharf and emerged onto a cobblestone street dusted with snow. The setting sun was nearly down, and the bluish hues of dusk only added to its dreamlike appeal. A tall Christmas tree decked in white lights was nestled snugly into the background like a painting. My pace slowed, and I stared in wonderment.

Nikki's arm tightened around mine. "I told you that you'd love it."

"It's beautiful. It really looks like it came straight out of a Christmas storybook."

"Landon?" Nikki glanced behind her. "Can you get a picture of me and Quinn?"

He kept his hands in his pockets and stared at his sister.

She scoffed. "It's a picture. Don't tell me you've sworn off taking pictures now, too?" Nikki huffed when Landon didn't respond to her chiding. "Fine. Kade, can you take it?"

Kade grabbed the outstretched phone. "I'm only not offended I was your second choice because Landon has mad photography skills." He backed up several feet. "Ready?"

"Here." Nikki repositioned me like I was a store mannequin, tilting my head and angling my body correctly. She tipped my chin up slightly and cleared the hair from my face. "Perfect."

Careful not to move, my gaze involuntarily flicked to Landon. Our eyes met briefly before he glanced away. Whatever I'd said or done the other night, he obviously had no plans to let it go.

Nikki returned to my side, put her hand on my back, and leaned her torso forward and slightly toward me. "Ready."

Kade held up the phone and snapped several pictures, squatted down for a different angle, moved closer for a few shots, and then handed her the phone. "Acceptable, or should I take a few more?"

She scrolled through the images, her eyes taking in each picture with focused attention. Then, she smiled. "Got it." She held the phone toward me. "You look stunning, Quinn."

I studied the picture, surprised that she was right. It was a great picture of both of us, but more than that, I appeared confident and happy and a complete contrast to the hundreds, possibly thousands, of selfies I'd taken and promptly deleted over the last year. I looked like my old self, just in a more flattering pose. "You look stunning, too," I said, eager to draw the attention away from myself. "You always do."

"Thank you," she said without a hint of reservation. "Are you okay if I post this to my stories, then?" Her gaze shifted to Landon, and she gave an impish smile before she looked back to me. "I'll tag your account."

"Sure," I said more casually than I felt. Nikki Aker—social media goddess—was going to post that glorious picture to her stories. No big deal. I could keep it cool.

Her fingers moved over the screen's keypad at lightning speed. "Done." Nikki tucked her phone in her back pocket.

"What's the plan for dinner?" Kade asked, stepping next to us. "Are we grabbing something here?"

"Oh, shoot!" Nikki stopped and glanced behind us. "I left my bag in the trunk."

Kade quirked his head. "And it has our dinner in it?"

"Yeah. Want to help me grab it?"

"You know I do."

"We'll be back in just a minute."

Kade waggled his eyebrows at us. "Unless we get distracted on the way."

Nikki laughed and latched onto Kade's arm. The two of them started back in the direction we'd come, looking the very picture of two people in love. Feeling awkward being left alone with Landon, I watched them until they disappeared around the corner.

"How have you been?" Landon asked, his tone polite but not overly friendly.

My gaze met his. "Good." I rubbed my frozen fingers together, repressing another shiver by tensing my body. "And how about you?"

"Fine. Thanks."

"That's good."

The awkward silence hung thickly around us in the cold evening air. Our conversation the other night had felt so natural. What went wrong? "Did you get enough sleep ... the night you left?" The question slipped out of me before I had time to filter it.

His jaw ticked. "I did."

"That's great. Sleep is important." I cringed inwardly. Sleep is important? Who says that? I mean, besides a doctor when you go in for a checkup, but in a regular conversation? No wonder Landon was intent on keeping his distance. Something was very much wrong with me. "Oh, and thanks for the groceries," I said, desperate to change the subject. "That was really kind of you."

"No problem."

No problem? That was all he had to say?

Fine.

Two could play at this game—as stupid of a game as it was. I blew out a breath, the white cloud of air dissipating as quickly as it had come, crossed my arms, and angled myself away from him. I could feel Landon's gaze settle on me, but I didn't give him the privilege of meeting it.

"What are you doing?" he asked, confusion in his voice. Or was that amusement?

I tapped my foot, growing all too aware of how numb my toes were. "Nothing."

"Then why do I feel like I'm getting the silent treatment?"

"Because you are."

In my periphery, I could see him nod, but he said nothing.

I spun back toward him. "To be honest, I'm kind of sick of your Dr. Jekyll and Mr. Hyde routine. I don't know what I did to make you upset, but I'm sorry—whatever it was."

"That had to be the shortest silent treatment in the history of silent treatments."

"I didn't realize how hard it is to be silent when the other person is acting like an imbecile and needs to be told."

"Weren't you the one who just apologized to me?"

I narrowed my eyes. "After I compared you to Dr. Jekyll and Mr. Hyde. That was the main point. Besides, I can't help it. I'm an over-apologizer."

"An over-apologizer," he said, accentuating each word. "I didn't realize that was a thing."

I gestured to myself. "Case and point."

"Case *in* point, actually."

"Ugh! You're so aggravating." Another shiver moved through me.

"And you're freezing. Let's wait for Nikki and Kade inside."

"Your diversion tricks won't always work, you know." I glanced longingly toward the store Landon had indicated, well aware it would work this time. "Eventually, we're going to have to figure this out because there's no way I'm going to your sister's wedding with you otherwise. I've had enough stiff conversations and second-guessing myself to last me well beyond Christmas."

"If you want, we can chat about it now, here in the cold."

I threw one last irritated scowl in Landon's direction, then allowed my frozen toes to carry me toward salvation.

NINE

LANDON

I LINGERED NEAR THE DOOR, WATCHING QUINN PERUSE the racks of women's clothing. Her shivering had subsided a few minutes ago, and she was now contentedly swaying to the Christmas music, even lip-synching the words occasionally. I chuckled quietly before rebuking myself. No. I wouldn't let her affect me. Not anymore. Especially since I again suspected Nikki really was trying to set the two of us up. Why else would Kade refuse to bring me home after the meeting in Boston? Unless he'd gone rogue with his own matchmaking scheme—or more like a *keep-me-away-from-his-cousin* scheme. But it made more sense that Kade was doing Nikki's bidding, and she was using the threat of Tyler and Rachel as an inciting factor to force Quinn and me together. She was probably stoked I'd asked Quinn to the wedding.

"Can I help you with something?" A barrel-chested man with a long beard and a sleeve of tattoos approached me. I was over six inches taller than him, but considering his arms were probably the same circumference as my thighs, I felt sufficiently intimidated.

I caught sight of his employee name badge. "Thanks, Jim, but I'm fine."

"Are you here to buy something?"

Was this guy desperate for a commission or something? "Nope. But I'll let you know if that changes."

His line of sight shifted to Quinn, probably realizing she was a more promising customer, and I followed it. She picked up a thick, black coat and held it to her with a mesmerizing smile before glancing at the price tag. Her eyes went wide, and she set the coat back on the rack like it had deeply offended her.

"Sir?"

I glanced back toward the voice, surprised to find Jim standing in the same spot as before.

He flicked his head in Quinn's direction. "Do you know that woman?"

"Why?" I asked, feeling suddenly defensive of her. Did this guy want me to introduce him? Because that definitely wasn't happening.

"Is there a problem, sir?" Quinn wove through the clothing racks, coming toward us.

"Do you know this guy?" Jim asked, his tone a lot friendlier with her.

Amusement lit Quinn's face at the same time I realized the reason for this man's interrogation. "We're friends," I said, waiting for Quinn to confirm my innocence.

Her lips pursed, like she was considering my claim.

I lifted my hands in disbelief. "Are you serious right now?"

A delighted smile danced on her face. "*Friend* seems a subjective term around here, but I guess I'll claim him."

Okay, I deserved that.

Jim sent me an apologetic look. "Sorry, man. With how intently you were watching her, you kind of gave off stalker vibes."

Quinn covered her mouth, her eyes bright with suppressed laughter.

"Nope," I said through a grimaced smile. An uncomfortable amount of heat flooded over me. "Just *friend* vibes."

Jim shook his head, a smirk visible through his beard. "No wonder she's confused about your friendship. I definitely don't look at my friends like that."

I opened my mouth to defend myself but shut it again when I couldn't think of an adequate response.

Quinn reached out and touched Jim's arm, and I refused to feel envious of him. "Thank you," she said. "I'm glad to know there are people willing to step in when they feel the need to."

He winked at her. "I'm glad my services weren't required. Though I'll be standing right over there"—he pointed to the register—"if you change your mind about him."

Quinn awarded him with her smile, then she turned it on me when he'd walked away. "You were watching me *intently*?"

My eyes flicked to the ceiling. "Jim exaggerated. I wasn't watching you that intently."

The laugh she'd apparently been suppressing finally escaped. "He thought you were a stalker. You're lucky I came to your rescue. Did you see the size of his arms?"

"You're going to hold this over my head, aren't you?"

Her expression turned mockingly thoughtful. "Yes, I think I will."

I started toward the other side of the store with purpose.

"What are you doing?" she asked, following me.

I stopped in front of the rack she'd been looking at earlier. "I'm making a deal with you."

Her face scrunched up in confusion until I grabbed the coat I'd seen her check the price on and held it up. "You won't say a word about any of this, and I'll buy you this coat."

She lifted her brow in challenge. "That coat is a hundred and twenty dollars."

I didn't budge. "Do we have a deal?"

"I already have a coat." She gestured to her jacket as proof. "I don't need another one."

I rubbed the material of her sleeve between my fingers, careful to not actually touch her. "That's not a coat. It's a snowboarding jacket. Those are two very different things, especially on the East Coast."

"And what would I do with that beastly thing when I get back to San Diego? I'll never use it."

"I don't care what you do with it when you get home."

She shook her head. "I'm not letting you buy me anything else. You've already paid for my medicine and my groceries."

"That was different. This is a trade, and I'd be very grateful if you'd agree—preferably before Nikki gets back and has more blackmail to use against me."

Quinn grabbed the coat, and I was sure it was a deal closure, but she put it back on the rack instead. "I won't say anything to anyone. I promise." Her expression was so sincere I nearly faltered. But this had never been about her not telling anyone. It was about her needing a real coat so she didn't freeze while she was here.

I grabbed the coat again and started toward the register.

"Landon, I won't accept it." She trailed behind me.

"That's fine. It can sit in the house, unused, if you don't want it."

She huffed. "You're ridiculous."

I passed the boot display and stopped. "What size shoe do you wear?"

She crossed her arms and attempted a glare.

"Best guess it is." Her low-top sneakers were tiny, so I grabbed the smallest pair of women's snow boots I could see. "Size five/six. Speak now or forever hold your peace."

She held her peace, and we continued to the counter.

"Is that everything?" Jim asked.

"Yep." The display behind the register caught my eye. "Actually, can I get a pair of wool socks and those gloves," I said, pointing to a gray wool ladies' glove, "and one of those beanies?"

"Which one?"

I looked over at Quinn. "Do you have a preference?"

She dipped her head to one side, her glower impressively endearing.

"I think the black one would match her current mood the best."

With a hearty belly chuckle, Jim rang up the items. "That'll be two hundred and forty-eight dollars."

"Two hundred and forty-eight dollars!" Quinn's hand settled on top of mine as I attempted to pass Jim my card. A shock raced up my arm, likely from the unexpected chill of her fingers. "Landon, that's way too much money."

The pure look of sincerity in her eyes confirmed it wasn't too much. In fact, if she wasn't careful, she might be leaving here with several additional items. Man, was I doing a poor job at remaining neutral to her charms. "Bail would have been a lot more if you'd let Jim here call the police on me. Plus, I would have had a criminal record."

A reluctant smile touched her lips. "Promise you won't buy me anything else? I'm already indebted enough to you."

"You're not indebted to me." If anything, with all the trouble I'd caused her, it was the other way around. I handed Jim my card, and he processed the payment.

"Here you go." I shoved my credit card back in my wallet and offered her the shopping bag stuffed to the brim. "They're yours to do with what you want, but if it were me, I'd probably put them on. It will be chilly out by the water."

The depth of gratitude in her expression made it difficult to remain unaffected by her, but I couldn't look away. "Thank you, Landon. Really."

I drew in a slow breath and took a step back. It was hard to respond with her standing so close. "You're welcome."

"There you two are." Nikki closed the door behind her and

Kade. Her gaze dropped to Quinn's bag. "Did you find something to buy?"

Quinn glanced at me, obviously uncertain what to tell them.

"She just got some winter gear, and I think she wanted to put it on quick." I walked to meet them. "You know how it goes, living in California. Coats there are for fashion more than utility."

Kade nodded. "That's a fact."

"Hey, Landon," Nikki said. "I was going to get hot cider for our walk along the water, but I need help to carry them. Want to come?"

I eyed her suspiciously.

"Please," she said, dragging up her bottom lip. "It will only take a minute, and Kade will stay with Quinn while she puts on her new ... winter gear. Won't you, Kade?"

"Happily." Without a moment's hesitation, Kade walked to join Quinn where she sat on a chair, removing her shoes.

"Impressive," I said when Kade was out of ear shot. "Did you hire out or did you train him yourself?"

"Haha. Very funny." She flicked her head toward the door. "You coming?"

I grumbled my acceptance and opened the door for her.

"Wow. Don't be too excited to spend a little quality time with your favorite baby sister."

"I know that look you're giving me. You're up to something."

"I'm not. Scout's honor." She put up two fingers in what looked to be a lazy peace sign.

"The Boy Scout sign is three fingers."

She only smiled and walked out the door.

NIKKI PAID for the drinks and handed me two of them. "You good? They're kind of hot."

I nodded, and we started back toward the store where Kade and Quinn were waiting.

"So, are you going to tell me why I was the selected errand boy?"

"Why did you ask Quinn to be your date for the wedding?" she asked with only the slightest hesitation.

I shook my head with a laugh, not surprised by her choice of topic. Fortunately, I was one step ahead of her. She wanted me to confess I was falling for Quinn, and I wouldn't.

Nikki went to take a sip of her drink but pulled back when the steaming liquid touched her lip. "That is hot!" She pressed her lips together and glanced over at me. "So are you interested in her or not?"

"Why does it matter?" I asked casually.

She stopped, her eyes moving back and forth between mine. "You know what I think? I think you asked Quinn as an excuse to not be set up with Rachel. And if I'm right, it's not fair to any of you."

I stared at her, suddenly unsure of everything. Especially how I was supposed to answer. "Quinn is great," I said, hoping a generic response would allow me to gather more information.

"She is. She's amazing. But you two couldn't be more different. You need someone driven and organized. She needs someone fun and playful."

"I'm fun."

She pinned me with a look that confirmed she disagreed. "If you like her, explain something to me. Why didn't you greet Quinn when we arrived tonight? You didn't say hello or even glance in her direction. And both times I've seen you together, you've hardly spoken to her. This might come as a bit of a shock, but that's not how someone acts when they're interested, Landon."

My mind was still reeling, trying to adjust to this unexpected turn of events. "Maybe for me it is."

Nikki shook her head. "I know you too well to buy that. When you're in, you're all in. Like you were with Eliza."

I scoffed. "And look where that got me." Pain. Regret. Heartache. I didn't want to give someone that power over me again.

We walked in silence for the next few minutes.

"I know Eliza hurt you, and you're scared to love again, but don't close out every opportunity for healing. Rachel is perfect for you. And Quinn deserves a chance to find happiness again, too. Don't stop her from having this chance."

"Please tell me you aren't referring to Tyler being *her chance?*"

"He's changed since college." Nikki's irritation leaked into her tone. "He's grown up."

Quinn was too guileless for the likes of Tyler Baker—grown up or not. "You never knew him like I did, Nikki. Trust me, I think your instincts are off on this one."

"They're not. Maybe you should let her make her own decision about him."

The thought of Quinn and Tyler together made me physically sick. His grabby hands wouldn't get anywhere near her. Not when I could easily do something about it. Well, not easily, with how attracted I was to her. But I could keep myself in check. I was confident about that. What I couldn't do was let Tyler fool Quinn like the dozens of other girls from our undergrad days, especially after everything she'd been through this last year. It looked like Quinn and I needed to up our game. If Nikki thought we really were developing feelings for each other, she'd drop this whole Tyler-and-Rachel thing. At least, I hoped she would.

"I'll let her make her own decision if you will," I said, meeting Nikki's gaze. "But I think we're a better match than you think."

Now, I just needed to run the plan by Quinn.

I SLOWED MY PACE, and Quinn unconsciously matched it, leaving more space between us and Nikki and Kade. The two of them were deep in conversation about seating arrangements at the wedding and what adjustments they needed to make now that Kade's sister would be bringing a plus-one.

"When was the Christmas boat parade?" Quinn's thick, blonde curls flowed out from under the black beanie in the sea breeze. With her new coat zipped to her chin, gloved hands holding a steaming cup of cider, and boots on her feet, I hadn't seen her shiver once since leaving the store. The realization made me smile.

"It's usually right after Thanksgiving."

Her gaze scanned the harbor, flickering between the handful of boats that still displayed their Christmas decorations. "I would have loved to see it."

"There's always next year."

Quinn laughed. "I don't see that happening—unless you and Rachel intend to have a Thanksgiving wedding and need some gingerbread turkeys."

"Hilarious." I shook my head. "But speaking of Nikki and her matchmaking attempts ..."

Quinn's smiling eyes settled on me. "Is that what she wanted to talk to you about?"

"She's not deterred from her plans. She thinks I only asked you to be my date to the wedding to keep her from setting us up with anyone else." I paused. "I mean, that is why I did it."

"I'm aware." Quinn's gaze returned to Nikki and Kade, the two of them still talking a few yards ahead of us. "So, should we confess and let her set us up with Tyler and Rachel?"

"Is that what you'd prefer?" I gripped my cup and watched her profile for any indication of what she really thought.

She shrugged. "If you do."

"I don't."

Her gaze met mine, her eyes narrowing slightly. "Why not?"

"I'm standing by what I said. Tyler isn't your type. And I refuse to let Nikki set me up again, so if you don't have a strong preference, I say we continue our plan ... with one or two minor adjustments."

"What adjustments?"

A lump of nerves formed in my throat, and I cleared it to get the words out. "We need Nikki to believe we're actually developing feelings for each other."

Quinn's laugh took me by surprise. "You literally wouldn't even make eye contact with me when I got here today, and you want to convince your sister we have feelings for each other?"

"I'm sorry about that. It had nothing to do with you." Not in the way she assumed, anyway. I debated telling her my frustration with Kade's meddling—his refusal to take me home after our conference—and how it had caused me to again question Nikki's intentions to set us up (which I'd been wrong about a second time), but it would all take too long, and I needed to get to the point before Nikki or Kade realized how far behind we'd gotten.

"What would these adjustments entail?" Quinn asked before I'd had a chance to bring it up again.

"The classic things—flirting, small touches, shared glances." I said it like my pulse didn't race at the mention of it.

A frown formed on her lips. "We'll probably need to spend more time together and go out a few times between now and the wedding, right?"

I lifted a shoulder, like her obvious concern didn't bother me. "It wouldn't hurt."

We continued on in silence, but with each step, I grew more anxious to know what she was thinking. Was the idea of a fake relationship—no, not even that—a fake interest in me so appalling?

"If we do this," she finally said, "I have one condition. No more silent treatments or abrupt behavior changes. We'll work things out like mature adults through communication."

I rested a hand over my heart. "My days as Mr. Hyde are behind me."

She smiled at the reference. "Then we'd better get started."

TEN

QUINN

I STARED AT MY PHONE. EIGHT HUNDRED AND SEVENTY-two new followers from a single story? And it had only been six hours since Nikki had posted it. That was amazing. No. That was terrifying. These were Nikki's followers—lovers of fashion, expensive vacations, celebrity friends. None of them would care about my silly baking posts. They'd followed me, but they would just as quickly unfollow when they realized I had nothing to offer but images of baked goods.

I dialed Ashlee and thanked the heavens she picked up. "I'm in a tailspin, Ashlee."

"From what? Cody? Did you look at his profile?"

"No. Nikki tagged me in a picture, and I have almost nine hundred new followers."

The line went silent for a minute. "Why am I inclined to think that's a good thing?"

"A year ago, it might have been, but now ..." I sighed. "They added me because I'm friends with Nikki. I doubt many of them even looked at my page, and next time they see one of my posts in their feed, they're going to unfollow me."

"First, you don't know that. And second, who cares if they do? Don't you want people following you who actually want to see your posts?"

"I'm not sure I can handle a mass exodus right now."

"You're worrying for nothing. People love your posts, Quinn."

"Then why is my engagement so low? It has to be my content. I need to make more reels or more elaborate—"

"What you need to do is stop stressing. How about we talk about something else? Try to get your mind off it?"

I released a pent-up breath. "That's a good idea. How is training the new team going? Any fun stories to share?"

"I have one about a new nurse that tried to place an IV, but before I tell it, I want an update on Hot Guy."

"Landon's good," I said, deciding how best to share my news. I didn't need Ashlee getting the wrong idea about us. "Remember how I told you he asked me to be his date for Nikki's wedding to prevent her from setting us up with other people? It turns out she saw right through that, so we decided to ... up our efforts."

"What exactly does that mean?"

"Just doing things that will make Nikki think we're developing feelings for each other."

"Wait. Let me get this straight. You and Hot Guy are fake dating?"

I groaned. I knew she'd take it wrong. "We're not fake dating. We're acting interested in each other."

"Do you need me to pull out the dictionary again? Because I'm pretty sure that what you two are doing would firmly be categorized as fake dating."

"Whatever it is, it's fake."

"All of it?" Ashlee asked, shining a light on the one reason I'd been hesitant to agree to his new plan. I had no interest in a relationship right now. None. And yet, sometimes, the way Landon looked at me made me forget that. To imagine him touching me ... The thought sent a shiver coursing through my body. How was I supposed to keep straight what was real and what wasn't? Especially if he stopped his brooding? But the bottom line was, I trusted Landon. Or more like, I trusted he had an unyielding death grip on his bachelor status.

"It has to be. Neither of us are in a place for anything more."

"If you say so. Have you already started?"

"Sort of. We flirted a little more than usual tonight at the harbor, but nothing too drastic. Landon was worried his sister would suspect what we were up to if we ramped it up too fast."

"And what's next?"

"I have a dress fitting tomorrow with a stylist friend of Nikki's. Landon said he'll show up at the end, and ... I don't really know. I guess we'll see from there."

Ashlee laughed.

"What?"

"How is this your life right now—that you're fake dating a GQ model?"

Despite her blatant misrepresentation of the entire situation, I smiled. "I have no idea. An onlooker might think my luck is finally changing."

But I knew all too well that wasn't the case.

I GLIDED from the dressing room like I was accustomed to wearing gowns that cost more than my monthly income—not that costing more was a hard feat with how little I currently made —and smiled at the sounds of adoration I received from my small group of onlookers.

"Stunning."

"The red is definitely my favorite."

I stepped onto a circular platform as directed, glancing at the dress in the row of angled mirrors. It was beautiful.

Sophia approached, looking every part the designer with her skin-tight black pencil dress, hair pulled back without a single bump, and her critical eye surveying every inch of me. She pulled at the fabric by my waist, pinning it behind me. "Three-quarters of an inch off the waist, but the height of the shoulders is perfect. The heart neckline is flattering for her small chest, but we'll need to add padding to prevent any unfortunate situations from occurring."

Her assistants nodded their agreement. I glanced down at my *small chest* and how meagerly it filled out the top before also conceding her point.

"High heels will be a must." Her admonishing gaze landed on me. "The higher, the better for you. The flower girls will be wearing a very similar shade of red, and we'd hate for anyone to mistake you for one of them."

I flinched at the comment, though it was also a valid point. If any of them were older than ten or eleven, there was a good chance they'd be as tall as, if not taller than, me.

The woman studied me a little longer and then sighed. "I wish I had enough time to custom-make you something. With your petite frame and wavy hair, a mermaid-style dress with some sheer draping would look exquisite on you."

"I'm just grateful you're letting me borrow something on such short notice."

"Oh, the dress is yours to keep. I won't be able to sell it after it's fitted to your body."

I lifted a hand to my mouth, my gaze darting to Nikki. "I didn't realize ..."

"Anything for a friend of Nikki's." She glanced over at Nikki. "I'd like to be tagged in any pictures of her wearing the dress, if you don't mind."

Nikki stood from her place on the chic black sofa. "I'm planning on an endorsement post for both this and the flower girl dresses you designed."

"Wonderful." Sophia's eyes sparkled when they turned their attention back to me. "Go undress, and we'll get started on the adjustments."

The chime on the front door of the shop dinged, and in strode Landon, looking like some kind of fashion god. His gaze met mine, then slowly trailed down my body, a smile creeping onto his lips. "Wow. You look amazing."

My heart felt like it had dislodged and risen to my throat. *It's not real. It's not real.* "Thank you," I said, unable to hold his gaze.

"What are you doing here?" Nikki stepped toward him and away from the gawking ladies around us.

"Quinn told me she had a fitting this morning. Since I didn't have plans for the day, I thought I'd come see if she wanted to head to lunch and then hit up the Cliff Walk. It's a beautiful day for it." He glanced between us. "Unless you already have plans?"

Nikki's distant gaze made it obvious she was having a hard time computing the situation. "You came all the way into Providence to see if Quinn wanted to go to lunch with you?"

He shrugged. "I don't have her number yet. And I figured you'd probably have other wedding errands you need to do while you're here, so now you don't need to run her home."

Nikki tilted her head to the side. "How thoughtful of you," she said dryly.

I stepped down from the platform. "I'll go change quick."

Landon's gaze remained on me all the way to the dressing room, and I sent him a conspiratorial smile before throwing the curtain shut. "Get a hold of yourself," I hissed under my breath. "He's acting."

Carefully, I removed the luxurious velvet fabric, returned it to the hanger, and got dressed. Nikki was talking to Sophia when I exited, and Landon was standing near the door, waiting. "Ready?"

"Just a sec." I walked over to Nikki and wrapped my arm

around her waist, waiting for her to finish what she was saying. "Thank you for this. And for coming with me."

She draped her arm around me and gave me a side hug. "You're welcome. Sophia says she has the perfect pair of heels for the dress. She just needs your shoe size."

"I wear a five."

Sophia's gaze flicked to my feet. "I think they have them that small. I'll double-check and let Nikki know."

I released Nikki and moved to Sophia, giving her a hug. "Thank you for everything."

Shockingly, she returned my embrace. "You're going to look amazing."

"Thanks to you."

Sophia flicked her hand toward the ceiling. "A dress can only get a woman so far. It's how she holds herself while wearing it that matters."

"That's true. But I'll be holding myself with more confidence because of your beautiful dress."

She dipped her chin in acceptance of my compliment.

"Have fun on the Cliff Walk." Nikki smiled at me, then glanced toward her brother. "Oh, and I talked to the nursing home. They said Grandma's more cognizant in the mornings if we want to visit her Saturday or Sunday right after breakfast."

"Conveniently, my schedule is free." He sent her a knowing grin. "Let me know what works best for you."

Landon opened the door, and when I stepped past him, he placed his hand on the small of my back to guide me through. Despite how my whole body tingled, I smiled up at him like it was the most natural thing in the world to have his hand on me.

"Bravo," I said when we stepped out of view of the large windows that looked out over the parking lot. "I think I underestimated your acting skills."

He unlocked the passenger door to a black, well-used truck, and I hopped in. "You looked great in the dress, so my reaction felt entirely natural."

He closed the door and walked around to the driver's side, and my breath seemed to freeze in my chest. He thought I looked great in the dress? "Nikki was adequately shocked to see you," I said when he'd climbed in, trying not to dwell on his indirect compliment.

"Hopefully." He grinned. "So where do you want to go to lunch? There are several places here in Providence, or we can head back to Newport."

I fidgeted with my seatbelt. "We don't really have to go out. I'm pretty sure we achieved what you came for."

Landon turned the key in the ignition. "She'll ask us about it later. If I don't take you, she'll know."

I had a lot of work to do on the gingerbread houses. Between the day I'd lost from my Benadryl-induced sleep, yesterday afternoon's trip to Bowen's Wharf, and now the dress fitting, I was no longer ahead of schedule. The wedding was in eight days, which meant all four gingerbread houses needed to be done and ready to be transported in six. I'd need at least a full day for decorating each of the houses and two for Rosecliff. One day of padding was all I had if anything took longer than expected. If I lost any more of today, then I'd be cutting it close.

He glanced at me out of the corner of his eye. "Unless you don't want to go."

"I do," I said, unable to disappoint him. "And I'm fine with whatever you want for lunch. I'm pretty easy."

LANDON PARKED the car along a narrow street, still grinning to himself as he pulled the keys from the ignition.

I leveled my gaze at him. "It's not that funny. I don't like fish ... or lobster. Really, anything that lives in the water."

He chuckled. "Which is completely fine, but why didn't you tell me that at *any point* before we ordered you a lobster roll?"

I released my seatbelt and shifted toward him in the seat. "I hate inconveniencing people, and you seemed so excited about the place. Besides, I'd thought there'd probably be something on the menu that wasn't seafood, and when that didn't prove true, I decided to just give it a try. I thought maybe I didn't dislike seafood as much as I remembered. But once it was sitting in front of me, the *fishy* smell confirmed I still did."

Landon watched me with a thoughtful expression. "You're a mystery to me. How can you hate inconveniencing people one minute and tell someone exactly how you feel the next?"

"Actually, with most people, I rarely blurt out whatever's on my mind."

"So I'm one of the lucky few?"

I sent him an apologetic smile. "Or unlucky, depending on how you look at it."

"I'll go with lucky." When he opened the truck's door, a burst of frigid air replaced the heated air. "Ready?"

I grabbed the handle. "How long is this cliff walk thing?"

"It's seven miles if you walk in and out again, but we'll take the trolley back to our car, so three-and-a-half from one end to the other."

I glanced toward the dashboard clock. It was already past two. "How long will it take to walk it?" I asked, trying to keep the panic from my voice. I didn't have time to spend another several hours touring like I didn't have a job to do.

He paused, studying my expression. "A couple hours. But if you're too busy, we don't need to go. I just figured you'd like to see the gilded mansions."

My lips parted. "The mansions? You can see them on the walk?"

"Several of them, and the ocean views aren't too shabby either."

"Can you see Rosecliff?"

"It's a little harder to see than some of the others, but we should be able to catch a glimpse."

I nodded, swallowing down my slight trepidation, and opened the door. I hadn't perfected the art of procrastination to forego a glimpse of Rosecliff. "Let's go."

The large ornate iron gate that started the Cliff Walk looked right out of a fairy tale. A thin layer of snow stuck to the ground where the crashing waves couldn't reach, and ice crystals engulfed the few plants brave enough to endure the cold along the narrow walking path. There were a few other adventurous souls out in the freezing weather, but not many.

I glanced behind us at the long stretch of beach. "I've never seen anything like that before—the snow and the sand together. It's beautiful."

Landon turned around on the path, taking in the sight as he walked slowly backward. "It's not quite like Christmas in San Diego, is it?"

"No. I mean, don't get me wrong, I'm not sure I'd be willing to trade warm weather for this, but I'm definitely not as strongly opposed as I would have been a month ago. Or a week ago, actually. Perhaps that's because I'm properly attired." I pulled my beanie a little lower over my head for good measure. "Thanks to you."

Landon turned to face forward again, letting his attention go to the horizon. "You're not an inconvenience, you know."

I studied his profile, but it revealed nothing.

"So, next time, tell me you don't like lobster before I'm forced to gorge myself sick." He gave a playful smile. "You might need to assist me out of here if that second roll doesn't start to digest."

"I was impressed you finished them both," I said with a laugh.

"Almost as impressed as I was when you put down that giant burger and every last fry."

"Fries are my kryptonite. I will finish *all* of them every time. And I refuse to share fries with anyone ... unless it'd be an inconvenience for me to have my own." I sent him a playful look. "But you better believe I'll be thinking all the evil thoughts as someone fists my fries into their mouth."

Landon laughed. "Your fry-hoarding tendencies have been noted."

We carried on in light conversation as we weaved around the coastline, walking down the Forty Steps overlook, and glimpsing an occasional mansion. Despite the chill in the air, I began to sweat—like, a lot. A solid stream ran down my back and another puddled under my non-existent chest. This coat Landon had bought me was insanely effective at not only keeping the cold out, but keeping my warmth in—every exercise-induced bit of it. I unzipped the top portion to let the frigid air flow inside and pulled off my beanie and gloves to zip them into my pocket.

"Getting warm?"

"Shocking, right?"

We entered a part of the path that wound between two tall rock walls. Before we reached a set of stairs to come out of it, Landon pointed to where a short, white fence lined the top of the wall.

My eyes widened with excitement. "Is it Rosecliff?"

"It is. But we can only see it through the chain-link fence up there." He gestured with a flick of his chin, but I was already taking the steps two at a time. "I see it!" The exquisite white two-story building came into view, blending in with the snow-covered lawn and gray sky. It was exactly like the pictures I'd poured over, except it was real and right in front of me. "It's incredible."

"Did you know a lot of these mansions were people's summer cottages?"

"Summer cottages?"

"Yep." Landon came behind me, grabbing onto the fence just above my hands and leaning in to catch a glimpse. His breath was warm on my cheek. "Would you want to live in a place like that?" He asked it in a way that made the question sound significant.

"Not a chance. It'd be too much work and way too expensive to keep up. Besides, think of all the people it takes to run a place like that." Something about his proximity made the words pour out of me. "They'd be coming and going at all hours of the day. I'd hate it. I wouldn't mind visiting, but I prefer a small house that's easy to take care of, as long as it has a decent-sized kitchen and enough storage for all my baking supplies."

"What are those?" Landon asked, and it wasn't until his thumb brushed across my bare fingers that I realized he was talking about the small scabs that dotted my fingers. "They aren't hives."

I stood perfectly still, hoping my quickened breath wasn't noticeable this close. "They're from the sugar-glue I used to build the gingerbread houses. You have to melt the sugar until it's no longer granulated. In its liquid state, it's scalding hot."

Concern lingered on his brow. "I have a first-aid kit at the house if you need it."

"The cold makes them look worse than they are. They usually heal up in a few days."

"Let me know if you change your mind." A couple started up the stairs behind us, and Landon put his hand on my waist and pressed against me to allow them room to pass. My breath hitched, and all I could think about was the pressure of his touch and how his body leaned against mine. I glanced up at him to find his inviting copper eyes on me. "Sorry," he whispered, but he didn't move. And I wasn't sure I wanted him to.

"Landon?" A female voice pulled both of our attention to it, and we turned. An older gentleman stood next to a rail-thin woman with perfectly sharp features and long, brown curls that defied the sea breeze.

Landon's jaw clenched, and his hand that clung to my waist went rigid. "Eliza."

ELEVEN

LANDON

I stared at Eliza, my heart drumming in my ears from the unexpected encounter. Or maybe it was from Quinn's proximity. Either way, what was Eliza doing here in Newport? Didn't she live in one of the Carolinas now? My gaze flicked to her new husband. He stood a little way off with his hands stuffed into his pockets like he was just as leery about the upcoming conversation as I was. For as much as I'd heard he was worth, it surprised me to see he looked like an ordinary man. An old one—easily twice her age—but an ordinary one.

"Landon, how are you?" she asked, her voice full of artificial sincerity. "It's been a long time."

I gave a stiff nod. I hadn't seen Eliza since the divorce, and her sudden appearance had blindsided me. Quinn watched me with an expectant look, but I couldn't think how to introduce her to my ex-wife and her *sugar daddy*. I wasn't sure I even wanted to.

"Hello. I'm Quinn." Quinn glanced between Eliza and her

husband, a casual smile on her lips. Apparently, she'd introduce herself.

"Mark," Eliza's husband said, holding out a hand for Quinn to shake. She accepted it without hesitation.

"It's nice to meet you." Her gaze shifted to Eliza. "And you're Eliza?"

Eliza dipped her chin, her gaze doing a once-over of Quinn. "I am."

"I'm Quinn," she said again. "I already said that, though, so ..." She released a quick breath. "Are you from Newport, then?"

"Originally, but we live in South Carolina now. We just came to visit my dad for Christmas."

Quinn aimed her smile at Mark. "I bet that's nice, having your daughter home for the holidays."

To Mark's credit, he chuckled, but Eliza's face flashed with annoyance.

Quinn glanced at me, obviously confused, and I suddenly found myself repressing a laugh for her sake. "Mark is Eliza's husband."

Quinn's hand shot to her mouth, her eyes rounding. "I'm so sorry. I just assumed with the age difference ..." She forced her lips together, like she was trying to stop herself from talking. "But that's great. My uncle married a woman thirteen years younger than him, so ... not quite as big of an age gap as between you two ..." She winced at her own comment. "But ... they seem happy. Like I'm sure you are." She glanced up at me with an apologetic look, and I gave her a smile. Despite what she likely thought, I was glad Quinn was here, filling the silence with her wonderfully awkward comments.

Eliza wore a forced smile. "We are very happy." Her gaze shifted to me with intention, and she set her hand on her stomach. "We actually will be welcoming our *second* child this summer."

Her revelation was a direct hit, and I placed my hand on Quinn's back as though her small frame could compensate for the blow. I could feel Quinn's gaze on me, but I couldn't meet it. All I could think about was the video Eliza had made before leaving me. A mix of lies with partial truths she'd posted for anyone to see. Instantly, my old, festering wounds seemed to rise to the surface, and I shifted uncomfortably, not knowing how to respond.

"Congratulations." Quinn's arm wrapped around my back, and she placed her hand on my chest, pulling me from my stupor. She looked at me with intention, and the depths of her blue eyes instantly calmed me. "It's crazy to think that could be us in a year or two—having a baby. Can you imagine? You're going to be the best father." She smiled at me like she meant it before turning her attention back to them. "Like Mark must be to your children."

I stared at her, not only because of the impromptu charade but how unprepared I was for the force her comment had on me. The sincerity of her smile. And how, even when she could have chosen the lower road and implied Mark wasn't a good father by her silence, she chose the higher one. Quinn was nothing like Eliza.

Eliza didn't acknowledge her comment. "So the two of you are together?"

It took me a moment to pull my gaze from Quinn. "It's still pretty new." I took Quinn's hand in mine, intertwining our fingers like it was the most natural thing in the world. And it kind of felt like it. "But with how fast it's been moving, it's only a matter of time before we have some big announcements."

"Wow. That's great." Eliza's tone was falsely upbeat. "Who would have thought we'd both be so lucky in love?"

"And yet, here we all are, living proof of that luck." Quinn's amused expression flitted to me, and something inside me shifted. Was I lucky? I suppose I was, but maybe I'd been too swallowed up in the pain to realize it. Eliza had moved on, and I clearly hadn't. Not that I was still in love with her by any stretch of the imagination. But the last two years since our divorce, all I'd wanted was to prove her wrong. To prove to everyone else she had been wrong about me. That I was everything she'd said I wasn't. But for what purpose? Eliza didn't care, and most people that had believed her lies likely hadn't given me a second thought. I would never be enough for her, but I didn't want to be. I just wanted to be enough for *someone*.

I looked down at Quinn, feeling an overwhelming amount of gratitude for this quirky, quick-thinking woman. "As much as we'd love to sit and reminisce about how happy we all are"—my gaze returned to Eliza—"Quinn and I had better get home. It was nice to see you, Eliza. Mark," I said, dipping my head in acknowledgment. "Best of luck with everything."

"It was nice to meet you both." Quinn gave a little wave. "And I'm sorry again about the whole dad misunderstanding. You two are perfect for each other."

Had I not known how genuine Quinn was, the comment could have been a well-delivered, back-handed compliment.

To Mark's credit, he chuckled again. "It's not the first time someone assumed I was Eliza's dad. It was good to meet you both."

With a final wave, I directed Quinn down the stairs and back the way we came to avoid any more encounters with Eliza and Mark.

When we were far enough away that they couldn't see us anymore, I released Quinn's hand and instantly regretted doing so.

"I can't believe I thought he was her dad." Quinn groaned. "Then I couldn't stop talking, and I made it so much worse. *Thirteen years younger.*" She did an exaggerated imitation of herself. "*Not quite as big of an age gap as between you two.* Honestly, who says something like that?"

"Technically, Mark's older than her dad, so it makes sense you thought what you did. And I probably shouldn't have, but I thoroughly enjoyed the whole misunderstanding."

Quinn nudged her elbow into me. "Yeah, because it wasn't you making a fool of yourself."

I laughed, realizing how heavy of a load the encounter had taken off my shoulders. I felt lighter. Freer. Quinn had not only made the whole conversation palatable but ... enjoyable? Introspective, even.

Quinn glanced at me as we walked. "What are you thinking about?"

"How I need to rethink my whole life."

"Oh, good. Nothing too impactful."

I smiled. "I've spent the last two years trying to prove people wrong who couldn't care less what I've achieved. And I just now realized it."

Quinn didn't respond, but her gaze remained on me.

I blew out a heavy breath. "Nikki set me up with Eliza. She was a friend of hers, and Nikki was positive we'd be perfect for each other. Between how hard Nikki oversold me, and that I was just about to graduate from law school, Eliza wrongly assumed I'd be able to provide the life she wanted instantly—a life that, I came to find out, looked very much like Nikki's. Turns out most attorneys don't make a portion of what one would expect—of what she'd expected.

"Right after we married, I was working at a small firm that didn't even have benefits. She used her dad's connections to get me a job at a bigger firm. I hated it—twelve-hour days and meager vacation time. But I did it for her. Except, it wasn't enough. It didn't take her much longer to realize she'd wasted her potential on me. Within a few months of our divorce being final, she married Mark."

"And that's why you're wary of Nikki setting you up?"

"Exactly."

Quinn released a heavy breath. "I don't blame you."

We walked in silence for a while before she met my gaze again. "I'm sorry that happened."

"Don't be. I think sometimes life brings you down a path to show you it's the wrong one. Now I know."

As we continued along the Cliff Walk, back to the truck,

Quinn was unusually quiet, and I hoped I hadn't said anything to cause it.

IT WAS PRETTY EARLY, but I could hear Quinn up and walking around, so I grabbed the large box sitting by the couch and started up the stairs. She opened the door and smiled. Then her gaze shifted to the box at my side. "What's that?"

"A hypoallergenic Christmas tree."

Her nose scrunched up in that adorable way of hers. "They make hypoallergenic trees?"

I shrugged. "You said you had a fake tree growing up, right? So the hope is this one should be hypoallergenic for you."

She crossed her arms. "You promised you wouldn't buy me anything else."

"First, I never promised that. What I said was you weren't indebted to me. And second, as your current landlord, it's my legal duty to provide this residence with a Christmas tree that won't cause any occupants to get hives."

"That is a strangely specific duty."

I gave an innocent shrug. "Legal precedent. You must not have been the first person to have a reaction."

She graciously laughed at my lame lawyer joke and opened the door wider.

When I carried the box inside, the collection of fully assembled gingerbread houses caught my eye. "You've been busy."

"I still have to decorate them all." She gave a small pout and returned to her seat.

"I'm sorry if lunch and the Cliff Walk yesterday put you behind schedule."

She smiled. "It was worth it. I'm still reeling over the fact that those mansions were people's summer cottages."

"The gilded mansions are some of the closest things the U.S. has to English manor houses. You know, like *Jane Austen*."

Her hand with the frosting dropped to the table, and there was a look of panic in her eyes. "Why did you say Jane Austen like that?"

I gave a casual lift of my shoulder. "I may have scrolled through your feed."

She groaned and tossed her head back.

"Interesting response. I'm not sure I've met an influencer who doesn't like people following them."

Her gaze snapped back to me. "You followed me?"

I laughed. "Should I not have?"

"No. It's fine. I just get weird when people from my real life follow me. How did you find my account, anyway?"

"Nikki tagged you in that picture from Bowen's Wharf."

She gave a heavy nod, like it wasn't the first time that picture had caused her grief.

I set out each section of the Christmas tree from the box. "Explain your handle to me: TheKookieCook. From what I could see on your feed, you don't cook—you bake."

"Kookie has a double meaning. The more evident part is that I'm a bit ... well, kooky. It's also cookie with a k, as a nod to all the baking I do. And Cook happens to be my last name."

"Ah. Is it strange that I didn't know that? I feel like it is." I paused, mustering the courage to continue. "That, and I don't have your number yet."

The corners of her mouth curled upward. "All things considered, that does seem like an oversight. We can't pretend we're developing feelings for each other and not have exchanged numbers." She put down her frosting, walked over to me, and extended her hand. "If I could see your phone ... I don't currently know where mine is."

I handed it over, and as I watched her add her number to my contact list, my gaze swept over her petite features and large blue eyes. She truly was stunning but in a way that was approachable.

"Numbers have officially been exchanged." She handed my phone back, and a distant ding sounded. "And you already texted me."

I glanced at the screen to find my texts open and one to Quinn that said: *Hey, beautiful. It's Landon.*

Quinn gave a mischievous grin. "In case Nikki sees." And with that, Quinn turned and walked back to her seat, my eyes trailing her the entire walk.

"I had an idea for your social media account," I said after a few minutes. I'd managed to get the bottom portion of the tree in place on the stand and was working on separating the branches to make it look more realistic.

Her head leaned to one side. "My attention is yours, as long as it doesn't involve any mentions of my earlier videos and posts."

"Like the *Harry Potter Potions* one and your *Personal Tribute to Hobbits—My Fellow Short People*?"

Her eyes grew wide. "How much did you watch?"

"Let's just say I stayed up later than I planned on. But that's the thing. I was hooked. Your older posts and videos were hilarious and endearing—"

"And embarrassing." The shade of red in her cheeks gave me far too much pleasure.

I positioned the next layer of the tree and dropped it into place. "They were you, Quinn."

Her mouth quirked to the side. "I'm not sure that's a good thing."

"It is. I promise. Not that your current posts aren't full of beautiful images and reels. They are just missing one significant element—you. The Kookie Cook. The girl who would hold tea parties and theme-night bakeoffs."

Her gaze turned distant. "I'm not even sure I know how to be that girl anymore."

"You don't need to be her. You just need to be you. The wonderful, crazy, genuine girl I'm lucky enough to be fake dating." I winked at her.

She laughed. "For the record, I don't think we're officially fake dating yet. You only just got my number."

"Point duly noted."

It wasn't long before I had the tree built and all the branches looking mostly decent. I checked to make sure the lights worked and threw on a few of the ornaments I had. It didn't look amazing, but it was something. When I finished, I glanced around the room, looking for something else to do. I wasn't ready to leave yet. But Quinn had already repositioned several of the Christmas decorations to spots around the house that were no longer covered in gingerbread pieces. "I see you fixed my garland," I said, pointing to the stair banister.

She glanced over her shoulder with a laugh. "Only because you did a terrible job putting it up."

"Fair." I moseyed over to the table, studying the familiar house she was currently decorating with an intricate pattern. There was no candy or colors, just the brown of the gingerbread peeking through a lovely frosted design that reminded me of white lace. "That's the house I grew up in."

Quinn smiled, keeping her gaze focused on her task. "I'm glad you recognized it."

I scanned the others. "What cabin is that?"

Her gaze flicked up briefly. "The one where Nikki and Kade met."

That made sense. I pointed to the next one. "Rosecliff, obviously, and ..." I shook my head. "I also don't know this one with the pillars."

"Kade's family home."

"Ah. That makes sense." I knew he'd grown up in a ritzy neighborhood outside of Boston, but I'd never been to the house.

"Nikki wanted each gingerbread centerpiece to represent the places that were most special to them—individually and as a couple."

I moved behind Quinn's chair, resting my hands on the back of it and trying not to overthink the gesture that suddenly felt too intimate. I kept them there. Her fluid motions were mesmerizing. She traced designs that she'd baked into the cookie and free-handed swirls and small hearts on the blank surfaces of the gingerbread.

"Did your grandma teach you to make these?"

"My grandma taught me to make a gingerbread house. The recipe is hers for the dough, the sugar-glue, and the royal icing. But her houses were a lot more traditional—you know, with the candy canes and gumdrops? I guess I taught myself the rest of it. Not that it's anything all that special."

"Are you kidding? It's amazing. My mom loved baking, too. She would have been in awe watching you." Exactly like I was.

Quinn dabbed a bit of frosting to end the section she'd been working on and leaned back in her chair to examine it. "Nikki told me how much your mom loved making gingerbread houses. How much she loved Christmas. It must be hard without her here."

I was unprepared for the emotion that caught in my throat. "It's been difficult for all of us. My marriage had just ended, and suddenly, my mom was sick. Really sick. It felt like the world was crumbling down around me. She'd only had the diagnosis a few weeks before ..." I drew in a deep, steadying breath, refusing to get emotional in front of Quinn. "... before she was gone."

Quinn shifted to one side in the chair so she could look up at me, and her hand settled over mine, her warmth penetrating into the darkest parts of my broken heart.

My next inhale shook, and I swiped a hand over my eyes. "It's hard to allow myself to remember her when all I feel is grief when I do."

She said nothing for a minute, her hand still on mine. "I don't know what it feels like to have lost a parent. I can't imagine how hard it must be. And I'm sorry. Hopefully, one day, that grief will turn into sweet recollection. And every memory of her will bring you joy, even if it's still mixed with sadness."

I gripped her hand in mine, unable to say any more.

She gave a timid smile. "Nikki mentioned you were going to visit your grandma soon?"

Grateful for the subject change to get my emotions in check, I nodded. "My whole family, actually. Julie should arrive in Newport today with her husband and kids, and my dad and Sandra are planning to come as well."

"Would you like me to make a gingerbread house you could decorate with her? It wouldn't be anything fancy, but Nikki said she also enjoyed making them."

I glanced at the undecorated houses. "You have lots to do. You don't need to add anything else to your day."

"It wouldn't take long, and I'd love to do it—unless that's not allowed at the care facility."

"I'm sure it's allowed." I studied her hopeful expression. "But only if you have time."

Her smile widened, and she gave a goofy salute. "Yes, sir."

I shook my head with a chuckle. "I'd better let you get to it, then, soldier." I paused when I reached the door. "And not that you're likely planning to go out, but there's supposed to be a storm tonight. Nothing too crazy. They're predicting a few inches of snow is all, but I thought you'd like to know."

"Are you going anywhere?" Her voice was casual, but a small crease formed in the middle of her brow.

It looked like I'd have to wait until tomorrow to see Julie and her family. "I'll be downstairs. Text me if you need anything."

The line between her eyes disappeared. "Even if it feels like I'm inconveniencing you?"

"Especially if it feels like that. Maybe then, you'll learn you aren't."

I stepped into the stairwell and locked the door so Quinn wouldn't have to get up.

TWELVE

QUINN

It had been hours since Landon had left, and my mind was still churning over all the events from today—the last few days, really. I typically enjoyed the mindless work of decorating so I could listen to music or put on a movie as background noise, but no movie sounded good, and I'd tried many a holiday tune, but it simply wasn't cutting it. I needed something to ground myself and quiet my thoughts. And with Landon a text message away, perhaps an episode of my favorite true-crime podcast wouldn't be too much to handle.

I found my phone and started the next episode, engrossed in the plot of a neighborhood killer that ended up being a seventy-four-year-old woman. Were there no demographics untouched by murderous rage? My phone rang, making me jump and pausing my podcast. I sighed. This was not the first time Mom had called, and if I didn't answer soon, she'd likely call the police and report me missing.

"Hey, Mom."

"There you are. Sheesh. I nearly called the police. I haven't heard from you in three days, Quinn."

I smiled to myself. "I texted you."

"Anyone can steal a phone and send texts from it. I needed to hear your voice and make sure you were alright."

"I'm fine. I've just been super busy."

"I hope part of that busyness was you asking about changing those airline tickets to come home on the twenty-third."

And this was the precise reason I hadn't answered the last few times. I hadn't even agreed to come yet, and here she was, implying her will into reality. "I'm sorry. I haven't seen Irene Garrity—the one who booked my tickets—since I got here."

"And you have no other way of contacting her?" Doubt tainted Mom's voice.

I winced. "I'll email her tomorrow."

"Every day you wait, the tickets are going up in price, Quinn. If we're the ones having to fly you home, Dad and I don't want to spend a fortune to do it."

"I'll email Irene tonight."

"Thank you, sweetie. I'm excited for you to see all the new Christmas traditions Margaret has planned for us. I don't know why we didn't do our own thing together sooner."

It suddenly felt as though I'd swallowed a paperweight with the way my stomach dropped. "Sounds great. I'd better go, though. I'm right in the middle of decorating one of the houses, and I need both hands."

I held my breath, waiting for her to say I could just as easily put it on speaker, but she didn't. I wasn't surprised. I think she felt like showing interest in my work was only prolonging something futile. "Don't forget to let me know the minute you hear about the plane ticket."

"Is that Quinn?" my dad's voice came through the speaker.

"Hey, Dad."

The sound muffled momentarily, like Mom had passed him the phone. "Hey there, sweets. It sounds like you need to go, but real quick, I wanted to touch base with you about the receptionist job at my office. I don't need to know right now if you want it, but I will soon—probably in the next week or two—so just keep that at the forefront of your mind. I think it would be a great position for you, and it has benefits."

I closed my eyes, drawing in a slow breath. "Thanks, Dad. I'll think about it."

"I hear the East Coast is hunkering down for a big winter storm. Do you have enough food to last you a couple of days?"

The beauty of non-perishable groceries. "I do."

"That's my girl. Stay warm, and—" The soft hum of my mom's voice in the background had me trying to hear what she was saying. "Yes, and let us know when you hear about the tickets."

I rolled my eyes. "Love you, Dad."

"Love you, kid."

It took me a minute to regather my desire to continue decorating, but once I put on the next episode of my podcast—a seasonal one about the Stalking Stuffer, who'd leave a stocking full of coal at the crime scene of those who had made his *naughty list* —the royal icing was flowing again.

Boom!

My hand stilled, the piping bag hovering above the roof of the gingerbread house. What was that sound? I muted the podcast and quieted my breathing, listening for any unfamiliar noises. The blood pumped through me, whooshing past my ears as it went. Besides the low hum of the wind, the house was quiet. I moved to the window and peeked out the curtain. Falling snow billowed in the wind. That must have been what the noise was— something blowing in the storm.

I let out a sigh of relief and started toward the table when another boom stopped me mid-step. That one sounded like it came from upstairs. But no one could be upstairs. I'd been here all day. Unless ... What if someone was trying to get in? It was an illogical thought, most likely prompted by the image of a Santa-like stalker entering houses through open windows. Or was it illogical? I'd not finished the episode. Maybe the Stalking Stuffer was still on the loose.

As silently as I could manage, I moved to the table and grabbed my phone to type a quick text to Landon. Before I pressed *send*, reason seemed to return, in part, when I noticed the time in the corner. Eleven-thirty? I couldn't text him this late about something that was most likely nothing. Besides, he was probably sleeping. And I was hesitant to keep him from his sleep —again. With new resolve, I put the phone down. If someone was trying to get inside, I doubted they'd try to enter through a locked third-story window in a snowstorm.

But there was a chance—though slight.

As some sort of middle ground, I retrieved the trusty iron skillet I'd threatened Landon with that first night and placed it next to me on the table. Perhaps it hadn't been the best night to break my true-crime podcast fast, however much it took my mind off Landon.

A third bang echoed through the house, and instinctively, I snatched up the phone and pressed *send* on the message I'd typed out. Landon could get sleep later.

Quinn: Hey! I don't know if you're still up, but if so, do you keep hearing that loud noise?

WHILE I WAITED for Landon's response, I stared at the stairs to the third floor, refusing to let a perpetrator catch me unaware. The phone chimed, and I startled.

Landon: I haven't heard any loud noises. Maybe it's the storm?
Quinn: Maybe.

Quinn: If I don't get murdered in my sleep tonight, we'll know that was it.

Landon: I'm on my way up.

LANDON'S KNOCK came so soon after his text arrived that I realized he'd probably already been planning to come to my rescue even before my melodramatic text.

"Is it you?" I asked through the door.

"It's me."

I opened the door, wearing a sheepish smile. "I'm sorry to bother you—"

A scent of warm spices lingered on his clothes, and I barely refrained from full-on sniffing him as he stepped inside. "I think we're going to need to write *I'm not an inconvenience* on an index card and attach it somewhere you'll be forced to read it several times a day."

I bolted the door behind him. "Thanks for coming."

"So, what sounds are you hearing?"

"I've heard it three times now. It's a loud—" I made a low guttural sound that barely resembled it. "I think it's coming from upstairs."

"Are all the windows closed?"

"I don't open windows and leave them unattended. Ever."

His lips curved upward at the corners. "I should have guessed that."

The lights flickered, and I glanced up, taking a step closer to him. "What was that?"

"Probably just the—" The lights dimmed, then went out, leaving his unspoken words hanging in the air.

"Curse words." I latched onto his arm, pressing myself against him. "Do you think someone cut the power to the house?" I whispered.

"No. It's just a power outage." There was the slightest trace of concern in Landon's voice as he lifted his phone flashlight and shone it around the room. "And did you just use 'curse words' as an expletive?" He started toward the sliding glass door, and I moved with him like I was a new appendage to his body.

"The few times I've sworn, I've used the words wrong, which kind of ruined the whole point of it. I've since resorted to *curse words*. It's an all-encompassing phrase, so it's difficult to use incorrectly."

"Brilliant." Landon opened the draping curtains, and a dim bluish light from the snow-filled night illuminated the darkness. He glanced down the street. "No one has power, and the street-lights are out," he said, the muscles in his arms relaxing at the real-ization. "But if you want, we can check upstairs. See if we can find what's causing that ... *demonic* sound you demonstrated."

I nodded, too nervous to react to his teasing.

The two of us made our way up the stairs, arm in arm—or more like my arm clutching onto Landon's with a death grip. "Do you want to stay out here?" he asked, opening the door to the first room.

I glanced down the long, dark hallway. "I'll come with you."

His light cut through the darkness, revealing a seemingly empty bedroom. I trailed behind him as he walked to the window and verified it was shut and locked. "On to the next?"

"Should we check under the bed or in the closet ... or both?" My thorough nighttime check always included a floor-to-ceiling check of each room—anywhere a person could hide and some places they likely couldn't.

Landon aimed his light toward me, as if to see if I was serious, before he lowered to his knees and checked beneath the bed. "All clear." The moment he climbed to his feet, I grasped onto him again, and we moved to the closet. Landon beamed his light at the closet full of clothes and shoes. "What's my stuff doing in here?" He didn't sound upset, just surprised. "Did you move it?"

"No. It's been there the whole time. I thought it was strange there would be a closet full of men's clothes in a rental, but I just assumed someone had left it." I'd actually had a whole story imagined for the lost clothes' owner. The poor man with no family who'd met his untimely demise here in Newport. And no one knew to look for him. It was quite a tragic tale, and several times, I worried I was wrong about the demise part, and he'd suddenly show up to reclaim his clothes. Until Landon got here. Then I realized they were probably his. "But it all makes sense now. Minus how they got here."

"Maybe Nikki had them moved in here so the closets in my room would be empty for you to use. I'll have to remember to ask her." He closed the closet. "On to the next room now?"

I nodded my approval. The next was also murderer free, as was the shared bathroom—shower, cupboards, and behind the door. The master looked especially eerie in the dark, or maybe it felt that way because if someone was hiding, it would be in here.

Boom!

I latched onto Landon like a cat trying to be given a bath. "See. That's the sound."

Landon went tense, his flashlight whipping across the room. "Anyone here?"

"Just for the record," I whispered, "people hiding from you won't answer that."

He sent me the briefest smirk before continuing his search. We—well, he with me towing behind in a way that couldn't have made walking in the dark an easy task for him—moved around the room in a logical order. We started to the left of the door, checked both closets and under the bed. All the windows were still locked. The bathroom was the last place to check. He opened the door and shined his light into the darkness.

My heart was racing, and my head was spinning from my shallow breaths as we crossed the bathroom floor. His hand settled on my waist, and he directed me behind him. I gripped his soft, linen shirt in my hands, holding my breath while I waited. Slowly, his hand reached out, and he flung the shower curtain back.

Empty.

"No one's inside the house," he said with a sigh of relief.

My shoulders relaxed. "I wonder what that noise was."

"Probably something blowing in the wind."

We started downstairs when the bang came again.

He headed toward the front door. "I'll be right back."

I hurried after him. "Where are you going?"

"Outside to see what that sound was."

Or who it was. "In the storm?"

"I'll be fine. Lock the door after me, and I'll be right back."

I gave a meager nod of agreement, and he slipped out. I bolted the door behind him when guilt riddled my mind. What if I was sending him to his death—unarmed and unsuspecting? That was a heavy burden to live with. Besides, I had no idea where my phone was, and the house was too dark for my comfort level. Without another thought, I pulled on my boots by the door and grabbed the iron skillet from the table.

When I stepped into the frigid night air, the snow whipped around me. I glanced around, but I couldn't see Landon. My body convulsed in some sort of intense shiver, and my teeth clanked together in repeated motion. Maybe I should have waited for him inside like he'd said. But what if he needed me?

Footprints in the snow caught my attention, and I carefully stepped where he had. Snow found its way into the tops of my untied boots, but I continued around the house, wishing I had thought to grab my coat. Landon stood toward the far side of the house, his shoulders rounded from the cold. He directed the unimpressive amount of light emanating from his flashlight upward. I continued forward, my gaze locked on what he was staring at—a long, thin piece of metal hanging from the roof. I glanced behind me to make sure no one was around.

After a minute, he turned off his flashlight and shoved the phone in his pocket, starting toward me with his attention on the snow in front of him.

"What is that?" I asked when he was close enough to hear me.

His eyes shot up, and he froze. "Jeez, Quinn." He released a puff of breath, and his expression softened. "What are you doing out here? It's freezing, and you don't have your coat."

I lifted the iron skillet as evidence. "I thought you might need my help."

He bit the inside of his lips as though trying to prevent a smile. "It's just the rain gutter that's come loose. But had it been something more sinister, you would have single-handedly scared the culprits away. One look at you and"—he tossed his thumb over his shoulder—"gone."

I scoffed. "Remember, I'm tougher than I look." As though my body wanted to mock me, it gave another uncontrollable shiver. "When I need to be, anyway."

He chuckled. "Let's get you inside."

With careful steps, we made our way back into the stairwell, and Landon locked the shared door behind us. "You going to be okay?"

I batted at the air. "Of course. It's not like I'm afraid of the dark." Mostly.

His hand hesitated on the doorknob to the downstairs apartment. "Are you sure?"

I started up the stairs to prove my point, glad the stairwell window let in a faint light. "Yeah. Besides, we both know you need your sleep," I said, hoping it sounded more playful than accusatory.

He laughed. "If something comes up, don't hesitate to call. I'll keep my phone by me."

Reaching the landing, I creaked the door open, staring into the dark house. I swallowed. Just because it was dark didn't mean it wasn't safe. Our house check had been thorough—at least, pretty thorough. There were a few places we hadn't looked on the main floor, and I had stupidly left the door unlocked while we'd been outside. I hadn't noticed any extra footprints in the snow to indicate someone had taken advantage of the opportunity, but how carefully had I looked? I hesitated, glancing over my shoulder to find Landon still standing at the bottom, waiting. "We didn't check the coat closet," I blurted before I could stop myself. "Or the broom cabinet in the kitchen. Or the laundry room."

Landon started up the stairs, his smile discernible in the dim light.

"And we missed the downstairs bathroom," I said, my voice catching as he stepped next to me on the landing. His warmth penetrated into me. Since when did my insides morph into a kaleidoscope of butterflies at the thought of being alone in the dark with a man? This was not good. I was not supposed to be having feelings like this for Landon.

When I bolted the door behind us, I felt oddly aware of Landon standing at my side.

"Anywhere else we should check?" he asked, only his shadowed features visible in the thin veil of light coming from the sliding glass door.

"No. I think that should be it." I hesitated, wondering how much to show the crazy card. But it was unnervingly dark, and since I had to sleep here by myself, I might as well mention my concerns to prevent Landon coming back a second time if my imagination got the better of me. "Unless, when we were outside, someone moved from one of the new hiding places to somewhere we'd already checked. Or came in through the unlocked door." There it was. I'd officially revealed an exponential growth trajectory on my crazy.

"The whole house it is." He retrieved his phone from his pocket again and aimed it downward. "Do you want to come this time?"

Yes, I absolutely did. And that was the problem. Since it was improbable that there was anyone hiding in the house (though it was always safe to double-check), it was growing clear to me why I wanted to go—the accidental touches, the sound of his laugh, and the memory of his hand on my waist. I didn't trust myself. Not at all. Not with these stirrings inside me. "I'll wait here."

"THE HOUSE IS SECURED." Landon had made quick work of the house check.

"Thank you."

He shined his flashlight around the room until he located me on the couch. I squinted when the beam of light hit my face, and he quickly shut it off and shoved it in his pocket. "Do you need anything else before I go?"

"No. I should be good?" It came out more like a question than a statement. Like I was still trying to convince myself that I'd be okay. And I guess I was. With the power out, I dreaded going to bed. Every night, I'd been leaving the hall light on while I slept. Between that and the lock, I'd be alerted to anyone trying to get into my room. But now ... it felt like I was in a setup for one of those awful horror movies that I'd regrettably watched before I realized they would permanently ingrain themselves into my brain.

"You don't sound very confident." Landon stepped around the end of the sectional.

My confession couldn't be avoided. "I picked a bad night to resume my true-crime addiction. Two weeks clean, all for nothing."

Landon plopped down on the far side of the couch, his shadowed frame barely discernible against the dark leather.

"What are you doing?"

He placed his feet on the coffee table, apparently settling in. "Keeping you company."

"It's probably past midnight. You need to go to bed."

"I won't be able to sleep knowing you're scared and by yourself, so we might as well stay up together."

I stared into the void of darkness around him, trying to convince myself to tell him I'd be fine. But being alone with Landon in the dark was a lesser concern than being alone in the dark by myself. Though it was still a valid concern, just for other reasons. "If you're sure. But you can leave whenever you get too tired."

"Can I ask you something kind of personal?"

My breath seemed to catch in my lungs. "Sure."

"Is there a specific reason why you're nervous all the time? Did something happen to you?"

I gave an airy laugh. "You'd think so, but not really. I mean, when I was little, there was a girl in my school that got kidnapped. It turned out it was her dad, who didn't have custody of her, that took her. And she was fine in the end. But I have a pretty vivid imagination that can quickly get out of hand. That, and my mom instilled a healthy dose of paranoia in me. I remember walking to my friend's house who lived at the end of our street, and when I'd see a car coming, I'd dive behind a bush so they wouldn't see me. Not just once, like every time I walked there. She moved away when I was nine, so I'd like to think I probably would have stopped doing that eventually, but it's up for debate."

"But you're so friendly when we're out, even to strangers."

"What can I say? I'm a living, breathing paradox."

Landon laughed. "You really are. In a good way, though."

I shifted, tucking my legs under me for warmth. "I think it comes down to when I'm with someone who I feel safe with, I can talk to anyone."

"That makes sense."

Another bang sounded, and I glanced out the glass door. "It's really coming down out there." The sight was beautiful—countless large flakes drifting downward in the darkness. If only it weren't so cold, I might appreciate it more. I ran my hands over my arms. "How long do you think the power will be out?"

He shrugged. "Hopefully not too much longer. Are you cold?"

"A little. But I'm okay."

"Here." He moved to the far end of the sectional and lifted the end, grabbing a blanket from a concealed storage area. He handed it to me and returned to his seat, passing in front of the fireplace.

"What about the fireplace?" I arranged the thick throw over myself, grateful for its warmth. "Does it burn wood or is it gas?"

"Oh, smart. It's gas." He hurried toward it, pulling out his flashlight and aiming it at the mantel, searching among the Christmas decorations. "Darn. Where's that key?"

"Key? Isn't there a switch or something?" That was how my parents' gas fireplace worked.

"No, this one has a metal key you use to turn on the gas." He dropped the light to the ground. "Huh. It's usually right here. I wonder where I put it." He moved over to the closet and started rummaging around.

"It's okay if you can't find it," I said, knowing all too well how elusive some items could be—my phone being one of them. "I'm warm enough for now."

He stepped back and ran a hand over his beard. "I swear it was just sitting on the mantel."

"What happens if you don't find it? Can you not use the fireplace anymore?"

"I can order a new one. It just doesn't help us right now." He moved back to his place on the couch, on the other side of the sectional from where I sat. "Sorry about that."

"Like I said, I'm perfectly warm at the moment. And I have my coat in the closet if it comes to that."

Landon leaned back, returning his feet to the coffee table. "I never thanked you yesterday for how you handled the whole Eliza situation."

"You mean my superior acting skills?"

He chuckled. "Yes. That's exactly what I mean."

"I know it was probably taking the whole 'pretend we're interested in each other' thing a little far, but when I thought about the roles being reversed—about how I'd feel if I ran into Cody and his new ... girlfriend—I couldn't help myself. Especially after Eliza had clearly used the whole *baby* thing to hurt you."

"Was it that obvious how I felt?"

My gaze dropped to my hands. "I would have felt the same."

He went silent for a minute. "It might surprise you to hear, but after Eliza and I got married, I was eager to start a family." He paused. "Eliza wanted to wait. She had all sorts of reasons for not wanting to have a baby, and I tried to respect her choice, but after a while, I realized that there was really one underlying reason for her wanting to wait. I couldn't provide the life she wanted for her children. Or her. We had money, just not enough for her tastes." He paused, his expression heavy. "When I mentioned converting our downstairs into an apartment to supplement our income, that was the last straw."

"But you were doing it for her."

"She didn't see it that way. She saw it as evidence of my inabilities." He hesitated. "Her comment about her being pregnant with their second child was her way of letting me know Mark—unlike me—was enough for her."

"The way she glared at me when she heard we were together seemed to imply the opposite."

"You think?"

"I'm positive." The hope in his voice nagged at me. "Would you ever think about getting back together with her? I mean, if things were different, and she wasn't married to Mark?"

"No." He didn't give a moment's hesitation. "Eliza is a part of my past, but there's no place for her in my future." He crossed his arms. "How about you? If ... is it Cody?"

I nodded.

"If Cody wanted to reconcile things between you, what would you do?"

"Honestly?" The question had been one I'd thought about constantly this past year, and rarely did I stick with the same answer for long. "I don't know. Cody has been such a big part of my life that it's hard to imagine it without him. And despite what you might think from the few things I've said, he's a great guy. He's smart and funny. He takes—well, *took*—great care of me for years. But I'm not sure I could ever forgive him for what he did. For walking out on me months after he'd vowed that he'd always be there. I wish he would have talked to me about why he was so unhappy. If I could have understood his reasons for leaving ... if I'd known what I'd done wrong ... I could have tried to fix it."

"Why do you assume it was you that was in the wrong?"

I gestured to myself. "Remember? I'm the Queen of Chaos. I always have been." I tipped my head from one side to the other. "Not exactly like I am now—this last year I've somehow taken all my worst traits and amplified them tenfold—but I've always been disorganized, and messy, lacking ambition, too passive, aimless, scared of everything—"

"Wow." Landon cut me off mid-sentence. "You really should try some positive self-talk."

A sardonic laugh escaped me. "I'm not sure I could think of many positive things to say about myself at the moment."

"I have plenty if you'd like to borrow mine for the time being."

I stared at him, my cheeks warming at what he implied. "Like what? My canned-chicken sandwiches?" Self-degradation had always proven a useful tactic to divert attention from myself.

"Those were surprisingly good. But, no. You're excessively honest, kind, forgiving, and creative. I could go the more superficial route and tell you you're beautiful—stunning, actually." In the following silence, I heard the click of his smile. "You can change the entire mood of a room in an instant."

The air between us shifted, and my body tingled under his thoughtful notice. "That's not true." Compliment rejection activated.

He pointed at me in mock warning. "You can't say anything. This is how I view you. You're just choosing which ones to borrow."

A smile tried to escape, but I managed to cover it with an overdone huff instead.

"You're undeniably endearing, especially when you huff like that."

I grabbed a decorative pillow and chucked it at him.

When it thudded into his chest, he gave an exaggerated grunt. "And you're definitely stronger than you look."

"Okay." Laughter brimmed behind my voice. "I think we're done now. But thanks for the ideas. They were very *insightful*."

He chuckled at my lack of enthusiasm. "I have plenty more, if you need them."

My attention drifted to the falling snow. "The truth is, I can't help but wonder if ... well ..." What was I doing? Landon didn't need to hear my deepest confession—one I'd only ever mentioned to Ashlee. And even that was done in a non-committal passing comment. My good sense must have gone out with the power. "Never mind."

He dropped his feet and leaned forward, his elbows coming to rest on his knees. "What?"

"Really, it's nothing."

"Quinn, you can tell me. I just might understand."

It was true. Of everyone I knew, Landon was the only one who'd experienced divorce after a whirlwind marriage. His scars, though well hidden, probably didn't look too different from my own. "I just wonder if I wasn't enough for Cody. You know ... in the ways a wife should be." My whole body flooded with an uncomfortable heat at my admission. "I mean, well ... not like that. Not exactly. It's just ... the girls he's dated since our divorce seem to be the exact opposite of me in ... looks, I guess. Tall, endless legs ... well-endowed." I groaned. This was not going how I'd intended it to. "You see, Cody posts to social media, where all of our friends and family see these gorgeous women he's with. And if *I* wonder if I was lacking in ... certain ways, I'm guessing they also do." I sighed. "And now, whenever I'm around anyone, it's all I can think about—the calculations of my failings that must be going on in their heads."

The room went unnervingly quiet, and I suddenly wished I

hadn't borne my soul to him. I had a tendency to take things too far. Admitted too much. And what did I expect him to say to that anyway? That it wasn't true? That I was enough? I'd forced him into a position where he'd have to be disingenuous in his answer —if he answered at all. There was no way around it.

After a minute, he leaned back in his seat again. "Looks like we have another thing in common. After Eliza, I've constantly focused on my failings. On all the ways others believe I failed."

Warmth poured into me at his simple admission, and I was instantly glad I'd trusted him. And though trust and vulnerability were dangerous ground for us, all things considered, it was still good to be understood. "I guess that's why we make such a great pretend couple," I said, showing Landon I remembered our boundaries perfectly. Okay, not perfectly, considering the unnerving feelings that consumed me every time he got close, but pretty solidly...ish. Solidlyish.

"I hope the power comes back on soon," he said, pulling my attention back to him.

My heart plummeted. One minute, I thought we were bonding, and the next, he wanted to flee. Again.

"Because of the heater, I mean," he clarified. "It's getting chilly in here."

"Oh." Relief flooded over me, like I'd given Landon complete power over all my emotions. I glanced down at the blanket covering me and then back at him, debating whether I should offer to share. It was his blanket, after all. "This blanket is big enough for two people." It was a compromise—not so much an invitation as it was stating a fact. Landon could make of that what he wanted.

"That's okay. It's not too cold yet."

I shrugged, pretending his refusal to bundle up in a blanket with me had no effect. "Suit yourself. More heat for me."

"Actually, it would mean more heat for both of us if we shared."

"True. I remember hearing that if you're trying to stave off hypothermia in someone, you're supposed to strip down and use your body heat to keep them warm."

He laughed. "I would have gone with penguins as an example, but that works, too."

"Penguins?" For the millionth time tonight, my whole face blazed in embarrassment, and I wished I could somehow bottle up the heat emanating from me. It would probably be enough to keep me snuggly warm all night. Or longer. When would I learn to think through my comments before saying them? Obviously never. "That definitely is a more appropriate answer. And a lot more applicable, seeing that neither of us has hypothermia, and we'll definitely be keeping our clothes on." I barely prevented a groan at my continued stupidity. "I'm sorry if I put an unwanted image of undressed people in your mind. Other people, not us, of course." My attempts to fix this conversation were futile. "You know what? I'm going to stop talking now."

"Don't stop on my account. I'm thoroughly entertained."

If he could see the scowl on my face in the darkness, I was certain he'd regret his amused tone. Unfortunately, he couldn't. "Just so you know, if you get hypothermia for refusing to share a blanket, that's on you. Don't expect me to come to your rescue."

"I'd better not get hypothermia, then." He stood up and started toward me, making me tense in anticipation. Was he really coming to sit by me? Because I was suddenly having serious doubts about this being a good idea. He stopped in front of me. "Or am I no longer invited to share your blanket?"

"You are on very thin ice."

"Hypothetically, if that ice broke, would you then be willing to stave off my hypothermia?"

My jaw dropped, and I shook my head, trying to keep my laughter from betraying me. "That's it. Your privileges of blanket sharing have officially been revoked." And I meant it. I couldn't be snuggling under a blanket with him if he was going to say flirty things that made me forget his feelings weren't real.

His deep, chesty laughter echoed in the quiet room. "I guess

I'll just have to soak in any excess heat you give off by sitting next to you." He dropped onto the cushion so close to me that my body sank toward him.

Quickly, I righted myself, then lifted up the blanket and tossed half of it over him.

He took hold of it and wrapped it over himself, leaving a small gap between our bodies to prevent us from touching. "See, there's that forgiveness I mentioned earlier."

I smiled at him. "That's where you're wrong. I'm actually using you."

"Really?"

"You are literally twice my size, which logically means, with your extra surface area, you'll be putting off twice the body heat that I can to fill our little *cocoon of warmth* here."

"But you're already warm. I still have to warm up before I can be of any use to you." He placed his ice-cold hand over mine where I grasped the edge of the blanket, but it didn't have the effect he was probably going for. Instead, my body did that strange thing where I felt oddly in tune with every internal sensation.

"You're freezing," I whispered, staring into his shadowed face. "Here." I guided his hand under the blanket and clasped it in mine, convincing myself this was me being helpful and nothing more. "Let me have your other one, too."

In the quiet, I could hear him swallow, but his other hand found mine.

Trying to ignore the buzzing in my chest and the pleasure of his skin against mine, I rubbed my fingers over his, starting at his palm and moving outward along each finger. For several minutes, neither of us spoke.

"Is that better?" I asked when I realized his fingers were no longer cold to the touch.

His gaze was fixed on me. "Yes. Thank you."

I'd just convinced myself to release his hands when his thumb caressed the top of my hand so gently I thought I imagined it. The second time, my breath caught. Then, his fingers intertwined with mine.

My heart trembled out a faster beat, and I stilled.

The air between us was electric, like the first time our hands had accidentally touched. I couldn't see him clearly in the dark, but he was only a breath away. I willed him to close the space between our lips. I couldn't remember the last time I'd wanted anything this much.

Landon exhaled. "We should get you to bed."

My pounding heart plummeted, and I retracted my hands from his. "Yeah, of course." I stood, allowing the blanket to fall from my lap. An overwhelming feeling of rejection chased away the flitting, invigorating sensation of anticipation from moments before.

"As long as it's okay with you, I'll sleep on the couch tonight." Landon's voice had an extra rasp to it. "That way, you'll know you're safe."

"If you're sure." I took a step backward. "I guess I'll see you in the morning."

Landon climbed to his feet next to me. "Quinn, I feel like I need to—"

I lifted my hands. "No, it's fine. Really. You don't need to explain anything or apologize ... or say whatever you were going to say. It's late and dark, and neither of us are thinking clearly. Well, you apparently are, seeing that you stopped us from doing anything we might regret. Not that we would have actually done anything to regret. I mean, more like ... complicating things." I cleared my throat. "So I totally get it."

"Quinn."

"I'm fine. Honestly. I'm just going to head up." I started walking toward the kitchen with careful steps. "Siri? Hey, Siri?" I gave a high-pitched giggle that sounded false even to my ears. "She never hears me at first. Hey, Siri," I said again, louder this time. Finally, a quiet chime sounded, and a flicker of light drew my attention to the counter. "There she is." I snatched up my phone and turned on the flashlight. "Night, Landon."

He gave a long exhale. "Night."

When I reached the room, I slipped into bed without getting ready. The darkness hardly troubled me compared to the way my mind looped through what had just happened. Again and again. The slight caress of Landon's thumb and his fingers intertwining with mine. Now that I saw it playing in front of me, I realized his gesture had been a way of letting me down gently after my whole awkward, hand-warming display. What an idiot I was. I definitely needed to swear off relationships for the rest of forever.

THIRTEEN

LANDON

MY PHONE BUZZED ON THE COFFEE TABLE, AND I rolled over, trying to get my bleary eyes to focus at the name on the screen. Nikki's name clarified.

"Hey." I picked up the phone and put it to my ear, too tired to sit up. I'd hardly slept all night due to a wicked combination of cold and guilt. "You're up early."

"Do you even know what time it is?" Nikki asked, sounding concerned.

My gaze slid to the corner of the screen. "Yeah. It's seven-forty-five. And being that I'm on forced vacation, my point remains valid."

"You're still planning on visiting Grandma with us at eight, aren't you?"

Crap. I sat up, rubbing the sleep from my eyes. "You bet."

"I'm completely convinced."

"Sorry. I didn't sleep well."

"Why's that? The storm?"

I thought to inform her it was because I'd spent the night hanging out with Quinn, but I was already feeling guilty enough about everything last night to play up our fake relationship at the moment. "Yeah. One of my rain gutters busted and clanked against the house whenever there was a big gust of wind."

"Did it also keep Quinn up?" Had I discerned an uncanny amount of interest in her voice?

"I'll let you know as soon as I talk to her this morning, which will now have to wait until after we visit Grandma."

"Actually, that's why I was calling. The nursing home called to ask if we could come tomorrow instead. The employee that clears their parking lot hasn't made it in yet today because of the snow, so there's nowhere for visitors to park at the moment."

"And you let me think I was going to be late? Thanks for that."

She laughed. "What would I be if not your annoying little sister? It would send me into an identity crisis if I ever stopped teasing you."

"Truer words have never been spoken." I yawned. "But the nursing home has power?"

"They didn't mention that they didn't. Why? Is yours out?"

"It went out at about eleven last night and hasn't come back on yet."

"You two must be freezing."

I certainly wasn't eager to climb out from under the blanket. "It's a little cold but bearable. It would help if I could find the key to my fireplace."

"When we were there the other night, it was on the mantel with the majority of your Christmas decorations."

I ignored her teasing and stood, wincing at the frigid air. "That's what I thought." I walked to the fireplace, searching the mantel in the morning light. "But it's not here anymore."

"What do you mean, it's not there? Are you in the house right now?"

I let my head fall back at my oversight. "It's not what you think."

"Landon, what happened?" Though Nikki's silence was momentary, it hit like a ton of bricks. "If this is to prove a point to me, I'm going to tear you limb from limb. Do not hurt Quinn."

"Jeez. Thanks for the confidence in me. You make it sound like it's a common practice of mine—breaking women's hearts for the fun of it. But for the record, I slept on the couch downstairs so Quinn wouldn't be scared. Besides, if we're pointing fingers here, it was you who put her in my house. Where's your blame in all of this?"

"In all of what? *Did* something happen between you two?"

"No!" I ran a hand through my mussed-up hair in frustration. "I just meant ... never mind."

"Sounds like you could use a nap today."

I grunted in reply, eager to change the subject. "I assume Julie and Josh got to Dad's without any problems?"

"Yep. The storm blew in from the northeast, so they missed it entirely—until they got here, of course."

"Good. I feel bad I didn't make it to see them last night."

"The kids were disappointed you weren't here, but it was probably for the best. With how intensely that storm hit, I would have hated for you to have driven home in it."

I smiled at knowing I'd been missed. "Unfortunately, depending on the state of the roads, I might not venture over to Dad's until tomorrow."

"We get it, even if the kids don't. All they can talk about is when they can see Uncle Landon. Kade is trying hard to win them over, but they're very loyal to you."

I chuckled. "It's going to be hard to displace me. My *favorite uncle indoctrination program* not only started early but has been intensely thorough."

Her laugh vibrated the phone. "Oh, there's one last thing. Can you ask Quinn what she wants to do when the guys show up Tuesday? I'd hate for her to be uncomfortable, so if she prefers, we can get her a hotel, or she's always welcome to join me and the other ladies at our Airbnb."

The thought of Quinn leaving was surprisingly hard to swallow. "I can ask her, see what she prefers."

"If she's too accommodating, see if you can push her a little. I really do want to make sure she's comfortable. Though with Tyler crashing there, it might be beneficial for her to stay, allow them to get to know each other a little better."

I was entirely caught off guard by her comment and couldn't decide what to respond to first. "I can't believe you're still trying to set Quinn up with Tyler when I've clearly stated my interest in her."

"It hasn't been clearly stated, actually. And the little I pulled out of you was not convincing. So yes, I'm going to continue trying to set her up with Tyler since I know your feelings for her are some sort of act of defiance against me."

"You're wrong," I said, feeling the weight of my comment more than she could know. "So please don't ruin anything by getting Tyler involved. Which brings me to my second issue. Why is he staying here? He's not part of the wedding party."

"He asked me if there was somewhere he could stay, and I figured since there were only eight groomsmen, that even if Quinn chooses to stay, you'll have extra space for him."

"And you just assumed I'd say yes?"

"Not a doubt in my mind."

I'd done this to myself, always giving in to everything Nikki wanted—except for my social media boycott. I'd not budged on that. That was, until Quinn. Now, it was only a matter of time before Nikki realized it, and I'd be back to helping her with her social media account. Either way, there was no point pretending I'd say no to her about Tyler staying. "He can stay, but he's sleeping downstairs, far away from Quinn."

"If you're not careful, Landon, you might just convince yourself you're falling for her."

"I've already told you I am falling for her."

"Let's not rehash your pathetic attempts to convince me. I just want to see you both happy, and my matchmaker instincts tell me you'll both be better off with the people I have in mind for you."

"Again, I think you should get your instincts checked. They've seemed a little off lately." And they'd certainly been off with Eliza.

"They're not off. Not this time. But, hey, I've got to run. Kade is searching Dad's cupboards like a hangry scavenger." Kade's voice neared the speaker, and Nikki let out a loud giggle.

"See you tomorrow," I said, eager to end the call before I was forced to hear wherever this was going between them.

"Yep," she said, obviously distracted. "I'll send everyone your love."

"Thanks." Another loud giggle had me tapping the *end call* button. In the quiet that followed, my thoughts drifted back to Quinn. I blew out a puff of air. What was I doing? This whole pretending-to-like-Quinn thing was turning into a disaster. And it didn't help that I was insanely attracted to her. I needed to knock off whatever this was I was feeling while somehow still acting like I was interested in her when we were around other people.

"Was that Nikki?" Quinn's voice sent me spinning toward her. Thick waves of hair hung wildly around her face, framing tired, blue eyes. It looked like I wasn't the only one that didn't sleep well, and I hated to think I'd done anything to cause it, but I probably had.

"It was. She called to let me know we can't visit my grandma until tomorrow."

Genuine concern lined her face. "Is everything okay?"

"Yeah. With the snow, they can't get their parking lot cleared for visitors until later today."

"I made that gingerbread house, so don't forget to grab it before you go."

"When did you have time?"

She shrugged. "Yesterday afternoon. It didn't take very long. I have extra dough in the fridge in case any of my pieces get damaged, so it was a matter of rolling it out and cutting it to the right shape. I also have extra royal icing for you to bring, but you may want to stop at the store to grab some candy for that more traditional look."

"You really didn't have to do that."

"I wanted to." She gave a light smile and moved toward the fridge. "Are you hungry?" She pulled open the door and reached inside, then her eyes darted to me. "It's warm."

I started toward her. "How about the freezer?"

She tossed the other door open and quickly shut it again. "It still feels cold in there. Hopefully, the power comes on soon."

"It almost feels warmer in there than it does in the room. Too bad I didn't think to set out all the food last night. It probably would have fared better." I touched a few of the lukewarm items when my eyes fell on the large, covered bowl. "Do you think your dough's gone bad?"

She sighed. "Probably. I guess it was a good thing I made that gingerbread house for your grandma yesterday. Thankfully, I shouldn't need any more since the houses are all built."

"What about your frosting?"

She tipped the smaller bowl to view its contents. "The icing uses meringue powder instead of eggs, so it's safe. I just keep it in here because I like the consistency of it when it's cold. I can always add a little more powder to thicken it up." She shook her head. "But all that food you bought for me—the milk, and eggs, and yogurt—what a waste."

"It's not a big deal. As soon as the roads get plowed, I can go grab some more groceries."

"We can at least eat the fruit." She grabbed a small package of berries, a bag of kiwis, and two pears.

While we washed and cut the fruit, I could sense Quinn was more guarded than usual. And I hated it.

I waited until we were sitting to breach the uncomfortable subject. "Quinn, can we talk about what happened last night?"

Her eyes shot up from her plate of fruit. "We don't need to. Really."

"I thought you wanted to communicate like mature adults."

"Yes, but I said that when you were the one who didn't want to talk. Now that I don't, I'm actually not opposed to brushing things over and pretending they didn't happen. Being a mature adult is significantly overrated."

"I'm sorry about what happened," I said, unwilling to be deterred. Quinn deserved an apology. "I shouldn't have—"

"You're sorry?" she interrupted. "I'm the one who should be sorry. Like I said, it was late and dark, and my feelings were all muddled because of it. It was like, one minute, I was partly rational, and the next, I—" She bit at her lip. "I don't know. I was awkward and things got uncomfortable."

And I'd caused it. It had only taken me a moment to realize my error—that I was crossing a boundary by clasping her fingers in mine—but apparently it was all it took. "I'm sorry you were uncomfortable. I should have stopped it before it got to that point." I ran a hand through my hair, frustrated with myself. "We need to reestablish our boundaries around this whole *fake-interest* thing. If you're even still wanting to do it?"

Quinn fingered the fruit on her plate, her gaze distant. "I think redefining boundaries would be helpful. We need to make sure we're on the same page."

That was acceptance enough for me. "Agreed. So what boundaries do we want to put in place?"

She didn't hesitate. "When we're alone together, we're platonic friends. No flirting. No touching."

So no holding hands or imagining what it would be like to kiss the other person. Got it. I popped a piece of kiwi in my mouth, hoping to appear casual instead of guilt-ridden. "Anything else you'd like to add to the list?"

"Could you not come over smelling like an intoxicating concoction of spices and the great outdoors? It's hard to focus when you're constantly wafting a scent that makes me want to take a romantic stroll in the woods with a cup of steaming cider in hand."

My head reeled back from the unexpected admission, and I was relieved her attention was on her food. Had I misunderstood her discomfort somehow? Had my breaking the boundaries not been the problem, but my unwillingness to break them? I was suddenly entirely confused. "So, I should stop showering?" I asked, testing the situation with humor, as dry as it was.

Her eyes sparkled when they met mine. "That would definitely help. Oh, and when you run your hand through your hair like you did a minute ago and leave it looking tousled ... that has to go. And the way you rub your hand along your bearded jawline, like this—" Quinn's hand traced over her chin and jaw dramatically, wearing a mockingly seductive expression.

I lifted a brow. "I do that?"

"All the time." Her head tipped from side to side. "Okay, I might have overdone the sexy look for theatrics. Yours is a little more subtle than that." She scrunched up her nose at me. "But not much."

This felt like dangerous ground. But if I was careful, maybe we could have a little fun without letting it go too far. "Well, if we're listing personal traits now, I need you to stop scrunching up your nose like that. No more biting your lip. And I wouldn't mind if you started using that calamine lotion as your morning moisturizer so I'm less distracted by you."

She tilted her head to the side and brought up her bottom lip. "I thought you said the calamine lotion was a good look on me."

I pointed to her pout. "And no more of whatever that was."

She scrunched up her nose again.

I tossed up my hands. "You're already breaking the boundaries."

Her gaze flicked to my hair. "Your hair is still tousled."

I patted it down. "Better?"

She studied me, her eyes scanning my features and then moving to my hair. "Have you ever considered shaving your head?

Because if we want to get serious and prevent any future lapses ..."
She gave a timid shrug, and I thought to ban that from her as well.
"Though you'd probably be one of those attractive bald guys. It's
basically hopeless."

"Are you saying you're attracted to me?"

She tucked both knees into her chest and leaned into the back
of the chair. "It would be a lie to say I didn't find you attractive.
But finding someone attractive differs from being attracted to
someone. One is an observation, and the other is rooted in desire.
I can acknowledge that lots of men are attractive without being
attracted to them."

Unable to squelch my curiosity, I leaned forward, resting my
elbows on the table. "Which category do I fall under?"

Her cheeks turned pink, but she held my gaze. "I'm pretty
sure it's supposed to be the platonic-friend category, remember?"

Supposed to be? Which meant it might not be. An unexpected ray of hope filled my chest. A ray that should not have
been there. What was wrong with me? It was definitely time to
change the subject. "Speaking of lots of men," I said, snapping
out of whatever trance I was under, "there will be nine guys
showing up here on Tuesday, including Tyler Baker. Nikki
wanted me to ask what your preference would be about where
you stayed once they arrive."

Her shoulders fell slightly, like she was as disappointed to be
leaving the previous topic of conversation as I was. "What are my
options?"

"You are welcome to continue staying here, since all your
stuff is here. But if you're not comfortable with sharing a space
with a bunch of guys you don't know, Nikki said she's happy to
get you a hotel. The other option would be to stay with Nikki
and her bridesmaids at the Airbnb. She said they have extra
room."

"I'm fine with whatever."

I sent her a pointed look. "You have to choose. Nikki specifi-
cally told me to not let you be overly accommodating."

Her gaze moved to the sliding glass door. "Regardless, I'm going to work on the gingerbread here, right?"

"You could always request a hotel suite. You'd have plenty of room to work there."

"I don't want Nikki to have to pay for that."

"This is about what you want. And I promise you, she wouldn't even bat an eye at the request."

Quinn's gaze locked on me. "Would that be your vote, then? The hotel room?"

It was better to let her decide, because I didn't trust myself to willingly let her go somewhere else. And I clearly needed to let her. "I'm not going to influence you. This is about what you're comfortable with."

She gave another small pout. "I don't like making decisions."

"You're not supposed to make that face."

She only intensified it, her large blue eyes adding to the effectiveness. "What do you think I should do?"

I lasted only a few more seconds. "Fine. If it were up to me, I'd have you stay." Darn. I wasn't supposed to have said that. "The guys will be gone a good portion of the time, and I could make sure the rowdy ones sleep downstairs. Your stuff is already here, and ..." My words trailed off. I couldn't admit outright that I simply wanted her to stay.

"It would be a lot harder to convince others we're interested in each other if we're not together," Quinn said, finishing for me.

I hadn't even thought of that. "Exactly."

She fidgeted with her spoon. "Are you sure that I won't be an incon—"

"Don't even say it."

"I don't mean an inconvenience to you, but what about to the rest of the guys?"

Honestly, I didn't care. If Quinn was comfortable with the idea, then the guys who didn't like it could get over it. It was my house.

She shrugged. "I feel like it will ruin the whole bachelor-pad vibe to have a girl lurking around, decorating gingerbread houses while you talk about women and make unseemly jokes—or whatever guys do when they're alone together."

I chuckled. "And that's exactly why I'd appreciate a balancing presence to all the testosterone, if you're up for it."

"Well, if you're sure." A shy smile lifted her lips, and I had to force myself to look away from them. "I mean, my stuff is already here." She said it like that was her main reason for staying, but the way color flooded her face again, I foolishly hoped it wasn't.

"I'm sure."

Quinn gave a small shiver. "Wow. It's cold in here."

A new desire to get the fireplace working sent me to my feet. "You really haven't seen a key anywhere laying around? Nikki said she saw it on the mantel the other night when she was here."

Quinn followed me into the kitchen. "Not that I remember. How big is it?"

I started opening drawers, searching through the utensils. "Seven or eight inches long."

"That's a big key to lose."

"You're telling me." I moved back to the front closet, finding nothing. "I wonder if I put it in the box of Christmas decorations."

Quinn was searching the island and looking around her gingerbread houses. "What does the top of the key look like? Just like a normal key?"

"No. It actually doesn't look like a key at all. It's a metal handle about an inch and a half long."

She spun toward me. "With a long bar coming out of it?"

"You've seen it?"

She walked over to the fireplace and stuck her hand in one of the stockings, pulling out the key. "I thought you were talking about a real key." Her hand clasped over her apologetic grimace. "I'm sorry. I put it in here when I was repositioning the Christmas decorations because I didn't know what it was."

"It's not your fault." I grabbed the lighter and hurried toward her. "I should have been a little more specific instead of assuming you knew what a fireplace key looked like." I grabbed the outstretched key and inserted it into the hole by the fireplace. Turning it, I heard a slight hiss. Then I pressed the lighter. A fire blazed to life.

Quinn kneeled by my side, stretching out her hands to warm them by the flames. "Oh, sweet warmth," she whispered, her eyes closed in pleasure. The golden light illuminated the angles of her face, and my gaze settled on her parted, full lips. What would it feel like to kiss those lips? Would she taste as sweet as she smelled —like vanilla with a touch of cinnamon? I forced my attention back to the fire before she opened her eyes and noticed me staring. I needed to get a hold of myself. I was already finding it impossible not to flirt with Quinn. I couldn't risk breaking the one boundary that seemed to be most vital in keeping us both safe from regrets —no touching. Except, currently, I was pretty certain I'd have no regrets if that boundary was broken.

I shook my head. That was not a helpful thought.

FOURTEEN

QUINN

"Look up here," Landon said.

My gaze flicked up to find him standing with his phone in hand, hovering just above me. "What are you doing?" I asked, re-situating the piping bag to build the pressure again.

"I'm just getting a few shots of you in action."

"Why?"

"You'll see. Just smile at me ... now keep working."

I sent him a playful glower but dipped my head and continued my icing pattern on the section I'd been working on. I didn't have time to waste. There were only a few more hours of sunlight, and if the power didn't come back on, that meant only a few more hours of decorating.

"It really is amazing what you do." Landon's camera was still out, but I wasn't sure if he was still filming or not. "Is the pattern in your head, or are you just making it up as you go?"

I smiled up at him. "A little of both."

He lowered his phone. "I'll let you get back to it."

I continued working until my fingers were too stiff to continue. I placed the piping bag on a plate and began opening and closing my hands to increase blood flow. The fire had warmed up the room some, but not enough to make a significant difference where I was sitting. "I think I need a quick break," I said, standing and stretching my back. "Want to join me?"

"Sure." He stood and tucked his phone into his pocket. "What are you thinking?"

I'd seen passing views of the winter wonderland all morning and found the idea of venturing out into it strangely tempting for a girl that typically preferred a consistent seventy degrees. "Could we go outside real quick? Maybe a walk down to the bay?"

"Do you have time for that?"

No. But that didn't lessen my desire to go explore since Landon would be with me. "I think I'll be fine."

Landon stood. "I'll go get my coat and boots. Whenever you're ready, you can meet me downstairs."

I already had leggings on under my yoga pants and was wearing two sweaters, so I put on my coat and boots and shoved my gloves in my pocket. My beanie wouldn't fit over my messy bun, so I quickly undid my hair and braided it in a massive side braid before shoving the beanie on and locking the door behind me.

Landon opened the door before I reached the lower landing. "Come on in for a second. I just need to find my gloves."

I stepped in and shivered when the cold air touched my face and hands. "It's freezing in here."

"That's why I've spent the day upstairs." He smirked at me. "At least part of the reason."

I pointed a finger at him, slightly confused by his admission. "Are you flirting?"

"After that super-intense boundaries talk, there's no way." He walked down the hallway toward the back room, his low chuckle trailing after him.

In his absence, I scanned the apartment. It had a decent-sized living room with a large television settled over a row of lower shelves and a similar-colored sectional to the one upstairs, though not as massive. There was a small kitchen and a hallway with four doors, two on each side. The decor was a nice, clean, nautical look with red accents among a lot of blue, white, and gray. "This is nice," I said.

"It's been a great rental," he called from the back room before reemerging with his gloves in hand. "But if you see Nikki, don't mention my lack of Christmas decorations. I need to get some up before the guys come."

"Why didn't you put up the Christmas tree you bought for upstairs?"

"I returned it to the lot. I didn't want to risk you having another *encounter* with it."

Why did he have to be so darn thoughtful? Maybe I should ban him from that as well. Though, with how many times he'd tousled his hair and run a hand over his beard in the last few hours, it wouldn't matter. He seemed as serious about keeping our newly appointed boundaries as I was.

He opened the door. "Ready?"

The afternoon sun shone off the snow, making it glisten like countless crystals covered it. I squinted at the sight. "It's crazy to think this much snow fell in one night." I glanced back at Landon, who locked the door behind us.

"Seven inches of new snow fell on top of the inch or two we already had. It's a decent amount."

We started up the shoveled drive to the unplowed street, and I did my best to not conjure up the memory of Landon shoveling snow earlier. I shouldn't have watched from the window as long as I had, not only because I had so much to do but because it hadn't helped my resolve in keeping our rules. "The snow won't affect Nikki's wedding, will it?" I asked, desperate to clear the image of him shoveling from my mind.

"It shouldn't. They'll have the roads clear in the next day or two, and as long as we don't get another big storm, which isn't on the ten-day forecast, travel shouldn't be restricted. Really, the timing of this one was pretty perfect. Had it been next weekend instead ..." Landon shook his head. "I'm not sure what Nikki and Kade would have done."

We reached the unmarred snow that covered the road. Each step caused a satisfying crunch beneath our boots. The sky was a bright blue, and only the slightest of breezes moved through the glistening, snow-burdened trees. "I'm sorry I've been lame today," I said, looking at Landon out of the corner of my eye. "I really need to get these gingerbread houses finished."

"Don't apologize. You have work to do. Besides, watching you has been extremely entertaining."

"I highly doubt that with how often you nodded off in the last few hours."

A smile slid into place. "I wasn't the only one doing the watching, then?"

I laughed. "Your constant shifts to sleep-breathing were hard to miss. It had a Pavlovian effect on me. I nearly joined you once or twice." My head whipped toward him. "In taking a nap. Not with you." My quick exhale came out in a puff of white air.

"You would've been welcome." Landon's smile widened, but he continued walking. "We'll see the bay just around this corner."

As I tried to keep up, my legs burned at the exertion. Right after we passed the fourth or fifth house, the view opened up to the left, an expanse of water glistening nearly as brightly as the snow. It was beautiful. Breathtaking, really.

"Easton Bay," Landon said at my side. "That right there is a popular beach in the summer." He pointed to the shore fifty yards in front of us, where only a thin line of sand was visible between the snow and the waves that drifted lazily in and out.

I drew in a long, frigid breath of salty air, as though I could inhale the beauty of it all. "I can't believe you live so close to this. It's incredible."

His gaze scanned the scene. "Sometimes I forget to pay attention, but it really is."

I felt my pocket for my phone but sighed when I realized I'd left it behind.

Landon's gaze slid to me. "What's up?"

"I was going to take a picture, but I left my phone at the house since it's dead."

"May it rest in peace."

I nearly snorted. "You are going to make a great dad. You've already got the jokes down."

He chuckled and pulled his phone from his pocket, handing it to me. "I still have some battery. You can use my camera."

"Thanks." I snapped a couple of pictures.

"Want me to grab one of you?"

"I thought you'd sworn off taking pictures." I glanced over at him, a teasing smile on my lips. "I'd hate to compromise you when you were so adamant about not taking a picture of Nikki and me at Bowen's Wharf the other night."

"It wasn't my best moment."

"So you typically aren't opposed to taking pictures?"

"I'm opposed to social media."

My smile wavered. "Oh. I didn't realize—"

"I'm not opposed to all of it. I just ..." Landon released a long exhale. "After my divorce, I deleted my account. I was done with social media and anything to do with it, including getting sucked into photographing pictures for someone to post. Even for Nikki. It felt easier to draw a hard-and-fast line."

I thought to ask him what had happened that left such a bad taste in his mouth, but I assumed if he'd wanted to tell me, he would. "How did you look through my feed, then?"

He chuckled. "Yeah ... I may have caved and signed up for an account again. It's a different handle, though, and this one's private."

"Why'd you change your mind?"

A mischievous grin emerged. "I think it's obvious."

I stared at him until a stupid smile betrayed me. "I'm not sure how I feel about making you break your solemn oath against all things social media."

"You look pretty amused by it." He removed his glove and grabbed the phone from me. "Now, let me take your picture."

"You might as well. I've already corrupted your integrity." I took a step back to the sound of his laughter, held out my arms wide, and smiled.

He snapped a few pictures and then lowered the camera. "Speaking of corrupting my integrity, want to take a couple with me?"

My brows lifted until they were hidden beneath my beanie. "Selfies? Like the two of us together?"

He shrugged. "I was thinking about what you said the other day after we saw Eliza. About why you told her we were dating."

"Because if the roles were reversed—"

"Exactly. And the roles are reversed, to some extent. It's not like Cody's here with his current girlfriend or anything, but you said he's posting pictures of himself with other girls on his social media."

Where was Landon going with this?

"I'd like to repay the favor. You wouldn't need to say anything about who I am or that we're together. Just post them to your account—if you wanted."

I found myself staring at him, again, while trying to wrap my head around his offer. Not only because a minute ago he told me he'd sworn off social media completely and was now offering to let me post a picture of him, but because of the repercussions of posting that picture. It wasn't only Cody who would see the pictures. My parents, my sisters, all my extended family, and friends. I'd get blasted with messages. Then, there were all my followers. What would they think if a random picture of some man—especially one as attractive as Landon—suddenly hit my feed? They'd expect to see more of him. And after next week, there would be no more. There was no logical reason to entertain the idea of a selfie shoot with Landon. So why did I want to say yes? "We could take a couple," I said, trying to keep the nerves from my voice. "I can always decide later if I'm brave enough to post one."

He held up his phone. "Do you want me to take them? Or do you want to?"

Without a tripod, I was no selfie expert, but it seemed less intimidating to be the one in control of the camera instead of the one thinking about how to pose. "I can."

He moved to stand behind me, our backs to the water. "And just so you're aware, I'm going to break the cardinal rule and touch you, but only for the sake of the picture." His ungloved hands settled on my hips, and despite my multiple layers, the sensation sent a chill through me and made my breath catch. I had one job: to take the picture. Well, smile and take the picture. I held out the phone, trying not to get distracted by the image of us on the screen or the pressure of his hands on me. Just smile and click. Smile and click. I took a few, then scrolled back through them. With Landon right behind me and my large head in the foreground, I looked like the luckiest bobble-head alive. I quickly deleted them to try again.

"Confession." I stretched out my arm a little farther to put more distance between my head and the lens. "I'm terrible at selfies."

Landon scooted closer, his hands sliding lower along my upper thighs in a blissful distraction. "You're a social media influencer. Isn't selfie-taking in your blood?"

My head was spinning, but I was determined to keep my wits about me. "My short wingspan is more conducive to a tripod and remote." I groaned at the new evidence and held it up as proof of my point.

He stood so close I felt his laugh vibrate against my back. "And to think, I was convinced there couldn't be a bad picture of you."

I nudged my elbow into him. "Not all of us can look like a Greek god at the snap of a finger."

"Here. Let me have the phone." He wrapped one arm in front of me from one shoulder to the other and leaned in until our faces were even. My heart pounded beneath his arm, and I hoped he couldn't feel it. Not wanting to simply stand there, I rested my hands on his forearm, knuckles out, and tilted my head toward him. He lifted the phone high in the air with his monstrous reach. He didn't press the capture button on the screen but squeezed both sides of the phone, and the phone clicked. And clicked again.

I looked over at him, planning to inquire about his little phone trick, but the question slipped from my mind when our eyes met. His face was inches from mine. His lips a breath away. My gaze lingered on them for a second too long. He nestled into me, his skin warm against mine. Shocks of electricity pulsed through my body when his beard tickled my neck.

I turned my face toward the screen, and another round of clicks sounded. It was a well-timed reminder—this was all pretend. Exactly like everything else with Landon. And yet, even as I repeated the truth in my head, my body was in a state of denial. I closed my eyes, allowing myself to suspend reality for a moment longer, before opening them again. I needed to get a grip. "Do you think we got a good one?" I dropped his arm and stepped out of his grasp, suddenly grateful for the freezing temps that had prevented me from melting into a puddle.

He handed me the camera. "You be the judge."

My chest buzzed as I scrolled through the images. This couldn't be us. The people in these images looked completely smitten with each other. Their feelings looked real, not pretend.

"Anything worth keeping? Or should we have a round two?"

The thought of being that close to Landon again made breathing difficult. I thrust his phone toward him. "Nope, I think we got it. Should we start back?" Before he could answer, I started up the hill, soon huffing and puffing from my chosen pace. It was time to get back to work. I was in desperate need of a distraction.

THE SUN HAD SET, and with how hard I was focusing in the low light, it was probably time to call it quits. But I'd not gotten enough done on the gingerbread house. I still had two to three hours of work before I could finish, and the thought of putting it off until tomorrow made my stomach churn. How was I ever going to finish the other three that were all more time-intensive than this one?

My gaze landed on Landon for the millionth time today. He sat at the far end of the couch, doing something on his phone. How he had any battery left, I didn't know. I just hoped we didn't have to spend a second night without power. Especially considering we only had one working phone—aka flashlight—between the two of us, and who knew how much longer Landon's would last at the rate he was using it?

Landon lifted his gaze, and I forgot to look away like I wasn't watching him. "When you have a minute, I want to show you something."

I looked back at the gingerbread house and sighed. I was not usually one to call it quits, but what was I supposed to do when I was straining to see as it was? I didn't want to risk messing up. Dropping the piping bag onto the plate, I started toward Landon, feeling suddenly overcome with exhaustion. The late nights, my aching eyes and hands, and the ambiance of the roaring fire made me want to curl up in a blanket and pass out. When I dropped on the cushion next to him, he glanced down at our touching legs and then back at me.

"Slight rule change," I said, too tired to move. "We can touch when we're alone as long as it's not intimate."

He gave a slow nod. "Is there a precise definition of intimate you'd like to give, or can we treat that with some subjectivity?"

"Are you lawyer-talking me?"

"I want to make sure I don't cross any lines."

"Fine." I pointed to our thighs. "This is okay."

He nudged me with his elbow. "How about that?"

"Also okay."

The hand that rested on his thigh brushed the side of my hand, sending a trill of pleasure through me that chased my exhaustion away. "That?" he asked.

I glanced over at him, confused about his intentions. "Less okay."

"And why's that?" Those darn brown eyes of his glinted with amusement in the firelight. What was he up to? "I'm just curious."

"Our hands touching feels more intimate."

He patted my hand stiffly and sent me a questioning look. "So, not fine?"

I laughed. "No, that's acceptable."

"Then what's the difference between this"—he transitioned from patting my hand to caressing the tips of his fingers over my skin—"and this?"

Fire filled my veins beneath his movements. I swallowed. The difference was clearly the feelings that one induced in me, but that was the last thing I wanted to admit right now. "I'm pretty sure you're smart enough to figure it out."

"You might be overestimating my intelligence. How can we be on the same page if it's not completely clear?"

I studied him. Currently, he seemed to want to break the boundaries we'd put in place, but last night, I'd also thought that before he abruptly ended things. Perhaps it wasn't me that was confused. Perhaps it was Landon. "I'm lost. Can you explain what's happening here?"

The corners of his mouth were twitching. "I'm simply asking for a little clarification."

Fine. Two could play at this game. And with how previous matches had gone, Landon was always the first to call it quits. Not that they were actual matches, but more like awkward situations where I'd been unable to correctly read his cues. But I was too tired to think rationally, and honestly, I was eager to see where he intended for this to go. "You're right. It's hard to know for certain. But with a few more scenarios, I think you'll get it." I smacked my outside hand down onto his thigh, giving it a light squeeze. "This is platonic." I loosened my grip and let my hand slowly and gently slide to his knee. I kept it there, rubbing my thumb in small circles. "Intimate."

He gave a slow nod.

I bumped my foot against his. "Platonic." My foot came to rest against his, and I seductively ran it along his and leaned into him, pretending I didn't feel a surge of excitement course through me. "Intimate."

His eyes narrowed. "I think I'm getting it. Maybe a few more examples."

He wasn't backing down. Did he really want me to keep going, or was he going to stop me soon? If I'd been thinking clearly, I would have hoped he'd stop me, but it was apparent I wasn't. I lifted my hand and gave him a quick pat on his cheek.

"Platonic," he said, his Adam's apple bobbing like he knew where this was going.

"Good. Now what about this one?" I set my hand on his jaw and ever so softly traced the line of it with just enough pressure to position his face toward mine. My gaze lingered on his parted lips, but I was uncertain if I had the courage to keep playing this game. Or if this was a game at all. What if Landon stopped me? What if whatever this was had gone too far? I couldn't take another rejection. My hand relaxed, but before I could drop it, his settled over mine.

"Go on." His voice was a husky whisper, and his gaze flicked to my lips.

A rush of adrenaline surged through me at his assurance, bolstering my confidence, fueling the desire within me. I guided his chin downward and brushed my lips against his. "Intimate," I whispered against his mouth.

He pulled back, and my heart dropped, until I saw the way he was looking at me. His eyes reflected the same desire that was threatening to consume me from within. "So let me see if I have this figured out." He tucked a loose hair behind my ear in a quick motion. "Platonic?"

My chest was abuzz with anticipation, but I managed a small nod.

His fingers stilled on my cheeks and then, ever so slowly, moved across my skin until his thumb landed on my bottom lip. The softness of his touch was my complete undoing. And when his lips found mine, I met them with eagerness. It had been too long since I had felt beautiful and wanted, and I was here for every glorious moment.

My hands moved through his hair, and I relished the feel of the thick strands between my fingers. I relished all of it—the taste of him, the way his hands couldn't decide exactly where to be on my body, and the scratch of his beard on my face. When our kiss intensified, Landon wrapped his arms around me and pulled me onto his lap. My body was on fire, but I wanted more. More closeness. More kisses. More Landon.

The lights flickered on.

Unbelievable.

Breaking our kiss, I glanced up with squinted eyes. "How's that for timing?"

Landon threw his head back and groaned, obviously feeling similarly about the interruption.

The curtains were still open from earlier, and the thought of what someone from outside might see if they looked in was unsettling. Not that I expected there to be a creeper outside in the snow, waiting for the power to turn on so he could see what we were up to, but perhaps a neighbor glancing out their own window to see if others' power had also returned.

Landon's hands dropped to the sides of his thighs when I climbed off his lap. "Where are you going?"

I gave him a playful smile and reached for the light switch when my gaze stalled on the nearly completed gingerbread house.

Now that the power was back on, I really needed to finish decorating it. Too bad I had zero inclination to do anything except cuddle up to Landon and continue where we'd left off.

"It's fine." Landon stood up from his place on the couch before I could flip the switch. "You have things to do. And honestly, it will probably be for the best if I leave."

My shoulders fell in time with my hand that had been on the switch. I hated that he was right.

He stopped when he reached me, and his mouth curved upward at the corners. "Of the two real rules we had—no flirting and no touching—I'm confident we broke them both."

"It's up for interpretation."

He chuckled. "How about we sleep on what transpired and reconvene tomorrow—see how we're feeling about those rules after some time to process?"

My gaze dropped from his, and I nodded. Did he already regret what had happened?

His hand came to my chin, and he lifted my face to his. "I don't regret anything," he said, like he'd read my mind. "I simply want to make sure you don't either. Okay?"

This time, I nodded with a little more confidence. Landon didn't regret kissing me. And I certainly didn't regret kissing him. At least, I didn't think I did.

IT WAS past nine when I finished the gingerbread house, and instead of starting on the next house like I should have, I quickly got ready for bed and jumped beneath my covers. My phone was charging on the nightstand, and I debated calling Ashlee to tell her what had happened, but I could see the wisdom in Landon's words—I needed time to process everything. Currently, I was still wrapped up in the memory of Landon's kiss and the pressure of his hands on my skin. But maybe in the light of a new day, I'd feel different, though I doubted it.

Instead, I grabbed my freshly charged phone to check in on my comments and see if anyone had tagged me in a post so I could repost it. Twelve new text notifications greeted me. Seven from Mom and five from Ashlee. I quickly scrolled through Ashlee's partially worried texts before responding that all was well and I'd call her tomorrow. I drew in a slow breath and opened the texts from Mom.

Her most recent messages were full of worry about the storm she heard was ransacking the East Coast. I quickly replied to ease her mind.

Quinn: Hey, Mom! Sorry. The power's been out since yesterday, and my phone died, so I couldn't charge it. I'm safe and warm (now), and I'm sorry if I scared you.
Mom: Thank heavens! I was searching the internet for Nikki's number.

Good thing I'd texted.

Mom: Did you figure out anything about the tickets?

Shoot! I'd totally spaced on it. Guilt pricked at me. Okay, I hadn't totally spaced on it, but the few times I'd remembered, I'd procrastinated. And I knew exactly why.

Quinn: Sorry, Mom. I don't think it's going to work. But don't feel like you need to get me a ticket. I'm fine spending Christmas here.

I dropped the phone in anticipation of her upset rebuttal. I knew it was selfish of me, and usually I'd comply with only the slightest bit of internal grumbling, but this year was different. I really wasn't sure I could face Christmas at home. Not this year. And not with a newlywed couple who knew no limits to their PDA. And not when I could be here with Landon. Not that we'd actually spend Christmas Day together. He'd need to be with his family. But I wanted more time with him whenever I could get it.

My phone pinged, and I peeked with one eye to see Mom's response, but the text that had just come in was from Landon.

Landon: Hey. In all the excitement, I forgot to show you this:

The second text was an image of me. Wait. No. It wasn't an image; it was a video. I pressed play, and a compilation of the clips Landon had taken of me earlier were edited together and set to music. One of me laughing. The gingerbread house from a bird's-eye view, then dropping around to pan across the portion of the roof that was finished. A snippet of me playfully scowling at him. And a zoomed-in one of my hands as they glided over the gingerbread, creating an intricate icing pattern.

Unexpected emotion stuck in my throat. In my real life, no one had ever taken an interest in my social media account. Not enough to do something like this. Sure, my family and friends liked my posts, occasionally even commented, but they weren't the ones getting excited about what I had just completed and what I was doing next. At best, they thought my ambition to become an influencer was a fun diversion. At worst, they viewed it as a time-wasting distraction. But with one small gesture, Landon had validated me.

Quinn: This is amazing. Thank you!
Landon: You're welcome. I was thinking you could post it to your social media account.
Landon: If you wanted.

I pressed play and watched the whole thing a second time.

Quinn: I can't believe you made that today. It looks professional.
Landon: Before my abstention from social media, I used to help Nikki develop content. She's a very thorough teacher.

The idea of Landon supporting Nikki pinged my heart. What would it be like to have someone you loved supporting you? I guess Ashlee did that for me, to some degree. But she was more an emotional support through the ups and downs. And Cody hadn't been unsupportive—at least, not outright—he'd just never understood why I spent so much time creating content. Even when I was bringing in a substantial side income those few months before he left, he didn't get it. But the truth was, I wanted to be an influencer because, for the first time, I felt like I had something to contribute. Something of my own. A small piece of the world that actually cared about what I loved. And they loved it in return—more so a year ago, but still.

So many people I knew digitally, and some I'd met in person, were making a living off their social media accounts. Why couldn't I? I had been so close, and I knew there was potential to grow. I just didn't know how to tap back into it.

Landon's comment the other day returned with full force. I glanced at the video on my phone. Could the first step to resurrecting my following's engagement really be that simple—posting videos and pictures with me in them again? I downloaded the video and opened Instagram. It was worth a shot.

FIFTEEN

LANDON

I TOOK THE STAIRS TWO AT A TIME AND KNOCKED ON the door. It still felt weird staying downstairs, especially after spending most of yesterday in the house with Quinn.

The door opened, and Quinn peeked around the side of it. "Hey." Her cheeks turned pink at the sight of me, like she was suddenly reminded of what had happened between us last night. She opened the door wider to let me in.

I tried to read her expression and determine if she'd woken up with any regrets. "How'd you sleep?"

"A little too well. I think all the *excitement* from ... yesterday exhausted me." She bit at her lip. "How about you?"

"Until I heard the snowplow early this morning, I didn't budge all night."

"Looks like we might need to start a new nightly tradition." Her full smile came out in all its heart-stopping glory. "Sleep is important, you know?"

Relief flowed over me, and I instantly brightened. She

wouldn't be smiling and teasing if she regretted our kiss. Or kisses. Plural. "I could definitely get on board with that."

"Thanks for sending those pictures of us at the bay. Oh, and I posted that video you made."

Pride swelled in my chest, but I didn't tell her I'd already seen the post. Not yet. "And how'd it go?"

"I think you might be right. Several people shared it, including Nikki, and I got a ton more likes and comments than I've been getting. My followers also seemed really excited to see me in a reel again."

"That is what the vast majority of the comments were saying."

She swatted at my arm. "You already saw it?"

"Did you not see my comment?"

"I haven't read through them all yet."

"It's okay. It would be difficult having to sift through hundreds of messages of adoration to find a random one from some guy."

"Yep. Just some rando." She laughed before her eyes widened. "You probably need to go. Here." She walked into the kitchen and grabbed the small, undecorated gingerbread house off the counter. "It's pretty sturdy, but I don't recommend dropping it."

I took hold of the cardboard base the house was centered on. "I can't believe you just whipped this up. It looks amazing."

"Thanks. Oh, and let me grab you the icing." She returned with two bags full of the frosting and set them on the side of the cardboard. "One is probably enough, but I didn't want you to run out. You can bring back any extra."

"Why don't you come with me?" The question burst out of me before I had time to stop it. All morning, I'd been thinking how fun it would be for Quinn to come along, but I hadn't actually planned on asking her.

Her gaze met mine. "I wouldn't want to intrude on your family time."

"It wouldn't be an intrusion. Since Nikki will be there, I

thought it would be a good opportunity to continue convincing her of our *feelings*."

Quinn's gaze dropped to the ground. "That makes sense."

"It won't be for very long. An hour or two at most. And to make up for lost time, I'll provide you with lunch and dinner today so you don't even have to cook." What was I doing? She clearly had things to do, and I was looking desperate. But I kind of felt desperate. No. I needed to dial it back a little. "It's fine if you can't. I'm sure I'll be able to teach my grandma how to do this." I lifted the house a fraction, nearly sending the frosting bags to the ground.

She reached her hand up to stabilize them. "Why would you need to teach her? I thought she loved decorating gingerbread houses."

"She has Alzheimer's. She doesn't remember much."

Quinn's brow creased. "I'm sorry. I didn't realize. You don't need to take this, then." Her hands settled on the edges of the cardboard, brushing against mine. The flow of energy that rushed through me made me want to scoop her up and carry her back to the couch. Who cared that I'd be a few minutes late?

Grateful my rational brain was still functioning to some degree, I kept hold of the gingerbread. "Just because she can't remember how to do it doesn't mean she won't enjoy it." I looked down. "So the gist, for us *typical* gingerbread decorators, is to cover the gingerbread house in frosting and stick candy to it, right?"

She gave a defeated huff. "Do I have time to change before we go?"

QUINN WAS UNUSUALLY quiet the last few minutes of the drive. When we got to the nursing home, I put the truck in park but didn't turn off the ignition. "Are you having second thoughts about coming? Because I can run you home."

The frosting rested between us on the middle console with the bags of candy we'd stopped to get, but she clung to the cardboard of the gingerbread house on her lap like it was a lifeline. "How are you going to introduce me to your family?"

"Probably as Quinn Cook, unless you have another name you'd like me to give them?"

She sent me a pointed glance. "Very funny. You know exactly what I mean."

"What would you prefer?"

"Maybe it's best if we just stick to me being Nikki's ... gingerbread house ... maker."

"Quinn Cook. Nikki's gingerbread house maker. Got it."

Quinn shifted in her seat. "But what if Nikki has already mentioned your interest in me? Or your pretended interest in me? Or maybe she didn't say anything so they'll assume we're together since you brought me." She lifted a hand to her face. "I shouldn't have come. I can't stop thinking about what they're thinking about about us."

I leaned against the driver's side window and studied her worried profile. "That's a lot of abouts."

Her head whipped toward me. "You're teasing me when I'm on the verge of a panic attack?"

I should never have asked her to come. "We don't need to lay on the *interested-in-each-other* thing too thick, if that's what you're worried about. Just tell me what you're comfortable with. Or if you'd prefer, I'll take you back to the house. It's really not a big deal."

She drew in a slow breath and released it from her mouth. "I don't want you to be late. And once I'm in there, I'll be fine. Most of the battle for me is the needless worrying." Her gaze flicked to my mouth. "Just no kissing me. Not that you would in front of your family ..." She tucked her lips inward briefly. "But anything else is fine."

"We really don't need to—"

"It's okay. Really. It's all pretend, anyway." She opened the door, not waiting for a response.

Her comment rammed into me like a lead ball, twisting and turning and making a mess of my insides. It should all be pretend. That was what we'd agreed on. But for some reason, her comment stung. Was she regretting the blurred lines between us? This muddied version of what we'd initially committed to?

She glanced around, looking for a place to set the gingerbread house while she climbed down.

"Hold on." I touched her arm, pausing her haphazard attempt to exit. "Let me come help you. The ground could be slick."

I turned off the truck and hurried to help Quinn out. Since she seemed unwilling to relinquish her hold on the gingerbread house, I steadied her arm while she climbed out.

"Thanks," she whispered, stepping past me to the sidewalk. I grabbed the bag of candy and frosting and shut the door. The walkway to the entrance had been salted, rendering my continued help unnecessary. When we reached the lobby, I glimpsed Nikki and Kade through the window. My hand automatically moved to Quinn's back when I opened the door for her, but her comment echoed through my mind, and I shoved my fist in my coat pocket instead.

"Quinn!" Nikki's questioning gaze skirted to me when she wrapped her arms around Quinn in a side hug to avoid the gingerbread house. "What are you doing here?"

"I made your grandma a gingerbread house, and Landon thought I should come help her decorate it. I hope that's okay."

Nikki glanced down at the house. "Of course it is. That was so sweet of you. And I loved the reel you posted last night. It was so good to see your beautiful face in your feed again." Her gaze slid to me. "Did you make it?"

"I did," I said like it wasn't some huge deal, and I nearly set my hand on Quinn's back a second time before lowering it again. "Where's everyone else?"

"Your dad and Sandra are already back with Grandma," Kade answered since Nikki was too busy analyzing me. "And Julie texted, saying they were running a few minutes late. They should be here soon."

"Should we head back, then?" I asked.

Nikki seemed to break out of her trancelike evaluation of us. "Kade and I were going to wait for Julie, but you two go on back."

When we were out of earshot, Quinn leaned toward me. "Did you see how intensely Nikki was looking at us? I nearly confessed the whole thing to her."

With how Quinn's eyes twinkled in shared humor, maybe I was overthinking her comment earlier. "You and me both."

When we reached Grams's room, I stepped through the door first so Quinn wouldn't have to. "Hey! I heard this is where the party is."

Grandma sat smiling on the chair, seeming delighted to have more visitors she likely didn't recognize. Dad and Sandra stood from their seats next to her and approached us, their curious gazes sliding from me to Quinn.

"Hey, son." Dad wrapped me in a tight hug. "Who is this gorgeous woman you brought along?"

"Quinn Cook." I smiled at her. "This is my dad, Marty, and my step-mom, Sandra."

"It's a pleasure to meet you both." Quinn still clutched onto the gingerbread house with white knuckles.

Sandra stepped up to Quinn. "What's this?"

"A gingerbread house. I thought we could decorate it with ... Grandma." She gave a shy smile, obviously not knowing what else to call Grams.

"Isn't that the sweetest thing?" Sandra gave my dad a meaningful look. "Can I take it from you and set it on the table?"

Quinn allowed Sandra to take it, then crossed her arms in front of her chest. Wishing I knew how to put Quinn at ease, I dropped the bag of candies and frosting next to it. "Speaking of Grandma ..." I started toward one of my favorite faces ever. "Hey, Grams."

She reached out for me as I approached, a welcoming smile on her face. "Aren't you handsome?"

I took hold of her hands and knelt down in front of her. "I'm Landon."

"Landon," she said, like she was trying to place the name. She pressed her hand against my cheek and studied my face. "You look like my husband when he was a little younger. Dear, come look at this young man ..." Her searching gaze moved around the room, making my chest constrict.

Dad stepped forward, catching her attention. "Dad's not here, Mom."

Grandma blinked, and her brow crinkled. Then she looked back at me.

"I'd like to introduce you to a friend of mine." I scooted back to make room for Quinn, and she squatted down beside me, one hand resting on the armrest of Grandma's chair and the other on my knee. It felt natural and real, but none of this was real. That was what she'd said. I swallowed and looked back to Grams. "This is Quinn."

Again, Grams's eyes widened. "She's beautiful." She reached out and set a hand on Quinn's face, rubbing her cheek with her thumb. "Are you two married?"

Quinn sent me an amused look. "No."

"Oh." Grandma's smile lessened. "Why not? You would have beautiful children."

I dipped my chin, fighting a laugh. "Well, if you think so, perhaps we should consider it," I said, unable to stop myself. "For the sake of the children, of course." I sent a sideways glance at Quinn to find her smile as bright as ever.

"Look who's here!" Nikki strolled into the room with Julie's kids bunched around her.

"Uncle Landon!" Chloe came running, and I shifted just in

time to catch my squealing nine-year-old niece in an embrace. Carson and Gavin followed close behind their big sister and immediately began climbing on me until I was nearly bowled over.

"Boys, what did I say?" Julie gave them her potent mom look, and they instantly dropped their arms, their expressions as forlorn as two scolded puppies.

"Later, boys." I winked at them.

"Hey, you. Where's my hug?" Julie reached over the top of her kids, and I stood to meet her.

My gaze fell on the empty doorway behind us. "Where's Josh and the baby?"

"Reid fell asleep on the drive over, so Josh is sitting in the car with him until he wakes up."

My gaze eagerly moved to Quinn. "Julie, I'd like you to meet Quinn."

Quinn stood, her hands clasped in front of her. She glanced behind her and took a small step to the side to make sure Grams could see. "Hello."

"It's good to meet you." Julie smiled before her gaze returned to me, and a familiar glint of mischief touched her eyes. "And how do the two of you know each other?"

The room went quiet.

I pointed toward Nikki. "Nikki actually introduced us. You know how she has a knack for matchmaking."

"Really?" Julie sent Nikki a knowing look, and I was pretty sure, with the varying degrees of smiles around the room, Nikki had informed them all about Quinn and possibly even the reason we were *together*. I thought of grabbing Quinn's hand as an act of defiance but couldn't get myself to do it.

It's all pretend anyway. Why had those words hit me so hard?

"Quinn is amazing." Nikki directed a sincere smile at her. "I wouldn't blame Landon for figuring it out."

Carson, the oldest of Julie's boys, tugged on my hand. "Mom said you have a new girlfriend. Is that her?"

Julie tussled Carson's sandy-blond hair. "I didn't say that."

"Yes, you did. You said he didn't come see us yet because he was with his new—"

Julie covered his mouth from behind and gave a forced laugh. "We're still learning when to repeat Mommy and when not to." She tipped his chin up and looked down at him. "Right now is one of the times *not* to repeat what Mommy said."

Carson crossed his arms. "Why am I in trouble? You were the one who said it."

Despite the color flooding Quinn's cheeks, she laughed.

I took a step toward Quinn, ensuring I also wasn't blocking Grams's view, and put my arm around her shoulder in a gesture that felt more friendly than anything. "To answer your question, Carson, I definitely have a crush on her." Not a prick of guilt followed the declaration.

Gavin and Carson glanced at each other, both curling up their lips in disgust, but Chloe looked up at us with doe eyes. "If you get married, can I be your flower girl, too?"

"Okay, time to say hello to Grandma." Julie directed the kids toward where Grandma watched with a pleasant, somewhat vacant, expression.

I leaned in close to Quinn. "Sorry about that," I whispered.

She smiled up at me. "It's okay. At least we know what they're all thinking."

"How tall are you?" Carson reappeared at our side, obviously having little interest in being introduced to Grandma again. He put his hand at the top of his head and moved it toward her at an upward angle. "I'm only seven, and I'm almost up to your shoulder."

Quinn laughed. "You are tall for a seven-year-old."

"Carson, come here," Julie hissed, pulling him back toward Grandma. "Sorry," she mouthed.

My hand settled around Quinn's waist, only so I could pull her closer to talk to her—or that was what I told myself. "I'm just going to give you a blanket apology now to cover the next hour or two."

"LET me help you to the table, Grams."

She allowed me to assist her to her feet, and her gaze met mine as she shuffled forward. "Well, aren't you a handsome young man? What's your name?"

"I'm Landon," I answered for the fifth or sixth time since arriving.

"You look so much like my husband when he was young. He was a dreamboat." She glanced around. "Have you seen him, by chance—my husband?"

My heart broke a little every time she asked for Grandpa. "Not today."

She nodded, and I helped her into the seat next to Quinn, their backs facing the rest of the room. Before I pulled away, my hand unintentionally brushed against Quinn's arm, and she smiled up at me.

"And who are you?" Grams asked, her eyes bright when they fell on Quinn.

"I'm Quinn." She said it like it was the first time Grams had asked her.

"Aren't you a pretty thing?"

Quinn laughed. "I thought we could build a gingerbread house together. I heard you enjoy decorating gingerbread?"

Grams's head shifted from side to side, taking in all the decorations set out. "I do?"

"Not only do you decorate them, but I also heard you are remarkably talented at it." She held out a frosting bag, and Grams wrapped her hand around it, looking a little hesitant. "Should we give it a go?" Quinn asked.

"Why not?"

Quinn laced an arm under Grams's and then cupped her hands around the bag and over Grams's hands. She squeezed the bag, and Grams gave an audible gasp of excitement when frosting made its appearance onto the brown surface.

"Well, look at that." Grams smiled at Quinn.

"You did it."

Quinn was a natural, tender and caring, and I couldn't take my eyes off her—until Nikki stepped in front of me and grabbed my wrist, tugging me into the hallway behind her.

"Whoa," I said when we were a few steps outside of the room. "What's got you all riled up?"

"You're putting on quite the show in there," she whispered, a smug look on her face.

I crossed my arms, feeling self-conscious under her glare. "First off, it's not a show."

She stepped close to me. "You expect me to believe that, in a week and a few days, you're this smitten with Quinn?" She shook her head. "I'm not buying it."

My head cocked back. I hadn't been doing anything to try to convince everyone of my pretend feelings for Quinn. Not today. And not with Quinn's well-planted comment still lodged in the back of my mind, making me second-guess everything.

Julie stepped out of the door and glanced between us. "Is something wrong?"

Nikki flung a hand toward me. "Landon is an idiot," she hissed.

I pointed at myself, my jaw hanging open. "What have I done?"

"Shhhh..." Julie shut the door before turning back toward us. "What is this about?"

"He won't admit it, but Landon didn't want me to play matchmaker, so he got Quinn to agree to"—Nikki did air quotes with her fingers—"date him."

Julie's hands went to her hips, and her glare settled on me. "That, in there, was all pretend?"

I threw up my hands, confused as to what they were even talking about. I mean, I had played up the part previously, but not today.

Nikki crossed her arms. "It was like I was watching some poorly executed romance movie with how overdone the staring was. And the excessive number of *coincidental* touches ..." She shook her head.

"And all the shared smiles and glances." Julie added with a frown. "How disappointing it isn't real."

Under the condemning stares of my sisters, I couldn't deny it. I didn't want to. I wanted to have it all out and be done. Quinn deserved better than to be forced to *keep pretending*. "It wasn't Quinn's idea." This was entirely on me.

Nikki jabbed her index finger into my chest. "I knew it. I knew you were faking."

My hands lifted in defense. "You are the reason we did it." I swallowed, realizing how stupid that suddenly sounded. "I told you I didn't want to be set up." And there was no way I would allow Quinn to be set up with Tyler.

"For such a smart guy, you clearly didn't think any of this through." The intensity of Nikki's scowl made me shift uncomfortably. "It takes anyone like 3.2 seconds to realize Quinn is the kindest, most genuine person on the face of this planet. She'd never say no to your scheme, even if she wanted to. And watching her, it's obvious she's conflating what's real and what's not. It might be pretend for you, but unless she's an Academy-Award-winning actress, it's not for her. She's obviously falling for you. Which brings us back to you being an idiot."

I stared at Nikki, my mind focusing on the only point I seemed to hear. "You think her feelings for me are real?"

"There's not a doubt in my mind." Nikki sighed. "But she deserves a man who will treasure her—not one who will use her to get out of a date. So if that's not you, you need to put an end to this. I don't want to see her hurt, not after everything she's been through this year."

I tensed like I'd just been given a round-house kick to the stomach. It was undeniably because of Nikki's blatant criticism, but it was also more than that. A lot more than that. The thought of ending anything between me and Quinn—pretend or not—made me feel hollow inside. Dread, even.

A man who will treasure her ... so if that's not you ...

Why couldn't that be me? In an instant, I was playing back all the excuses I'd used to keep my feelings in check while Quinn and I had spent time together. Only one still seemed to hold true: Quinn wasn't ready for a relationship. She'd stated the fact from the beginning, and I needed to respect that. But what if Nikki was right? What if Quinn's feelings for me were real? Like my feelings for her had clearly become.

A stampede of running feet on the tile floor forced our attention down the hallway.

Carson ran toward us, waving a package of chips in the air, with Gavin and Chloe close on his heels and Kade rounding the corner a good distance behind them at a casual stride. "Mom, look what Uncle Kade bought us at the vending machine!"

The nurse at the nearby station rose from her seat at the computer. "No running, please."

"Sorry," Julie said before turning her gaze on her children. "You heard her. Slow down."

Undeterred, Carson speed-walked the rest of the way to us. "Look. Kade got me my favorite chips—sour cream and cheddar."

Chloe gave an exaggerated eye roll and stepped up next to him. She looked so much like Julie when she was a little girl, from the dark hair and eyes down to the splash of freckles across her nose. "Those aren't his favorite chips, are they, Mom?"

Carson stuck his tongue out at Chloe. "They are, too."

"Are not."

Julie lowered to their level. "I don't see why this matters, so unless you two want me to take your chips—"

"I have M&Ms." Chloe lifted the bag to show her mom. "Not chips."

Julie blew out a steadying breath. "Fine. Unless you two want me to take away your *snacks*, stop arguing. Please."

"Look what I got." Gavin's chubby, four-year-old fingers were wrapped around a sealed, hard-boiled egg.

She laughed. "Oh, neat. An egg."

Kade shrugged. "That's what he wanted."

Julie stood and smiled at Kade. "That was sweet of you to let them pick a treat. Thanks."

"I have to become their favorite uncle somehow." He mussed Gavin's hair and glanced around our small group. "What's up with the impromptu hall meeting?"

Nikki sent Kade a meaningful glance. "We were just discussing *Landon's crush*."

"Oh." He nodded and lifted a thumb to me. "I applaud the top-notch acting. Very nicely done."

I ran a hand through my hair. "You are all ridiculous."

The door opened, and Dad poked his head out. "You guys okay?"

We nodded in unison.

He didn't look convinced, but he waved us to him. "You should come see this. Here." He stepped out into the hallway. "I can stay with the kids."

Intrigued, all four of us quietly filed back into the room. Sandra stood next to Grams's bed with her phone pointed at Quinn and Grandma, like she was recording them. When my gaze fell on Grams, my feet froze to the floor. With slow, careful movements, Grams was frosting the gingerbread house without Quinn's help.

She moved the bag of frosting along the seam of the roof. "One year, when Julie was around five, we put all the different candies in bowls. Nikki was an infant and needed feeding before we could begin decorating. We made the mistake of leaving Julie alone with the candy."

"What happened?" Quinn asked, her chin resting on her propped-up arms and her attention glued to Grams.

"She had a candy feast." Grams's airy, familiar laughter filled the room. How I missed that sound. "Except for the black licorice. She'd tried one piece of it and spit it out, back into the bowl."

"I don't blame her. I'm not a black-licorice fan either."

"That's because they don't make it like they used to." Grams dabbed a few dots of frosting on the roof of the house, and then, with concentrated effort, she picked up a few Dots and placed them along the top.

Quinn's gaze met mine, and she gave a timid smile that warmed me straight through. "Did Landon ever help you with one of the gingerbread houses?"

Grams's back was still to us, and a part of me wanted to walk to where I could see her face, but I wouldn't risk pulling her out of the moment. Out of the memories. "He wasn't ever particularly interested in anything but the candy, but there was one year, when he was around ten years old, that he got an idea for a gingerbread house—well, not a house, but a rocket ship— and he was determined to make it. His mom and I tried our best, but I don't think we quite understood his vision. After a few failed attempts, he finally made something he was pleased with. I can still remember how proud he was of himself. It didn't really look like a rocket ship, but I was proud of him, too. I always have been. All three of them. They're such good kids."

"I know they all think the world of you," Quinn said. "They love you a lot."

Grams nodded. "I love them."

Nikki's hand found mine, and she smiled up at me, tears brimming in her eyes. I glanced to my other side, where Julie wiped at the tears streaming down her cheeks. I wrapped an arm around her, and the three of us stood there together, relishing the moment—the glimpse of the grandma we'd missed so much.

"A gingerbread house?" Carson walked past us and toward the table before any of us could stop him. "I want to help."

Julie stepped forward. "Carson, sweetie. Come here."

He paused next to Grandma's chair and looked back at Julie. "Can't I help?"

Grams's gaze landed on him. "Hello there, dear. What's your name?"

"Carson. Remember? We already met. A couple times, actually."

"We did?"

He nodded. "Can I help with your gingerbread house?"

She glanced back to the table and then to the frosting in her hand. "My gingerbread house? I don't think it's mine."

And just like that, she'd slipped away again. But we'd been given a gift. Quinn had given us a gift. And it was in that moment I knew my feelings for her were definitely not pretend. Not anymore. Now, the problem was what to do about it.

SIXTEEN

QUINN

THERE WAS SOMETHING BLISSFUL ABOUT A MAN DOING the dinner dishes. Especially when he was also the one who'd prepared dinner. And more especially when he was as attractive as Landon. With the drying towel thrown over his shoulder, I was finding it difficult to concentrate on my decorating.

He glanced up to find me watching him—again. "How's it going over there?"

"Good." I bobbed my head up and down. "It's good."

He turned off the sink and wiped his hands. "What are you thinking about?"

"Nothing." I needed a diversion. "Just wanted to say thanks again for taking me today to visit your grandma. I had a great time. With her. With your family. They're all wonderful."

He walked around the kitchen island toward the table. "It's you who deserves my thanks. I haven't heard Grams talk that much in years. After my grandpa died is when her Alzheimer's set in. The doctors said, sometimes, when someone experiences trauma, like a loved one dying, it can physically damage the brain." He shrugged. "I don't know if that's what led to it, but she hasn't been the same since. And it got worse after my mom died."

"It broke my heart that she kept looking for your grandpa."

Landon nodded. "Mine too. But it's always a joy to see her. I mean, how many times did she excitedly ask you your name, then tell you how beautiful you were? A dozen? Two?"

I laughed. "Something like that. And I'm not going to lie, I kind of feel like a million bucks now."

"Ah. So that's the trick."

"I'd prefer if you remembered my name, though."

He pulled out the chair next to me at the kitchen table and sat down. His serious expression felt out of place with our teasing. "Quinn." He paused in a way that left my stomach in knots. "I told Nikki the truth today."

I studied him, unable to form a response.

"Well, actually, she insisted—again—that she knew we were faking, and I couldn't find it in me to deny it this time. With how muddied the waters are getting in this whole thing, I don't think we should keep this going."

My gaze dropped to my lap, my chest constricting around my sinking heart. "Yeah. That's totally fine."

"I don't want you to misunderstand—"

"Really." I lifted my gaze, putting on a smile. "It's fine, Landon. You don't need to offer an explanation or feel bad or anything. I knew exactly what I was agreeing to—"

"Considering where I think you're headed, I do need to explain." His eyes were locked on mine. "Quinn, I don't want to continue with our scheme because I've realized I'm not pretending anymore. I can't stop thinking about you. When I'm not with you, I wish I was. That's not pretend. I want this. For real."

I stared at him, trying to make sense of his admission despite the distracting celebratory reactions alighting through my whole body. "You do? Like, for real?"

"A ridiculous amount."

"I want this, too." I grabbed his hand on the table and intertwined my fingers with his. "Also a ridiculous amount."

His knees turned toward me, and I mirrored him until we were facing each other in our chairs. The air felt heavy, and both our chests lifted in near sync with each other. His gaze slid to the side, and he tilted his head toward the partially completed gingerbread cabin. "You need to finish that one tonight, right?"

I gave a small pout, thinking of a hundred different ways I'd rather spend my evening, and they all included Landon. "I didn't realize how early Irene wants them at Rosecliff on Thursday. If I'm going to make it to Nikki's bachelorette party on Tuesday, I have to get this one finished tonight."

He nodded and stood up. "That's my cue."

"No." I kept hold of his hand. "It wasn't a hint you should leave."

"I know. But I promised that if you came with me to visit my grandma, I wouldn't distract you. And considering that's all I want to do ... I should go." He lifted my hand to his mouth and pressed his lips against my palm, keeping hold of my fingers. Despite how gentle the kiss was, it caused an explosion of electricity to pulse through me. "Night, Quinn."

When he took a step away, instead of releasing his hand, I tightened my grip. His gaze moved to our interlaced fingers and then to me. I pulled him back toward me, craning my neck to look up at him from my chair. "I'm of the opinion that there's always time for a kiss."

A smile slowly stretched across his handsome face, and he bent toward me but stopped right before our lips touched. "Are you sure?" His breath was warm and sweet, and I could almost taste him.

I closed my eyes and nodded. "I'll always make time for this," I whispered, my voice breathless.

Then, his mouth was on mine, his lips intertwining with my lips. His hand came to the nape of my neck, softly pressing me toward him to compensate for the increasing strength of our kiss, of our movements. I ran my hands over his chest and up around his neck, but still, I wasn't close enough, so I stood, lifting onto my toes. Landon's hands settled on my hips, the tips of his fingers making contact with my stomach and sending a rush of desire through me. I tightened my grip on him, needing to get even closer.

Suddenly, Landon stepped back, letting his kiss linger for a moment longer before pulling away. His chest was rising and falling in quick bursts. He opened his mouth, then closed it again. He ran a hand across his beard and let out a slow exhale. "Wow. That was ... amazing, which is why I should go. And you need to work, so ..."

My face flushed with heat at his meaning, and as much as I wanted to convince him to stay, I knew that wouldn't have been a good idea for more reasons than I wanted to admit. "If I can get started on the third house tonight, we could probably plan to do something tomorrow night—for a little while, anyway."

"I actually have somewhere I'd love to take you." He took a step closer again, his hands coming to my arms and then trailing down them slowly. Goosebumps spread over my skin.

"Where?"

"You don't want to be surprised?"

"Surprises make me anxious."

He smiled, and my gaze unintentionally went to his mouth. "One of the mansions does tours by candlelight. They deck out the whole place in Christmas decorations, and it feels like you've traveled back in time a hundred years. I think you'd love it."

I beamed up at him. "That sounds amazing."

"So you're in?"

I nodded.

"Perfect. Then I'll see you tomorrow." He placed one, gentle kiss on my lips and stepped away.

"Night."

With one last smile, he disappeared out the door, locking it behind him and leaving me alone with the gingerbread houses and my reeling thoughts.

"I'M NOT GOING TO LIE." The speaker on my phone vibrated as Ashlee spoke, and I repositioned it. "When I didn't hear from you for an entire day, I thought Mr. GQ might be a psycho killer after all. See how you've rubbed off on me?"

I laughed. "Nope. Not a psycho killer."

"What's going on with the two of you? Is the fake-dating thing working out?"

"So, about that ..."

"What happened?"

I hesitated, trying to think how best to word it. "It turns out it's not fake anymore. Landon told me tonight his feelings for me are real."

"I knew it! I knew this was going to happen. I mean, how could it not—you're amazing, you're both gorgeous, and those fake-dating schemes are basically an invitation to get together. I mean, look at every romance ever with that as a plot device. The characters end up in love. Every time." She hummed thoughtfully. "Why have I not tried that yet?"

I laughed. "I highly recommend it."

"So he just told you and left? Or did anything else noteworthy happen?"

"Maybe."

"Girl, spill it."

"Which kiss do you want to hear about? Tonight's or last night's?"

"Hold up. He kissed you last night?"

"Yeah. Well, I kind of kissed him first, but he *really* kissed me after that."

"Shut the front door! And you're just telling me about it now?"

I picked up the phone and walked into the kitchen, grabbing the extra icing to refill my nearly empty bag. "I was exhausted—"

"From your make-out session?"

"We didn't make out. We only kissed for a minute or two."

"Anything in the minute range is totally a make-out session."

I scooped a spoonful of icing into the bag and pressed it down to one end. "Do you want to hear about it or not?"

"Shutting up."

I added another scoop and twisted the end of the piping bag. "It was sweet and perfect ... and maybe a little passionate. Then the power came back on, and—"

"You switched the lights back off?" Hope filled her voice.

I laughed. "No. I only have three more days until all the centerpieces need to be done. I'm nervous I won't get them done as it is."

"Stupid work getting in the way of your kissing." Ashlee laughed. "Speaking of the centerpieces, though, that video you posted ... did Landon film it?"

"I didn't realize that's what he was doing when he was recording me."

"Oh, my gosh. I just got chills. You two love each other."

My heart fluttered at her declaration. "We've known each other less than two weeks, and half that time, he hardly talked to me. So no, I'm pretty sure neither of us loves the other."

"Pretty sure?"

"It's been fun, and I like him. A lot."

"So ... what's the problem?"

"It just feels like it's happening too fast. I mean, when I'm with him, I want it to happen faster, but then he leaves, and I start second-guessing everything."

"Like what?"

"Like whether I'm emotionally ready for another relationship. Until a few days ago, I was still pining over Cody and our failed marriage, and now it feels like I'm setting myself up for another failure—that as soon as Landon realizes what a mess I am, he'll be running as fast as he can away from me."

"I thought you've been super open with Landon about everything."

"I've tried to be, but me informing him of my issues and him actually seeing them are not the same thing."

"You know what I think?"

"Hmmm?"

"I think you overthink everything. Landon likes you. You like him. That doesn't mean you need to decide right now if you're going to get married and have a ton of babies. It means you just have fun and see what happens." She paused. "And you are having fun, aren't you?"

My phone chimed, and I glanced down to see a text message from my mom.

Mom: Dad and I bought you a return ticket for the 23rd. Can't wait to see you!

I groaned. "Are you kidding me?"

"What?"

"My mom bought me a return ticket to San Diego for the twenty-third."

"I thought you wanted to stay in Newport."

My stomach twisted. "I do. I probably should have worded my refusal a little more strongly."

"What did you say?"

"That she didn't have to buy me a ticket."

"Yeah ... that's not a refusal. That's what you say when you feel bad someone has to pick up the tab for you, but not too bad because you actually want them to."

"What was I supposed to say? *Sorry I don't want to spend*

Christmas with the family this year because I'm carrying a large load of emotional damage, and I dread the thought of being around Margaret and Michael on the anniversary of when Cody walked out on me?"

"Yeah, that probably would have worked better."

I carried my piping bag back to the table and sank down in the chair. "What am I supposed to do?"

"Do you want to stay in Newport?"

I propped the phone back up on the table. "Yes."

"Then stay."

"What about the ticket? It probably cost my parents a fortune. And they'll be so disappointed if I don't go. Not to mention Margaret won't talk to me for, like, a month."

"You know I adore your family, so I'm saying this from a place of love, but it's kind of their fault. You're a grown woman. You can make your own decisions, and you don't need to feel bad every time you don't bend to everyone's expectations."

"But maybe I should just go home. It's not like I have plans here, anyway."

"Wow. I think you missed what I said. Like, every word."

"No, I heard you. And I love you for it. But I think I'm just being selfish and petty, and I need to suck it up. Besides, I honestly love being with my family at Christmas."

"So, if in the end you decide to go home, that's fine. Just be the one making the choice."

"I don't like making choices."

"Then your life will never be your own. Your parents will happily keep making choices for you—flying you home, getting you a job, telling you what to do and what goals to have. Exactly like Cody did when you were together." Ashlee paused and let out a heavy breath. "I'm sorry that was probably sucky to hear, but I love you, and I want the best for you."

I stared vacantly at the phone, Ashlee's words gnawing their way into my conscience. "I know you do."

"Despite what you've been led to believe, Quinn, you are extremely competent. Trust yourself enough to see it."

ASHLEE'S WORDS circled around my mind for hours as I finished the cabin and started on the replica of Kade's childhood home. I didn't get much done on it before my eyes grew heavy and my fingers ached too much to continue, but it was probably enough to justify going out with Landon tomorrow night.

When I climbed into bed, I needed to decompress. I started by scrolling through my comments, responding to some and liking all the others. This was the problem with social media for me. I never felt like I could only interact with a handful of followers and not feel guilty. But I was learning that interacting with every last one was an unrealistic goal. And thankfully, Landon had exaggerated the number of comments on my video, and it took me only about thirty minutes to scroll through all one hundred and forty of them, responding to the occasional one.

Then, I found Landon's.

I could watch this all day.

My heart pattered about recklessly in my chest. I clicked on his name and saw that he had zero followers and one account he followed—mine. A smile burst onto my lips. He really had created an account for me. Not that I expected it to remain like that, especially once Nikki discovered he'd ended his social-media fast, but for a moment, I was the sole reason he was on there. The contrast to Cody seemed stark. Cody had set up an account years ago, but until he'd left me, he'd never really used it. Now, in the past year, his feed was full of selfies and images of him with beautiful women. And apparently a new girlfriend. One I hadn't even seen yet.

That familiar itch in my finger urged me to look at Cody's

account.

I dropped the phone. It had been two or three months since I'd last peeked. There was no point in ruining the streak now. No good would come of it.

Except, maybe if I looked, it wouldn't affect me like it did before I'd met Landon. My heart seemed to be relinquishing the grasp Cody had on it, so maybe I was finally ready to move on, and this could be the test to prove it to myself. Resolved and feeling confident in my resolution, I typed in Cody's handle.

When his feed filled my screen, my heart sank, and I instantly knew I'd failed the test. A big, fat F-minus. Cody's new girlfriend was stunning, her crop-top shirts fitting her like nothing had ever fit me before. Her long, tanned legs went on for miles, and her curves were in all the right places. But I was a glutton for punishment, and I clicked on her linked profile. Though Cody was more of a cameo on her feed than she was on his, her most recent post had an image of the two of them wrapped around each other. The caption read: *Can't wait to spend Christmas in the Caribbean with this hunk of mine.*

A wave of shock surged through me, gutting me to my core. Cody was going to the Caribbean with some girl he'd only been dating for a month or two at most? I couldn't draw a breath. This had been a bad idea. A really bad idea. I turned off the phone and tossed it on the bed, trying to calm myself through my downward spiral. Cody and *Ms. Legs* would be in the Caribbean together exactly a year after he'd walked out on me. Would they be sharing a room? A bed? The thought made me physically sick. Then hurt. Then angry.

I grabbed my phone and opened up Instagram. Creating a new post, I scrolled through the pictures Landon had sent of the two of us together until I found my favorite—the one where Landon looked at me like a love-stricken Odysseus—and I posted it to my account with the caption: *Sometimes the bumpiest roads lead us to the most exquisite places.*

It was poetic and beautiful. And written entirely out of spite.

SEVENTEEN

QUINN

I'D NEARLY FORGOTTEN MY POOR, LATE-NIGHT POSTING decision until I took my phone off silent mode the next morning. Notifications chimed like it was about to detonate. Missed voicemails. Missed texts. Loads of social media alerts.

Curse words. I usually dealt with my bouts of insecurity with a good cry session and sleeping in until noon, not posting a revenge picture on Instagram for tens of thousands of people to see. I covered my face with my hands. What had I been thinking posting that?

Before I could form a reasonable answer, my phone rang.

Mom.

No. No. No. I dismissed it and went into the bathroom. But the fourth time it rang, I realized avoidance probably wasn't the correct coping mechanism.

"Hey, Mom."

"Hey, Mom? That's all you're going to say? Not, *I posted a picture on social media with a guy that I forgot to tell you about?*"

My chest tightened, like a heavy weight pressed against it. "I told you about him. It's Landon. The owner of the house."

"That's who's in the picture? The Christmas tree landlord?" Quick bursts of air from Mom's stress-breathing vibrated through the speaker. "Are you two dating?"

I shifted. "Yes, but it's super new. Like, last-night new."

"Then what are you doing posting pictures of you together, Quinn? Do you know how many calls and texts I've gotten this morning? And it's only eight here."

I glanced at the clock. It was already eleven here? Apparently, I'd nearly gotten the sleeping-till-noon portion of my self-pity reaction correct. Too bad I didn't have time for it. "Mom, I'm a grown woman," I said, trying to tap into Ashlee's confidence in me.

"Why are you acting like a child, then? A reasonable adult doesn't post pictures of herself with some man before they have the decency to explain to their family who he is."

Mom's words were a perfectly placed knife. Not only because I'd not told them about Landon, but because I had been acting like a child—or, at best, an immature adult. I'd posted that picture because I was hurting. Because I wanted to hurt Cody. Instead, I'd caused some kind of extended-family drama and possibly undermined any credibility in my feelings for Landon. It had been a stupid choice.

Mom released a long sigh. "Please, from now on, talk to us before you share news like that with the entire world."

I bit at the inside of my cheek, feeling every bit the scolded child. "I will."

"So besides Landon being Nikki Aker's brother and your current downstairs neighbor ..." She paused. "He is still sleeping downstairs, right?"

"Of course." At least until he moved upstairs tomorrow, but that was different. There'd be a houseful of guys sharing the space with us.

"Okay. So besides those things, tell me about him."

"Umm ... He's got a JD and is general counsel for Carrigan Enterprises, a multi-billion-dollar firm."

"And is he good?"

"At being a lawyer?"

"No. Is he a good person?"

"Oh. Yes, he's wonderful."

Mom gave a thoughtful hum. "Just be careful, Quinn. You need to make sure you're in a better place before you get into anything too serious." Before I had time to ask her what exactly she meant by a *better place*, she continued, "You never responded to my text about the plane ticket. I emailed you the confirmation. Did you get it?"

I opened up my email app to see it near the top. "Yep. I got it."

"And does that work?"

My throat grew tight. Considering I'd already maxed out my selfish quota for the day, now didn't seem like the best time to mention I wanted to stay in Newport. "I think so. Thanks."

Within a few minutes of getting off the phone, I'd responded to Ashlee and explained to both my sisters via text who "the guy in the picture" was. Despite my need to get going, I was now scrolling through the well wishes of my followers, feeling less repentant with all the hilarious comments about how attractive Landon was. My phone chimed, and a text notification dropped from the top. My heart nearly fumbled to a stop at the name on it.

Cody.

With shaking hands, I pressed on the message.

Cody: Thinking about you today. I really miss you. I miss us.

I'm not sure how long I stared at his message. A thousand responses flew through my mind, ranging from hostile to ecstatic to passive. In the end, I simply wrote:

Quinn: It's been a long time.

I'D BEEN SO LOST in thought while decorating the gingerbread house that it took me a few seconds to register that the sound reverberating in my mind was actually a knock.

"Coming." I placed my piping bag on the plate and hurried to the door to glimpse Landon through the peep hole. Drawing in a quick, calming breath, I opened it.

The smile Landon gave that usually set my heart fluttering constricted my chest with guilt instead. Not that I had a reason to feel guilty. Not really. Yes, I'd posted the picture of us together, but he'd suggested taking them for that very reason. And Cody and I had texted a few times off and on today, but it wasn't like I'd gone crawling back to him. He'd mentioned he'd missed me and would love to find a time to talk. I'd kept my cool and reluctantly agreed a conversation was in order. So why did I feel like I'd done something wrong?

"Hey!" The false cheer in my voice sent his brows raising.

"You okay?"

"Yeah." I pointed behind me. "Just working."

He nodded, his eyes settling on the partially decorated gingerbread house behind me. "How's it going?"

"Ummm ..." I cleared my throat. "I got kind of a late start."

His gaze returned to mine. "Should we postpone our tour? We could do it after Nikki's wedding, since you'll be here through Christmas."

"No. Let's do it tonight," I said, not sure I would be here for Christmas anymore. "Let me just grab my stuff."

He waited silently as I hurried to put on my boots and coat and grabbed my phone off the table. "Ready?"

His head tilted to the side. "Really, Quinn, if you have stuff to do—"

"I can stay up late to finish it." I forced a smile. "I want to go." And I really did. Not only because the idea of touring one of the gilded mansions in candlelight was alluring, but as confused as I was, I wanted to spend time with Landon. I'd missed him all day.

We walked to the car in silence. The chill of the night penetrated through my jeans and blew across my face. Landon opened the door for me and helped me into the truck before hurrying around and starting the engine. A strong gust of air blew out of the vents, and Landon quickly turned it down. "It will be warm in a few minutes, and I'll turn it up."

I nodded.

His gaze remained on me. "You sure you're okay?"

"I have some things on my mind is all."

"Want to talk about them?"

I blew out a breath that clouded in front of me. "Not really."

"Does it have to do with the picture you posted of us?"

My gaze slid to his, my heart pounding in my chest. Of course he'd seen it. "Maybe."

He leaned back in his seat and faced me, letting the truck idle.

I glanced down at my lap, too embarrassed to look at him. "Last night, before bed, I got on Instagram to respond to comments, and I made the mistake of looking at Cody's feed. I thought, with how things were going between us, that maybe if I saw his pictures and didn't care, I'd pass some kind of self-dictated test. Evidence I was moving on." I paused, hating what I was about to confess. "I didn't pass the test. Seeing him with his new girlfriend gutted me."

Despite my hesitation, I met Landon's gaze. "I posted that picture to hurt him like I was hurting. He must have seen it, because he texted a few hours ago. He told me he missed me. That he missed us. And he wants to talk."

Landon gave a slow, thoughtful nod, but he said nothing.

"I've felt horrible about it all day. And then, knowing that we were going out tonight ... I like you, I really do, but I'm ..." I blew out a heavy sigh. "I'm confused about why I'm feeling this way."

The cab was silent for a good minute or two, and I waited for him to tell me what a disaster I was. That he couldn't believe I'd done what I did.

"We don't need to rush anything, Quinn." Landon grabbed my hand, not in a romantic way but in a gesture of reassurance. "The last thing I want is for you to feel guilty about anything. You've been honest from the start about where you are in your life. If you need time to figure things out, that's okay."

My aching heart swelled at his generosity.

He smiled, a touch of playfulness to it. "Though we may need to reestablish some of those boundaries for the time being. Until you know what you want."

I laughed, and it was like a heavy weight lifted off my chest. "Thank you for understanding."

He released my hand and put the truck in gear. "It's one benefit of having recently been right where you are."

EIGHTEEN

LANDON

QUINN'S EYES LIT UP AT THE SIGHT OF THE EXTENSIVE ballroom, and I couldn't repress my smile. It amazed me how her joy bubbled out of her until it filled wherever she was or whomever she was with—especially me, it seemed.

Her hand came to my arm, and her light touch sent a tremor of pleasure through me. "Can you imagine having attended a ball here?" she whispered.

I leaned down to whisper in her ear. "Sort of. We had our high school prom here one year."

Her widened eyes turned to me, the candlelight glinting in them. "That's amazing. Ours were always at convention centers and had the most awful themes. Our senior prom was decorated to look like a casino, and they gave us gambling chips when we entered. Whoever's idea that had been obviously had not the slightest romantic inclinations."

Quinn quieted when the tour guide explained how this floor had originally been built for stables and was later converted into a ballroom, but I missed most of what she said after that. I couldn't take my eyes off Quinn or quiet my thoughts.

I wouldn't pretend that Quinn's confession about Cody had been easy to hear. I'd been falling so fast for her I hadn't taken a moment to consider we might not be falling at the same speed. But I also knew where she was coming from. The hurt and self-doubt that came after divorce was all-consuming. Some things just took time. I could give Quinn that.

"Are you coming?" she asked, her voice pulling me from my thoughts. The group was moving to the next room, and we trailed behind at a leisurely pace.

"So, what do you think?"

"It's amazing, though I definitely wouldn't want to live here either. To think of sharing a house with ghosts."

"Ghosts?"

She giggled. "Weren't you listening? The guide said the place is haunted."

Apparently, I'd missed more than I thought. "That sounds like a story for a Halloween tour, not a Christmas one. I guess unless the ghost is a jolly, giant man in a green robe that shows you where you're failing in life."

Quinn laughed. "Are you a Dickens fan?"

"If by Dickens you mean the musical adaptation *Scrooge*, then yes. Watching it is a long-standing yearly tradition at the Aker house."

"I don't think I've seen that version."

I feigned offense. "Unpardonable. We are going to right that wrong immediately. Well, maybe not immediately since you need to finish your gingerbread houses, but soon."

"Deal."

The woman guiding the tour stopped our group in the corridor and began sharing something about the furnishings.

"As scary as it would be," Quinn whispered, "I wouldn't mind if the three ghosts of Christmas visited me. Not if I could get some clarification on my life like Ebenezer Scrooge."

"What sort of clarification are you looking for?"

A man standing next to us sent a look in our direction that said he didn't appreciate our chatting.

Quinn mouthed a quick, "Sorry," and his scowl turned to a polite smile and a wave of acceptance. I was pretty sure Quinn could back over a stranger's foot with a car, and the minute she sent her dazzling, contrite smile at them, they'd apologize for having stood too near the tire.

When the group continued forward again, she leaned in close. "All of it. Whether I should take a *real job* and give up my social media account—"

"Why would you quit? I thought you said it was the one thing you loved doing."

"It doesn't currently provide enough for me to live on. I know it's possible to do it—before my divorce, I was earning a decent amount—but since my engagement fell at the beginning of the year, my affiliate links aren't performing like they once did, and it's been a lot harder to get sponsorships. Even when I do get one, because of my lower engagement rates, I only get a portion of what I used to, hence the living off my best friend's kindness. But I can't do that much longer."

"Maybe I could help you grow your account. My undergrad was in marketing. And before I boycotted social media, I'd spent years helping Nikki." I hesitated. "I also helped Eliza start a successful account." Which she then used against me. "I'm sure I could come up with a few things for you to implement or different income streams to consider."

Quinn glanced over at me. "You don't need to do that. You obviously have a good reason for swearing off social media."

"I want to help—if you want it, that is."

Her lips pursed in thought. "Considering your advice about putting myself in the posts again seems to already have worked wonders, I certainly won't refuse to hear any ideas you have. Though the uptick in interest could be because your video was amazing, and your attractive face was in my second post." Her teasing grin landed on me, then her gaze moved to my beard. "My followers apparently love a man with a well-groomed beard."

I chuckled. "So I read."

Quinn's focus remained on me as we followed the group several yards behind. Her gaze darted to my mouth before she looked away again. "Maybe that's the rule we should instigate—having you shave your face instead of your head. It feels like a happy medium."

"Aww. So you also love a man with a beard?"

"I do now." Her eyes widened. "That's not how that was supposed to come out. I only meant I didn't realize how much I liked beards until you. Not that I love ..."

I chuckled. "I know what you meant."

She shook her head, and I was certain, in the low light, I glimpsed a tint of red in her cheeks. "I didn't realize you helped Nikki with her account."

"I did a lot of filming and photographing for her in the beginning, but I was probably more useful to her as a sounding board for her ideas, helping her see different angles or ways to do things."

Quinn's lovely features were illuminated as we passed another lit candelabra. "I love that you helped your sister. And Eliza."

"It gave me an appreciation for how much work it takes." And with Eliza, what someone was willing to do to get ahead. "People think these successful influencers just fall into it—and maybe some do—but Nikki worked incredibly hard to get where she is. She still does. Just like you do. And like you're going to continue doing because you love it." After two years of hating on social media, it felt strange being the one to convince someone to keep at it. But here I was, certain that a small corner of the world would be darker without her influence. "What you share is important. It brings joy into people's lives."

Quinn sucked in a quick breath, and her gaze dropped to the wooden floor. I worried I'd said something wrong, but then her arm laced through mine, and she leaned her head against my arm.

We caught up to the group as they started up the stairs. When we reached the top foyer, the group moved into another large, open room. A giant Christmas tree sat centered in front of a large window, its white lights the only light in the room besides the candles.

Quinn's gaze darted about the room. "What a beautiful tree. And look at all the decorations. It's so festive."

"We'll enjoy it from back here," I said, taking a few steps back and pulling her with me. "I don't want tonight to end in another Benadryl overdose."

"Oh, good call. I almost forgot, and I'm not sure how I'd manage to get my decorating done with another six-hour nap forced in there."

I actually tried to pay attention this time as the tour guide talked about the uses of the room and the modern updates different owners had implemented, but it was pointless with Quinn still latched onto my arm, nodding her head and smiling up at me excitedly every few minutes as the woman spoke.

When the group continued forward, I planted my feet.

"What are you doing?" Quinn asked, sending a worried look in the direction of the group disappearing through the far door.

"I thought you might like a few more minutes in here— without all the people."

She bit at her lip. "Will we get in trouble?"

I shrugged. "Some things are worth a little trouble."

She laughed but seemed to relax at my nonchalant attitude. "This really is amazing. Ghosts or no ghosts, I think I could spend a night here, soaking this in. Not too close to the tree, of course, but right here. Or maybe on those couches right there."

We stood in the silence, Quinn enjoying the scenery and me enjoying Quinn.

After a minute, she looked up at me. "Your turn. If you had a visit from one of Dickens' Christmas spirits, what would you want to be shown?"

I hesitated, nervous my answer would be a little too forward after her confession earlier. But just because I'd told her I'd give her time, it didn't mean I wouldn't be upfront with what I wanted. I needed Quinn to know that I was here and willing to give us a try whenever, if ever, she was ready. "I'd want to be shown what I could do to win you over."

She stared up at me with those large blue eyes, her gaze darting to my lips, and her body unconsciously leaned closer to me. My hand came to her face, and she drew in a slow inhale, her chest rising and falling in time with mine.

"We should keep going," I whispered, my voice coming out hoarse. "And, for the record, it's not because I want to. It's because I meant what I said about giving you time."

Even if it took every bit of willpower I possessed not to kiss her.

"DO you think this will be enough?" Nikki glanced over the stash of food and drinks I was about to haul inside from the bed of my truck.

I grabbed out two boxes of soda and stacked them on a package of water bottles. "Considering the guys are only going to be here a couple of days, and most of that time we're scheduled to be places, I'd say it's more than enough."

"Okay." She checked her watch. "I have to run. I'm meeting Irene over at the Airbnb in half an hour to make sure everything's good to go."

I started toward the door with my load. "I'll see you tomorrow."

"Oh, Landon."

I stopped in the doorway and looked back at Nikki.

"Quinn is coming to the bachelorette party tonight, right?"

"She said she was planning on it."

"Good. Sophia is going to bring her dress by, so I'll have it there. Do you think you'll have time to drop her off before you have to leave, or should I have Julie come grab her?"

"I can drop her off."

Nikki smirked. "Of course you can."

I heaved a breath. "I know you might not believe me after my confession—why I asked Quinn to be my date for the wedding—but the truth is, I really do like her. And you're right. She does deserve to be treasured. I want to be the one who gets to do that —to treasure her. So whatever you have planned in that match-making brain of yours, please know that my feelings are genuine, and I'd very much appreciate it if you didn't interfere."

Nikki studied my expression. "You're being honest?"

I nodded.

A smile filled her face. "Then, where the two of you are concerned, I'm officially resigning as matchmaker extraordinaire. You will have no future interference from me. I promise."

"Thank you."

Nikki turned to her car with an added spring in her step, and for the briefest moment, I wondered if she'd accomplished exactly what she'd set out to do.

When I stepped into the shared stairwell, Quinn was at the top of the stairs. "Can I help carry stuff in?"

"Don't you have to be decorating?"

"Are you underestimating my strength again?" She started down the steps toward me and grabbed the top case of soda, the weight of it sending her forward slightly when she slid it from my stack. "Upstairs or down?"

"Either. I'll follow you."

She started back up the stairs. "I spiffed up the kitchen and got the fridge cleaned out so you'll have room to fit whatever you need."

"You didn't need to do that. I was planning on doing it."

"Well, I finished my third gingerbread house, so I took a little break."

I propped the door open as I entered to make our task of going up and down easier. "And that's what you did with those precious few minutes—cleaning? I'm offended."

She glanced over her shoulder, a playful smile on her lips. "You were shopping."

"Are you still on a break?" I asked, admiring the three finished gingerbread houses as we passed.

Quinn put the pack of soda inside the fridge and grabbed the other one off the top of my diminishing pile, shoving them in as well. "I think I can spare a few more minutes."

"And do you have any thoughts for how you want to spend those minutes?"

She grabbed the water bottles from my hold and set them on the ground with a loud *thunk* before stepping onto them like a step stool. She was now only a few inches shorter than me. Her hands wrapped around my neck. "I might have an idea."

My heart hammered in my chest, and I stood there, unmoving. "Are you sure it's one you won't regret?" I willed her to say yes.

Her fingertips stroked the back of my neck in a way that made my hands clench into fists at my sides to keep from taking hold of her. She pressed against me, and her lips brushed against my neck before her lips settled by my ear. "I know what I want," she whispered.

NINETEEN

QUINN

LANDON'S HANDS SETTLED ON MY WAIST, SECURING ME against him. And when his lips found mine, they were soft and warm, his kiss gentle. He pulled back, his eyes searching mine. "What changed?"

"I overheard what you said to Nikki downstairs. And it was like my mind clarified. I instantly knew what it was I wanted." It was Landon. He was good, and kind, and thoughtful. In the few weeks I'd known him, he'd supported me in ways that Cody had never done.

"So you want to give this a shot ... with me?"

I nodded, feeling shy under his focused attention. "If that's still what you want."

Landon threw his arms around my waist and picked me up. I wrapped my legs around him and laughed. "Where are we going?" I asked when he started walking.

He set me down on the counter but didn't answer. His lips

settled over mine with eagerness, and his hands moved to the outside of my thighs. I returned his kiss with equal intensity, running my fingers through the hair at the base of his neck.

"Whoa! Sorry." A man's voice sent both our gazes flying to the doorway, where a guy stood, watching us from the propped-open door, a look of utter amusement on his face. He pointed at the propped-open door. "It was open."

Landon cleared his throat. "Tyler." My gaze shot to his, and Landon gave a subtle nod of acknowledgment. This was the Tyler Nikki had wanted to set me up with. "I didn't expect you for another few hours."

"Obviously." He chuckled. "But that was awesome what you had going on there. I could feel the sparks from here."

My whole body was blushing, if that was even a thing. It sure felt like a thing.

Landon helped me down off the counter and took hold of my hand, leading me toward the door. "Tyler, this is Quinn." He flicked his chin at Tyler. "Quinn, Tyler Baker."

"It's nice to meet you." I set my free hand around Landon's forearm so I wouldn't have to shake Tyler's hand. My whole body was still trembling from Landon's kiss, and Tyler seemed like the last person I'd want to know that.

"It's nice to meet you. And Landon, buddy"—Tyler's hand came down hard on Landon's shoulder—"it's been a long time. Thanks for letting me crash here."

"Of course. Nikki wouldn't have it any other way." His words seemed to carry an additional meaning.

"She's the best." He clapped his hands and rubbed them together. "So I'm assuming by the heated moment I just walked in on, I'm the first to arrive?"

Landon nodded. "And your timing couldn't be better. Actually, it could have been better, but I have a load of things out in the truck I could use some help carrying now that you're here."

"What are those?" Tyler glanced behind us at the table. "Gingerbread mansions?"

"They're the centerpieces for Nikki's wedding, so don't touch them, or she'll murder you."

"Got it." He stepped closer to inspect them, lifting his hand in the air as if to show he was being careful. "Oh, wow. Look at the detail on these things." He leaned forward, resting his hands on his knees. "I wonder how long it took for someone to make those. It's incredible."

"Quinn made them. And they've taken her weeks."

Tyler's gaze flew to me. "For real?"

I nodded.

"Wow. Not only beautiful, but talented." He straightened and started back toward us. "Landon always gets the good ones."

Landon's hand tightened around mine. "Here. Let me show you where you'll be staying downstairs. Then, you can help me carry in the rest of the stuff." He turned to me. "You'll be okay?"

"Yeah. I'll start on Rosecliff."

He let go of my hand and turned to follow Tyler out. A moment later, he reappeared in the doorway, strode over to me, and gave me a parting kiss that made my toes curl and my breath catch.

SOON THE WHOLE house was overrun with men. They all seemed nice enough, even Tyler, but I couldn't help but feel like my presence put a damper on their party. The loud laughter coming from downstairs would likely be up here, too, if I hadn't set up camp in the middle of the room. As it was, guys would wander through, checking the fridge and cupboards, before heading back downstairs to congregate.

"What would you think about moving the finished ginger-bread houses up to my room ... well, your room?" Landon watched at my shoulder while I slowly plodded along on the decorating of Rosecliff Mansion. "I'm worried they're going to get damaged somehow."

I put down the piping bag on the plate. "Yeah. That's fine."

"Anthony," Landon gestured to an athletically built guy rummaging through the fridge. "Can you help me carry these upstairs?"

"Sure." He closed the fridge door empty-handed.

"All but this one," Landon said, pointing to Rosecliff. He looked at the house they were going to start with. "Is there a special way to do this? Or do we just carry it by the cardboard under it?"

"The cardboard should be thick enough to support it. I used a few layers."

As they picked it up, I held my breath, but the transition went smoothly. "Here, let me go upstairs and clear a space for it." Upstairs, I moved a few of my things off the long dresser in the master in time for the guys to walk in with the gingerbread house. "Right here."

They headed down again, and I waited for them upstairs until all three gingerbread houses were safely delivered—two on the dresser and one on the desk.

"Sorry to have you do that." Landon came to stand in front of me when Anthony had gone, his discerning gaze taking me in. "You okay?"

"I'm just feeling bad."

Landon's brow furrowed. "About moving the gingerbread houses?"

"No. About being here at all. I probably should have gone to a hotel."

"I promise you, the guys are glad to have a free place to stay. None of them care they have to share the space with a beautiful woman."

I sent him a disbelieving glance. "I'm sure that's not true. And you're sharing a room with Anthony when you could be in your own room"—I paused—"if I was at a hotel, I mean."

Landon wrapped his arms around me. "True, but then you'd be at a hotel instead of in the room next to me, and I couldn't see you whenever I wanted. So I'll gladly share a queen-sized bed with Anthony."

"The two of you are sharing a queen-sized bed? How is that logistically going to work? You're not small guys." I glanced over at the king bed in here. "Why don't we switch rooms now that you're staying upstairs? You can have the king, and I'll take the queen."

"This is the only door with a lock."

I nodded, conceding his point, then nuzzled into him and his wonderful scent. It was amazing how natural it felt being with Landon. If I stopped to think about it, it kind of freaked me out a little, but when I was with him, everything seemed right in the world. "Is it bad I don't want to go to the bachelorette party tonight?"

"Only if it's bad that I don't want to go to the bachelor party, and I'm the one throwing it."

"That is bad." I looked up and wrinkled my nose.

He cupped my face in his hands. "I never had a chance to apologize about Tyler walking in on us earlier."

"I'm the one who instigated that one."

"I did appreciate that more than you know." His thumb brushed across my cheek, and he leaned down to kiss me but then paused. Footsteps sounded down the hallway behind us. "And one of these days, I'm going to kiss you without being interrupted."

"Hey, Landon." A guy whose name was possibly Brian came through the door and paused mid-step when his gaze fell on us. "Sorry. The door was open, but I can come back later."

"That's okay," I said with a smile and stepped out of Landon's hold. "I should get ready."

Landon sent me an apologetic smile and then turned toward the guy. "Did you need something, Adam?"

Okay, so not Brian, but I was pretty sure there was someone here by the name of Brian.

"The toilet's clogged downstairs."

"That didn't take long." Landon sent me one last smile and followed Adam out, stopping at the door to lock the handle and shut it behind him.

THE AIRBNB NIKKI had rented for her and her bridesmaids was filled to the brim with chatting, laughing women. The large room opened out onto a deck overlooking the water, and a heated swimming pool let off steam into the cold night air. This was nothing like the perfectly simple bachelorette party Ashlee had thrown for me, and I was amazed, and a little overwhelmed, at how many friends Nikki had.

I grabbed a sparkling water and found an armchair in the corner, trying not to think about how much I could be getting done on my last gingerbread house if I were home. Or how late it was and how tired I was getting. Or how comfy I'd be in yoga pants and an oversized sweater instead of my tight jeans and this professional blouse. I'd literally packed one nice outfit for when I was going to meet Irene at Rosecliff to help set up the center-pieces. Now, it looked like I'd be stuck wearing this same outfit for multiple occasions, including the rehearsal dinner.

"Hey!" A woman approached who looked straight off the pages of a magazine, her deep-red hair shining in the light. I glanced around to see whom she was talking to before realizing it was me.

"Hey," I repeated in a nearly identical tone, like I was some kind of human recorder.

She wore a small strappy dress that hugged her body in all the right places and made her legs look like they went on for days. The strappy heels only added to the effect. I was seriously under-dressed. She smiled. "I saw you over here and thought I'd join you if that's okay?"

"Of course."

She took a seat on the chair next to mine, crossing her legs in a way that proved not all women had cottage cheese on their upper thighs. "I'm not a fan of big groups of people I don't know."

"I'm not a fan of big groups of people, period." The admission sounded different in my head. Not quite as anti-social as it came out. "But especially when I don't know them." Nope, that didn't help.

"So how do you know Nikki?"

"Umm ... through social media. I'm doing the centerpieces for her wedding."

"The gingerbread houses?"

I nodded.

"You're Quinn, TheKookieCook? No wonder you look familiar!"

I nodded again, amazed someone here knew me. The other influencers Nikki had introduced me to throughout the night, as kind as they were, hadn't seemed super interested in me once they realized my interest was in baking and not beauty, fashion, or travel.

"I love your account. I've been following you since Nikki shared one of your posts, like a year and a half ago or more. I can't believe some of the things you make. They're incredible."

"Thank you. That's sweet of you to say." I took a sip of water to make it look like I was nowhere near freaking out that someone in the big vast universe not only knew who I was but actually loved my account. "How do you know Nikki?"

"I'm Kade's cousin, Rachel."

The water I'd started to swallow went down the wrong pipe, and I started coughing. Rachel? This was Rachel? Why was I not surprised Nikki had wanted to set her up with Landon?

"Are you okay?"

I nodded, putting up a finger until I could find the ability to breathe again. "It just went down the wrong pipe," I said in a strained voice. I cleared my throat and forced out a smile. "So what do you do, Rachel?"

"I'm a senior architect for a big firm in New York, but I'm hoping to start my own firm soon."

That was not what I'd expected. Model. I wouldn't have been surprised. Social media influencer. Absolutely probable. Lead architect. It never crossed my mind. "That sounds amazing and like a lot of work."

"That's kind of why I'd like to start my own firm—a healthier work-life balance. Right now, it's hard to travel as much as I'd like."

My stomach tightened, remembering that Landon said he also wished he had more time for it. "You enjoy traveling?"

"I live for it."

"And where's your favorite place to go?"

She sighed like I'd asked if she preferred to die by fire or ice. "That's hard. Europe—Spain, France, Croatia. Basically anywhere along the Mediterranean. But the East is incredible, too. I wouldn't mind going back to Thailand or Laos. Vietnam." She pointed at me, her eyes brightening. "I've also been to New Zealand. The Hobbit village where they filmed the Shire in *Lord of the Rings*."

I couldn't fight my smile. "You got to go there?"

"It was magical. You have to go. You could recreate that personal tribute you did to the Hobbits—your fellow short people. Your followers would love it."

I clearly needed to take that video down. "That would be fun."

"And where is your favorite place to travel?"

"I've not traveled much. I went to Arizona once when I was little, and I've driven through Nevada up to Utah. I have been to Mexico, but via a cruise, so I didn't actually get off the boat at that port—my mom had heard about a recent kidnapping." I pinched my lips together, refusing to say anything else about my pathetic amount of traveling, but I couldn't leave it on the kidnapping comment. "And then all over California. Oh, and even into Oregon once, but barely over the border."

Rachel nodded, not a hint of judgment on her face. "I love California."

It was the right answer after my awkward rattling off of all the places I'd been—or lack of places.

"And I've never been to Utah. I've always wanted to go, though. I've seen pictures of Zion, and it looks insanely beautiful."

"I've not been ... but it does look beautiful."

"So these centerpieces," Rachel said, having mercy on me. "How big are they?"

"They're all slightly different sizes, but the three smaller ones are somewhere around three by two feet. And Rosecliff is almost four by three."

"Do you have some sort of background in architecture?"

I tucked an obstinate curl behind my ear "No. Not at all."

"I remember the gingerbread house you posted last year. What was it again—a cottage of some sort?"

"Good memory. It was a Cotswold cottage."

"That's right. In the reel, you showed blueprints of the design. Did you just come up with those on your own?"

"I watched a few videos on YouTube."

Rachel laughed. "Of course you did. Do you still have the blueprints you created for your centerpieces?"

"They're at the house where I'm staying. You're welcome to look at them sometime."

Rachel gave a mischievous smile. "How about now?"

"Now?"

Rachel glanced around and shrugged. "My introvert battery is tapped out and needs to be rejuvenated before tomorrow's activities. So, if you're ready, I can get us a car."

I glanced toward Nikki, who was standing next to Julie in the middle of a large group of women. "Let me just grab my dress from Nikki's room, and I'll meet you at the front door."

TWENTY

QUINN

To my relief, the lights were all off when we got to the house, which meant Landon wasn't home yet. Not that I was worried about him meeting Rachel, it was just that ... Okay. I was a little hesitant to let him see this goddess of a woman his sister had intended to set him up with, especially because she was proving to be every bit the *whole package* Nikki declared she was.

"Wow. Talk about prime real estate, right next to the bay like this." Rachel glanced up at the house when we got out of the hired car. "And the house is lovely."

I led the way inside, flipping on the light switch when we reached the shared stairway. Her gaze roved over the setup, like she was taking it all in.

"There's an apartment down here with three bedrooms," I said, gesturing to the door as we passed. "I'm upstairs."

When I opened the door and turned on the lights, Rachel's attention went immediately to the replica of Rosecliff on the table. "It looks just like it." She walked around the table, studying

225

it from different angles. "Look at the detail in the gingerbread. Your icing work on the part you've done is incredible, too. It all is. Constructing scaled-down models is no easy task, and you do it with gingerbread. I'm beyond impressed."

"The blueprints I made are in my room upstairs. I can go grab them, or you're welcome to come up. The three finished gingerbread houses are up there."

She shrugged out of her coat and draped it over the back of the chair. "Lead the way."

I placed my dress and shoes from Sophia in the closet and grabbed the blueprints. As I sifted through the papers, getting them in order, Rachel studied each of the other gingerbread houses. "I recognize this one. It's Kade's family home in Boston. How did you get the dimensions?"

I handed her the paper I'd drawn out the plans on. "A combination of pictures, Zillow, and Google Maps. There's a tool where you can measure things on the aerial view. Once I knew the size of the roof, the other parts weren't too difficult to calculate. It's definitely not exact, but it's close enough to capture the look of it."

Rachel's gaze moved across the design. "Honestly, you could teach our interns a thing or two." Pride swelled in me at her compliment, and she handed it back to me. "Can I see the others?"

I handed her the papers, and she moved to the bed, taking a seat on the corner of it. She nodded, her eyes roving over each one with careful consideration. "If you ever decide baking isn't for you, you could always look into architecture. You've got a talent for it."

Footsteps sounded on the stairs, and my heart nearly jumped into my throat. I spun to face the hall to find Landon walking toward me.

"Landon."

He smiled. "I didn't think you'd be home already, but I saw the lights on. How was the party?"

My gaze shifted to Rachel, sitting on the bed, her legs crossed and the slit in her dress perfectly exposing her thigh. "Good," I said.

He stepped into the room, and his gaze fell on Rachel. His feet came to a stop and his eyes met mine. "Sorry, I didn't realize you had ..."

"Landon, this is Rachel." I gestured to her, forcing the corners of my mouth upward.

"We've met." Rachel glanced up from the papers in her hand, smiling at Landon. Thankfully, neither of them looked at me to witness my confusion. When had the two of them met? "Hello, again, Landon."

Landon dipped his chin in greeting, not denying her claim. "Did you ladies have a good night?"

"Julie threw a stellar bachelorette party for Nikki. They're still going strong over there." She placed a hand on the bed—his bed—and leaned back with a seductive smile. It might not have been intentionally seductive, but the very essence of sexiness seemed to emanate out of her. "How was the bachelor party? Nothing too eventful, I hope."

"It was good." Landon's gaze remained locked with hers for a moment longer, before it dropped to the floor. "Unfortunately, I'm not sure they're done for the night either. I drove a couple of the guys home who'd had a few too many. The rest will be dropped off soon."

"Thanks for the head's up." Rachel stood. "Nothing ruins a night like the unwanted attention of intoxicated men." She handed me back my stack of papers. "Will I see you tomorrow at any of the planned festivities?"

I wrapped my arms around myself. Standing next to Rachel, I felt frumpy and short in my blouse, jeans, and low-top sneakers. "Possibly. Depends on how much I can get done on Rosecliff."

"I hope you come. It's been so much fun talking with you. And thanks for letting me peek at the centerpieces." She turned to Landon, running a hand through her silky, straight hair and pulling it over one shoulder, leaving the other completely bare except for her thin strap. "I'll see you tomorrow." Maybe I'd imagined it, but there was something in her eyes when she looked at him that made my insides churn.

Landon gave her a closed-lipped smile. "You will."

She gave a finger-wave over her bare shoulder and headed out the door, her heels echoing along the wooden floor as she went.

"So you had fun tonight?" Landon asked.

I gave an absent nod, still trying to lift my spirits from the pits of despair. "I couldn't believe how many people were there."

"That's one thing about Nikki. She hates excluding anyone, which gets hard when you have as many friends as she does."

The sound of the front door opening and closing carried up the stairs. "Rachel is really nice."

His gaze was set on me. "She is."

"I didn't realize you'd met her."

"She was over visiting Kade at my dad's this morning."

And he hadn't thought to mention that he'd been introduced to the girl Nikki had actually wanted to set him up with? "Fun."

"Did she want to see your designs?" He pointed at the papers gripped in my hands.

"Yeah. She did. She's an architect, but you probably knew that already."

Landon took a step toward me, his hand brushing along my arm. "You okay?"

I forced my gaze to meet his. "Perfectly. Everything's great."

His eyes narrowed. "You sure?"

"I'm just stressed. I have a lot to do."

He glanced at the alarm clock next to the bed. "It's almost midnight."

"I know. I just need to get more done on Rosecliff before I go to sleep." I took a step back, still wearing a false smile. "I'm going to change real quick, and I'll be right down."

"I guess I'll go check and see if the rest of the guys arrived."

He shut the door behind him, and I dropped onto the bed. Why hadn't Landon told me he'd met Rachel? It seemed insignificant but also monumental. Was he regretting not having listened to Nikki? Did he want to ask Rachel to the wedding instead?

No. I was being petty. I knew that.

But that didn't mean the thought hadn't gone through his mind once or twice. And honestly, I wouldn't blame him if it did. Rachel didn't only look fresh off a Milan runway, but she had a successful career and was kind. And she loved to travel, just like Landon. They even wanted to go to some of the same places. I, in contrast, was chaos personified. And an uncultured chaos at that. I hadn't even had the sense to bring more than one presentable outfit to wear on a three-week trip. It was only a matter of time until Landon realized all my faults, just like Cody had.

My phone dinged. I stood up and grabbed it from the corner of the dresser where I'd apparently left it. As if Cody had sensed my thoughts turn to him, his name appeared on the notification for a new text. I felt not even a hint of excitement.

Cody: Thinking of you. When can we talk?
Quinn: I'll be home after Christmas.
Cody: Can I just call you now? I'd love to hear your voice.

With thoughts of Rachel and Cody's Ms. Legs sauntering through my mind, I wasn't in an accommodating mood. Besides, I wanted Cody to look me in the eyes and tell me why he'd left. I wanted to see the truth of it in his expression and know, once and for all, what had been so wrong with me that he couldn't keep the promises he'd made to me. The vows we'd taken.

Quinn: I'd prefer to talk in person. How about you text me when you're home from your vacation to the Caribbean, and we'll figure something out.

My pulse raced when I pressed send, and I momentarily regretted my passive-aggressive text. But the truth was, I had no intention of reconciling anything between us. Like Landon had said about Eliza, Cody was a part of my past, not my future. I knew that now. But I deserved answers. I deserved to have a chance to fix whatever I'd done wrong before I risked driving Landon away.

MY EYES WERE GROWING HEAVY, but I couldn't stop. I had one side-face decorated and had just started on the front-face of Rosecliff, which meant, once I went to bed, I'd have to finish the rest tomorrow. Well ... today, considering it was well past the middle of the night. Realistically, I was looking at another twelve to fifteen hours. There was no way I was going to be able to do anything tomorrow besides stay home and decorate this thing.

"This is why I'm here." My audible reassurance fell flat, especially considering, while I was here working, Landon was going to be enjoying the events tomorrow without me. And possibly with Rachel.

Loud laughter wafted up from the vent. I was grateful Landon had managed to confine all the guys to the apartment downstairs for the time being. It was difficult enough to concentrate on what I was doing with images of Rachel and Landon exploring Newport together. I hated what a beautiful couple they made in the theatrical imaginings of my mind.

The door creaked open, and Landon stepped inside. "You're still up."

I drew in a long breath. "Yep."

He pulled out a dining room chair and scooted it next to mine. "How's it going?"

"Slow."

"I'm sorry." He hesitated. "Do you think you'll be able to join us tomorrow?"

An unexpected stinging behind my eyes made me blink. There was no way I was going to start crying now. "No. Probably not."

"If you get done earlier than you think, I could always come and pick you up between events. Maybe before the trolley tour or the harbor cruise?"

I kept my gaze focused on the icing as it clung to the ginger-bread. "That would be fun. I'm just not sure I'll finish in time."

He leaned forward in his chair, and his hand settled on my leg. "I could stay here with you."

I glanced at him, suddenly wishing he could stay. But that was me being petty again. "Nikki would be so sad. Besides, you're going to have fun."

His thumb moved in a small circle on my inner thigh just above my knee, sending heat pulsing through me. "It'd be more fun if you were there."

With the way he looked at me like I was the only person in the world he wanted to be with, I almost forgot about Rachel. Almost. "I'll try to finish early."

He leaned back in his chair, his arm draped across the back of mine. His fingers mindlessly played with my hair while he watched me work. And each time I looked over at him, he'd meet my gaze with a slight smile.

When I reached a breaking point, I turned toward him and rubbed a hand over his cheek. "You look tired."

He yawned and covered his mouth, but it was too late, and I yawned, too. "I feel tired," he said, clasping my hand in his. "But I think it's best if I wait until the party dies down before I head off to bed. Besides, you're still awake, so there's no way I'm leaving you unguarded in a house full of inebriated men."

"You can't know how much I appreciate that." I shot him a smile. "Is Kade having a good time, though?"

He chuckled. "Josh gave Kade a ride home after the bar. Kade said he didn't want to be *too tired* tomorrow. But, yeah, I think he had a good time before abandoning me." A loud thud from downstairs sent Landon to his feet. "Speaking of having a good time ... I'll be right back."

Poor Landon.

A few minutes later, the door opened again. "What happened?" My gaze lifted to find Tyler standing there instead of Landon. "Oh, Tyler."

"Sorry, I didn't realize you'd be here." His voice was a notch louder than usual. "The bathrooms downstairs are both occupied."

I gestured behind me. "This one's free."

He walked toward the table, a slight smell of alcohol lingering on him. "It really is amazing that you made that."

"Thank you. It sounds like you guys are having fun downstairs."

He ran a hand through his hair. "I'm kind of impressed Landon pulled it off. He's more of the designated-driver type, so my confidence in him managing a bachelor party of this caliber wasn't high. But I've got to say, he pulled through for Kade."

When he stood there, unmoving, I tried to think of something to fill the silence. "Landon mentioned the two of you went to the same college for undergrad?"

"We did. Not intentionally, though. Our dads were friends back in college, so we both pledged for the same fraternity and ended up living together for two years. Not roommates, but in the same house. Even then, I was always closer with Nikki. But Landon's a great guy. All the ladies loved him—the handsome, stoic type."

The thought of *all the ladies* loving him wasn't surprising, though I was ready to move on from that thought. "He is great."

Tyler took the chair Landon had occupied next to me and turned it to sit on it backward, facing me. He draped his arms over the back of the chair and leaned closer. The smell of fermentation grew more potent. "How long have the two of you been dating?"

"Not very long," I said, not sure how else to answer that. I could sense Tyler's gaze on me, but I didn't stop to meet it. I hoped Landon wasn't going to be too much longer. Not that I was uncomfortable, but if he got any closer, it would definitely be pushing my limits.

"Well, he's a lucky man. Always has been. Except for the whole Eliza thing, I guess."

"Did you know her?"

"Yeah. She's from here originally. She and Nikki were friends. That's how I first met her." He shook his head. "She really had us all fooled, though. I don't think I even know the full extent of what she put Landon through, but from what I do know, I don't envy him."

In his current state, Tyler seemed like he'd spill everything he knew with only the tiniest bit of prodding, but if Landon wanted to tell me about what happened with Eliza, he would. To prevent Tyler from seeing how curious I was, I returned my gaze to Rosecliff and kept decorating.

"From what I gathered," Tyler said, apparently not needing any prodding, "Eliza kept demanding more, and he kept trying to make it work. I mean, there are two sides to every story, right?" He gave a loud laugh that made me flinch. "But from what it looked like on this side, Eliza had some serious issues. She's a good actress, though. When I saw the *sob story* she posted before she left Landon, I remember calling Nikki. She was livid. But honestly, had she not assured me Eliza was a narcissistic liar, and had I not known Landon myself, I might have believed all the things Eliza had said about him. I think a lot of people did. Nikki lost a group of followers after the whole thing—but not as many as Eliza lost when Nikki made her own post defending Landon and ousting Eliza. It was intense there for a while."

No wonder Landon had gotten off social media. I turned my attention back to Tyler, debating whether or not it was a violation of trust between me and Landon to ask about what Eliza had said. The heavy feeling in the pit of my stomach confirmed it probably was.

Tyler gave a heavy blink. "I think Nikki feels responsible for the whole thing."

"She didn't know Eliza would turn out to be so awful."

"That's what I told her. And honestly, every other match she's arranged has been spot on."

I allowed myself a quick glance at Tyler. He was a very attractive guy with his hazel eyes and sandy-brown hair that nearly matched the color of his tanned skin. But with the cocky confidence he radiated, I was positive Nikki was wrong about the two of us. Maybe she was also wrong about Landon and Rachel.

The door opened, and Landon stepped inside, his gaze moving from Tyler to me. "Everything good?"

I nodded. "Yep."

Tyler smiled. "Don't worry. I was behaving myself. Your girl and I were just having a little heart to heart." Tyler stood up, gesturing to the chair. "Your seat, sir. I'm just going to use the bathroom, and I'll be on my way back downstairs."

When Tyler shut the door behind him, Landon's gaze returned to me. "He kept his hands off you, right?"

"Yes," I whispered, not wanting Tyler to hear us talking about him. "He was just telling me about college ... and Eliza."

Landon gave a slow nod, like he understood what might have been said. "That doesn't surprise me. He's always been a talker when he drinks."

"So what was that noise?" I asked, hoping to lighten the scowl on Landon's face. Now wasn't the time to ask him about what Eliza had posted—not with Tyler on the other side of the bathroom door.

Landon released a breath. "I'm not even sure. I checked in all the rooms, but everything seemed fine, and none of the guys fessed up. Though it's only a matter of time until something breaks with that many guys together. Several of them probably should have been done drinking hours ago."

The bathroom door opened, and Tyler came strolling out. "Do you mind if I grab a quick drink of water?"

Landon pointed toward the kitchen. "Cups are in the second cabinet to the left."

A ruckus on the stairs sent Landon back to the door. "What are you guys doing?" he asked, looking down into the stairwell before opening the door wider.

Two guys stepped through, supporting a third man between them. "I think Vince here is done for the night," one of them said.

"I'm perfectly fine. And I know how to walk myself," Vince mumbled, pushing out of the guys' supporting hold. He took a few haphazard steps, supporting himself on the back of a dining room chair when he reached it. "Whoa, dude. Is the floor moving?"

Trying to be discreet, I scooted Rosecliff out of arm's reach of Vince. The last thing I wanted was for him to flail his arms again and accidentally hit it.

"You guys can go back down," Landon said to the others. "I'll make sure he gets upstairs." He stepped between Vince and the table. "Here, Vince. Let me help you."

"I don't need help." His words slurred together, making it hard to understand him. He lifted up a finger. "I'm still thirsty."

Tyler stepped toward him with his large cup of water. "I'm pretty sure water's the only drink you should be having right now. Here."

"I don't want water." Vince's hand flew up and batted the cup out of Tyler's grasp, directly toward me.

I squeezed my eyes shut, bracing for the impact. A spray of water hit my face, but the brunt of it, along with the cup, hit the side of Rosecliff—the only side I'd already decorated. I froze, unable to move. Unable to look at the damage.

"Look what you did," Tyler yelled. "You just got her house all wet."

Vince glanced over at me, but his blank gaze didn't focus.

My vision blurred with tears, and my ears hummed.

"Get him upstairs," Landon said to Tyler, pushing past both of them into the kitchen.

I needed to look. I needed to see what damage had been done, but I felt dizzy with the thoughts racing through my mind. There was no more dough—it had gone bad in the power outage. I could always make more, but I was already low on time. I'd never finish. Besides, how would I get the ruined piece free? The sugar-glue might as well have been cement, and I could easily damage another piece in the removal process.

Just look.

My heart was in a frenzy, beating soundly against the walls of my tightened chest, when I leaned around to view the side of the house. The icing was beginning to run in the wetter spots, and a portion of my design had been crushed by the impact of the cup. I drew closer and dusted some of the broken icing away. A sigh of relief escaped me. There was no physical damage to the gingerbread.

Landon was back at my side with a stack of towels, drying the water from the table and off the edge of the cardboard. "What can I do?"

I rubbed the sleeve of my sweater over my eyes, clearing away the tears pooling there. Whether they were from despair or relief —or a mixture of both—I wasn't sure. "We've got to get the water off before it starts dissolving the gingerbread."

Landon handed me a towel and started sponging up the water on the roof with careful movements. "What about the frosting? I don't want to touch it."

Slowly, I dabbed at the places the water had hit. The icing was saturated, and it smeared at my touch. I ran my pinky finger along the outside of one of the areas to see if I could maybe fix it, but the moisture in it confirmed my fear. With a swift motion, I ran the towel over all of it.

Landon's gaze shot to me. "What are you doing?"

"The icing is saturated, which will make the gingerbread soggy if I leave it. I'll just have to start over once it's dry."

"That took you hours."

I shrugged, still fighting back the tears as I continued to scrub off the icing with brisk motions until every bit of it was off, and only a faded white dusting remained among the darkened spots of slightly damp gingerbread. But it would dry. I hoped. "Looks like I'm not going tomorrow."

Landon stood there, obviously unsure what to say.

I soaked up any remaining water I saw. "I should have just gone to the hotel."

"I'm sorry. I shouldn't have—"

"It's not your fault that I'm incapable of making the right choice. Ever." The tears sprung from my eyes, no longer willing to be dammed.

Footsteps sounded on the stairs, and Tyler reappeared. "He's in bed."

Not wanting him to see me cry, I turned away and dried my face with my sleeves. Though, the way my shoulders trembled with my silent sobs, there was no hiding the truth.

The room was silent, and I was positive Tyler was noting the damage to the gingerbread and my current state.

"I'm sorry, Quinn. Had I known—"

"It's fine," I interrupted, still unable to look at him. "It's no one's fault." No one's but mine. If I were a competent, rational person, I never would have chosen to stay in a house full of random men to finish the gingerbread. I had put a damper on their whole party, and now some of them were forced to feel bad about what had happened, all because I'd wanted to stay here with Landon.

The silence continued, soon followed by retreating steps and the sound of a closing door.

Landon stepped up behind me. He didn't say anything, but he wrapped his arms around my ribcage, securing me into him, and rested his chin against my shoulder. I leaned my head against his, allowing his strength to bolster me and his support to calm me.

After several minutes locked in his embrace, I glanced up at him. "I'd better get to bed. I've got a long day ahead of me."

He pressed a gentle kiss to my forehead. "I'll see you in the morning."

THE SOUND of Landon's truck pulling in sent me to the window. I glanced out to see several guys unloading, quickly dropped the blinds back into place, and hurried upstairs.

It wasn't that I didn't want to see Landon. I did. For the most part. But it was late, and I'd had a rough day. Not only because I'd been up before the sun to start over on decorating Rosecliff—which meant I'd spent almost twenty-two hours straight on the darn thing—but I'd also been alone with my thoughts for way too long. Thoughts that constantly shifted with each new tag on Nikki's account from all those who had been able to spend the day celebrating with the soon-to-be bride and groom. The play-by-play of what I'd been missing had sent me spiraling on more than one occasion, especially when I saw Landon among the faces in the photos. But apparently, I was a masochist, because I'd kept looking. All day.

I locked the door behind me and switched out the lights, wishing I'd thought to do a quick glance around the room beforehand. It was too late now. I could hear male voices downstairs. But if there *was* someone hiding in here, they would end up on one of those *dumbest-criminals-ever* podcasts. I'd literally been inside and alone all day long, and now I was one scream away from several guys breaking down the door to save me. The odd thought calmed me as I crept toward my bed in the dark and hopped beneath the covers.

Heavy footsteps sounded on the stairs, and one guy laughed.

"Shhh. Quinn's sleeping." Simply hearing Landon's voice made me want to go unlock the door and pull him inside. But instead of kissing him like I currently had the urge to do, I'd probably start bawling like the emotional wreck I actually was. I wouldn't ruin his perfectly wonderful day with a dose of crazy.

The bathroom door opened and shut several times as the guys readied for bed, and after the last one, footsteps paused by my door, and I was sure it was Landon. After a few slow breaths, the footsteps retreated again. For the second time since lying here, I wanted to get up and unlock the door. I wanted to see Landon and thank him for having lunch and dinner delivered to the house so I wouldn't have to cook today. I wanted to tell him that, as hard as today was, his sweet text messages kept my spirits up. But I couldn't.

For Landon's sake.

Because if there was one thing I'd realized during my day of forced introspection, it was that I really wasn't in a place for a serious relationship. I was still very much a mess. And where Cody had walked away, I was beginning to think Landon might not. He would suffer in his stoic kindness. And he deserved better than that.

TWENTY-ONE

LANDON

WHEN I FINALLY HEADED DOWNSTAIRS IN THE morning, Quinn was already at the table, working. Tyler and Vince sat next to her, the compliments rolling off their tongues. I knew they both felt awful about what had happened, so between that and the fact that Tyler kept a healthy distance from Quinn, the sight didn't irk me too much. And it didn't hurt that just seeing her lifted my spirits. It had been a long day yesterday, made longer by the fact that she'd already been asleep when I'd gotten home.

"Look who's joining the land of the living," Tyler said when he caught sight of me.

Quinn glanced over her shoulder and sent me a brief smile. A generic smile. Or maybe I'd read it wrong.

"How's it going?" I asked, resting my hands on the back of her chair.

"I'm just finishing up, with only a few minutes to spare before the driver gets here to collect the houses."

I scanned the building, amazed anew by her talent. Not only was the gingerbread replica of Rosecliff impressive, but the detail work was stunning. Until Quinn's creations, I hadn't realized gingerbread houses could look like this—classy and artistic. No wonder Nikki had hired her. "It turned out amazing."

"It really did," Vince said, nodding in agreement.

"Thanks." Quinn smiled at him, and I tried not to feel slighted that he'd been rewarded with her gratitude.

"Do you get to come to breakfast with us, then?" I asked. "Since you're done?"

Quinn kept her focus on the house. "I was actually going to go with the driver to make sure the houses all get there in one piece."

"I could follow him over so—"

"I thought I'd stay and see if I could help with the setup." She glanced up at me with an apologetic look.

I shrugged. "That's fine. I'll go with you."

Her brow creased. "You can't miss breakfast."

"Nikki won't even be there. She's going to be at Rosecliff with Irene. And I'll let one of the guys take my truck so they don't have to hire a car."

"You should go with everyone else. You don't even like decorating."

Why was I getting the feeling she didn't want me to come along? Was she upset about not being able to go yesterday? Or could it have been what Tyler had shared with her about Eliza? Had she found the video yesterday and watched it? My stomach twisted. I should have explained the whole situation before it was blurted out by a partially intoxicated man, but knowing that the video was still up on Eliza's feed—even as deeply buried as it now was—I couldn't bear the thought of Quinn seeing it, of Quinn believing any of the things Eliza had said about me.

"Despite what you seem to think," I said. "I'm not going for the decorating."

She didn't respond but returned her gaze to the gingerbread.

Tyler stood, avoiding my gaze. "I'm going to go grab my things from downstairs." Apparently, the awkwardness of the situation was getting uncomfortable.

Vince followed him to the door. "I'll come with you."

When the door closed behind them, Quinn went rigid in her chair.

Taking the chair Tyler had just vacated, I looked over at her. "Is it time for another one of those *adult conversations*? Because I'm getting the vibe that something's bothering you."

Her eyes were full of uncertainty when they met mine, and for a split second, I was certain she had seen Eliza's post. "Doesn't it get exhausting, always having to ask me what's wrong?"

I quirked my head to the side, not expecting that question. "No. I guess I don't feel like I'm always asking you that."

"But you do. Constantly. And it's not your fault. I'm just—"

The door opened, stopping her revelation. Tyler poked his head in. "Sorry to interrupt, but the driver's here. Should I send him up, or do you two need a few more minutes?"

Quinn bounded to her feet, obviously eager for the interruption. "Yes. That's fine. Thanks, Tyler."

He kept the door propped open and gestured to the driver, who must have been standing at the bottom of the stairwell. A few seconds later, a man in his early fifties stepped through, his gaze falling on Quinn. "I'm here for the centerpieces."

"Hello. I'm Quinn," she said, sending him one of her contagious smiles.

Instantly, he brightened. "Wally. It's nice to meet you."

"Thanks for doing this. There's one." Quinn gestured to the table. "And the other three are upstairs."

He glanced toward Rosecliff. "Oh, wow. That's bigger than I expected. I might need some help to get them in the van if anyone's available."

"I can help," Tyler responded before I even had a chance to offer. "And I'm sure Vince would be willing."

"I can as well," I said, feeling like quite the dunce, still sitting at the table by myself. I stood.

"Great." The man pointed. "Let's start with this one."

In less than fifteen minutes, we had all four gingerbread houses safely stowed in the large van and were following behind Wally on our way to Rosecliff—Quinn in the front seat of my truck, and Tyler and Vince in the back.

"Thanks again for coming, guys." Quinn sent a sweet smile over her shoulder.

"It's the least we could do," Vince said.

Quinn glanced at him over her shoulder. "After this, promise never to feel bad about what happened again. It was an accident. And it turned out alright."

"An accident that prevented you from coming out with us yesterday," Vince said, blowing out a breath.

Tyler nodded. "It didn't help our guilty consciences with Landon as a visual reminder of our stupidity. He moped around all day."

I glanced at his smirk in the rearview mirror. "All things considered, I thought I did a pretty good job staying positive."

Tyler leaned forward in his seat until he was directly behind Quinn. "It was pathetically obvious how much he wished you were there," he whispered.

Quinn's gaze landed on me. I could see the warring emotions in her expression, but the amusement seemed to win out with how her eyes danced.

I suddenly didn't dislike Tyler as much as I'd thought. Maybe he had grown up in the last six or seven years.

The van pulled onto Rosecliff's private drive from Belvue Avenue, and I followed. I left enough room between my truck and the van to allow Quinn to see the building as we approached.

Her whole face lit. "It's incredible," she whispered. "I can't believe I'm actually here."

When I parked, she was still taking it all in as Tyler jumped out of the truck to assist her out. So I didn't dislike him as much, but I definitely didn't like him either.

"Are these the centerpieces?" A woman with a distinct New York accent came out of the front entrance on the right, a clipboard in hand.

Wally opened the back of the van. "Yep. Where do you want them, Miss Garrity?"

Her gaze landed on us. "Who are all of you?"

Quinn gave a small wave. "I'm Quinn Cook. I made the gingerbread houses."

Irene gave her a quick once-over, followed by a stiff nod that said Quinn was exactly what she expected—and not in a good way. "Of course you are."

I stepped forward, placing my hand on Quinn's back. "I'm Nikki's brother, Landon." I hated having to pull the Nikki Aker card, but the way Irene's expression immediately flashed with regret made me glad I had the card to pull. Quinn deserved respect, especially after all the work and sacrifice she'd put into the houses. I flicked my head toward the others. "These two are friends that came along to get the gingerbread houses inside in one piece."

Irene lifted her chin like it pained her to acknowledge our help. "Well, in that case, thank you. Go ahead and unload. I'll meet you inside."

Quinn watched with a worried expression as the four of us carefully unloaded the first two houses—two on each house— and carried them through the slush to the entrance. When we stepped onto the carpet just inside the door, Quinn's shoulders relaxed.

Irene waited inside the entrance. She glanced at the houses, and the corners of her mouth pulled into a near smile. "I admit those are not what I'd envisioned when Nikki mentioned gingerbread houses as centerpieces. They're actually going to look exquisite surrounded by greenery and flowers." She motioned toward a long table in the lobby. "One will go over here. Probably the largest of the four."

"That would be the replica of Rosecliff," Quinn responded.

"But it's still in the van. These two are the family homes of Kade and Nikki."

Irene nodded. "Let's set those two together right here, then." She pointed at two smaller tables of different heights near each other. She scooted one a little closer and patted the top. "And we'll put the third on the table across the entrance where the guests' gifts will be placed."

We did as she said, then went to grab the other two. Wally and Vince took the cabin, and Tyler and I hauled in Rosecliff with Quinn guiding our every step. When they were safely in place, I handed Tyler my keys. "I know you have your car at the house, but once you get there, you can have one of the other guys drive a group to breakfast in my truck. We'll get a ride-share or have Nikki drop us off."

He took the keys. "Sounds good. We'll see you two lovebirds later."

"Thanks again, guys." Quinn's cheeks flushed with color, but instead of looking at me, she started toward Irene. "We were going to ask Nikki if there was something we could do to help."

"I have everything taken care of, but Nikki should be here soon. Feel free to walk around until then. I'm going to go see that the chairs from the terrace have been moved out of view of the windows."

Quinn's gaze remained on Irene until she'd disappeared through the ballroom doors. Something was definitely wrong, but with how intentionally she avoided me, it probably wasn't the time to have the looming conversation, no matter how much I wanted to clear the air between us.

I thrust my hands in my pockets, trying to appear casual. "Do you know why Nikki picked Rosecliff?"

Quinn glanced over at me, studying my expression like this was some sort of trap to get her talking. "No."

"When we were younger, my parents took us on a tour here. She was probably ten or eleven. And when she saw that staircase right there"—I pointed to the heart-shaped staircase Rosecliff was famous for—"she declared she was going to get married here one day. Even back then, she was always a hopeless romantic."

Quinn's gaze followed mine, a smile lighting her face. "It is beautiful."

"Well, being the annoying older brother, I felt it was my duty to tell her that was a pipe dream and would never happen. And here we are."

Quinn laughed, but before I could fully enjoy the glorious sound of it, a cold draft sent our attention toward the door.

Julie and Nikki stepped inside, chatting, but stopped when their gazes fell on us. "Morning, you two." Nikki came to give us both a hug, with Julie right behind her.

"I was just telling Quinn the reason you chose this venue," I said, pulling out of the embrace and shifting to Julie's.

"And why's that?" Nikki asked.

"That you chose it to spite me."

"It wasn't the only reason I chose it." Nikki sent me a knowing smile. "But it was probably the main one."

Julie glanced around the entryway. "I still can't believe you're getting married at Rosecliff tomorrow. Mom would have loved to be here."

A moment of silence fell over all four of us.

"She's here," Nikki finally whispered, her gaze settling on the gingerbread houses. "Oh, Quinn! Look at how those turned out." Nikki hurried over to where the replica of Rosecliff was, her eyes eagerly taking in every detail of the house, the elaborate white pattern intricately free-handed across every surface of the gingerbread.

Julie joined her. "When you said gingerbread houses, I was thinking like the ones we used to make—like the one Quinn made with Grandma—not these. They're perfect."

Quinn's hands were clasped in front of her, her knuckles blanching from her grip and her cheeks a beautiful pink. "I'm glad they turned out alright."

Nikki scoffed. "Alright? They're exquisite. And to think you had to start over yesterday morning on Rosecliff. I was sick to my stomach when Landon told me about it. I'm so sorry that happened."

Quinn gave a small shrug. "It all worked out."

"Well, we missed you." Nikki's gaze slid to me. "Didn't we, Landon?"

"She's already been informed of my moping."

"That is the perfect word for it," Nikki said with a laugh.

Julie nodded, smiling at Quinn. "It really is."

Quinn pulled her lips inward. "I'm sad I missed it."

Nikki stepped toward Quinn and took her hand. "At least you'll be able to make it to the rehearsal dinner tonight. Do you know what you're wearing yet?"

Quinn glanced down at her outfit—the same one she'd worn to the bachelorette party. "This, I guess. Again. I didn't really pack anything else."

Nikki brightened. "Not that I don't love the outfit, because I absolutely do, but Julie and I adore playing dress up. What do you say? Can we take you shopping?"

Quinn was shaking her head with vigor. "I'm sure you both have so much to do today."

Julie stepped to Quinn's other side. "Actually, after this, we have nothing planned until our nail appointment at two. Honestly."

Nikki pulled out her imploring pout. "And Julie was just saying that she wished we had an excuse to be gone a little longer from the kids."

"I left a bottle for Reid, and my dad and Sandra keep giving the other three loads of sweets." Julie rolled her eyes. "So between them and Kade's over-the-top spoiling, they've turned into demon children."

Quinn looked from one pleading expression to the other, and I already knew there was no hope of her refusing. My sisters were frighteningly adept at the art of persuasion.

Quinn finally gave a timid nod. "Only if you're sure you have time."

Nikki and Julie shared triumphant smiles. "We're positive," Nikki said, and her gaze moved to me. "The two of you didn't have plans, did you?"

"Nope." And I had zero problem tagging along to watch Quinn's fashion show, especially if it was going to be anything like her dress fitting. An image of Quinn in her floor-length red dress sent my heart pounding. "Kade's babysitting the guys, so my day is free as well."

"Perfect," Julie said. "Because you can go help Josh with the kids. They've been begging for you to come see them since you stopped by the other morning."

I opened my mouth to protest but quickly closed it again. Maybe an afternoon out with my sisters was exactly what Quinn needed, especially if they planned to use their persuasive abilities in my favor. Besides, I had been meaning to go see the kids. "Sounds great."

Julie threw me her keys. "You can take my car."

"I NEED A BREAK," I said, pushing off the floor and huffing for dramatic effect as all three kids clung to my back. "You three have gotten too strong."

The three siblings sent each other proud, knowing glances but didn't budge.

"Who wants hot chocolate?" Sandra called, sticking her head around the corner. "I have whipped cream and sprinkles for the top."

The kids relinquished their hold on me and took off running without a backward glance. That woman was a saint. I lay back down on the carpet, turning onto my back and tossing my arms to the side. "I don't know how you do it, Josh."

Josh stood in the doorway, bouncing Reid in his arms. "My wrestling matches rarely go sixteen rounds."

"Touché." I closed my eyes, wondering how likely it was that one of the boys wouldn't do a cannon ball onto my stomach in the next ten seconds. It was a risky choice to stay, but I was too worn out to move. "Chloe sure is getting big."

"And sassy." Josh laughed. "I used to wish I could have seen Julie as a little girl, but now that I face the sheer determination and stubbornness of her nine-year-old self daily, I'm wondering if the universe didn't play a trick on me."

I chuckled. "If she turns out half as great as Julie, you'll be alright."

"That's what I keep telling myself in the hard moments—which are often."

"Is Reid asleep?" I asked, opening my eyes again. "I need a form of protection from getting mauled when those kids come back in."

"Almost." Josh walked over and placed a heavy-lidded Reid on my chest.

I cradled one arm over him and patted at his back until his eyes closed. "Thanks. I could use a good oxytocin dose right now."

Josh sat on the couch. "Things not going well with Quinn?"

I drew in a deep breath, and Reid moved up and down with it. "She got divorced about a year ago. It's not been easy on her. I think a part of her is ready to move on, but the other part of her is stuck in regrets and insecurity."

"Do you know what happened in her first marriage? Why it went south?"

"I don't even think she knows. But she, of course, blames herself."

"Sounds like someone I know."

I rested my hand on Reid's back, but he squirmed, so I started patting again. "Divorce can really shatter a person's self-confidence. That's why I'm trying to be patient and understanding, because I get it. I was just there. I still am, in some ways. Though seeing Eliza the other day was liberating for me."

"You saw Eliza?"

I glanced over at him. "Quinn and I were on the Cliff Walk, and we ran into her."

"And?"

"I realized how lucky I was, standing there with Quinn instead of Eliza. I mean, maybe it took me a minute to get all the way there in my thought process, but I eventually got there." I paused, smiling at the memory of how unexpectedly freeing the whole conversation had been. "She thought Eliza's new husband was her dad."

"She didn't say it to them, did she?" Josh's tone was hopeful.

"Oh yeah." I laughed at the memory, which sent Reid's arms flailing out. "Sorry, buddy."

"I like her even more now."

Dad walked into the room. "Who are you two talking about?"

"Quinn," Josh said without a moment's pause.

Dad took a seat next to Josh on the couch. "She seems like a real special girl."

I nodded. "She is."

"And there might be a lot I'm missing, but I honestly don't remember you looking at Eliza like that."

"Like what?"

Dad smirked. "Like she's the sole giver of all happiness and good things."

I gawked at him. "Where did you even come up with that line? It's ridiculous."

"No." Josh laughed. "It's actually a perfect description for the way you stare at her."

I cringed inwardly. "I guess it makes sense why I'm scaring her away, then."

Dad's gaze narrowed. "What do you mean?"

"I don't know. One minute, it seems like things are going

really well, and the next, she becomes super guarded. I was telling Josh I think it mainly has to do with her divorce. It's only been a year."

"Ah." Dad nodded, like that was all that needed to be said. "At least you're the right guy to be there for her."

It was true—all the pain I'd gone through with Eliza had made me the right guy for Quinn. A guy who could understand her hurt and give her the time and support she needed to heal. And to hopefully love again. The thought made me oddly grateful for the rocky path I'd been made to walk. "I hope so."

The room went silent, and all I could hear were the little huffs of Reid's breathing while he slept.

"Does she have plans for Christmas?" Dad asked, breaking the silence. "She did mention she'd be here for it, right?"

"Yes, but she doesn't have plans."

"You should ask her to join us. She'd be welcome."

"I thought about it, but spending Christmas with the family seems like kind of a big deal. Not for us, necessarily, but I'm worried it might freak her out."

"So the alternative is to let her stay at your house by herself and spend Christmas alone?"

"Point taken." I let out a breath. "But if I invite her, and she comes, I need you two to spread the word that no one should assume anything. Or if you make assumptions, just don't speak them out loud in front of her."

Dad gave a nod. "I think we could manage that."

"Speaking of managing things ..." I glanced at my dad. "Did you, by chance, move all of my clothes into one of my guest room closets?"

His silent smirk told me everything I needed to know.

"Awesome. It's good to know where your allegiance is."

Dad laughed. "It was for the greater good."

"The greater good?" I chuckled, causing Reid to squirm on my chest. "I could have been killed by frying pan. And you would have been an accomplice."

"An accomplice to what?" Julie asked, stepping into the room with Nikki at her side.

"To my untimely death had I been hit over the head with a frying pan." I craned my neck to see if Quinn was with them, but I didn't see her. "And I'm guessing you'd be on the accomplice list, too—not warning me about what Nikki was up to."

Julie tucked her lips between her teeth and sent Nikki a knowing glance. Guilty.

"Such a conspiracy theorist." Nikki stepped over me and lifted Reid off my chest. "Sorry. My turn."

"Where's Quinn?" I asked.

"We dropped her back off at your house," Julie said. "We texted you to see if you were still here, but you never answered."

I sat up, leaning back on my hands. "Sorry. I think I left my phone in the front entryway." Apparently, Quinn was rubbing off on me. "Must be on silent."

Nikki swayed, smiling down at Reid. "You'd better hurry home. With how amazing Quinn looks in her new dress, I'm not sure you'll want to leave her unattended in a house full of handsome men."

She didn't need to tell me twice. I hurried to my feet. "Tell the kids I'll see them soon."

"Oh, and Landon ..." Nikki's voice paused me mid-flight. "Instagram recommended I follow an account that, strangely, looks like it belongs to you, except it's private and it's only following one other account. Do you know anything about that?"

I grimaced. "Maybe."

A slow smile spread across her lips. "You'd better accept my request to follow you, especially if you're planning to post any photos like the selfie Quinn posted of the two of you. It was beyond gorgeous."

And just like that, a weight slid from my shoulders. Nikki knew about the end of my social media boycott and was happy for me. Now, I hoped seeing Quinn would have a similar effect in lightening my load.

TWENTY-TWO

LANDON

Quinn's door was closed when I got home, and I decided, instead of interrupting her, I'd hurry and get ready for the rehearsal dinner myself. That way, if she finished early, we could find a little time to talk. I was eager to see how the afternoon with my sisters had gone and to attempt a non-committal approach at inviting her to spend Christmas with my family. And possibly, if timing and circumstance permitted, see if she would tell me what had been bothering her earlier.

Oh, and most of all, I was dying to see her in her new dress.

The motivation to be there when she came out had me setting a new personal record on getting ready. But she still hadn't emerged when I came out of the bathroom in my slacks and button-down shirt with a gray blazer worn over it. I neared the door and listened, but I couldn't hear anything. I typically prided myself on my patience, but after a few more seconds of just standing there listening, I rapped my knuckles lightly on the wood.

"Just a minute." The mere sound of her voice sent my heart racing, and when I heard her walking toward the door, I was gripping my hands in fists at my sides, trying to get a hold of my nervous energy.

The doorknob turned, and then Quinn was standing there, looking like a deity in a mid-thigh, white dress with a low V-neck and short sleeves. The gold thread that made geometric patterns on the fabric perfectly matched her golden hair that was pulled back in a wavy mass at the nape of her neck. A few tantalizing curls hung around her face.

I swallowed, trying to find the words. Any words. "Wow!" My voice came out breathless, which made sense but sounded ridiculous.

"Is it too much?" she asked, glancing down at herself.

"No. You look ... I don't know if there's a word to describe it." My thoughts were still taking a moment to compute. "Wow! Again. I mean, you're always beautiful, but had I known what those oversized sweaters were hiding ..." I pressed my eyes shut. "That didn't come out right. I just mean ... It's probably best I didn't realize that ..." I huffed. Words were hard things.

"Smooth, Landon." Anthony leaned out of the room behind me like some sort of judgmental, eavesdropping Casanova. "What he means to say, Quinn, is you're absolutely stunning, and he's the luckiest guy alive."

Quinn laughed. "Thanks for the translation."

"Let me know if he has another brain lapse, and I'll do my best to interpret it."

"Very funny," I said, sending a scowl over my shoulder in time to see Anthony disappear into our room again. "But yeah. What he said."

Quinn made a point of looking me over. "You look very handsome yourself."

"Thank you." I hesitated at the threshold of the door. "Can I talk to you for a minute?"

The same guarded expression from earlier flitted over her

features, but she nodded and took a step back, allowing me into the room.

I closed the door behind me. "How was spending the afternoon with Nikki and Julie?"

"Your sisters are too sweet. I really enjoyed myself. We were at Rosecliff long enough to see the florists decorating around the gingerbread houses. All the flowers are white—ranunculus, roses, muscari, and these little white blossoms. I think they called them waxflowers, but I could be wrong. With all the greenery and the pinecones, it was exquisite. And I didn't even see it finished."

"I look forward to seeing it tomorrow."

"I did feel bad that Nikki paid for my dress and shoes." She lifted her hands to show me the tops of them. "And my nails. She said it was her *thank-you* gift for everything I put up with."

"I am a lot to deal with."

Quinn laughed. "I'm pretty sure she mentioned the last-minute gingerbread fiasco, but you're not wrong." She stopped, her teasing smile still in place. "Want to see the shoes?"

If Quinn wanted to show me, then I wanted to see. "Absolutely."

She hurried toward her closet, then turned back toward me, a pair of strappy gold heels in her hands. "Aren't they glorious? I'm not very practiced in heels this tall, but they were surprisingly comfortable when I tried them on, so hopefully, I won't embarrass myself and break an ankle or trip in front of everyone."

She took a seat on the edge of my bed and slipped her foot into the shoe. I watched, transfixed as she buckled it around her petite ankle. How had I never realized how sexy putting on a shoe could be? How many missed opportunities had there been? By the time she was buckling the second, I forced my gaze away, far too aware of how I was staring like she was the *source of all happiness and good things*.

"There," she said, standing up. "What do you think?"

I swallowed and bobbed my head stupidly, unable to convince my eyes to lift from her sun kissed legs. "Yep. Those work."

The smile that danced on her mouth told me she knew exactly what I thought of them. "So, you wanted to talk?"

"Did I? I'm having a hard time remembering at the moment. Here, let me try this." I turned around, taking an exaggerated breath, which made her laugh again. The sound was as sweet as music. "Oh, yeah. Now I remember. I was going to ask—"

A knock sounded at the door.

"What?" I called, trying not to sound irritated.

"Landon, are you in there?"

Obviously. I walked to the door and opened it to find Brian standing there. "What's up?"

His gaze moved to Quinn, his eyes widened, and a small smile lit his face. "Sorry to interrupt, but I need an iron."

"It's in the top-right cabinet in the laundry room. And the ironing board is in the tall cabinet to the left of the washing machine."

He nodded and took a step back, but when I went to shut the door, he put out a hand to stop it. "Where's the laundry room?"

I took a steadying breath, realizing I'd better help him or he might interrupt us again when he couldn't find it. "You know what, I'll show you." I glanced back at Quinn. "I'll be right back."

She smiled and nodded.

"Great dress, by the way," Brian said, his gawking eyes lingering on her for too long. "It looks *really* good on you."

"Okay, that's enough." I grabbed his shoulder and turned him around to the sound of both him and Quinn laughing.

A few minutes later, I stepped back into the room. Quinn sat on the bed, flipping through social media, her legs crossed at the ankles. Again, I had to force my eyes from them.

"Sorry about that."

Quinn set her phone face-down next to her. She took a quick breath in, as though bracing herself for the conversation. "So, you were saying?"

I moved to the bed and took a seat next to her, trying to keep my thoughts focused on what I was going to ask her. Not her legs. Not the delicious scent she was emanating. Not the soft-pink color of her lips. And certainly not that we were sitting on my bed. The bed she'd been sleeping in for the past few weeks that suddenly seemed much too inviting a place to discuss anything. I stood back up. "Sorry. I'm just going to stand if that's okay."

She nodded.

"What I wanted to ask you was—"

Another knock.

"Are you kidding me?" I moved toward the door and flung it open.

Vince's expression held immediate remorse. "I'm sorry. I didn't realize you were back yet. I was just going to ask Quinn if she could tie my tie. I can't ever remember how to do these things, and she'd said earlier she'd help me." He paused, his eyes taking in my expression. "But you know what? I'll come back in a few minutes—"

"I can help you." Quinn came to stand in front of him, pulling up his collar in a way that made me wish I hadn't known how to tie my own tie.

While she pulled the tie to the appropriate length, his gaze slid to me. "Sorry," he mouthed.

I nodded my acceptance of his apology, though I was ready to push him out the door the moment she tightened the knot around his neck.

"There you are," Quinn said, smoothing out his collar. "You look very handsome."

"Thanks." His gaze dropped to her dress, and I nearly groaned out loud. "You look incredible."

Quinn's cheeks pinked. "Thanks, Vince."

"We good here?" I asked, glancing between the two of them.

Vince gave a quick shake of his head, like he was coming out of a trance. "Yep. I'll leave you two to it."

I shut the door and locked it this time, as though that would prevent more interruptions.

Quinn's eyes were full of amusement when her gaze met mine. "Continue."

"I was wondering if you wanted to join my family for Christmas," I blurted, wanting to have it out before we could get interrupted again.

Her whole countenance fell with her smile.

"No pressure or anything. I just don't want you to be alone on Christmas. And my family is super relaxed, so it wouldn't mean anything to them either." Okay, I was way underselling my intentions. "Not that it wouldn't mean anything to me, but it doesn't have to ..."

Her gaze locked on mine. "My parents bought me a return ticket to San Diego for the morning of the 23rd."

A knot formed at the base of my chest, making it difficult to breathe. Why hadn't she told me? Had she asked them to buy it? I knew she was going to have to go home after Christmas, but I'd thought we'd have a few more days together. "And that's what you want to do?" I asked, realizing that her answer had the potential to break me.

"No, but I can't help but wonder if it's best."

I nearly choked on my next question. "Why would that be what's best?" Had she seen Eliza's post? What else would cause her to doubt my intentions? But before I could explain, a light rap on the door about drove me to madness. "Give us a minute, please," I called.

"Yeah, so ..."—Tyler spoke through the door—"a few of us were just getting ready to leave, and some guy pulled in the drive asking for Quinn. No rush, but he's waiting downstairs."

I met her confused gaze. "Do you know who that could be?"

She shook her head.

Well, there was obviously no point in trying to have this conversation until the house was empty and I could get a few moments alone with Quinn. We might be a little late to the dinner, but it was better than being interrupted every other minute. "Guess we should probably go figure that out first."

"Probably."

I opened the door, and Tyler gave an apologetic look before his gaze settled on Quinn. "No wonder random guys are showing up on the doorstep for you. You look—"

"Amazing, incredible, wonderful, stunning, all the things." I put my hand on her back, if only as an excuse to touch her, and gently guided her forward. "She is already well aware."

"Yikes. Someone's a little possessive of his woman." Tyler gave an amused look and Quinn shot him one back before she started down the stairs in front of us at a careful pace, her hand on the railing.

"There's a lot more to Quinn than her super-attractive body and heart-stopping face, but apparently, I'm the only one who can remember that when she looks this insanely good."

To my relief, Quinn laughed and glanced over her shoulder when she'd stepped down the last stair. "Or maybe you should share with Tyler the *turn-away-from-me* strategy. That seemed to help you think more clearly a minute ago."

Tyler nudged his shoulder into me, and I chuckled. "Okay. I may have had to utilize other measures to turn my thinking brain back on once or twice." I took another step and bumped into Quinn, who had come to a dead stop in front of us. Her gaze was locked on the guy at the door, appraising her with far too much pleasure. A guy I recognized from a few of her older posts.

What was Cody doing here?

TWENTY-THREE

QUINN

"What are you doing here, Cody?" I heard the quiver in my voice.

His gaze flicked to Landon and then Tyler before returning to me. "I need to talk to you."

"You came all the way to Rhode Island to talk to me?"

He shrugged, his hands in his pockets. "You said you wanted our conversation to be in person, and I didn't want to wait any longer."

I stared at him, trying to make sense of the fact that he was here at Landon's house. "How did you even know where to find me?"

He shifted his weight, obviously uncomfortable with either his answer or Landon and Tyler's presence. "The location tracker app I installed when you took that road trip to visit colleges with Xena."

I had a vague recollection of him doing that. "Why didn't you just call and let me know you were here?"

One side of his mouth quirked into that endearing side smile that used to turn me to mush. "Would you have taken my call?"

I wrapped my arms around myself, feeling completely out of sorts. "Probably not."

"Which is why I had to come." His gaze darted to Landon and Tyler behind me again. "Can we go somewhere to talk? Please?"

A stampede of footsteps from the third-floor stairs echoed through the open space, and Anthony, Vince, and another guy—who wasn't Brian but possibly Chad—came to a halt at the bottom of the stairs. Their gazes shifted over the scene in front of them: Landon and Tyler with their arms crossed, the stranger at the door, and me, barely holding myself together.

"Who's that?" Vince asked, glancing at Landon.

"This is Cody," I said, not wanting this to become something more than it needed to be. "My ex-husband."

"What's he doing here?" Anthony asked, a hint of hostility in his voice.

"He just came to talk with Quinn," Landon said, dispersing the tension with his calm demeanor. His gaze settled on me. "What do you want to do?"

I glanced at Cody, then around the room at our onlookers, feeling entirely uncertain. I wanted to go to the rehearsal dinner. I felt like I owed that to Nikki after everything she'd done. And even though things were complicated between me and Landon at the moment, I didn't want to miss out on my second-to-last night with him. But I needed to talk to Cody. He was here, and if I refused to talk to him now, I wasn't sure I'd be given another chance. "I need to talk to him."

Landon rubbed a hand over his beard and breathed out a slow, intentional breath. "Yeah. You should."

I looked back at Cody, who wore a victorious smile that made me want to change my mind, but I was doing it for myself, not for Cody. I needed answers. "Let me grab my phone. I'll be right back."

The guys parted for me as I made my way through them.

When I got to my room, I glanced around, searching for my phone. "Siri." I listened for the familiar chime but didn't hear it. "Siri."

A floorboard creaked behind me, and I spun around, my hand clasping my chest.

"It's just me." Landon put his hands up, reminding me of the first night we met.

"I'm sorry. I didn't hear you follow me up."

"Your phone's on the bed," he said, pointing toward it.

Sure enough, there it was, laying face-down on the throw draped over the end of the bed. "Thanks." I scooped it up. "Tell Nikki I'm sorry, and I'll hurry over to the dinner as soon as I'm done."

"Don't worry about the dinner. Take your time, and get the answers you need."

I reached out for his hand. "Thanks for understanding."

His hand clasped over mine, his thumb brushing across my skin, keeping me spellbound. "Before you go, I need to explain about the video Eliza posted before she left me. As convincing as she was ... it's not true. I always tried to support her. I didn't withhold anything that I had an ability to give her, which wasn't much, or at least not as much as she wanted, but I tried. I really did. I know I wasn't perfect, but I gave that relationship everything I had. And yes, I wanted to have kids, but I didn't overpressure her. At least, I don't think I did. I just—"

I squeezed his hand. "Landon, I didn't see her video. I don't need to. I know what kind of a man you are. You are the best of everything."

"But if you didn't ..." He searched my eyes. "Why would you think it's best if you go home?"

"I'm a mess, Landon. It's not fair to make you suffer while I figure out how to function again." Not even again, actually. That was half the problem. Cody leaving me had brought on a whole new battle of insecurities, but if I was being honest, I'd never really had a firm grasp of this whole *life* thing. I'd just been more naïve about my weaknesses in the past.

He took a step closer and let his hands come to my arms. "I told you there's no rush. And I meant it." The way his fingers moved across my skin nearly had me forgetting all of my worries. It nearly made me forget that Cody was waiting downstairs. "But you deserve someone who will adore you exactly as you are. Every quirk and every crazy, beautiful piece of you." His hands lowered to his sides, leaving a void of warmth in their absence. "I'm not going to pretend that I don't really want that man to be me. But if it's Cody—"

Without another thought, I placed a hand on the back of Landon's neck, pulling him toward me. My lips met his with tenderness and adoration equal to what he'd shown me. Though our kiss was brief, it was perfectly wonderful. I locked my gaze with his. "I'm going for answers, Landon. That's all."

He gave an uncertain smile. "I'll wait to hear from you, then."

CODY OPENED the car door for me, and I slid into his sleek rental. Despite the car being different, the rest felt entirely familiar —and yet wrong.

"By the way"—he started the ignition, his gaze sliding over my body—"you look absolutely divine. I nearly forgot how insanely gorgeous you are."

I looked out the window, gripping my coat in my lap and shooting a last glance at Landon's house before we drove away. "Where should we go to talk?"

He shrugged. "Do you have a place in mind?"

He wouldn't talk if he felt like people could overhear us, and my emotional stability seemed a little shaky at the moment. The last thing I wanted to do was have a breakdown in front of a bunch of strangers. "Not really. Just somewhere private."

The way he smiled at my comment made it seem like I'd implied something I hadn't. "We could always head back to my hotel room—if you wanted."

"That's fine."

"Do you mind if we grab a bite to eat first?" He pressed the digitized screen above the middle console, scrolling until he found the maps. "My treat."

My stomach rumbled at the thought of food, but I didn't want to postpone our talk. I wanted to get to the rehearsal dinner. Not that I'd mention that to Cody. "I'm good, but thanks."

"Well, I'm starving. And I hear Newport has amazing lobster rolls. It seems a shame to come all the way here and not taste one."

Something fast would be okay. Landon and I had been in and out with our food in twenty minutes last week. "Go ahead."

"Would you mind looking up a place and putting it into the map?"

I pulled out my phone and started searching when a low-battery warning flashed on my screen. I glanced around the middle console. "Do you have a charger in here?"

"No. I do at the hotel, though."

Scrolling through the restaurants listed, I tried to remember which one Landon had taken me to, but I hadn't really been paying attention. Go figure. I clicked on one with a massive collection of good ratings and leaned to enter the address into the car's system.

Cody glanced over at me. "So who were all those guys?"

"Kade Carrigan's friends, here for the wedding."

"And why were they at the house with you? That's where you're staying, right?"

I didn't feel like I owed Cody an explanation, but I also didn't want him to shut down and refuse to talk to me. He likely thought there'd be a reconciliation, or he wouldn't have flown across the country to chat, and a part of me didn't want him to find out the truth yet. Had I always tiptoed around him, or was I just nervous? "The house belongs to Nikki's brother. I've been staying there the last few weeks. The guys just arrived a few days ago." Except Landon, but I didn't say that.

"You'd think with all the money she and her fiancé have, she'd spring for a hotel room for you when the guys came into town. It seems like the decent thing to do."

I bit my tongue, refusing to mention it had been my choice. "How's your family?"

His gaze flicked to me. "Good. Courtney graduated this last June and started at UCLA. And my mom still talks about you all the time."

"I miss her. I miss them all." His family had been a huge part of my life for years, and to suddenly have them gone from it was devastating. I'd lost a lot more than just Cody when he left.

"They think I really screwed up, walking out on you like I did." He paused, his thumbs tapping against the steering wheel. "I think they were right."

I met his gaze. "They were."

BY THE TIME Cody and I got to the hotel, the rehearsal dinner had been going for over an hour and a half. It wasn't even Cody's fault I was so late. I'd made the mistake of putting in an address to a lobster shack that was seasonal, and we didn't realize until we'd parked and walked a good distance—which was made slower by my being in heels—to a boarded-up building next to the water. The next place was open, but the line was atrocious, and it took nearly forty minutes to order and get our food. By the time we got back to the hotel, waves of panic were rushing through me.

"Are you sure you don't want me to order you something?"

Cody asked, closing the doors behind us. "There's a menu for room service on the dresser."

"I'm good. Really."

"So ..." He smiled, reaching out for my hand. "I've missed you, Quinn. I've missed this—us just being together."

I pulled my hand free. "You can't just show up and assume you can fix what happened between us. You left me. Without even an explanation."

"And I'm sorry. If I could go back and do it differently, I would. I swear to you."

I felt nothing at his declaration. "Why did you leave?"

"Because I was an idiot."

"Don't tell me what you think I want to hear. Tell me the truth."

"The truth?" He released a quick breath. "The truth is, I really don't even know."

I stared at him. "What do you mean? There has to be a reason. Something I did that would make you break your vows to me— your promises."

He shook his head and shrugged.

"Was it that I'm disorganized ... or paranoid ... or not driven enough?" I was reeling, grasping for any reason he might have left, but he shook his head. There had to have been something. I released a shaky exhale, nervous to ask my next question. "Was it our intimate relationship?"

His hands came to my arms, his fingers tracing patterns over my skin, but all I felt was a distant memory of how his touch had once affected me. It didn't anymore. "It definitely wasn't that."

His confirmation loosened my tightly knotted chest, and I took a step back, breaking his contact with my arms. "Then what, Cody? Someone doesn't walk out on a person they love for no reason. There had to be something."

He shrugged. "Marriage wasn't what I thought it would be."

My body trembled from my heightened emotions. "You've said that. But what do you mean?"

By the look on his face, I could tell this wasn't turning out for him like he'd wanted. It wasn't for me either. "I don't know what you want me to say. I wasn't ready for marriage, but everyone was pressuring us. And I get it. It was the natural step after five years of dating, but I didn't understand what I was committing to when I made all those promises. But I understand now, and I intend to keep my word to you."

I gawked at him. "You already broke your word. Please tell me you see that?" His expression was guarded, but I wasn't sure the answers I'd come for were there regardless. "You know what? I've got to go. I have somewhere I need to be."

He flung a hand toward the door. "You're just going to walk out of here before we can fix things?"

I stilled. "Did you really just say that? That *I'm* going to walk out? Like the fault of this somehow lies with me when I've been waiting for almost a year for you to come *fix things*?" I threw up my hands. "It's too late now. You shattered my heart, and you weren't the one to put it back together again."

"So this is about that guy in your post—the one who was there today?"

"It's why you came, isn't it? That photo I posted? It was okay for you to go date whomever you wanted and fill your whole Instagram feed with pictures of other women, but you couldn't stand the thought of me being with anyone else."

"Yes, I admit, that's why I came. Seeing you with him hurt in a way I wasn't prepared for. But being here with you has reminded me of how perfect we are for each other. I want to make this work, Quinn. I care about you more than you know."

Is this what care looked like? Because I suddenly realized it looked like food deliveries and buying a poor SoCal girl a real winter coat and boots so she wouldn't freeze. And making a video. And losing sleep to keep a nervous wreck of a woman company in a winter storm. And appreciating talents and wanting to help someone succeed in something they loved.

My gaze locked with his. "You never once asked me about the

gingerbread houses I built for Nikki. You didn't ask me about my social media account or any of the projects I'd been working on. Not once in the last two hours did you care enough to ask about anything in my life." Which, sadly, didn't surprise me as much as it should have.

"I had other things on my mind." Cody's hands lifted at his sides. "But fine. How'd it go? Your gingerbread houses?"

The laugh that escaped me sounded empty, exhausted. "You could never stand that my attention was on anything but you. You didn't want me to have something of my own. You wanted to keep me for yourself."

He gaped at me like I'd slapped him across the face. "That's not true."

"It is." My gaze turned distant, and I thought about Landon, about all the ways he'd shown me he cared in the last few weeks. "The people we love are supposed to support us, help us grow and thrive, not try to hold us back." I grabbed my phone and coat off the dresser. "I've got to go."

"Wait. I flew across the country to see you ... for this?"

"I never asked you to come."

Cody pushed a hand through his hair in frustration. "Well, wish this *new guy* luck for me. He'll need it."

I hesitated on the threshold of the open door. He knew where to place his final blow, but the sting was momentary. He'd lost, and he knew it. He wanted to hurt me, like I'd hurt him. And I understood that petty desire more than he knew. I glanced over my shoulder. "Goodbye, Cody."

TWENTY-FOUR

QUINN

THE DOOR CLICKED SHUT BEHIND ME, AND I COULDN'T help but think how symbolic it was, closing this chapter of my life. I could finally put Cody firmly in the past, and though my whole body was shaking from the encounter, I felt like I was floating as I made my way down to the lobby. Or maybe that was my anxiety.

I tapped Landon's contact number and waited. The phone rang several times before going to his voicemail. My heart sank a little, disappointed he wasn't eagerly waiting for my call like I'd assumed. But the dinner was probably loud, and he'd return my call when he realized he'd missed it. My phone beeped a low-battery warning—less than ten percent. "Shoot." Why hadn't I remembered to charge it when I got to Cody's room? Not that I'd been in there long, but anything would have helped. I headed toward the reception desk. "Excuse me?"

A woman looked up from her monitor. "Can I help you?"

"By chance, do you have a charger for an iPhone?"

She shook her head. "I'm sorry. We don't."

"That's okay. Thanks."

I glanced around the empty lobby, hoping that someone would emerge soon so I could beg a charge off of them. All I needed to do was muster the confidence of a used-car salesman and keep my mind from creating some vivid backstory for the targeted individual that would prevent me from actually speaking with them. That didn't sound entirely impossible.

Hoping the last missed call had been a fluke, I dialed Landon again. When it went to voicemail a second time, I tried not to let it get me down. I was still on a high from finally having closure, from knowing that Landon wanted to give a relationship a try, and that I did, too. I needed to talk to someone—at least, until I heard back from Landon.

The phone rang, and Ashlee picked up. "Hey! How was the rehearsal dinner?"

"I didn't go." Before she could question me, I blazed forward. "Cody showed up at Landon's right before we left. I've spent the last two hours with him—"

"With Cody?" Worry saturated Ashlee's voice.

"Yes, but it's over between us. For good."

Ashlee released a sigh of relief. "You got your answers, then?"

The receptionist glanced up from her monitor, and I realized she probably didn't want me chatting next to the front desk. I gave her an apologetic smile and wandered into the lobby, taking a seat on a chair facing the windows by the entrance. "Not directly, but I got closure. I think Cody doesn't know how to love someone—not yet, anyway. And I don't want to be the one he hurts while he learns—*if* he learns."

A slow, steady clapping came through the speaker. "Truer words have never been spoken. Cody wasn't a bad guy. He was actually great in a lot of ways. But he never loved you right, Quinn. Not like you deserved."

I smiled. "All this time, I thought it was me. That it was something I did that had made him leave."

"Wow. You said that like it was new information and not like I've spent the last year trying to convince you of that very fact. Of course, it wasn't you! Cody was with you for five years. That's plenty of time for him to have known what he was getting himself into."

My smile faltered. I knew exactly what she'd meant—Ashlee had never been anything but supportive—and yet the truth behind her comment made me pause, sending Cody's parting message for Landon pinging around my brain like some kind of volatile pinball machine. *Wish this new guy luck. He'll need it.* A seedling of doubt settled into my tightening chest. Had my confidence that I'd not been the problem been incorrect? Could Cody not tell me a specific reason he'd left because there wasn't just one thing? Or a few? But several?

"Are you still there?" Ashlee's voice pulled me from my thoughts.

"Sorry. Did you say something?"

"I asked if you decided whether you're going to stay for Christmas."

I tried to muster my confidence from a few minutes ago. "Yeah. I think so."

"You've had one heck of a night. First, closure with Cody, and now taking charge of your own life. I'm proud of you, Quinn. That's huge."

That irritating voice of self-doubt grasped the opportunity presented. For the second time, Ashlee's intended reassurance shifted into something that left me feeling empty and hollow. Had I been a capable, productive person, she'd never need to tell me how proud of me she was for taking charge of my life. For finally finding some closure in a relationship that had ended almost twelve months ago.

Or maybe I was just exhausted. I hadn't slept well in days, and I'd hardly slept at all last night. I was tired and hungry and had just gone through an emotional experience. An experience I'd waited a year for. Self-doubt was taking advantage of my temporary lack of judgment.

"Thanks," I said, trying to keep my tone upbeat to prevent an interrogation. She knew me too well, and though I wouldn't mind her talking me out of my current downward loop, I didn't have the battery life for it. As if the universe agreed, the phone flashed another warning. Less than five percent battery. "Hey, Ash. I've got to get off. My phone battery's almost dead, and I want to make sure I can get ahold of Landon."

"Yeah. Go. But call me later! And I want a full update on all the kissing that is about to go down. Every. Single. Detail."

Even in low moments, Ashlee could always make me smile. "I'll take notes."

"I'd appreciate that ... from memory, though. Don't pull out a notebook and pen mid-kiss or anything."

My laugh was real, if a bit flat. "Thanks for the clarification. Talk to you soon."

I dropped the phone to my side, my gaze distant as I cycled through the unsettling thoughts still circling my mind, trying to expel them. They could wait until tomorrow when I was thinking more clearly and could decipher which ones were worth considering. Except, they wouldn't wait. Ashlee had mentioned that five years of dating Cody was adequate time for him to know what he was getting himself into. Or had it been? But Cody would have told me if there'd been something about me that had caused him to leave. Maybe not at first, but once he knew I didn't have any intention for us to get back together. When he'd thrown out the generically vindictive comment, he could have—*would have*—added his other reasons if there'd been any. Wouldn't he?

The phone rang in my hand, and I quickly lifted it to my ear. Landon's reassuring voice was exactly what I needed. "Hey!"

"Hey, sweetie." Shocked to hear my mom's voice, I looked at the name on the phone, as though to verify it really was her. "I was just calling to see how your gingerbread houses turned out. Did you get them to the venue without any issues?"

"I did."

"And Nikki paid you for all your work?"

"Yep. She sent it over on Venmo this afternoon."

"Well, congratulations. I still can't believe she paid you that much for gingerbread houses."

It was a back-handed compliment, but I'd take it. "Thanks."

"And I hope you still have a little more gingerbread building in you. Margaret wants you to make some for us to decorate when you get here."

The time had come. I pulled back my shoulders and took a slow, deep breath, mustering every ounce of confidence I had. "About that ..." My throat tightened, and my voice faltered.

"What about it, Quinn?" Accusation and suspicion touched every syllable of Mom's question.

"I'm going to ..." What was I doing? She would think I was crazy for wanting to stay for Christmas. Crazier than she already thought I was. And maybe there was something to it. I'd only known Landon a few weeks, and just because I wanted to spend Christmas in Newport didn't mean it was the right choice. Like staying at Landon's house instead of going to a hotel like I should have. And look where that had gotten me—a few extra hours of work on Rosecliff, no sleep, and a heap of anxiety. "Am I difficult to live with?" The question shot out of me before I could stop it.

Mom hesitated. "What does that have to do with you making gingerbread houses?"

"I just need to know." Ashlee might tell me what I wanted to hear, and possibly even Cody, but my mom would tell me the truth. She hated lying, and she had an uncanny ability to hint at all the ways I could improve. "Am I difficult to live with?" I repeated.

"Well ... it might take some getting used to for most people." She cleared her throat. "But that's true for everyone ... to some degree."

"But for me, to a higher degree?"

"Where's this coming from? You aren't thinking of moving in with Landon, are you?"

"No. I just ..." I didn't even know. I felt suddenly restless, and I stood, starting toward the large Christmas tree on display in front of one of the lobby windows. "Is it only living with me that's hard, or are there other things about me, too? Reasons that possibly contributed to Cody leaving? That might make someone else leave me in the future?"

Mom's side of the line was quiet, and I glanced at the screen to make sure my phone hadn't died. "Mom?"

"I don't know why Cody left, sweetie. But if this line of questioning has to do with Landon, like I suspect, I'd urge caution. This past year has been a rough one for you, and you aren't ready to jump into another relationship." She paused, blowing out a small breath. "You need to take some time to figure some things out—like who you want to be and what you want to do with your life—before you complicate it by adding another person to the equation. Not that you couldn't stay in contact with Landon. It's just ... it's probably better for you ... and for him ... if things don't get serious between you."

And for him. Especially for him.

Everything he adored about me came with another side to the coin. A side that apparently wasn't easy to live with. Or be with. Cody had known me for years and still wasn't prepared for what it would be like.

Tears brimmed in my eyes, and I reached out to touch a large glass bulb hanging on the tree. It reflected a warped image of who I was. Was that what I'd given Landon? A warped idea of what it would be like to be with me? I'd tried to be honest, but until he saw it all firsthand, he wouldn't know. And when he did, it would probably leave him running like Cody or suffering in silence like he'd done with Eliza.

My phone issued another warning. Three percent battery. "Hey, Mom, my phone is about to die. Tomorrow will be a busy day, but I'll call you from the airport Saturday morning."

"We can't wait to see you. Fly safe."

"Will do. Love you, Mom." I ended the call.

It was official: I'd completely deflated. My momentary hope of spending Christmas with Landon was gone. But worse, my hope of a future with him was fading again. But maybe it was for the best. Landon deserved someone who had her life together. That might eventually be me, but it wasn't right now. And it probably wouldn't be anytime soon.

A bright set of headlights pulled into the drop-off area outside, momentarily blinding me. When I caught sight of the truck they belonged to, my heart stopped.

Did Landon have a tracker on my phone, too? How on earth would he know I was here? Before I could think what to do, the passenger-side door opened, and a pair of long legs descended from the front seat. For a minute, I'd thought I was mistaken about it being Landon's truck until the woman shut the door, revealing her gorgeous red hair and perfectly symmetrical, model-worthy face. Why was Rachel with Landon? Is that why he hadn't answered my call?

It was dark outside, and the brightness of the lobby lights suddenly made me feel like I was standing in a glowing fishbowl, waiting to be observed. I ducked behind the Christmas tree. But curiosity pressed too hard, and I peeked around the edge of it like a joke of a spy—or a creeper, depending on how you looked at it. Landon had rolled down the window, and Rachel leaned against the truck, her arms resting on the door, the two of them talking.

He was probably just giving her a ride home after the rehearsal dinner. He was kind like that, and I knew he wouldn't have said those things to me earlier if he hadn't meant them—if he had any feelings for Rachel. But Cody had said similar things to me, and that obviously hadn't turned out well.

Besides, Nikki's intuition was never off—that was what Tyler had said. What if Landon hadn't realized his mistake in prematurely falling for me? What if he was only now realizing that Rachel was exactly his type—not only gorgeous and kind, but that she was driven and successful and loved traveling, just like he did? I wouldn't blame him for having a change of heart. In fact, he probably should. She was absolutely perfect for him. I gripped an arm over my stomach, suddenly feeling like I might be sick. Or maybe that was the hunger and exhaustion.

Rachel stepped away from the truck, shooting Landon one last look over her shoulder and sending a dainty wave in his direction. The automatic doors to the lobby opened. I pressed myself more firmly against the tree, shimmying toward the window but not close enough to be seen by Landon who was still parked in the front. Was he watching Rachel? I couldn't look. The click of Rachel's heels sounded on the tile floor. For a brief moment, I saw her shiny, thick hair swaying behind her before she exited the lobby.

I stood there, unable to move, the pine needles pressed to my cheek. I needed to figure out my next course of action, and it couldn't include Landon seeing me on my rollercoaster of self-doubt. There was always the option of going back to Landon's and faking sick, insisting he couldn't see me to prevent him from getting sick, but I was an awful liar. Besides, Landon would probably show up at my door with half a pharmacy and yummy food, which wouldn't help my current resolve at all. But where else could I go?

My gaze drifted to the woman behind the front desk, who thankfully hadn't noticed me assaulting her hotel's tree while I waited for Landon to leave. Or, if she had, she'd decided to pretend she hadn't. Either way, now that I'd been paid for the centerpieces, I could get a hotel room for the night and ... what? Stay here until I left Saturday? I couldn't miss Nikki's wedding—not after everything she'd done for me. And I was supposed to wear Sophia's dress. But how could I go? There was no way I could be Landon's date now. No way I could see him in person and still maintain my resolve. If I went, he'd feel an obligation to me that would prevent him from spending time with Rachel. I'd probably ruined everything for him. Everything Nikki had hoped for. She'd understand why I had to miss the wedding when I informed her of my reason. She might even be grateful.

Or maybe I should wait until morning to decide. I could feel myself spiraling, which always led to premature decisions that weren't my finest.

My phone rang, and Landon's name lit the screen.

I dismissed it, refusing to peek around the corner of the tree and risk him seeing me.

It rang again.

I didn't have the willpower to hear him say we could take things as slow as we wanted. I didn't want to take things slow with him. I wanted to keep following the same rapid trajectory we'd been moving along. And that was exactly the problem. What I wanted to do and what I needed to do were completely contradictory. The moment I heard his voice, I'd blurt out all my feelings and insecurities. I'd forget all reason and rationality. And I'd forget that, one day, he might leave. Or worse, he'd want to leave and he wouldn't.

A text message it would be. I'd just chalk up my immature response to another example of why I wasn't ready for a relationship.

Quinn: Hey. My phone is about to die, but I just called to let you know I'll be staying at a hotel tonight. Nothing to do with Cody. I just think it might be better if I do.

I shoved my phone in the pocket of my coat, trying to ignore the guilt that pricked me. The phone rang again.

I pulled it out enough to see his name lighting the screen. My thumb hovered over the *dismiss* button, but I couldn't get myself to press it. Landon deserved better than a cryptic text. "Hey."

"Hey. I'm sorry I missed your calls. My phone was somehow set to silent. Is everything okay?"

There it was again—him asking me if I was okay. And like always, I wasn't. The evidence was plentiful for why I shouldn't be in a relationship right now. But I couldn't say that. I simply needed to say I was fine and inform him that I couldn't go as his date to the wedding. "Actually, I'm not okay." Oh, great. I knew it. I knew I couldn't resist his soothing voice and caring tone. I should have dismissed his call again.

"Do you want to talk about it?"

I hesitated, rubbing a hand over my cheek. "I've told you from the beginning, I'm not ready for a relationship."

"And we talked about that. We don't have to rush—"

"I know. But I don't know when I'll be ready. It'll probably be years before I'm functioning like a normal person again ...and even then ... Landon, I really am a mess. Cody dated me for five years and wasn't prepared for what a life with me would be like."

"Is that what he said?"

"No. He didn't need to. But when I was leaving, he told me to wish you luck because you'd need it."

Landon cursed under his breath. "He was mad you wouldn't take him back, Quinn. If what he said was true, he wouldn't have flown across the country to try and fix things between you."

I hadn't thought about that. Except, jealousy did strange things to people. And that was really why he'd come—because of that darn picture I'd posted. The evidence against me was getting so high it was going to topple over and crush me beneath it. Besides, if it had just been Cody that implied how hard I was to be with, it might have changed something. But it hadn't been. Both Ashlee and my mom had unknowingly hinted at the same conclusion. "Maybe. But maybe not. I feel like, until I figure a few things out, we shouldn't date ... each other, I mean." My hand settled over the ache in my chest. "You're welcome to date whomever else you want." *Aka, the gorgeous redhead that just got out of your truck.*

"I don't want to date anyone else."

My heart floundered stupidly. More proof why I shouldn't

have taken Landon's call. Exactly why I couldn't see him in person. He somehow made everything seem right in this crazy world. He made me feel like I was right in *his* world. But I wasn't. And he'd realize that soon enough. "I'm sorry. I just can't ... not now." I risked a glance out the window. The cab of his truck was dark, but I could see the glow of the phone against his lowered head. "Maybe you could find someone else to take to the wedding." I pulled in a long, slow breath. *I wasn't doing this for me. I was doing this for Landon.*

"Are you not coming to the wedding?"

"I think it'd be best if I didn't."

The line went intensely quiet, and I waited, willing myself to not confess everything I was feeling in the unnerving silence.

"I'm sorry, Landon. I really am."

He still didn't answer.

"Landon?"

I glanced at my screen to find it had gone black. Oh, shoot. I clicked the power button, but nothing happened. The movement of headlights drew my attention upward, and before I fully processed the situation, it was Landon's taillights that filled my vision. A sense of dread pulsed through me when the red glow disappeared into the darkness. "It's okay," I whispered to myself. *I can do this.*

I returned to the receptionist's desk, emotion swelling in my chest. "Do you have any rooms available?"

"How many nights?"

"Just one."

Her fingers raced across her keyboard. "We do have one available."

"I'll take it."

"Wonderful. That will be two hundred and eighty-six dollars."

My mouth parted. Since when did hotel rooms cost so much? "Is that your cheapest room?" I asked, trying to keep my tone level.

Her gaze lifted to mine. "It's our only room."

I handed her my card, holding my breath while she ran it. I'd nearly maxed out my credit card, but I had some wiggle room. Fingers crossed it was two hundred and eighty-six dollars of it.

She ran the card a second time, her brow creased, and then she handed it back. "I'm sorry. The card was declined. Do you have another form of payment?"

I shoved the credit card back into my phone case. "Do you take Venmo?"

She shook her head. Not that I had a way to access it with my phone battery dead. "I just got paid today, so if I can find a charger ... then I'll transfer the money into my bank account and pay off my credit card bill." I spoke my plan as much to myself as to her.

The skin on her neck tightened with her apologetic grimace. "With processing times, I don't think that will work. At least not for tonight."

My skin itched with frustration, and I rubbed a hand over my cheek, but the itch only spread to my neck. "Could I possibly pay for it tomorrow?"

"Unfortunately, we need payment in full at the time of arrival."

Looks like I'd be giving Mom more proof of how not ready I was for a serious relationship. Or really just life in general. "Could I call my parents and have them book the room?"

She gave a sharp nod. "That would work."

I glanced down at the hotel phone next to her and pointed at it. "My phone's dead. Could I possibly use yours?"

Her smile was tight, but she handed me the phone. "What's the number?"

Oh no! I closed my eyes, trying to conjure up some memory of what their new numbers were. 858-39 ... Nope. *Come on. Think.* My brain was like a tire stuck in the snow, spinning endlessly with no progress forward. Nothing came. "I actually don't remember.

They switched providers a few months ago and had to change numbers."

She reached a hand out, and I placed the receiver back in it.

And there it was. Hard proof that Landon was better off without me. What functioning adult couldn't even get herself a hotel room for the night? Tears of frustration and disappointment welled in my eyes. "You really don't have a charger I could borrow?"

Pity lined the woman's face. "I didn't bring mine to work today, or I'd let you use it."

I gave a slow nod and took a step away from the desk. In retrospect, I should have told Landon where I was or gone out to talk to him in person. But I hadn't. And I had no way of getting in touch with him. If only I'd remembered to charge my phone while I was in Cody's room.

Cody.

I could always ask to use his charger. But I'd walked out of his room with my head held high. To go back now and beg for his help ... No. I'd prefer to try my luck at asking complete strangers to borrow their charger or sleep in the hotel lobby if I had to. I assessed the still empty room, and a tear slid down my cheek.

Then another. And another.

"Quinn?" The gentle female voice approached from the hallway, and I glanced over to see Rachel walking toward me, her face full of concern.

Of course it would be Rachel.

"What's the matter?" she asked, coming to stand next to me. "Is everything alright?"

"My phone died ... and I was going to ..." I sniffed. "... get a hotel room. But my credit card ..."

She wrapped her arm around my shoulder. "I have an extra bed in my room. You're welcome to come stay with me."

I wiped a hand over my tear-streaked face, mascara remnants marking up my hands. "I don't want to inconvenie—"

"It's not an inconvenience. I'm happy to have you."

The universe had some sort of twisted humor, but going with Rachel seemed a better option than eating a big slice of humble pie to go the Cody route. "Are you sure?"

"I'm positive." She turned to the woman at the reception counter. "I just need a new key. This one's on the fritz."

"Sorry about that. What's your room number?"

"Two zero three."

The woman typed the numbers into a small machine and handed Rachel a new hotel key. She looked at me. "I hope you find a charger."

"Thanks." I attempted a smile and followed Rachel from the lobby.

"What type of charger do you need?"

"An iPhone."

"Darn. I have an Android."

I wasn't at all surprised by my luck.

As we started up to the room, Rachel glanced at me out of the corner of her eye. "Is everything else okay?"

I nodded, the tears still rolling down my cheeks, causing my skin to sting.

"Anything you want to talk about?"

I owed her some sort of explanation. "My ex-husband unexpectedly showed up at Landon's house right before the rehearsal dinner. He wanted to talk. And in my current state, I didn't want to go back to Landon's and ... ruin all the fun."

She gave a slow nod, and I wondered if Landon had mentioned anything on their ride over about us. "I'm sorry."

I pulled in a quick breath, still trying to regulate my breathing. "It was actually good. I needed closure, and I got it."

"Either way, it probably wasn't an easy conversation."

We continued the rest of the way in silence, and by the time we got to the room, my tears were falling less frequently.

"Is all of your stuff still at Landon's?" she asked when she'd closed the door behind us.

"Unfortunately."

"I have a nightdress you could borrow, and I'm sure house-keeping could bring up an extra toothbrush." Her gaze landed on my cheek, and her eyes narrowed. "What's that?"

I lifted a hand to the spot she stared at, and dread filled me at the lifted patch of skin under my fingers. "Curse words!" But how? I hadn't touched a Christmas tree.

My stomach dropped at the memory of me hiding from Landon and Rachel, pressed against the pokey boughs of the tree in the front lobby. No wonder my skin was itching so fiercely. I hurried to the mirror over the desk, and I nearly reeled back at the sight of myself. My eyes were swollen, my nose was red from crying, and mascara was smeared across my face, but it was the raised spots dotting my left jawline and cheek that I couldn't pull my gaze from.

The itch was spreading down my arms and legs. I scratched, and new hives popped up in the wake.

Rachel turned on the lamp for more light and came closer, her gaze fixed on the raised welts.

"They're hives," I explained before she thought I had some contagious ailment that would leave her regretting sharing a room with me. "I've recently discovered I'm allergic to Christmas trees."

Rachel's brows lifted like she couldn't understand what that had to do with anything.

"I forgot and touched the Christmas tree in the lobby."

"What do you do for them?"

"Last time, Landon got me Benadryl and some ointment, but I don't—"

"There's a small pharmacy downstairs. I'll be right back." Before I had a chance to insist I could go, she was out the door.

I locked eyes with my reflection. "You are a mess. A ridiculous, awful mess."

Rachel was back a few minutes later. "They didn't have any kind of cream, but they did have Benadryl. If I need to, I can go try a store. There might still be one open."

"I think this will be fine. Let me know your Venmo so I can pay you back."

"Don't worry about it. It was only a couple dollars."

"Still. You've already done so much." I opened the bottle and took the appropriate dose this time. "Thank you, by the way. For everything."

She smiled. "I'm happy I could help."

My heart twisted. She and Landon really were perfect for each other.

"QUINN?" A hand settled on my shoulder, shaking it. "Hey, Quinn?"

With great effort, I peeled open my eyes to find Rachel, her hair and makeup already done, standing over me, wearing an apologetic smile. "I'm sorry to wake you. I just wanted to make sure you hadn't changed your mind about coming to the wedding."

My head was groggy, and all I wanted to do was close my eyes and go back to sleep. So much for feeling refreshed in the morning. Stupid medicine. Medicine! My hand flew to my face, suddenly remembering my reason for having taken it. I rubbed a hand over my cheek, relieved to find that the raised bumps had disappeared, along with the itch.

"They're gone," Rachel said with a smile.

"Thank heavens."

"So you still don't intend to come?"

"No. I don't think I should."

Rachel gave a disappointed smile but didn't ask me my reasons for ditching. "Do you still want a ride to Landon's to get your stuff?"

I lifted myself onto my elbows, still not willing to climb out from beneath the warm blankets. "If you don't mind, that would be great."

"Not at all. You can ride with me over to Rosecliff, then the driver can take you wherever you need. And feel free to come back and hangout here. You're welcome to spend the night again, too. The hotel actually has a free shuttle we could take to the airport in the morning."

"You're an absolute lifesaver. And I'm going to find a way to repay you for your generosity."

"Don't you even think about. I enjoy hanging out with you."

I glanced at the clock with bleary eyes, squinting so the numbers would clarify. When they did, I was sure I was seeing them wrong—or I was hoping I was. "It's 11:40?" I flipped the covers down and scrambled from the bed, only to remember that I was wearing Rachel's silky, green nightdress that was a few sizes too big for me. I wrapped my arms around myself to keep everything sufficiently covered. "The wedding starts in just over an hour. You've probably got to get going."

Rachel was already in a gorgeous gold dress with sequins that hugged her in all the right places. Her hair was curled and pinned back on one side. "We still have a little time."

"I'm so sorry. I should have warned you that Benadryl knocks me out, and you had complete permission to dump water on my head or do whatever you needed to wake me up."

She laughed. "My boyfriend always takes it before a long flight, and he's out for hours."

My gaze flew to hers. "What did you say?"

The intensity of my reaction made her brow quirk and her smile falter. "Maybe I shouldn't admit that he uses it off label."

"No. I mean, you have a boyfriend?"

She nodded, still looking confused.

I stared at Rachel, trying to make sense of the revelation. "But ..." I shook my head.

"Is something the matter?"

"No." I hesitated. "Except ... I was under the impression

Nikki wanted to set you up with Landon." Rachel having a boyfriend didn't change anything, though. Did it? This had never been about Rachel—not really. It had been about Landon needing someone who wasn't a disaster.

"Considering she set me up with Todd, I'm positive that isn't her intention." Her lips pursed. "But when I was visiting her and Kade the other day, he hinted that Nikki had someone in mind for Landon. And from what I understand, that's a huge deal after everything that happened. Nikki must be certain of whoever it is." Her gaze went distant. "But I can't think of who it might be. I haven't seen him interacting with anyone in particular."

Rachel's words swirled around my mind. If Nikki hadn't intended to set Landon up with Rachel, why had she acted like she was unless ... my gaze lifted to hers. "It's me. She's been trying to set me up with Landon. This whole time. Landon was right."

Rachel's eyes lit with excitement. "Of course it's you! That's why Nikki kept sending him concerned glances throughout the rehearsal dinner and during our day around Newport—because you weren't there." Her shoulders dropped at the same time as her smile. "Now I feel bad for asking him to give me a ride back to the hotel. He was probably eager to get home and check on you after your ex-husband showed up at his house." Her eyes widened, and her hand flew to her mouth. "But you were here. Does he know that? He's probably worried sick."

"He knew. I talked to him right before my phone died." I purposely left off the fact that it had been a pitiful conversation that probably hadn't helped to ease his worry.

"But the two of you aren't dating?"

"No." I nearly gave myself whiplash with how intensely I shook my head. "I'm afraid Nikki was wrong about us—about me, anyway. Landon needs someone who has her life in order. Someone like you ... except, not you, because you have a boyfriend, it turns out."

"It might surprise you to hear this, but I don't have my life in order. Honestly, I'm not sure many people do."

"But on the spectrum, everyone's a lot further along than me. Even those who know me best doubt I'm ready for another relationship." At least, my mom doubted I was.

"And do you think that?"

"I don't know what I think." I glanced at the clock. "Except for that I'd better get changed so you're not late." I gathered my stuff and scurried into the bathroom, trying to avoid overthinking everything again.

Before I put on my dress from last night, I held it over the bathtub to give it a good shake, holding my breath and closing my eyes. I hoped any remaining Christmas tree remnants would fall off with the brisk motion. I didn't want to spend the day in a Benadryl-induced sleep. Though another allergic reaction might be a valid excuse for missing the wedding.

My stomach knotted at the thought of not being there today, especially now that I was nearly certain Nikki had been trying to set me up with Landon this whole time. So, instead of being relieved I didn't show up, she'd now be utterly disappointed. On her wedding day. Why in the world had she picked me for Landon? Out of the countless women she knew—all of whom were a lot more ... *everything* than I was—she'd chosen me. What did she see that I didn't?

But it didn't matter. My window of opportunity had passed. The wedding started in an hour. And besides, I couldn't think about what Nikki wanted. Or my mom. Or Cody. Or Ashlee. Or even me. I needed to think about what Landon *needed*. Not now, but years from now when the novelty of being with me wore off, and he was left to deal with the repercussions of my crazy in his everyday life.

When I finished dressing, I opened the door, and Rachel glanced up from her phone. "Quinn, you need to see this."

A tinge of nerves shot through me. "What?"

"Here." She handed me her phone. It was paused on an image of Nikki's face, smiling.

I sat on the edge of the bed, my finger hovering over the video.

Then, I noticed my account had been tagged in the video. I glanced up, feeling slightly uneasy. "What is it?"

"Just watch it. It was posted a few hours ago."

Hesitantly, I clicked the image, and the video began.

"Hey, Instagram family." Nikki's hair was done in an elegant updo, but her face was still bare of makeup. Not that she needed it, but with the white robe she wore, I was guessing she was mid-getting ready for the wedding. "Today is the big day. I get to marry the man you've all watched me fall in love with, and I couldn't be more excited."

She sent a subtle nod to someone off-screen before returning her attention to the camera. "And you can expect my feed to continue to go crazy with pictures and videos throughout the rest of today, but that's not why I'm doing a live stream right now. I'm actually here to lend one of my most loyal supporters my platform. A guy who's not only been with me since my social media debut, but one that has been integral in my success. And he also happens to be one of my most favorite people on this planet."

Kade hadn't been there since her debut. Was she talking about Landon?

The camera shifted, and my heart's anxious rhythm stalled out entirely. Landon looked dreamy in his formal white shirt and black tie, his hair perfectly styled. And apparently, I wasn't the only one to think so with the explosion of heart emojis trailing up the side of the video. But why was Landon on Nikki's live stream? I thought he'd sworn off social media.

He ran a hand through his hair, and the heart emojis went crazy again despite how unsettled he looked.

"Landon," Nikki's voice came from behind the camera. "Is there *something* you'd like to say to *someone*?"

He drew in a slow breath, and his gaze shifted behind the camera to where Nikki must have been standing. "When I came up with this idea, I didn't realize what an idiot I'd feel like."

Nikki's laugh trickled through the speaker. "Pretend there aren't thousands of people watching at this very moment."

"Thanks for that." His gaze dropped, and I willed him to keep going, to say what he'd gotten on here to say, despite being certain I shouldn't want to hear it. I was already too close to wavering. "Okay." He nodded, and his eyes lifted to the camera again. "Quinn ..." He'd said my name! In front of tens of thousands, eventually hundreds of thousands of viewers, he was talking directly to me. It took every bit of focus to not get wrapped up on that one point alone. "I know we haven't known each other long, and it feels crazy how fast I'm falling for you ... it certainly looks crazy to everyone ... but I don't care. I'm tired of living my life by other people's expectations. I've done that long enough. Now, I want to embrace what makes me happy. And it turns out, that's you. Every wonderful, messy part of you.

"Because honestly, who isn't a mess? I know I am. Life is complex. People are complex. The key is to find those who not only see our positive traits—and I could go on and on about yours—but those who truly appreciate the messiest parts of us. The parts that have shaped us into who we are. I'd like the chance to adore you like you deserve, Quinn. All of you. However long that process takes. From the first moment you threatened me with that frying pan, I was captivated, and every moment since has only made me more certain this is what I want. You are what I want." His gaze dropped and then lifted again, and I felt like he was looking directly at me. "I really hope that's one more thing we have in common."

The video ended in an explosion of hearts and crying emojis. And I could see why. I felt like my own heart was going to explode, and tears were running down my cheeks. Thousands of people had already commented on the video. Tens of thousands had loved it. It was only a matter of time until my family and friends would all see it. My breath caught. That was why he'd done it. Landon had declared to anyone who cared to listen that I was desired. That I was worth being loved. I looked up in stunned silence.

A smile danced on Rachel's lips. "Are you sure you don't want to date him?"

I blinked. "Landon doesn't realize what life would be like with me," I said, though the rationalization was slowly slipping from me. The voices of doubt in my head had been chased away by Landon's voice telling me I was enough for him.

"He seems to care more about what life would be like without you. Besides, isn't that the whole idea of falling in love—having someone that complements you? Someone whose strength makes up for your weaknesses, and your strengths make up for theirs?"

"What if one person has all the strengths?"

Rachel moved to sit beside me on the bed. "I'm pretty sure a man doesn't fall that head over heels for someone who has no strengths." She smiled. "It sounds to me like you just need a little reminder about why he *adores* you. And I know a great way to get that." She shifted to face me and covered my hand with hers. "Come to the wedding."

My heart squeezed, finding a faster, heartier pace. "Okay."

Rachel dipped her chin with eyebrows raised. "Okay?"

I nodded and glanced at the clock. "But we'd better get going, or we'll both be late."

I TAPPED my foot nervously on the floor of the car, my searching gaze finally recognizing the neighborhood the ride-share driver had turned into.

Rachel rested a hand on mine, pulling my attention to where she sat on the backseat next to me. "You can still make it. The wedding doesn't start for another forty minutes."

"But it takes almost twenty minutes to get there, and I'm not even dressed."

"Let me wait for you, then."

I shook my head adamantly. Rachel had already done enough for me—going so far as to bring me to Landon's before going to Rosecliff—there was no way I was going to let her risk being late. "Absolutely not."

"Well, then text me when you're on your way, and if I need to, I'll cause a scene."

Despite my jitters, I smiled. "How do I hire a ride-share? Is it a website?"

"An app." She opened her phone and pointed to two icons. "I've used both Uber and Lyft. Just download whichever one you want, put in your credit card information and your location"— she opened the app, pointing at how to do that—"then hit request a ride. The closest driver available will come and get you."

"Okay," I said, "I can do that." At least I hoped I could. And I really hoped I had enough credit to get the charge approved. I was pretty sure I did as long as it wasn't a couple hundred dollars. A ride-share didn't cost that much, did it?

When we pulled into the drive, I leapt from the car with my heels in my hand for a quicker exit. "Thank you," I called to both the driver and Rachel at the same time for efficiency.

"Your coat." Rachel dangled it out the window.

I hurried back to the car, grateful she'd noticed it sitting there. The key to get inside was in the pocket, which could have been devastating if they'd driven off before I'd realized. I shuddered and pushed the thought from me. "Thanks. I'll see you in a few minutes!"

I bounded up the stairs two at a time. After a night away, walking in felt like I was coming home—until I thought about how eerily quiet the house was, and the moment was lost. With a quick scan, I was appeased that everything appeared secured. But hidden murderers or not, I didn't have time to worry.

The charger was sitting next to the bed where I'd left it, and once I plugged in my phone, I hurried to the closet and pulled out my dress. The velvet fabric was perfect for a quick change, and it felt wonderful against my skin. My hair was the real challenge.

The updo I'd done last night had taken me almost an hour, and I didn't have that kind of time. A quick comb-through would have to suffice, and I'd just sport my natural waves. By the time I'd applied mascara, my phone chimed, signaling it had powered on.

A flood of notifications sent my phone into detonation mode again, but I ignored them all and opened Landon's texts. There were a few new messages from him.

Landon: Considering my call went straight to voicemail, I'm guessing your phone died. Call me whenever you get this. I'd love to talk.

Landon: I hope you slept well. I wanted to let you know I'm leaving for all the pre-wedding stuff. I don't know if you got your phone charged, but since your things are still here, I'm assuming you haven't left Newport. I'm hoping you don't before we get a chance to talk. If you need anything, call me. I'll make sure my phone isn't on silent this time.

Before I could convince myself of what an awful person I was, I wrote out a message:

Quinn: You still in need of a date for the wedding?

Quinn: Even if she's a little late?

Quinn: And a lot sorry?

My last text had barely sent when the phone rang, and Landon's name appeared on the screen.

"Hey," I said, trying to keep the flood of emotions from altering my voice. I wasn't sure which would win out, and I didn't want to smear my mascara again. I didn't have time to fix it.

"Hey. Where are you? I'll come get you."

"I'm at the house, but you can't come. There won't be time before the wedding starts. I'm going to take a ride-share and pray really hard I don't get a murderer for a driver."

"Did you already request a car?"

"No. I have to download the app still. My phone just powered on, and I thought I should text to make sure you hadn't found yourself another date before I risked my life."

He chuckled. "Well, no need. I just requested a car. The driver is five minutes away."

"For real?"

"I'm far too desperate to see you to be joking."

I feared my cheeks would cramp with how big my smile was. "I'll be there as soon as I can, but don't wait for me. I'll find you after the ceremony."

"Quinn?"

"Yeah?"

He hesitated, and there were voices in the background. "Thanks for coming."

Again, I didn't trust my emotions enough to tell him how much his public declaration had meant to me. But I'd find the time. "How could I not? After that video Nikki posted of you, there are probably ten thousand desperate women waiting to get their hands on you. Who's going to protect you from all of them if I don't?"

He chuckled. "Good point. You'd better bring the frying pan."

TWENTY-FIVE

QUINN

MY HEART RACED AT AN UNWAVERING GALLOP, BUT I wasn't sure if it was from how fast I'd gotten ready, my anticipation to see Landon, my sliding into the backseat of a car alone with a driver I didn't know, or the fact I had a necessary—and dreaded—call to make. It was probably a wicked combination of all of those things. I stared at my phone. The battery was still low since I'd only charged it for fifteen minutes, which meant I couldn't put off my call like I wanted to. And we'd already been in the car for over ten minutes, so the ride was more than half over.

I pressed Mom's name and brought the phone to my ear.

"Hey, sweetie. I'm so glad I saw my phone light up. I've been out all morning, running errands, and didn't realize I had my phone's ringer off." Mom's upbeat voice had the opposite effect it usually did on me, and I squirmed in my seat. "Aren't you supposed to be at the wedding?"

"I'm on my way there now."

"Doesn't it start in a few minutes?"

299

Okay, not a strong start to what I needed to say. "Yeah, but I needed to call you first because my phone is about to die again, and I'll be out late."

"And it can't wait until tomorrow?"

I cleared my throat, my gaze darting to the driver who seemed to be absorbed in the soothing sound of Bing Crosby's voice drifting out of the speakers, singing about tree tops glistening and children listening. "About that. I'm not coming home."

A brief but heavy silence followed my declaration. "You're kidding, right?"

"I'm not. And I'm sorry, but I want to stay in Newport and spend Christmas with Landon."

"Sweetie, just because you want to do something doesn't mean it's the right decision. You're not in a place—"

"You're not wrong. I'll be the first to admit it—I'm a mess. I know I have so many things to work on, but that's just one side of it. I also have so much to offer to someone. To offer Landon." I swallowed, finding it hard to channel my self-confidence. "I'm kind and can get along with anyone. I forgive easily, and I'm honest," I said, borrowing some of the positive traits Landon had listed about me. Though, with each spoken attribute, I could feel the truth of it take hold inside of me, and the idea of adding to the list grew easier. Was that the power of positive self-talk? "I might be messy and forgetful, but I'm creative. I love learning new things, and for the most part, they come easily to me. I can bake with the best of them. I'm thoughtful and loyal. And I love deeply and whole-heartedly."

"I know, Quinn. That's what worries me. Do you understand how hard it was for your dad and me to watch you suffer this past year? I can't do that again."

Emotion welled in my chest. "I don't doubt it must have been hard for both of you, but Landon's not Cody. Can you trust me?"

The line was quiet for what felt like forever, and I glanced at the screen to make sure my phone hadn't died.

"Okay."

"Okay? Like you're okay with me staying in Newport for Christmas? Or you're okay with the Landon/Cody comparison?"

"I'm okay with allowing you to do what you think is best, so … if that's staying there for Christmas"—she released a long, slow exhale—"I'll support you in that."

A wave of relief washed over me. "Thank you."

"But if this is as serious as it sounds, your dad and I will need to meet Landon soon."

I was literally beaming. "I'm sure we can arrange something."

"Well then," Mom sighed. "I'll break the news to the family. I doubt we'll be able to get a refund on the ticket, but I'll call the airlines and see if we could get a credit or something."

"I can help pay for it if not."

"No. I shouldn't have bought it without confirming with you first. Live and learn, right?" She gave a small laugh. "Make sure you charge that phone of yours. I want regular updates on how things are going, and I expect a decently long video chat on Christmas."

"Done." My overactive imagination had come up with a dozen different scenarios for how this would go, but none of them had ended with my heart swelling in gratitude. "I love you, Mom."

"I love you, sweetie."

When I ended the call, I saw the driver's icy blue eyes flick to me in the rearview.

I swallowed down my trepidation. "I don't usually boast about all my good qualities when I'm talking to people. I feel like that needs to be said."

He chuckled. "Parents—our harshest critics and our biggest cheerleaders."

I nodded. "Isn't that the truth?"

His gaze met mine again. "You headed to the Aker/Carrigan wedding, then?"

I could hardly deny it, being that our destination was Rosecliff, but the question unsettled me. Why would a middle-aged man know about Nikki's wedding? Unless he'd driven others there already. "I am."

"My daughter follows Nikki Aker on Instagram. She's sixteen, and the majority of accounts she follows don't seem to care if their influence is good or bad, but I wouldn't mind my Kaela learning a thing or two from that woman."

I relaxed slightly at the turn of the conversation. "She is just as kind in real life. Kinder even."

"How do you know her? Are you a social media influencer as well?"

It felt like small talk, but I wasn't ready to let my guard down and pass out information to a complete stranger. Obviously, I knew strangers followed my account all the time, but it wasn't because they'd gotten my handle from me personally. "I'm dating her brother," I said casually.

His widened eyes flashed back to me. "The one from the live stream this morning?"

My mouth parted. "Umm ... yeah."

"What are the odds? My daughter and her friends were going bonkers over that video. And here you are, in my car. I'm going to be the coolest dad on the block when I tell them I drove the girl Nikki's brother loves to the wedding."

I laughed, not correcting his slight exaggeration.

"Do you think I could snap a selfie with you when we get there?" He paused, glancing over his shoulder. "Sorry. That's totally unprofessional of me, but there aren't many things I do that impress my daughter these days."

That wasn't a request I'd ever gotten before. "I'd be happy to take a picture with you," I said, trying to remain vigilant despite his kind flattery. "We'll just need to take it quick, since the wedding starts in eight minutes."

"We're almost there." He pointed up ahead. "Rosecliff is that second drive."

When we got closer, he slowed and then passed the turnoff

Landon had taken last time that put us right in front of Rosecliff. "Looks like they have that entrance blocked. I'll take you to the parking lot and pull as close as I can. It's about a hundred yard walk from there."

I nodded, my heart rate accelerating in anticipation of trying to make it inside before the wedding started. Less than five minutes. Landon would already be with the wedding party, but I'd see him after.

The driver put the car in park and hurried around to open my door. His phone was out, and he held up the camera for a selfie shot. I smiled up at it, and he gave the most dad-vibe face and thumbs up with his free hand. When the camera clicked, he pointed down a small walkway through a copse of trees. "Just on the other side of that, you'll hit the drive in front of Rosecliff."

"Thank you." I picked up the skirt of my dress and hurried in the direction he'd pointed. For all the beauty of my heels, they didn't make moving over damp gravel any easier. I bent over and pulled them off. It was time to run.

"Quinn!"

I looked up to find Landon jogging toward me, and I stopped mid-step. "What are you doing out here?"

"Hello to you, too." He smiled that smile of his that made my heart patter recklessly. "I was tracking your driver on the app. You know, in case he deviated from his course to murder you."

"Thanks for that. You would have made a great primary witness as to where my body was buried."

He laughed.

"But what I meant was, I'm pretty sure you're going to be late to your own sister's wedding."

"Nikki had a last-minute wardrobe malfunction."

I lifted a hand to my mouth. "Oh no!"

"Honestly, I think she was buying you a little more time."

"She's stalling the wedding for me? Holy curse words. We need to hurry." With my shoes in one hand and the skirt of my dress in the other, I started toward Rosecliff again, Landon pacing me, chuckling from what I assumed was my chosen expletive.

"Your feet must be freezing. Here." He wrapped a hand around my waist, lifting me up into his arms with ease. And suddenly, cradled against his chest, I wasn't the least bit upset with being nearly child-sized. He smelled divine, and all I wanted to do was reach my arms around his neck and warm myself with his kisses.

"Here we are." He placed me down at the entrance. His breaths were coming out in white puffs of air.

I used his arm for balance as I slid my shoes back on. When I straightened, I rubbed my hands down my figure. "Looking at me, would you guess I haven't showered and the combination of my nerves and this velvet are making me sweat?"

He took his time assessing me, and I blushed under the concentrated efforts. I pushed at his chest. "A simple yes or no would be fine."

He chuckled. "You look stunning."

"So do you."

His hand went to the door. "You ready?"

I nodded, but before the door opened, I put out a hand to stop him. "One last thing."

"What's tha—"

Before he could get his question out, I wrapped my arms around his neck and drew him to me. The kiss was supposed to be a quick reassurance, but the moment our lips touched, his hands slid around my waist, and I momentarily forgot everything but how it felt to be adored. And treasured. And crazy, head-over-heels in love.

Now, both our breathing came out in quick bursts. "Anything else?" he asked, a mischievous twinkle in his eye.

"I'm staying for Christmas, if that's still okay with you?"

His hand brushed across my cheek, sending my insides into a state of torturous, wonderful commotion. "Christmas with you sounds absolutely perfect."

This time, I allowed him to open the door, and when we stepped into the gorgeously decorated lobby—my gingerbread houses sitting as focal points amongst the luxurious greenery and flowers—a muted cheer erupted. My gaze flew to the heart-shaped staircase where the entire bridal party was lined up, their collective expressions of amusement on us, as they waited for Nikki to arrive so the procession could begin.

Kade stood near the closed salon doors and sent us a knowing grin before his gaze slid to the top of the stairs and his eyes glistened with tears. My gaze followed his to where Nikki stepped into view, looking like an absolute vision in her white dress. She stepped next to her dad and waved at us, and no one's smile was brighter than hers. Then her gaze met Kade's, and their shared look was filled with so much love and intimacy, I had to look away.

"By the way, I think you were right," I whispered as Landon and I started toward the group. "Your sister intended to set us up all along."

"Oh, I'm certain of it." Landon took my hand in his. "And I'll forever be grateful for her meddling. But don't tell her that."

My quiet laughter melted into the sound of organ music starting.

"Sandra has a seat saved for you right up front on the bride's side," Landon said, gesturing to which side that was. "I'll see you after the ceremony."

I gave Landon a quick kiss and slipped through the closed doors into the salon where the rest of the guests waited for one of the most anticipated weddings of the year.

TWENTY-SIX

LANDON

I KNOCKED QUIETLY ON THE DOOR AND PEEKED MY head inside the familiar room—the room that had been mine when I'd lived at home with my parents. Quinn's muffled groan made me smile, and I squatted down next to the bed. "Hey, Sleeping Beauty. Merry Christmas."

She cracked an eye open and gave a tired smile. "Hey, you! What time is it?"

"Almost six."

Her other eye opened, but she pulled the comforter under her chin like she had no intention of getting up. "Are Chloe and the boys awake? It's still so quiet."

"Not yet. I wanted to include you in one of my favorite traditions—if you want to join me."

She lifted herself onto her elbows. "You bet I do. What is it?"

"Come, and I'll show you."

She pushed the comforter off and stood, our matching plaid jammies—a Christmas Eve gift to everyone in the family from my dad and Sandra—looking much better on her than they did on me. She yawned and lifted her arms up above her head to stretch, the tiniest bit of her stomach showing. But it was enough of a glimpse to chase any lingering sleep from me.

I stepped toward her, slipping my arm around her waist and pulling her toward me. Before our lips touched, she turned her head and offered me her cheek. "You don't want to kiss me until I brush my teeth."

"Wanna bet?" I took hold of her face and pulled it toward me. She tightened her lips as I pressed mine against hers, her giggling thwarting her efforts to wriggle free.

She swatted at me. "You're going to wake up the kids."

"Fine." With a playful huff, I released her and nabbed the comforter off the bed. "Ready?"

Her gaze moved to the blanket draped over my arm before it dropped to my bare feet. "We aren't going outside, are we?"

"No. The blanket's for cuddling."

"The magic words have been spoken. Lead on." She took hold of my hand and followed me to the family room with quiet steps. The large Christmas tree sat like a glowing watchman over the presents scattered around the room in small piles, a personalized stocking that marked who each stack belonged to.

"It's magical." A smile danced on Quinn's lips, her eyes lit with the reflection of the tree.

"Growing up, my mom and I were the only early risers in our family. Every Christmas morning, we'd come and sit together on the couch, wrap up in a blanket, and enjoy the Christmas magic before everyone else woke up and it slipped away in the busyness of the day." I led her to the couch on the other side of the room, where I had two mugs of hot chocolate awaiting us on the side table.

She took a seat on the couch, and when I spread the blanket over our laps, she nuzzled into me. "I love that tradition. Thanks for letting me be a part of it this year."

"Thanks for being willing. And for being here on Christmas."

"I wouldn't want to be anywhere else."

I handed Quinn a cup of cocoa with a candy cane hooked over the side of the mug. "Just keep your distance from the tree. It's a real one. At the wedding, when Sandra found out you were coming for Christmas, she insisted she was going to take the tree down and replace it with an artificial one."

Quinn took a sip of her hot chocolate. "I'm glad she didn't. She had enough to worry about with the wedding and hosting everyone for Christmas."

"That's what I told her you'd say. Plus, I assured her, on the off chance you touched it, I would gladly keep you company during your medicine-induced stupor again."

Quinn nudged me in the stomach. "I'm pretty sure I've had enough *medicine-induced stupors* these past few weeks to fill my quota for the year."

I stared at her. "Did you have a reaction I'm not aware of?"

She bit her lip. "The other night at the hotel, I had a slight run-in with a Christmas tree, but it was fine. Rachel got me Benadryl, and the hives were gone by morning."

"How did you manage to have a *run-in* with a tree?"

A soft groan emanated from her. "I may have been in the lobby when you dropped Rachel off ... hiding behind a tree. I mean, in my frazzled state, I didn't remember the fact that I was allergic to it. I was just desperate to not let either of you see me."

"Wait. You saw me pull up at the hotel and didn't come out?" I wasn't upset, only confused.

Her gaze lowered to her mug. "I was having a moment of doubt, then Rachel got out of your truck." She shook her head. "She seemed perfect for you—minus the whole boyfriend thing, but I hadn't known that at the time." Quinn's eyes lifted to mine. "I worried I'd gotten in the way. That you would be better off with someone like her."

That explained Quinn's seemingly random comments about dating other people and me finding someone else to take to the wedding. But Rachel had been so far off my radar it hadn't even crossed my mind that Quinn might worry about her. Though, after what Cody had put her through this last year—and the fact that he had posted a selfie with him and his new girlfriend in the Caribbean yesterday—I couldn't blame her. I knew it would take Quinn time to fully trust me. And that was okay. She would eventually, and I was in this for the long haul. "Don't get me wrong, the few times I spoke with her, Rachel seemed like a great person, but she's not for me. She's not you."

"But what if, eventually, you realize how difficult it is to be with me? I'm not very good at keeping up a house, or organization, or remembering to do things. And I can't—"

"I'm not worried about it." I shrugged, setting my mug back on the table. "In fact, I look forward to it. All of it. The good. The bad. The messy. As long as we're together for it all."

She shifted more fully to face me, tucking her legs against mine. "But when we have kids"—she paused, her eyes going wide —"I mean, *if* we ever get married and have kids ... one day ... a long time from now ... no pressure or anything."

I chuckled. "I know what you meant."

Her shoulders relaxed. "I'm nervous I'll be the most scatter-brained, paranoid mom in the history of moms."

A brief glimpse of Quinn as a mom filled my mind, warming me straight to my core. She had no idea yet what she had to offer as a mother. But I would give her all the time she needed for that, too, *when*—not *if*—the day came to add to our family. I brushed my thumb across her cheek, relishing the softness of her skin against mine. "You're going to be an amazing mom, whenever that day comes. And we already know we'll have beautiful babies —Grams said so."

"True." She reached across me to set her hot chocolate on the table next to mine. "Just don't say I didn't warn you."

"I consider myself amply warned."

Her eyes returned to mine. "It's not too late to back out."

"For me, it is." I held her gaze. "I'm all in."

She stared at me like she was trying to make sure I was serious.

"This is crazy, right? I mean, we've only known each other a few weeks, but I feel surer of this—of us—than I have been of anything ... maybe ever."

"I feel the same."

"I think I love you," she blurted, her cheeks glowing red in the dim light.

My eyes darted across her face. "You think, huh? Because I'm positive I love you."

Quinn's eyes danced, and a breathtaking smile lit her face. She leaned forward, closing the space between us. "Let me rephrase that. I'm absolutely, entirely, completely positive that I love you, too." Her lips were soft and malleable against mine, and her kiss tasted like hot chocolate and peppermint. I pulled her tight against me, and we melted into the couch beneath the blanket, fully embracing the Christmas magic.

CHRISTMAS MORNING HAD BEEN absolute perfection. Quinn and I had enjoyed our time by the tree for a solid fifteen minutes before Chloe, Carson, and Gavin came running into the room in wide-eyed anticipation of what awaited them. Thankfully, their gazes were on the presents and not on Quinn and me cuddled under the blanket, kissing. Julie and Josh, however, who'd appeared a moment after their kids, with baby Reid in arm, didn't miss our eager scramble to sit up. And Quinn's guilt-ridden giggle did nothing to exonerate us.

My whole family had stayed the night at my dad's, and several of Sandra's kids had come over to open presents and have breakfast with us. Dad had even brought Grams over to spend the day with us, her pleasant smile and excited eyes taking in the chaos with amusement. Unsurprisingly, Quinn fit into the makeshift group perfectly and somehow helped ease our two families into feeling like one. If there truly was Christmas magic, she was it.

And the magic wouldn't have to end when she flew home. Quinn's parents had invited me to come stay for New Year's, and since I was already headed to LA to work, I decided to fly home with Quinn the morning of the twenty-seventh and get a rental car to commute to LA for the few days I needed to be at the office. Even Quinn's sister, Margaret, and her husband were extending their trip to meet me, and refusing to be the only person left out, Ashlee had booked a flight right after we got off Facetime with her earlier.

I took it as a good sign that they all understood how serious the two of us were. It probably helped that they'd all seen the viral live stream where I'd mortified myself for the sake of love in front of thousands—now millions—of people. The thought made my stomach twist, but I'd do it again in a heartbeat. Quinn needed to know how worthy of love she was. And I wanted others, her family and friends particularly, to know it as well. And now they did ... along with a significant number of people who likely didn't need to know but enjoyed the pronouncement of love all the same.

When Sandra's kids had left, and the house had quieted down, the adults sat around the family room, watching the kids play with their new toys. Quinn was tucked up next to me on the couch, holding Reid and collecting all of his smiles and newfound giggles, and completely melting my heart.

"Auntie Quinn." Chloe came toward us, an excited smile on her face.

"Auntie Quinn?" Julie said with an amused smile. "That's sweet."

Chloe looked at her mom. "You said Uncle Landon was going to marry her. That makes her my aunt, right? Like, with *Uncle* Kade when Auntie Nikki married him?"

Julie's lips parted. "I think your daddy and I had better stop having adult conversations in front of you and your brothers."

"It's fine," Quinn said, chasing Chloe's frown away. "You can call me Auntie Quinn if you want."

Chloe threw her mom an I-told-you-so look, which made all of us laugh, before returning her smile to Quinn. "Can we show Uncle Landon his present now?"

"Present?" I asked, sending Quinn a look. "You promised you wouldn't get me anything."

"I promised I wouldn't *buy* you anything, which, in retrospect, seems unfair considering you bought me a present—several, actually. The selfie stick." She ticked up a finger, then another. "Those cook books—*Meals of Middle Earth* and *Jane Austen's Tea Time Delights*—and that gorgeous new sweater. Oh, and *Scrooge*, the musical."

"Those gifts were all small."

Quinn shifted Reid on her lap to more fully face me. Her look told me my argument was moot.

I dislodged a piece of Quinn's hair from Reid's tightened fist. "Small items were part of an exclusionary clause on our agreement. You need to read the fine print next time."

"Verbal agreements don't have *fine print*, Mr. Fancypants Lawyer."

The entire room burst out in laughter. Even Grams laughed when she realized everyone else was.

"I think we have a new nickname for Landon." Nikki smiled. "All in favor?" She glanced around the room, and all the adults, including a delayed hand raise from Grams, consented.

Quinn stood, handing Reid to me. "Well, *Mr. Fancypants Lawyer*, I'll be back in a minute with your present." She reached toward Chloe. "Ready?"

Chloe eagerly grabbed her hand, and the two of them left the room.

When my gaze finally left the spot she'd disappeared from, all eyes were on me. "What?"

"Nothing. We are all taking pleasure in how enamored you are with Quinn," Dad said, and Sandra nodded at his side. "And we don't blame you. She's something else."

"She is, isn't she?"

Nikki smiled, her shoulders lifting in a small shrug. "I hate to say it, but since you haven't yet, I'm just going to get this over with—I was spot on with you two. And you're welcome."

I chuckled, leaning Reid up against me and patting his back. "For being so easily manipulated by you? That whole set-us-up-with-other-people-to-force-us-together routine was well-played. And to find out you all knew about it"—I shook my head—"it's shameful. Who can a man trust if not his own family?"

"Are you kidding me?" Nikki blinked, her gaze darting from me to Kade. "We literally just had to stick you together, give you one reason for the two of you to *team up*, and that was it. There was zero manipulation."

"What about those conversations you had with me at Bowen's Wharf and Grams's nursing home? It was reverse psychology at its finest."

She dipped her chin. "Telling you that Quinn deserved a guy that would treasure her was not reverse psychology. It was the truth."

"You told me not to date her."

"I told you not to date her *unless* you were being sincere, which you weren't at the time. You were being an idiot. Thankfully, you figured it out pretty quickly after that—precisely as I hoped you would."

Kade wrapped an arm around a smiling Nikki. "A simple, *thanks-Nikki-I-owe-my-very-happiness-to-you-and-will-forever-be-in-your-debt* is all she's looking for, man. Just give it to her."

I laughed, shaking my head, but sobered when I met her eyes. "Thank you. For real. I'm sorry I was such a Grinch about the whole thing. Had I known ..."

"Had you known, you would have let me set you up with her while you were working in L.A."

I paused. "Quinn was *the friend* you wanted me to take out?"

Nikki nodded. "But honestly, I'm not sure you would have had the emotional bandwidth to realize the opportunity I'd handed you—and I wasn't even sure I could convince Quinn to go out with you. So, as luck would have it, she happened to be an extremely talented baker, I was in need of some beautiful center-pieces for my wedding, and you had the perfect place for her to bake the gingerbread houses. It all worked out perfectly." She turned to Kade. "And I couldn't have done it without you."

Kade tipped his head from side to side. "I do make a wicked sidekick to your scheming."

Nikki kissed his cheek. "You do."

"When does your flight leave again?" Julie asked, glancing at her watch.

"Not until eight tonight," Kade answered. "We've got a few more hours until we have to head to the airport."

Julie leaned forward onto her elbows and gave a sigh. "Thailand sounds dreamy."

"Our resort caters to honeymooners." Nikki sent me a meaningful glance. "We'll let you know how it is. You know, so you can start gathering ideas."

I smiled, recalling where Quinn had mentioned wanting to travel. "I was thinking England might be a good option. When the time comes."

"Uncle Landon." Chloe's voice brought my gaze to the entryway. She stood by herself but glanced to the side, like Quinn was just out of sight. "Are you ready for your present?"

"Here." Nikki stood and scooped Reid out of my arms. "I'll gladly take this dapper little man."

"Ready," I said, feeling a twinge of nerves. I had a vague idea of what Quinn's surprise present was—the whole house had smelled like ginger and cinnamon yesterday while Quinn, Sandra, Julie, and Chloe were holed up in the kitchen—but besides it being made of gingerbread, I had no idea what they'd made.

Chloe nodded, and Quinn appeared around the corner, taking careful steps as she carried her present toward me.

I stared in awe, a grin creeping onto my lips.

"A rocket ship?" Grams said, smiling brightly from her chair. "My grandson Landon tried to make a gingerbread rocket ship a few years ago. It wasn't very good, but I'm guessing that's what he wanted it to look like."

Laughter filled every corner of the large, crowded room.

"You're right, Grams," I said. "Except, this one is even better than the one I imagined."

Quinn's cheeks glowed pink, and she set it down on the table next to me. "I know it isn't much—"

"It's amazing." I stared at it, taking in all the intricate details. "Did you do that NASA logo?"

"Yes, but don't look too close, or you'll find all the imperfections."

I held her gaze. "It's absolutely perfect—imperfections included."

She beamed at my compliment—at my meaning behind it—and I knew I would do whatever it took to always make her feel cherished and worthy of the love she wholly deserved. I reached up and grabbed Quinn's hand, pulling her onto my lap. Then, in front of my whole family and my disgusted nephews, I kissed her like she deserved, for being the sole giver of all happiness and good things.

EPILOGUE

SEVERAL YEARS LATER

QUINN

I GLANCED AROUND THE CROWDED COUNTER OF Landon's Newport house—our home, now—forgetting what I was looking for in the dimly lit room. The morning light had barely begun to push the darkness from the sky. "What was I looking for?"

"Your laptop charger." Landon handed it to me. "And here's your wallet."

I shoved them both in my bag. "Thanks. I feel so scatter-brained this morning." I paused. "Well, I always feel like that, but it's worse today. I think I'm nervous about the conference. What if I say something stupid while I'm presenting?"

"You won't."

I sighed. "And why aren't you coming again? You're the one who knows everything about growing a successful social media account."

"That's not true. You're the expert now." Landon wrapped

his arms around me. "That's why Nikki asked you to put on this conference with her. Just be yourself, and they'll love you."

I bit my lip, attempting to be persuasive, or cute, or something that would convince him to come. "They'd love me more if you were there."

"Who would watch the kids?"

"Julie said she would." But even when I said it, I knew we wouldn't ask that of her. Not when she'd just watched them a month ago while Landon and I took our annual week-long anniversary trip, this time a return trip to England where we'd spent our honeymoon.

"By the time I got them there, your conference will be half over. It's only four days."

"Four days feels like a long time to be away from you. Maybe I could tell Nikki I'm sick and I can't make it."

"And what about Ashlee? I'm sure she'd love to get off the plane in Florida to realize you didn't show up to a conference she isn't even attending."

I shrugged. "I don't know. She'd probably love a few days in a hotel room by herself, not having to work or act as emotional support to her crazy best friend."

"Correction: *kooky* best friend."

"Right? They're totally different."

Landon chuckled and tightened his grip on my waist. "We're going to miss you, but I want you to try and enjoy yourself. Promise?"

"Fine," I said, giving him an overdone pout.

Landon kissed me so tenderly it instantly calmed my nerves.

A pitter-patter of pajama-clad feet sent Landon and me glancing to the stairs. Bethany rounded the bottom step and came walking toward us with sleep-heavy eyes.

Landon moved toward her. "What are you doing up already?"

"I don't want Mommy to go."

Before I could agree to stay, Landon reached down and

scooped her up. Her tiny four-year-old body was swallowed up in his embrace. "Mommy has to go, but she'll be back soon."

Bethany frowned. "Can I go with her?"

I ran my hand through her sleep-matted hair. "Who would help Daddy with Oscar if you're not here?"

Bethany glanced at Landon. "Will she miss the boat parade?"

Landon's brows lowered. "The Christmas one?"

She nodded.

The corners of Landon's eyes crinkled. "No, sweetie. It's only May. We still have a little while before the boat parade." Apparently, Bethany hadn't only gotten her blonde curls and blue eyes from me, but her general sense of time—or lack of it.

"Okay." She reached out for me, and I held her close, never wanting to forget the feel of her little body in my arms and how she smelled like strawberries.

Landon watched us, a smile on his lips.

A cry sounded from upstairs, and Landon sent me a pointed look. "You willed him awake, didn't you?"

I shrugged, handing Bethany back to her daddy. "And here I thought you didn't believe in manifestation."

Landon laughed. "Well, your ride-share's almost here, so you'd better hurry and go love on him. And don't worry, I marked the not-a-murderer box for the driver."

"You are too good to me."

Landon nuzzled into Bethany, and she giggled, tucking farther into him to avoid his beard. "It's going to be a long day without Mommy here, isn't it?"

I smiled, hurrying the rest of the way up to get Oscar. When I opened the door, he stopped crying and smiled through the bars of the crib.

"Hey, baby. I'm glad you woke up before Mommy had to go."

I wrapped his warm little body into me, and we started back downstairs. I hated being away from my babies, but Landon was right. It was only a few days, and I'd be back before I knew it.

"What should we do today?" I overheard Landon ask Bethany.

"Make cookies."

"I can't compete with Mommy's cookies. How about we take a walk down to the bay?"

I cleared the last step in time to see Bethany nodding her head.

"Just be careful," I said. "And make sure you sunscreen them. And that you have Oscar in a wrap so that you can keep hold of Bethany's hand. Oh, and don't forget water and a snack, in case they get thirsty or hungry. And there's a first-aid kit in the diaper bag—"

"Don't worry, my love. I've got this." Landon placed a reassuring hand on my back and gave Oscar a morning kiss on his baby-fuzzed head. "I've been trained by the world's greatest mother."

I laughed. "That's a drastic exaggeration if I've ever heard one."

He pointed at me in mock warning. "You can't say anything. That's how I view you." The phone chimed, and he glanced at the screen. "Your ride's here."

"Thank you for letting me go." I lifted onto my toes and placed a soft, lingering kiss on his lips. "You really are the best of everything."

When I dropped down, his eyes opened slowly, like he was still relishing the feel of my lips against his. "I love you."

"I love you. *And* you." I kissed Oscar and then Bethany. "*And* you."

Landon took Oscar from me. "Call me when you get there."

"I will."

I grabbed my suitcase and started toward the door.

"Quinn?"

Landon's voice made me pause, and I glanced over my shoulder. "Yeah?"

He gestured with his foot to my laptop bag sitting on the floor. "You probably don't want to forget that."

"Oh, heavens. That could have been devastating." I took hold of the bag and slung it over my shoulder, pausing when I reached the door. My gaze moved across the three faces I loved most in the whole world. The ones who loved me despite the fact that I was still a mess. A perfectly wonderful and absolutely adored mess. "See you all soon."

Read the rest of the Christmas Escape Series

All standalone, sweet, closed-door romances that can be read in any order

Christmas Baggage

Deborah M. Hathaway

Host for the Holidays

Martha Keyes

Faking Christmas

Cindy Steel

A Newport Chirstmess

Jess Heileman

A Not-So Holiday Paradise

Gracie Ruth Mitchell

Later On We'll Conspire

Kortney Keisel

Cotswolds Holiday

Kasey Stockton

BOOKS BY JESS HEILEMAN

Regency Romance:
Abigail: A Novel
A Well-Trained Lady
The Nabob's Daughter

Contemporary Romance:
A Newport Christmess

AFTERWORD

I'm not going to lie, writing this book was a challenge for me. A good challenge, but a challenge all the same. As a historical author, my brain apparently thinks in antiquated language that I was constantly needing to rephrase into less formal, modern language. And even though I tried to keep this as light and fun as I could, true to my style, a few more serious themes snuck in that I'd like to mention briefly.

First, was that my main characters are divorcees. I've had several people ask me why I chose to have both Quinn and Landon experience recent divorces. Having watched several of my very dear friends go through a divorce, this was one small way I felt I could show my support. A way of saying: I see you, and I love you, and I full-heartedly believe each of you fully deserve a second chance at love—to find someone who can love and appreciate you unconditionally.

Second, I included a character with Alzheimer's Disease. I didn't make this choice lightly. Having had family members with this disease, I know how difficult it can be for people who have experienced watching their own family members suffer with it. But the love and the beauty in the experience is what I wanted to focus on—not the disease itself. Landon's Grams was actually inspired by my wonderful Aunt Rini who had a way of making her family feel special even when, at the end, she had no idea who we were. The comments of "Who are you? You are so beautiful," were taken directly from her. I will forever love and adore her, and I hope you can feel that love in how I handled this delicate situation.

Lastly, my main character has a dose of paranoia that might seem strange to some, but I assure you, she's not too different from myself in this aspect. As a person with anxiety, I thought it would be fun to make a wild imagination a part of Quinn's character. Since she's already a disorganized mess like me, it only seemed natural she should have this quirk of mine as well. Authors are currently being told to write what we know, and I guess this is what I know.

So, all of that being said, thank you for reading my debut into the contemporary world. Though I don't currently have plans for another contemporary, I'm not closed to the idea either. If a story comes to me that I want to tell, and it so happens to be a contemporary story, then I'll be back!

ACKNOWLEDGMENTS

Writing the acknowledgments is something I always put off until the very last moment. I suppose it makes sense, so I can ensure everyone who assisted with the publishing process is included, but the real reason is because I'm so overwhelmed by the task of thanking all of those who gave of their time and talents to support me. To thank those who made my book better. And those who made me better. My words of gratitude feel inadequate, but I don't know a better way to express my deepest thanks. So, here I go ...

First and foremost, I want to thank God for the talents He has given me. Despite how much I doubt myself and my abilities, He is unwavering in His support. I would be nothing without Him. He is my guiding compass in both my career and in my life, and I will be eternally grateful for the unwavering love and forgiveness He shows me.

A close second in support and love is my sweet husband. You have seen me through some of my most difficult moments, my constant self-doubt, my anxiety, and all the craziness that comes with being the spouse of an author. And you've done it all with unconditional love and endless support. Thanks for being my biggest cheerleader, my best friend, and the person I want to spend every day of forever with. I love you!

To my darling kids, I'm grateful for your patience as I figure out how to balance my writing with the rest of life's responsibilities. How blessed I am to call you mine. How blessed I am by your sweet smiles, your "oxytocin" hugs, and your uplifting, if somewhat biased, encouragement. I'm so proud of each of you!

I'm so grateful for my wonderful family, my amazing parents, and my in-laws. I'm especially grateful to Craig and Cindy for your help in selecting a location—Newport, Rhode Island—and your willingness to answer my questions when they came up. Also, Sheri, my sweet mother-in-law, thanks for being a sounding board for my baking/cookie decorating questions. It was such a help to have an experienced baker around when I encountered something I was unsure about. And I couldn't forget to mention my sister-in-law Maren, whose gingerbread building talents gave rise to the idea of Quinn building gingerbread mansions for a Christmas wedding. And to my nieces and nephews, thanks for unknowingly letting me borrow your names for the sweet children in this story.

To the fabulous group of authors in the Christmas Escape series, what a pleasure it has been working with each of you! Deborah Hathaway, Martha Keyes, Cindy Steel, Gracie Ruth Mitchell, Kortney Keisel, and Kasey Stockton, you ladies are seriously the best! I'm going to miss our constant texting about the series and collective dislike of making reels (especially when it involves dancing). Good thing we all are great friends now, so this won't be the end of our interactions.

To my amazing critique partners and dear friends—Deborah M. Hathaway, Kasey Stockton and Martha Keyes--I honestly adore each of you and am so immensely grateful for your friendship. You constantly lift, support, and share your immense knowledge of publishing with those of us that aren't as far along in their journey. I've become a better writer by reading your work and through the feedback you've so generously given. I've become a better person through knowing each of you. You are truly an elite group of ladies!

Jennie Goutet, these last few years wouldn't have been the same without your support. From the plot sessions and beta swapping to the endless cheerleading, you not only made my books cleaner and my stories better but you have been a light and a true friend to me. As I've told you many times, "I'm sorry, but you're stuck with me forever now."

A hundred thanks to my wonderful beta readers—Tawnie West, Cindy Steel, Kasey Stockton, Martha Keyes, and Jennie Goutet, I'm so grateful for how your feedback strengthened my story and my writing. Your knowledge of stories and characters is incredible. This story wouldn't be what it is without each one of you!

To my incredible editors: Emily Poole and Jenn Lockwood! You make me look like I know what I'm doing, which is a huge accomplishment so thank you for your feedback. And to Susan Kuechenberg, my amazing proofreader, I am exceptionally grateful for the work you did to polish my manuscript at the very last minute. I feel so much better putting this book into the world knowing it was first read by you!

Melody Jeffries you were a God-send. I'm not sure you knew what you were agreeing to when you took on all seven of our covers, but you rocked it! Thank you for sharing your talents with us. Thank you for the beautiful covers, going the extra mile, and for being so great to work with.

Another huge help with this release has been Tasha Bradford. You not only love my books and cheer me on when I'm in desperate need of it, but the whole release would be so much more difficult without your help. Thank you for always being willing to be the hand that I clutch during the rollercoaster ride that is putting a book into the world!

My early readers: Nancy Madsen, Tasha Bradford, and Ashley Weston, thanks for insisting I send you my book before it was edited and polished. Thanks for loving it despite all the errors! And to my amazing launch team—I am so grateful for your willingness to read my book early and help spread the word about it. There are so many incredible bookstagrammers and reviewers that stepped up to help, and I will forever be grateful to each of you!

Launching a book into this big vast world is so much easier knowing I have you guys in my corner!

I'm also grateful for the generosity of The Newport Preservation Society who not only gave me permission to use Rosecliff in my story, but answered several of the questions I couldn't find answers to online. I'm eager to make a trip there as soon as I can make it happen!

And last, but certainly not least, a huge, heartfelt thank you to my readers. Without you, I couldn't do what I love. So thank you for reading my stories. Thank you for your sweet emails and comments. Thank you for supporting us authors!

ABOUT THE AUTHOR

In kindergarten, Jess won a first prize ribbon for her original creation Pigs in Wigs. It was a solid storyline: there was this pig that wore a wig—and it rhymed. Not impressed? Neither were her children when shown the very masterpiece that influenced her to become an author. "You won a ribbon for that?" Yes. Yes, she did.

Thankfully, life has since exposed her to a thorough education with its share of awards and accolades—and, more importantly, to the trials and human experiences that form the heart of a storyteller and the substance of great stories.

Besides her love of writing, Jess is an avid reader, shameless people observer, international cafe loiterer, and partially retired photographer. She loves being a mother to five amazing humans and a wife to the greatest man she knows.

facebook.com/authorjessheileman

instagram.com/authorjessheileman